CA
US
THE
FOXES

Nicola West

SIMON &
SCHUSTER

London · New York · Sydney · Toronto · New Delhi

CATCH US THE FOXES
First published in Australia in 2021 by
Simon & Schuster (Australia) Pty Limited
Suite 19A, Level 1, Building C, 450 Miller Street, Cammeray, NSW 2062

10 9 8 7 6 5 4 3 2 1

Sydney New York London Toronto New Delhi
Visit our website at www.simonandschuster.com.au

NATIONAL LIBRARY OF AUSTRALIA

A catalogue record for this book is available from the National Library of Australia

ISBN: 9781760857479

Cover design: Sandy Cull/gogoGingko
Cover images: © Aleksey Tugolukov / Alamy Stock Photo (girl); © Kim Christensen / Alamy Stock Photo (treeline)
Typeset by Midland Typesetters, Australia

Printed and bound in Australia by Griffin Press.

FSC MIX Paper from responsible sources FSC® C009448 www.fsc.org

The paper this book is printed on is certified against the Forest Stewardship Council® Standards. Griffin Press holds chain of custody certification SGSHK-COC-005088. FSC® promotes environmentally responsible, socially beneficial and economically viable management of the world's forests.

To the best mum in the world*,

I didn't join a cult. I started one.

---

* If you're wondering why I dedicated my book to *your* mum (because you think *she's* the best), I have terrible news for you. She might be a pretty good mum, but she's not as good as mine. If you disagree, let's meet at the bike sheds after school. Don't worry, I'm not going to fight you – my mum will. She's always got my back. It's why she's the best and why I dedicated this book to her. Love you, Mum.

PROLOGUE

'Tonight's speaker needs no introduction, but I'm paid to give one, so here we go.'

The presenter paused for laughter, but little came.

'She's a bestselling author, a former Young Australian of the Year, and Walkley Award winner. At just twenty-nine, those are particularly impressive feats. However, she is best known for exposing one of Australia's most insidious and prolific killers.

'Tonight, on the seventh anniversary of Lily Williams' tragic death, we talk to the tenacious young journalist who uncovered the truth that shook not only her small town, but also the entire nation, to its core. You're really in for a special treat this evening. So please welcome to the stage author, journalist, and co-creator of The Lily Foundation, Marlowe Robertson.'

She mistook their applause for rain.

Instinctively, Marlowe turned her head towards the concert hall's sweeping ceiling before she realised the sound could never permeate the Sydney Opera House's concrete sails. No, it wasn't rain, it was the crowd – and they were applauding for her. She inhaled deeply. She still wasn't used to the attention – the ovation – the people clambering for a selfie or a signature, and the sold-out events.

Her publicist's bony finger prodded her spine, and her eyes fell on the flustered stagehand attempting to usher her out of the wings.

'Sorry,' Marlowe mouthed, unsure whether or not her microphone was on.

When she walked out onto the stage, she was blinded by the spotlights. The roar of the audience reverberated through her body, but she couldn't see them. She paused, shielding her eyes from the lights. One by one, individual people came into view, all wearing the flower crowns that had become synonymous with Lily Day. She stood, dumbfounded at the sea of white before her, and raised her hand to her own crown. Tears bit at the corners of her eyes, and her lips quivered. The applause grew louder.

'It's quite the sight, isn't it?' the presenter asked, placing her hand on the small of Marlowe's back.

Marlowe turned to face the woman. She was a former breakfast-show host with immaculately styled hair and the pinched features of someone who'd had one too many cosmetic procedures.

'I just –' her voice broke, and she turned back towards the crowd.

'We love you, Lo!' an audience member called out.

A small smile tugged at Marlowe's mouth, but she was interrupted by the presenter pushing her towards the interview chair. She winked in the general direction of the call-out – prompting further cheers – before heading to her seat.

As she sat down, she adjusted her leather jacket. The January heat made it an impractical choice, but her publicist had insisted. She'd long grown out of the grungy aesthetic she'd favoured in her early twenties, but it had become a part of her brand.

The jacket, boots and dark, femme-fatale fringe were expected of her. They all served to remind people of that infamous photo – her and the dead girl: Lily in a flower crown and floor-length gown, and Marlowe looking like a biker moll. The striking juxtaposition had made it the perfect cover for her book. Though she may have reconsidered it if she'd known she'd have to dress like that for the rest of her career.

'Thank you so much for being here today, Marlowe,' the presenter said, a false smile plastered on her plastic features.

'Please,' Marlowe replied, smiling warmly, 'call me Lo.' The nickname was another remnant of her youth that she wished she could leave behind.

The lights in the concert hall dimmed and two small screens illuminated at their feet. One showed the camera angles being broadcast live, while the other contained a countdown to the event's end. It was going to be a lengthy interview, but they had a lot of ground to cover. The presenter jumped right in.

'I want you to take us back to that date – the nineteenth of January 2008 – the night Lily Williams was killed.'

Marlowe took a deep breath. The memories were still so vivid. After all, she'd been reliving them for years via her bestselling book, *The Showgirl's Secret.*

The Showgirl's Secret

by

Marlowe Robertson

CHAPTER 1

The night air was punctuated by screams.

Familiar locations whizzed by – the beach, the harbour, the park. By the time I'd identified one, the next would already be in view. The comfortingly familiar landmarks that made up the seaside township of Kiama took on an uncanny air, reduced to nothing more than a nauseating blur. The showground beneath me only added to the chaos. Blinking lights. Pulsing music. Hordes of people lining up for showbags, sideshow games or carnival-style food.

I could just make out the other rides among the blur. They were all named after dances or natural disasters. The Cha-Cha, Avalanche and Break Dance were equally as nausea-inducing but lacked the spectacle of the Hurricane. It towered over the showground – its six octopus-style arms fanning out – and was accompanied by the deafening hiss of the pneumatic air compressor that powered its ascent. I could cope with the heights; it was the speed the rocket-shaped shuttles gained as they returned to the ground that was the issue.

On the upswing, Rachael's body would slam against mine. It would be her cue to raise her hands above her head as the centrifugal force lifted her from her seat. For that split second, she was weightless – floating above the town – screaming giddily. Her joy was tangible. Probably because it was the closest she'd ever get to escaping the bucolic little hellhole we called home.

'Put your arms up, it's more fun,' Rachael yelled, attempting to pry my vice-like fingers off the shuttle's safety bar.

I held on even tighter as my stomach lurched.

I'd almost managed to get out of having to go on the ride, telling my friends that I couldn't risk leaving the backpack containing my DSLR camera unattended. Unfortunately, and to my horror, one of them had agreed to fall on his sword and become the designated bag holder. After making a big song and dance about it in front of our friends, Dan had placed his hand on my shoulder and looked deep into my eyes, before saying, 'You work too hard, Lo. You deserve some fun.'

To anyone else, it would have seemed like a sweet gesture, but only I could see the deviant glint in his eyes as a cruel smirk carved its way up his cheeks. We'd been the kids to avoid on school excursions – dubbed the 'Chunder Wonders' – because we both suffered from severe motion sickness. He wasn't helping me. He was saving himself.

When the ride finally came to a stop, I hauled my body out of the shuttle and attempted to ground myself. My friends were excitedly talking about a potential round two, and I knew I had to make my escape. I scanned the crowd for Dan, swaying wildly, while trying to prop myself up on the ride's flimsy railing. The entire showground was spinning but, even in my disoriented state, I could tell that he'd vanished. Two days' worth of work was on that camera. My rage and nausea intermingled – a potent combination – and my foot reached for a step that wasn't actually there.

Fortunately, the quick reflexes of the ride operator saved me from face planting.

'Whoa. You right, love?' he asked, his hands firmly grasping my shoulders.

'Yeah,' I replied, quickly pulling away from his touch and steadying myself. 'Thanks.'

'Your mate's round the back, by the way.'

Relief washed over me, but it wasn't enough to quell my queasiness.

Despite the ground appearing to undulate beneath my feet, I was able to tiptoe through the vine-like wires between the Hurricane and the ghost train. When I reached the other side of the trailers, I saw Dan and the ghost train operator sharing a joint, staring out over Surf Beach. The carny saw me first and loudly cleared his throat before nodding in my direction. He looked uneasy.

'Don't worry – she's cool,' Dan said, turning to face me.

'Can't be too careful,' the carny replied. 'Fuckin' pigs everywhere.'

'Yeah, I know,' I said, flopping facedown onto the ground next to Dan. 'My dad's head pig.'

'What the fuck, man? I thought you said she was cool?'

'She is.'

'I am?'

'Stop fucking around, Lo,' Dan snapped. 'You're freaking him out.'

'I will not dob anyone in if they promise to make the world stop spinning.'

'Here,' Dan said, passing me the joint.

'No, I'm gonna puke.'

'It's good for nausea,' the carny said. 'Half my business comes from cancer patients going through chemo.'

He had a point.

I inhaled deeply, and my stomach heaved as the acrid smoke hit my lungs. I clamped my eyes shut, but the darkness just exacerbated the feeling that I was still hurtling through the air. The Hurricane had restarted and the roar of the air compressor reverberated through the ground, making things all the more disorienting.

'See?' Dan said to the ride operator. 'She's complicit now.'

'I was never going to narc on you in the first place.'

'Good,' the carny said, bending down to stare me straight in the eyes. 'I've had enough trouble tonight.'

I raised a quizzical eyebrow at him, but it seemed to send another wave of nausea coursing through my body. I groaned loudly, inhaling the scent of the oval beneath me. The grass was surprisingly cool.

'Lo actually might be able to help clear things up,' Dan said. 'She works with her.'

'Well, you tell that psycho bitch she's lucky he's not pressing charges.'

'What?' I asked.

'The whole thing with Lily on the ghost train,' Dan replied. 'You saw it, right?'

I closed my eyes and sighed. Lily's face was still etched behind my eyelids.

I hadn't just seen it; I'd photographed it.

CHAPTER 2

As part of my internship with the local paper, I was tasked with documenting the show for an online gallery. Normally, the job would have gone to Lily but, as she was this year's showgirl, she was required to be in front of the camera rather than behind it. It pissed me off that I was in her shadow once more, but it was also the most responsibility I'd had during my entire year of interning. I wasn't going to let it go to waste.

I'd spent the last two days photographing the sights of the show, hoping to capture its essence. I was already thinking of an angle for my photo essay and had landed on 'competitiveness'. Because, at the end of the day, that's what the show was all about. It wasn't about 'family' or 'community' or 'rural identity'. It was about winning.

I'd scored some great shots too. The triumphant fist-pump of the winning woodchopper; a young equestrian kissing the muzzle of her champion showjumper; a wall of submitted artwork covered in prize-winning ribbons; and – of course – the most victorious competitor of all: the showgirl and her sash.

I'd been given full creative control over my coverage of the show, save for the showgirls. The paper's editor, Mark, had insisted on overseeing everything involving them. So, instead of the candid shots I'd been taking all weekend, I was forced to capture awkwardly manufactured moments. I was loath to admit it but, surprisingly, I'd found myself enjoying taking pictures of Lily. There was something about her – there always had been – and it became more obvious when observing her from behind the lens.

She'd always been striking. Not to mention, my complete antithesis. Her statuesque form towered over my average height, while my pale skin looked ashen against her bronzed tan. Even my favourite feature – my poker-straight jet black hair – appeared to deflate next to her mass of honey-blonde curls. But her most arresting features were undeniably her eyes. She was born with heterochromia. Her right iris was green, while her left was blue. It was something she was bullied about as a child but, as an adult, it gave her an other-worldly air.

So, when Mark insisted I take photos of the showgirls as they emerged through the saloon-style doors of the ghost train, I reluctantly obliged. I set myself up in front of the train's exit and snapped a few test shots, while Mark loaded Lily and two of the runners-up into a small cart. I held my finger on the camera's shutter. To get the shot that I needed I'd have to react the second the doors pushed open. The ride operator was already getting antsy that we had commandeered the ghost train, which put even more pressure on me to get the shot on the first go.

Suddenly, my finger pressed down. I'd reacted to something but it wasn't the doors opening. There had been a scream – a loud one – and it had come from inside the ghost train.

I raised my eye from the camera and realised that the exterior lights had all been extinguished. The animatronic ghouls dotting the ride's outer wall had also stopped moving – their piercing laughter silenced. In the line out front, people talked in hushed whispers, while the ride operator disappeared through the ghost train's entrance. I caught Mark's eye and he aggressively pointed at the camera. I sighed, lining up the shot once more.

The exit doors flung open and I held my finger down, capturing bursts of images. Through the lens, I realised that I hadn't got my shot. Instead, the images were of Lily running from the ghost train – a look of genuine terror imprinted on her features. She ran straight towards me. For a moment, I thought she was going to bowl me over but she changed her course at the last second and our shoulders lightly brushed. I spun around, but she kept running like a woman possessed.

My mind was racing. What the hell had happened in there? I quickly realised that the two runners-up were yet to emerge from the ride and thought the worst. But, as I spun back around, the doors flung open again, revealing them both. They were still seated in the cart – which was being pushed along by the ride operator – and seemed fine, albeit a little embarrassed. I snapped a few pictures. But, without Lily, they were pointless.

'Sorry, folks,' the carny announced to the waiting queue. 'We've lost power. Hopefully she'll be up and running soon but any pre-purchased tickets can be used for other attractions.'

I watched as Mark offered his hand to the two girls, apologising profusely, and escorted them out of the cart. I also watched him disappear through the doors of the ride, arguing with the carny. While I waited for them to sort things out, I scrolled through the photos of Lily. They were stunning, yet genuinely unnerving.

She was looking particularly ethereal that night, wearing swathes of white lace with a crown of calla lilies set on top of her waist-length hair. In the photos, her loose curls were fanned back from her face from the force of her movement. It made her expression seem even more stark. That was fear – real fear – the type that takes over your entire body. It was palpable, even in photographic form.

I felt a hand on my shoulder and jumped a mile.

'Fuck!' I made eye contact with Mark and immediately chastised myself for appearing unprofessional. 'Sorry, you scared me. I was miles away.'

'She has that effect on people, doesn't she?'

I frowned and he gestured at the camera's screen.

'What happened?' I asked.

'The circuit tripped. From the sounds of it, Lily had a panic attack and needed to get out.'

'Jesus.'

'Yeah.' He sighed. 'I'm going to try to find her. Or at least her parents. You're done for the night. The gallery will go live first thing Monday morning, so I'll need the photos and your copy to approve by lunchtime tomorrow.'

'Will do!' I replied before cringing at my over-enthusiasm.

'Maybe leave that one out, yeah?' he said, gesturing at the image.

'Yeah. It doesn't really fit with my theme.'

'Theme?'

'I was hoping to explore the nature of competitiveness and what it means to us as a town. Every aspect of this whole show is based on winning or losing –'

'Whoa, calm down there, Lo. There's no Walkley for internet galleries. Don't make this more complicated than it needs to be. Check out the ones Lily has done and replicate that, okay? We want people to actually click on the bloody thing.'

'Sure,' I nodded, trying not to sound as deflated as I felt.

'I've really gotta go, darl,' he said, staring off into the crowd. 'Say hi to your dad for me.'

He headed off in Lily's direction and I looked at the photos I'd taken of her. My finger hovered over the delete button, but I couldn't go through with it.

CHAPTER 3

'To be fair, if I were trapped inside some creepy ghost train when it blacked out, I think I'd freak out too,' I told the carny and Dan.

'Look, I told your boss the carts weren't designed for more than two people, but he wanted to squeeze three in for the photo. Besides, the circuit didn't trip until after your friend had her little freakout. *After* she assaulted one of my men.'

I shot Dan a puzzled look and he nodded before taking another drag on the joint.

'And besides,' the carny continued, 'since Luna Park, we have backup generators for all the internal emergency lights. It was bloody brighter in there than it was outside!'

'What do you mean she assaulted someone?' I asked.

'The stupid bitch gave Steve a black eye.'

'In the ghost train?'

'Yeah,' Dan interrupted. 'He's one of the scarers. Y'know, wears a mask, taps people on their shoulders to give them a fright. Apparently Lily didn't take it too kindly.'

'That's a bloody understatement!' the carny spat. 'She swung her elbow back and hit him square in the face. Then she starts screaming and tries to get out of the cart. You're not supposed to get out of them while they're still moving! Add that to the extra weight, the whole circuit blew. Fuckin' nightmare.'

I held out my hand for the joint and took a drag. None of that explained the fear on Lily's face. 'You sure your man only touched her on the shoulder?'

'What the fuck sort of question is that?'

'I'm just trying to work out what would make her freak out so much,' I shrugged. 'Lily's not like that.'

'Yeah, well neither are my men. This is a family business – hell, we work with kids – if anyone showed even a *hint* of that type of behaviour, we'd sit them on their arse and make sure they never worked again.' He hocked a ball of spit onto the ground, perilously close to my face. My nausea resurfaced. 'Your town's precious showgirl is just a nutter.'

I shut my eyes again. My vertigo was as strong as ever, but there was something else that was making me uneasy. Lily's fearful face. There was more to the story. I knew it.

My phone buzzed in my pocket and I pulled it out and squinted at the screen – a text from my dad containing nothing but three question marks. I looked at the time.

'Shit.' I sat upright and punched Dan's shoulder. 'I told you to tell me when it was a quarter to.'

'I'm not your friggin' secretary.'

'Goddamn it, I've got to go. Give me my bag.' I snatched my backpack out of Dan's hands and ran off towards the pavilion.

'Oi,' the carny yelled behind me. 'You can't go that way!'

I gave him the finger and kept running.

I wasn't exactly what you would call 'close' with my dad – especially after my mum died – but we shared a few rare rituals that stoked the fire of familial connection. One of those rituals was watching the show's fireworks together every year. We had the best seat in the house – the bonnet of Dad's police car – where we'd dump out the contents of our showbags and eat cheap lollies as the fireworks erupted around us.

As a kid, I'd typically be clutching a stuffed animal almost as big as me. My birthday was on the twelfth of January and the show always fell in the following week, so my dad would win me a bonus present at the shooting gallery every year. He never missed a shot, and it was one of the only times I was actually proud to be a cop's daughter.

My dad was a man of few words and our conversations always seemed stilted. My mum had been the bridge between that gulf but, with her gone, we'd drifted further and further apart. So, to be able to share each other's company without uttering a word felt like the closest we'd ever get to having a real relationship. I would never have admitted it out loud, but I cherished those moments.

Which was why I was now sprinting between the showbag trailers to loop around the back of the pavilion. The ride operator was right; the area was technically off-limits to the public while the carnies' caravans were parked there. But it was the shortest route to the other side of the show ring and my only hope of reaching my dad before the fireworks started. It was creepy around there on the best of days, even more so when it was deserted like now, but I kept running.

The entire showground had fallen into disrepair over the years and was soon to be part of a multimillion dollar renovation. This show was the last hurrah before the old pavilion and its grandstand would be torn down. The only thing that would remain would be the historic stables – two long rows of parallel stalls – that had housed the show's competing horses for over a century and a half.

The stables were now eerily empty. All the animals had been removed before the fireworks. The only sound came from my boots reverberating against the concrete floor and rattling the rusted locks that adorned each stall. The ground was covered in brown needles from the towering Norfolk pines that dotted the showground, and I had to slow my pace to avoid slipping.

There were no lights among the stables, but the moon was almost full – its glistening snail trail reflecting off the ocean in front of me. It always surprised me how close the perimeters of the showground were to the cliff's edge and the roaring ocean below. I still felt nauseous, even with the cool sea breeze. The air was brined. Sticky with that salty scent.

I don't know why, but from the second I noticed the foot protruding from the stall I knew I'd stumbled upon something I wasn't supposed to see. My gut reaction was that it was two people sharing an intimate – though apparently passionless – moment. I even contemplated retracing my steps and running behind the stables to avoid any awkwardness, but there was something about the foot's stillness that signalled something was wrong. The fact that I recognised it made me all the more uneasy. I'd taken enough photographs of her that day to identify those gold gladiator sandals anywhere.

'Lily?' I called out.

I strained my ears to hear something – anything – but it was completely silent. I took a step forward. The stall's opened door was blocking my view of anything more than that motionless foot. The answer to my question was centimetres away from me, but I couldn't bear to answer it myself.

'Lily, it's Lo. Are you okay?'

Again, nothing.

'Lily?' I repeated, reaching towards the door.

BANG, BANG, BANG, BANG, BANG.

I gasped, stumbled forward and clutched my chest. Above the stalls, magenta fireworks bloomed. The air smelled of gunpowder, and the disembodied voices of the crowd oohed and aahed. I awkwardly laughed at my skittishness, before realising that I had fallen directly in front of the stall. I was a glance away from my answer. I slowly lifted my head.

From the second I saw her, I knew.

CHAPTER 4

Lily looked shocked by her own death – those polychromatic eyes frozen in surprise – her lips parted as if gasping at a particularly scandalous secret. But beneath her flower crown and halo of golden hair, a pool of blood had blossomed. She was lying on her side, in the foetal position, with one arm outstretched as if she were reaching towards something – or someone – unseen.

Her matching lace top and skirt were still a pristine white, both seemingly spared from the blood that had slowly drained from the deep wound on her temple. Had her head not been resting in the gelatinous red pool, I may have never even noticed the injury, hidden beneath her curls.

It struck me as fitting that, even in death, she inspired awe. The whole scene seemed staged. It was too perfect. Too pretty. A meticulously constructed tableau.

I'd seen bodies before, though never in real life. My dad had a nasty habit of leaving open copies of the *Police Journal* lying around the house. On the kitchen counter, the dining room table or next to the toilet. As a child, I was never quite sure when or where I'd inadvertently catch my next glimpse of a corpse. I grew desensitised to the bodies and eventually became fascinated by the articles behind the pictures. It was one of the main reasons I aspired to be a crime reporter. One person's early childhood trauma is another's career catalyst.

But none of those bodies looked like Lily's. They were all gruesome, macabre and – above all else – ugly. The trauma of the crime seemed to permeate every aspect of the body. Faces frozen in distorted depictions of fear. Blood and viscera spewing from necrotising flesh. Extremities awkwardly contorted in agonising positions. They lost all aspects of their humanity. They were nothing more than meat.

A surge of nausea took over my body, and a watery, acidic feeling stung the back of my throat. I sprang to my feet and ran to the edge of the stables before projectile vomiting into a pile of pine needles. Above me, the fireworks kept erupting – the sound echoing around the stables like gunshots. When I turned back towards Lily's stall, I finally saw the ugliness.

Lily's top had ridden up underneath her sash, exposing the small of her back. A patch of her skin was missing, but the wound didn't look fresh. As I walked towards her, I noticed seven strange symbols had been carved around the flayed flesh. I could only just make out the markings when the fireworks exploded and they faded into obscurity in between bursts. I looked around. The area was still deserted. I placed my backpack on the ground and carefully reached inside, retrieving my camera.

I only took a few photos. Enough to be able to see the markings clearly. My instinct told me they were the key to her death, and the reason behind her fear on the ghost train. I was careful, though, trying to time the flashes with the fireworks so as not to draw attention.

Looking at the symbols on the camera's screen, I struggled to recognise them. Some were letter-like, but others were made up of strange intersecting lines. Much like the patch of missing flesh on her back, they didn't look fresh.

In the distance, rapturous applause broke out. The fireworks had finished and the show was officially over. I removed the camera's battery and placed it in my pocket – so no one would be able to tell I'd taken the photos – before returning the camera to my backpack and slinging it over my shoulder. I had to tell my dad about Lily. Her killer must have been at the show and everyone was about to leave. I began walking away but hesitated, turning to take one final look at the body. I raised my hand to the shoulder Lily had rammed into earlier that evening. It was the last time I saw her.

I rounded the corner of the stables and walked up the incline, spotting the police four-wheel drive about halfway down the show ring. My dad was still sitting on the bonnet, staring up at the sky as if waiting for more fireworks to erupt. He looked smaller than he should have and I realised that was a thought I'd been having more and more lately. It seemed connected to the grey overtaking his sideburns and the deep lines embedded in his jowls. A wave of guilt overwhelmed me.

Already, the crowd was slowly filing out of the grandstand, making their way towards the exits. I struggled to think that Lily's killer could be among them. While Kiama was a tourist town, the show was predominantly attended by locals. It was our way of reclaiming our home after spending the summer holidays being swamped by strangers. Which meant, as unfathomable as it may have seemed, that I likely knew the culprit. I quickened my pace.

'I don't want to hear it, Lo,' my dad said as I finally reached the car. He sounded genuinely hurt.

'But –'

'It's fine.'

'No –'

'You're twenty-two –'

'Dad –'

'You can make your own choices about who you spend –'

'Jesus Christ, Dad, shut up! There's a body!'

His brows knitted in confusion. 'What?'

'It's Lily. She's dead. In the stables.'

His eyes scanned my face, searching for answers. 'What happened?'

'I don't bloody know – I only found her. But we've got to hurry; her murderer could be walking away with the rest of the crowd.'

He seemed taken aback. 'What makes you think she was murdered?'

'Well, I don't think she bashed her own brains in! And she has these weird symbols carv–'

'Get in the car,' he said, sliding off the bonnet.

On the short drive back to the stables, my dad questioned why I had been there. It was only then that I realised how suspicious it seemed.

'I didn't kill her!'

'I know. But you're going to be interviewed and you need to get your story straight.'

'I was taking a shortcut. The queue for the Hurricane was really long and, by the time we finally got on, I'd lost track of time. I didn't want to miss the fireworks so I took the shortest route.'

'So, you've been with people all night?'

I replayed everything I'd done that evening. 'Yeah. The only time I was alone was running from the Hurricane to you.'

'Did you see anyone else there?'

'No, it was deserted.'

We pulled up near the stables and my dad asked me to retrieve a pair of latex gloves from the glove box while he searched for a torch in the back. Acquiring both, we returned to the scene of the crime. Immediately, he spotted my pile of vomit at the edge of the stables and shone the torch's beam over it. My nausea returned.

'That's mine,' I sheepishly admitted.

'Oh, are you okay?'

'Yeah. As I said, I went on the Hurricane. You know how I get.'

The torch's beam swept along the concrete floor of the stables and the padlocked doors until it spilt into the open void of Lily's stall. From that angle, you saw the symbols before you saw anything else. The crimson etchings almost shimmered in the torch's light, and the strange misshapen patch of missing flesh looked even more horrifying illuminated.

'Shit,' my dad murmured.

I watched as he examined her body – squatting down beside her, his eyes meticulously scanning every millimetre of her flesh – but his gaze always returned to the symbols. He carefully pulled the gloves over his hands before turning to face me.

'Lo?'

'Yeah?'

'I need you to do me a favour. It's gonna sound bad, but you have to trust me.'

There was something in his voice that scared me – like I was talking to a completely different person.

'What?'

'You can't tell anyone about the markings.'

'But –'

'Marlowe, listen to me. This is important. I'm going to pull her top down and that's going to be how you found her. The rest of your story will stay exactly the same, you just never saw the marks, okay?'

'Dad, you're really –'

'You did *not* see the markings.'

The ferocity behind his words shocked me. I'd never seen him act like this. I found myself slowly backing away from him; my eyes swaying from his stern face to Lily's corpse. I didn't know what to do.

He sensed my fear and softened. 'I'm sorry, but I promise there's a good reason for this. I wouldn't put you in this position if there weren't. It won't impact the investigation, but it will keep you out of it, and that's what matters here. Please, Lo, trust me.'

I felt as if a pair of hands had wrapped around my throat, slowly crushing my windpipe. I could feel my heart thumping against the wall of my chest. None of it felt real, like the crescendo of a nightmare just before you woke up. It wasn't real. It wasn't happening.

But she was there, and so were the marks.

Between ragged breaths, I was somehow able to utter two syllables.

'Okay.'

CHAPTER 5

As the crowd streamed from the showground's gates, sirens pierced the cool night air. I was sitting in the back of my dad's police four-wheel drive, my legs dangling over the towbar, with a musty picnic blanket wrapped around my shoulders. The moon had risen since I'd last looked at it, and the calmness of the ocean belied the chaos occurring behind me. Police officers and detectives had taken over the showground. By that stage, many others had seen Lily's body, but no one appeared to have seen the markings.

My dad had sprung into action the second I'd agreed to lie about them, and I was already regretting my decision. But I was now complicit. From the second he'd carefully pulled her top down the timeline had shifted and the world where I'd seen the markings had ceased to exist.

I wanted to trust him, but he hadn't done much to gain that trust. In between radio chatter, he asked me to repeat my story again and again. He only stopped when I told him it was going to sound rehearsed.

He set me up in the back of the car, gently wrapping the blanket around my shoulders, before telling me that someone would eventually drive me to the station to be interviewed. He wouldn't be able to accompany me, he'd said, as he was running point on the crime scene, but he assured me that the detectives were all 'top blokes'. They were always top blokes, even when they clearly weren't.

My phone was buzzing in my pocket continually. The show's exiting crowds had all seen the police cars arriving and everyone wanted to know the gossip. What better source than the daughter of the town's top brass?

I reached into my jacket pocket and pulled out my phone, surprised by the small pieces of paper that exploded from the cavity like confetti. My spine was iced as I carefully unfurled each crumpled raffle ticket and I felt guilty that I had unceremoniously stuffed them in there in the first place. I felt a tickle on my cheek and, as I brushed it away, I was shocked to find that my fingertips were wet with tears.

Lily had given me the tickets – not long before she'd hopped into the ghost train's cart. It had all started when we were young; way back in the day when my mum was alive and our two families were still close. My mother had not only been responsible for ensuring I had a relationship with my dad, she had also been the conduit between him and the rest of the community. When she was alive, we'd socialised with people like the Williamses, but when she died all those ties were suddenly severed. My father just didn't have the energy to maintain them. Not that I was one to complain – being a loner had always suited me.

The yearly raffle was always to win a pony, and I can remember throwing the mother of all tantrums when my parents refused to buy me a ticket when I was younger. In all fairness, our former backyard-less home was hardly the best place to keep a farm animal but try telling that to a young kid who was giving Veruca Salt a run for her money. What can I say? I didn't care how – I wanted it *now.*

I'd been particularly upset because Lily had received multiple tickets from her parents. Sure, it was because her family actually had the space for a pony but, to my young mind, it was further proof that a gross injustice had been committed. To her credit, Lily did what she could to right the injustice – by giving me half of her tickets. Neither of us won that night, but it was enough to sate me.

Every year Lily repeated the gesture – going so far as to *only* buy tickets for me – and, despite my protestations the older I grew, it became something of an inside joke between the two of us. But, surprisingly, the joke was never at my expense. Anyone else would have held it over my head and used it to remind me of what an obnoxious brat I used to be. But that wasn't how Lily worked – she gave me the tickets because she genuinely wanted me to win. She was selfless like that.

We never won but I always felt a surge of hope when the winner was drawn. I didn't even want a pony any more, but you'd never know it as I carefully memorised each ticket number and silently willed it to be read aloud. I'd missed the drawing that night, but deep down I knew my number hadn't been called.

I wiped my tears away before carefully placing the tickets back in my pocket. I pulled out my phone and scrolled through the messages. Each was more desperate than the last, but I couldn't blame the townsfolk for their callous curiosity. The carnies getting drug-busted or caught up in a brawl was seemingly the most logical guess. After all, it had certainly happened before. But no one would have suspected there was a body; least of all Lily's. That sort of thing just didn't happen here.

Only Dan's message inquired about my own safety, so I replied to him, confirming that I was fine. I wanted to tell him more, but the words never felt right. It just wasn't the kind of news that could be conveyed via text. I came up with an alternative.

Don't worry, your carny mate didn't get busted.

He replied.

i was kinda hoping he would tbh
that stuff was shit

I sniffed my hair to make sure it didn't reek of pot – after all, I was about to spend the next few hours in the company of police officers – but was instead greeted by the faint scent of my coconut conditioner. I inhaled deeply. There was something comforting about it.

'The mo looks good on you,' a cocky voice teased.

I dropped the strands of hair that I'd been holding to my upper lip.

'At least one of us can grow one,' I replied, smirking at the baby-faced constable who'd appeared by my side. He feigned offence, but I knew he actually loved it.

CHAPTER 6

I'd known Nathan since he'd graduated from the Goulburn police academy several years earlier. He was a typical country boy with a broad accent and a less broad perception of the world around him. He'd apparently struggled academically but excelled at the physical and practical work the academy offered. He was also rumoured to have raised a few red flags during his admissions process, leading him to be assigned a mentor during his first station placement. That mentor was my dad.

He'd never outright said it, but I always believed my dad saw Nathan as the son he'd never had. With my own interest in the world of policing dwindling the older I grew, my dad needed someone to look up to him again. Nathan was the perfect candidate, enthusiastically listening to the stories I'd long grown tired of hearing.

Sure, he wasn't the brightest crayon in the box, but he was the kind of guy who'd have your back when a situation turned violent. My dad had spent years bemoaning the quality of recruits coming from the academy – more book-smart than street-smart – and so he always had a soft spot for those who would unthinkingly put their lives on the line. Some would call it bravery, others stupidity.

I got along with Nathan fairly well, all things considered. We'd both lost a parent young and clearly bore the scars in adulthood. We had the same type of combative and competitive relationship a brother and sister would have, but things seldom turned nasty.

We were both prone to foot-in-mouth moments and wore our emotions on our sleeves. The only difference was that I had learned how to handle the aftermath. In contrast, I don't think I'd ever heard Nathan say the word sorry.

Which was why I shouldn't have been shocked when I hopped into his police car, and he began rummaging through the fast-food packaging littering the floor. Naively, I thought maybe he was embarrassed by the mess and was haphazardly cleaning up but, when he threw a Red Rooster bag at my face, I realised my mistake.

'If you need to spew, do it in there. If even a speck of it gets on the car, I'll bloody clean it up with your hair.'

'Piss off,' I said, throwing the bag back at him.

'I really thought you were made of tougher stuff, Lo. That was the most beautiful body I've ever seen in me life, and you're spewing your guts up like a pussy.'

'Beautiful? That's the creepiest thing you've ever said, and that's saying a lot!'

'S'true though. Did your dad ever tell you about my first body?'

I sighed. 'Probably . . .'

'Oh, you'd remember it if he did. Ninety-eight-year-old woman with no family. Was dead for a month before anyone noticed anything. During a real bad heatwave, too. She was fuckin' liquefied.'

My stomach lurched.

'She'd sunk into her mattress – like, she became her mattress. Human bloody soup.'

He saw the look on my face and threw the bag back at me. I was worried I might actually need it.

'Worst thing I've ever seen in me life, but I didn't spew, and neither did your dad.'

'Do you want a fuckin' trophy?' I snapped. 'Besides, I didn't throw up because of Lily, I threw up because I'd just got off a ride. I get motion sickness. It's got nothing to do with me being a "pussy".'

He held his hands up in surrender, 'All right, calm down.'

'And you didn't even know soup lady. So you can't possibly know what it's like to suddenly find the body of someone you've seen almost every day of your life, can you?'

I didn't let him answer.

'I mean – fuck – up until my mum died, Lily was my bloody best friend! So even if I *did* throw up because of her, I think it's justifi–'

Tears bit at the corners of my eyes, and I quickly turned my head away. The last thing I wanted was for Nathan to see me cry. He sighed deeply, and we sat silently for what seemed like an eternity. Finally, he broke the silence.

'Fuck, Lo. I dunno what to say. I'm really sorry.'

'Just take me to the station.'

The trip was short, but the awkward silence was making me impatient. The main street of Kiama scrolled past my window – desolate and decaying – a ghost town in the making. There was a palpable tension in the air, and Nathan awkwardly shifted in his seat. He was obviously uncomfortable but finally deployed a trick he must have learned from my dad – he pretended nothing had happened.

'There's probably a reason why your dad never told you that story.'

I ignored him, but he continued.

'I might not have spewed but I really struggled with the whole thing. The smell stayed with me for days, no matter how many showers I had or how much deodorant I sprayed on meself. I couldn't eat, I couldn't sleep. It was affecting me real bad.'

In the reflection of the passenger window, I caught myself rolling my eyes.

'And because I kept talking about it, suddenly I've got a mandatory appointment with the bloody department shrink, who says it's all in me head. Saying I have PTSD or some shit.'

I slowly turned to face him, caught off guard by the admission. He kept his eyes on the road and pulled the car into the station's driveway.

'Finally, your dad tells me to use a nostril trimmer because the smell's stuck on the hairs. Only problem was, I'm not an old fart like him so I didn't have one. So I go rooting underneath me bathroom sink and find me girlfriend's Nair . . .'

'Oh, god,' I said, trying not to laugh.

'Yeah, dunno how you ladies put that shit on your undercarriage, it would melt a bloke's balls off in a second. But I didn't know that, did I? So, I start sticking it up me nose, and the next thing you know I'm in emergency with second-degree burns.'

I started cackling wildly. A genuine guttural laugh that descended into a coughing fit.

'All right, it's not that funny, Princess Pukey. Still haven't lived it down at the station. But you know what? The smell went away, didn't it? Shows what those psychologist fuckers know.'

'It also explains why you can't tell that this car smells like the tip.'

'Oh shit, really?' he said, reaching into the centre console.

He pulled out a can of cheap deodorant and began spraying the car. I dived out the door to avoid smelling like a high school locker room.

CHAPTER 7

We may have arrived in the driveway of the police station, but – technically – we were also in the front yard of my home. My dad and I had lived in the station's neighbouring lock-up cottage since my mum died. It was supposed to be a temporary measure – a way for my dad to still work while he raised a child on his own – but the town soon grew accustomed to having a police officer on the grounds 24/7. Kiama police station was never intended to be constantly manned and before we moved in the nearest permanent police presence was over twenty minutes away.

The cottage and the station both dated back to the late 1800s, and it certainly showed. Our home was in a constant state of disrepair, cold and damp on even the hottest days of the year. But the thing I hated most about it was my dad's open-door policy. My home was never truly a home. Instead, it was a glorified extension of the police station, perennially filled with strangers from all walks of life. It was not uncommon for me to leave my bedroom and discover a high-ranking police official raiding my fridge, a grieving widow using my bathroom, or a crim in cuffs curled up on my lounge.

And yet, as I stood in the driveway that evening, the cottage never looked homelier. The distinction between it and the station was now like night and day. One contained a soft and cosy bed where I could sleep off the night's horrors, while the other contained a harsh and sterile interview room where I'd be required to relive them over and over again.

'Come on,' Nathan said, interrupting my thoughts. 'The detective's waiting.'

I begrudgingly followed him.

The detective had a large coffee stain on his shirt, a splotchy shape that tugged at my mind like an inkblot test. There was something eerily familiar about it, but I couldn't put my finger on it. It added a dishevelled air to a person who was supposed to command authority but it also put me at ease. This wasn't the hard-boiled interrogator cop shows had led me to expect.

'G'day, Lo,' he said, standing up from the desk and extending his hand. 'Nice to see you learned how to do your hair yourself.'

I shook his hand hesitantly, and we both took our seats. I had no idea what he was talking about.

He sensed my confusion. 'You don't remember me, do you?'

'No,' I said, shaking my head. 'Sorry.'

'No worries. S'pose it's been a while now. I'm Bob Leary.'

The name was familiar – Dad had obviously spoken about him before – but I still couldn't place him.

'What's this about my hair?'

'Oh, when you were little I found you by yourself, bawling your eyes out. When I asked you what was wrong, you said you couldn't do your hair.'

'When was this?'

'It was at your old house, so it's going back a bit. Must've been . . .'

He paused and scratched the coffee stain. I finally realised what it reminded me of – the pool of blood emanating from Lily's skull.

'Uh, it was Tabitha's wake, actually.'

'Oh,' I said, trying to dull the all-too-familiar gut punch I felt at the mention of my mother's name.

'Yeah, sorry, didn't mean to be such a downer.'

'No, it's okay. I just don't really remember anything from back then.'

He nodded slowly. 'From memory, the issue was that your dad didn't know how to do your hair how you liked it – only your mum could – so you were upset that you didn't look your best for her.'

'Oh,' I repeated. I didn't know how else I was supposed to react.

'I found my wife. Well, ex-wife now – I've since traded in for a younger model,' he winked, 'and she did it for you.'

'Yeah, I don't remember any of that.'

'Do you remember Tabith . . . uh – your mum?'

'I'm not sure,' I admitted. 'Sometimes I think I have memories of her, but I realise they're just based on photos or stories I've been told. I guess I have memories of other people's memories?'

'Well, she was a beautiful woman. Inside and out. You look a lot like her actually.'

I shifted uncomfortably in my seat.

'Anyway, I'll try to get this over as quick as possible, Lo. I know you've had a rough night and just want to go to bed.' He paused and smiled. 'At least you don't have far to go.'

I retold the night's events to the detective in the exact way I'd recounted them to my dad, obviously omitting any mention of seeing the markings. I had also not told either about my brief encounter with the carny and Dan behind the Hurricane. I'd promised them I wasn't a narc and I was determined to keep my word. Besides, it wasn't pertinent to the case in any way so I wasn't too worried.

When the detective found out I had taken photos of the show that night, he asked me to show him on the camera. I thanked my lucky stars that I'd been smart enough to take out the battery. My dad still had no idea I had taken photos of Lily's body, and anyone else finding them would know it had been tampered with. I carefully removed the camera from my bag, placed it on the desk in front of me, and went to great lengths to show I was trying to turn it on.

'It must be dead,' I said, with feigned frustration. I was terrified he was going to ask for the memory card. Technically it belonged to the paper and wasn't mine to hand over, but I didn't know if that would fly as an excuse.

'Aw, no worries,' he replied. 'I'm sure there's nothing there, but make sure you keep all of them just in case we need to corroborate anything.'

'Will do,' I said. I hoped I didn't sound too relieved.

While the detective wrote up my statement to be signed, I asked him what I needed to do with my clothes. He looked bemused.

'Wash them?'

'Aren't they evidence?' I asked.

'I mean, did you touch the body?'

'No!'

'Then they're not much use as evidence.'

'What about my shoes though? Don't you need to rule them out with other footprints at the scene?'

He sighed loudly, rubbing the crease between his eyebrows. 'You watch too much TV, Lo.'

A knock on the door startled me, and Nathan appeared. He was holding a plate of Vegemite toast, cut into triangles, and a mug of hot chocolate.

'Before you go, you need to finish these,' he said, placing them in front of me. 'Your dad insisted.'

'Oi, where's mine?' the detective asked, before stealing a piece off my plate.

I stared down at the blackened toast, sliced into perfectly manageable portions, and realised that I would never be taken seriously by anyone in that station. I'd forever be a child – that little girl crying at her mum's wake because her hair wasn't right.

CHAPTER 8

After I'd read and signed my statement, and begrudgingly finished my meal, I was finally able to leave the station and go home. The interview hadn't been what I'd expected. They hadn't asked me anything about my relationship with Lily, just the cold, hard facts of how I'd come to discover her body. I guess I should have been relieved that they clearly didn't consider me a suspect, but it seemed sloppy. Wasn't the entire point of a murder investigation to treat everyone with a certain level of scrutiny? I felt uneasy. If they were that lax with everyone they'd never find her killer.

It wasn't like I didn't have a motive. Anyone who knew us would know we'd been competing since childhood. For the most part, things had been pretty equal, particularly at school, but once we entered the real world Lily kept pulling ahead. After a mere month of us both interning, she'd been granted a paid role at the local paper. She was also awarded a prestigious scholarship at uni, despite us both having the same high distinction average. And the real kicker? She'd been offered a cadetship at a national newspaper and had been due to start in a few weeks.

Sure, her role at the local paper would need to be filled – and likely by me – but that didn't mean I wasn't frustrated. She was finally going to escape this town while I was still trapped. Hell, people have certainly killed for less.

I obviously didn't do it. But they didn't know that, did they?

I opened the front door of the cottage and was greeted by the damp smell that I'd come to associate with domesticity. No one was home but that wasn't surprising. I knew my dad would likely be at the showground well into the morning.

I kicked off my boots and flopped down on my unmade bed, landing on something hard. I stared up at the horror movie posters that lined my walls then pulled my laptop from under my spine and opened it. A gallery of the previous day's photos appeared on the screen. I removed my camera from the backpack and plugged it into the laptop. Before I knew it, I was looking at Lily's body again.

The wounds on her back looked even more gruesome on the screen, and the gravity of what I'd done finally hit me. It was wrong to have taken the photos in the first place, let alone now that my dad had made me promise not to tell anyone about the markings. And yet, in a way, his behaviour almost justified the photos' existence.

I saved them in a hidden folder on my hard drive, before backing them up on a USB. As a final precaution, I emailed them to myself. I then erased them from the camera's memory card. To an outside observer, it was like they'd never been taken. My dad's secret was safe – for now – and so was mine.

I looked at the time. It had been almost five hours since I'd discovered Lily's body, and yet it felt like both more and less time had passed. It was early in the morning and I should have been asleep but I knew I wouldn't be able to. My gallery for the paper was due in a mere matter of hours but I was unsure if it would actually run given the night's events. Still, it was probably best if I got it done. It would show my editor, Mark, that I could make a deadline under any circumstances.

The newspaper's office and printing press were just around the corner from me and I considered physically going in. It was likely that Mark was already there. After all, he had enough ears on the ground to know when something big like this had gone down. Normally, I would have expected a call – one of my only advantages over Lily was that

I lived much closer to the paper than her – but Mark also likely knew that I'd found the body and would assume I was unavailable. But I wasn't, and I was undeniably the story's biggest asset. I just had to convince him of that fact.

To my surprise, when I arrived at the office the main lights weren't on but a faint glow was coming from somewhere in the back – the editor's office. Mark must have been there, but he clearly hadn't called anyone else in. I smiled. It was the perfect opportunity for me to pitch my angle for the story on Lily. I tried the door. It was unlocked.

I carefully navigated my way through the pitch-black bullpen. The paper was another relic from the 1800s but, as the office lacked the familiarity of my home, I found it slightly unnerving. The only other time I'd been here this early was on printing nights, and right now I missed the comforting drone of the press whirring out back.

I managed to make it to the editor's office without bumping into anything. The door was open, so I peered in and saw that the space was empty. There was an opened bottle of rum on the desk, as well as Mark's mobile phone and keys. It was odd for him to have left them.

'Mark?' I called out.

'What are you doing here?' a voice croaked from behind me.

I spun around, shocked, but couldn't make anyone out among the darkened desks.

'Mark?'

'Bring the booze,' the voice commanded. It was definitely him.

I grabbed the bottle off the desk and walked back out into the bullpen. I still couldn't figure out exactly where he was seated, so I flicked on one of the large banks of lights. One by one, the fluorescent tubes illuminated, casting a blinding light over the room.

'Don't!' He covered his face with his arm.

But it was too late, I'd already seen him.

Mark was hunched over Lily's desk, looking dishevelled. His eyes were red and puffy. He'd obviously been crying. He'd been drinking too. The bottle of rum was far lighter than I'd anticipated, and the ruddiness of his face suggested it had been a fresh bottle only hours before. I knew he was close with Lily's parents, but his behaviour seemed like an odd response to her death.

I plonked the rum down on the desk, trying to avoid the random clusters of crystals Lily had accumulated. She'd recently been going through a hippy phase, extolling the supposed virtues of shiny rocks and other mystical paraphernalia to anyone who'd listen. She'd bought me an expensive-looking necklace with two large blue stones for Christmas. I was never a fan of statement jewellery, so it had remained in its gift bag on my dresser at home. I'd intended to wear it at least once in her presence and I felt bad that I would never get the chance.

'You shouldn't be here, Lo,' Mark grumbled.

'I couldn't sleep,' I said, leaning up against the desk next to Lily's and removing my camera from my bag. 'And I thought I might as well get my gallery done.'

'We're obviously not going to run it now.'

'Well then, I'm here to help,' I said, removing the memory card from the camera and inserting it into the computer. 'What better person to write the article than the one who found her?'

'Jesus.' He looked at me with repulsion and took a swig of the rum. 'Go home, Marlowe.'

I was shocked by the vitriol in his tone, but I was determined to persevere. I knew the story could be my big break. On the computer screen, pictures from the show flickered as they were uploaded. For a split second, I saw Lily's horrified face as she ran from the ghost train. It gave me chills.

'Think about it,' I began. 'This story will be national news in a matter of hours. Out of town journalists will soon be swarming. If we don't act quickly, *they* will be the ones who control the narrative. We owe it to Lily to be the ones shaping her story.'

He rolled his eyes. 'Nice try, but we both know you don't actually believe that. For god's sake, Marlowe, her body's still warm. I would have thought you knew that better than any of us.'

'Which is precisely why I should be the one to write the story.' I could feel myself getting desperate. 'I know things. Things that I know the cops won't release to the press.'

He rubbed his eyes and sighed. 'I know that you've had a shitty evening, but you need to leave before you embarrass yourself any further. For the last time, *go home.*'

Panic began to grip my body. I could feel my only chance to leave this town slip away. Before I knew it, I'd blurted it out.

'There was something strange on her back!'

He sprang to his feet, almost pinning me against the desk. His flushed face was mere millimetres away from mine. 'You are a vulture!' he shouted. 'This – *this* – is why she got the job over you.'

With every syllable he uttered, I was drowned in the scent of rum. My heart pounded against the wall of my chest.

He seemed to sense my fear and lowered his tone, but I was still trapped against the desk. My entire body was shaking.

'You're dangerous. You'd do anything for a story, and that's a liability. People can sense your desperation and they know you'd throw anyone under the bus if it got you what you wanted. I need people in my newsroom I can trust. You can forget about Lily's job, and you can forget about your internship. You're *done* here. Forever.'

My mouth gaped. But, looking into Mark's rage-filled eyes, I knew there was no point in arguing. The unnerving feeling I'd experienced since I'd walked into the paper's office had become suffocating. And Mark had snapped the moment I'd mentioned the markings. It was clear that I needed to get out of there as soon as possible. I picked up my camera and backpack and left without saying a word.

As the front door swung shut and the cold night air engulfed me, streams of tears began pouring down my cheeks. My shaking became even more violent, and my teeth chattered loudly. I slumped against the office's front wall, trying to calm my breathing, but I was on the brink of hyperventilating. I could still feel Mark's inebriated breath caressing my throat. It made my skin crawl. I knew I had to get back home, but my legs felt like jelly.

Nevertheless, I ran.

CHAPTER 9

I never dreamed before she died. Or if I did, I never remembered it. Which was why I was so unnerved when I awoke in my bed hours after I'd fled from the paper. I hadn't realised how exhausted I'd been, and when I crawled under my covers – still fully clothed and sobbing violently – I never anticipated I'd actually fall asleep.

But, before I knew it, I was back at the showground.

I was running between the showbag trailers again, heading towards the stables. I knew what I was going to find, yet my pace didn't slow. Something kept propelling me forward, even though I didn't want to go any further. She'd be there. She'd always be there. I didn't need to see it to realise it.

I tried to stop myself, but I had no control over my body. It was on a predestined path and it was pointless to resist. My pace finally slowed as I reached the stables. But still, I edged forwards – straight towards the opened door of Lily's stall. I tried to close my eyes, but I couldn't. And, as I rounded the corner of the door, the nausea I'd felt in that moment made a disorienting comeback.

But the first thing I saw was not Lily's body. Instead, it was my dad, hunched low to the ground over her corpse. He was doing something to her. Something I wasn't supposed to see. Something far worse than just covering her markings. I began backing away but fireworks erupted above us. He turned, surprised, and locked eyes with me. My blood turned cold.

Because it wasn't my dad, it was Mark. And when I looked at the body in the stable, I realised it wasn't Lily.

It was me.

I ran. Just as I had run from the paper's office but, in my dream haze, the chasm between the two rows of stalls stretched on, seemingly forever. It was as though I were running on the spot because I could see the end of the stables and the edge of the showground but I couldn't get any closer. I could also see her, standing on the cliff's edge, that crown of lilies still perched on her windswept hair. Her back was to me, so I screamed out her name.

'*Lily!*'

Slowly, she turned to face me, that haunted look from the ghost train etched on her features. She was alive. I finally stopped running. Relief washed over me. It was okay, it was all going to be okay. But she still looked so scared – staring through me like I didn't exist. I looked over my shoulder. There was nothing there. Not my dad, not Mark and not my corpse.

'It's okay,' I called out. 'You're okay.'

Tears were streaming down her cheeks, she shook her head from side to side, and then she jumped.

I screamed her name, but it was too late. I ran to the edge of the cliff, terrified of what I'd see. When I stared down at the roaring ocean below, there was no sign of her. But something else caught my attention. The jagged rocks weren't rocks, they were crystals. In fact, the entire cliff face was made up of the glistening gemstones that had adorned her desk.

I knew what I had to do.

I jumped.

I awoke with a start. I was drenched in sweat, tangled up in my sheets, with my body awkwardly contorted. I looked at my hands. My fists had been clenched so tightly that there were nail marks imprinted in my palms. It felt like I hadn't slept a wink, but the pale light filtering through my window had an afternoon quality. My brain reminded me of the previous night's events, and I felt something in my chest drop like a stone. I just wanted to go back to sleep.

I hauled myself upright and dragged my fingers through my hair. I was still groggy, but I knew I had things to do. I spotted the golden gift bag that had been sitting – untouched – on my dresser since Christmas Eve. It was elegant and understated, just like Lily. I grabbed it and sat back down on my bed, carefully digging through layers of tissue paper to reveal a large velvet pouch. I removed the necklace, admiring its lustre.

It was a silver lariat pendant with two stones: one triangular piece that rested in the hollow of the neck and one long shard that hung past the sternum. The crystals were a deep blue, with flecks of gold and white that looked like land masses and clouds over a vast ocean. A satellite image of the earth captured in stone.

I hadn't appreciated its beauty at the time; too caught up in my own personal taste. I remembered being frustrated at her for buying it. Not only did it not fit my style, but it was also clearly expensive. It had made my gift look paltry in comparison.

And yet, she'd smiled so warmly when she opened the trio of leather-bound journals that I couldn't help but feel pleased with my choice. I'd told her she could use them during her cadetship, but she'd said they were too nice for that and that she had a better use in mind. She always had a way of making things seem special, even if they weren't. After all, even Dan had said they were a lame gift when I'd shown them to him.

I noticed something else in the pouch and carefully pulled it out. A small card embossed with gold-foil letters. On the front, it said:

Crystal Clear
Gift Shop
The Terrace Houses, Kiama

And on the back:

Lapis Lazuli.
The stone of truth.
Expose secrets, reveal hidden realities,
unravel the mystery.

I ran my fingers over the card's embossed letters, a small smile creeping up my cheek. Combined with my dream, the whole thing felt prescient – like I was being guided by something or someone unseen. But, before I had sunk too far into my flight of fancy, my pragmatic side kicked in. Had there been more to Lily's sudden interest in mysticism? And, if so, was it connected to the symbols on her back? At least I now had a starting point. I fastened the pendant around my neck. As pragmatic as I was, I knew I needed all the help I could get.

CHAPTER 10

I typically avoided the town on Sundays. The main street of Kiama became almost impenetrable, the footpaths clogged with tables and chairs full of alfresco diners soaking up the sun. Brunch became an endurance sport, as breakfasts stretched into lunches and lunches transformed into dinners. The tourist/local divide was always in full effect, with locals retreating to hidden hole-in-the-wall establishments over the flashy yet overpriced tourist traps. In most cases, it was best to avoid Terralong Street altogether. Even the best coffee in town wasn't worth a half-hour wait.

I paused on the corner of Shoalhaven Street, staring up at the paper's offices, and tried not to think of my encounter with Mark. It still hadn't quite sunk in that he'd fired me. Across the road, Daisy – a life-size papier-mâché cow – stood guard outside The Old Fire Station Art Gallery. Locals painted her once a month, and she was currently a striking black with colourful bursts of fireworks and the show's dates emblazoned on her body. I could feel the town's prying eyes, so I kept walking.

I hated running into people on the best of days, let alone when I knew everyone would want to grill me about my discovery. But I had no choice – to get to the gift shop at the terrace houses, I'd have to run the gauntlet of brunchers. I'd resorted to wearing the international signs of 'don't talk to me' – a hoodie, visible headphones and obnoxiously large sunglasses – but Kiama was anything but international. There was no such thing as personal space or privacy in a small town.

Which was why I was so surprised when I made it down the first half of Terralong Street without so much as a single greeting thrown my way. Don't get me wrong, I'd spotted locals and they'd certainly spotted me. But no one attempted to interact with me. Instead, they stared and whispered, elbowing their fellow tablemates and surreptitiously nodding in my direction. It was an unnerving, yet not entirely unwelcome experience.

I thought of the text messages. There had been so many before anyone knew that someone had died. Before they knew *she* had died. It was clear from their faces that the news had since made the rounds. Sure, people were still brunching, but there was a sombre atmosphere hanging over the street, and my presence was clearly not helping. I was a reminder of what had happened; that the town was not what they thought it was.

I imagined the conversations that had been occurring while I'd slept the morning away. They all broke down into two phrases: 'Not *here*' and 'not *her*'. People didn't get murdered in Kiama, least of all people like Lily Williams.

Continuing down the main street, the sickly smell of freshly made waffle cones filled the air and I instinctively scratched at my forearms. As a teenager, I had worked at the town's self-professed 'famous' ice-creamery and had the war wounds to prove it – crisscrossed scars – from the industrial-sized waffle maker. It was something of a rite of passage for the town's teens, and I had fond memories of my friends and me playing tic-tac-toe on each other's grid-like welts. My mind floated back to Lily's markings. We'd both been scarred by the town, in more ways than one.

As I passed the ice-creamery – trying not to make eye contact with anyone inside – I froze. I hadn't been expecting to see those two-toned eyes again. And yet, I shouldn't have been shocked. After all, the photos from the show ball had been on the photography lab's windows for the past two months. I'd long stopped noticing them as I walked past, but they were impossible to ignore now.

A large number featured Lily. She hadn't been crowned showgirl at that stage, but there were far more photos of her than there were of her competitors. I suppose it was unsurprising. She was a shoo-in for showgirl, and everyone knew it. Not only was she beautiful, well-spoken and intelligent, she was also the by-product of two of the town's most prominent agricultural families.

Both families had always been part of the town. And while Lily's dad, Michael, had forsaken the Williamses' dairy heritage for a career in psychiatry, Lily's mum, Sharon, was living up to the Roses' farming roots as the owner of a prize-winning vineyard and winery. She also happened to be an ex-showgirl herself – further cementing Lily's apparent destiny. The other entrants hadn't stood a chance.

I looked at a photo of the three of them. There had long been rumours that Lily was actually adopted and, looking at them, it was easy to see why. She looked nothing like either of her parents. Her mum was prim and birdlike, with blanched skin and long auburn hair. In contrast, Lily's dad was a wiry and intense-looking man, with thin lips and piercing blue eyes.

They both dressed far too formally, as if to constantly remind the townsfolk that they were better than them. Sharon in old-fashioned dresses, and Michael in suave three-piece suits. They both lacked Lily's warmth and approachability; that special *something* that commanded attention. The fact that Sharon was older than Michael had done little to quell the gossip that she'd been infertile long before Lily was born. However, if she had been adopted, it was a secret the family were determined to keep.

My eyes fell on a photo of Lily and me, our arms around each other's waists, both smiling warmly. It was the only picture of me taken at the event and, to my surprise, I didn't hate it. I had always preferred being behind the camera rather than in front of it, but there was no denying that it was an arresting shot.

I thought back to the moments leading up to the picture. I hadn't wanted to be in it, but Lily's dad had insisted. Even then, there was no denying his powers of persuasion.

CHAPTER 11

The show ball was held at the end of November, to raise money for the main event in late January. It was a special night in Kiama's social calendar when the local leisure centre's main hall was magically transformed from an indoor basketball court to an indoor basketball court sparsely covered with a few tacky decorations.

But it didn't really matter how unimpressive the transformation was since the guests were always too plastered to tell the difference. Despite members of the show committee earnestly declaring that the night was all about 'charity' and 'community spirit', deep down they knew the only drawcard was the open bar.

Unsurprisingly, I'd never been to a show ball before, and having to attend my first one sober was akin to torture. I'd been shadowing the showgirls for the paper since the entrants had been announced earlier in the month, and had photographed them visiting farms, getting makeup lessons and hosting high teas. Each event was as tedious as the last, but nothing could compare to having to watch them that night smile politely as drunken locals groped them during photo ops. I couldn't fathom what it must have felt like to play nice while your former primary school teacher 'accidentally' grabbed you on the arse.

Lily seemed to be the only one who escaped that kind of treatment. I'd love to say it was because they respected her, but it was far more likely due to her parents both being on the show committee (and almost always close by). It was interesting how the men were miraculously able to keep their hands to themselves when they were accountable, but I felt terrible for the other entrants.

I sighed deeply. I needed to get away from the locals and away from the show ball. I clearly wasn't as courteous as the showgirls, and I was concerned I'd make a scene.

Thankfully, along with Sharon Williams' winery, the hotel Dan worked at was supplying the booze that evening, and he and a few of his colleagues were tending bar. He and I had agreed to sneak into the leisure centre's pool at a designated time. He'd bring the drinks and I'd bring the snacks. It was the only thing getting me through the night.

When the clock struck eleven, I made a beeline for the ambitiously named 'canapé' table. It was covered in supermarket deli platters containing delicacies such as mini frankfurts, cheese cubes and generic brand crackers. I placed my camera down on the table and began piling two plates full of food. If I couldn't get my money's worth in booze, I was going to make up for it in cheese.

Unfortunately, I was a little too enthusiastic and accidentally knocked over an empty wine bottle while trying to reach a particularly elusive cheese cube. With both hands otherwise engaged, I watched in horror as the bottle rolled off the tabletop and shattered on the wooden floor. So much for not making a scene.

'Shit,' I mumbled to myself as every person in the hall turned to face me.

'I'm going to have to cut you off, Miss Robertson,' a mellifluous voice murmured somewhere close to my ear.

Lily's dad had always made me uncomfortable. It was the way he looked at me. Like he was drinking me in from head to toe. And yet, strangely, there was nothing sleazy about it. His eyes didn't linger over specific body parts longer than others, and he certainly didn't talk to my chest. Instead, when he looked at me, he seemed to be able to see everything I was and would ever be. It creeped me out.

Of course, I may have been slightly biased. I had never been a fan of shrinks, particularly after I was forced to see one after my mum died.

My experience hadn't even been that bad. I just didn't like the thought of someone getting into my head. Unfortunately, that seemed to be Michael Williams' favourite pastime.

'The sad thing is, I'm not even drinking,' I said, turning to face the voice in my ear.

'Why not?' Michael asked.

'I don't drink when I'm working.'

'Interning,' he corrected.

'Even more so.'

'Come on. Mark hasn't met an open bar he didn't bleed dry. I was under the impression it was the only perk of the job.' He held out the glass of champagne he'd been holding. 'It's fresh, I was bringing it to Sharon before *someone* made a mess that I now need to clean up.'

'Sorry, I'll do it.'

'Don't be silly. And seriously, take this.' He proffered the champagne once more. 'I don't know how anyone could make it through one of these things sober.'

I laughed and took the glass, allowing myself a small sip. Michael got on his hands and knees to pick up the pieces of the bottle while I found the nearest garbage bin and brought it to him.

'What do you think of the new labels?' Michael asked, holding up a large shard of the bottle. The torn label featured the top of the town's lighthouse.

'Uh, very Kiama-ish?'

Michael laughed. 'Sharon *despises* them. Had to fight tooth and nail to retain her family's original crests, but her investors were adamant she include the town's iconic buildings as some branding push.'

'I mean, that small town shit definitely sells, especially to the tourists.'

He nodded, seemingly satisfied. After I'd offered him a few napkins to wipe up the residue, the floor was once more fit for the under twelves basketball team.

'Sorry again, Doctor Williams,' I said as he got to his feet.

'No, I should be thanking you.' He leaned in close like he was about to tell me a secret. 'Anything that gets me out of schmoozing with these pissheads.'

I laughed. 'Well, in that case . . .' I picked up one of the other empty bottles and pretended to smash it against the table.

He was shocked but then laughed heartily. 'You're full of surprises, aren't you? Always a pleasure, Marlowe.'

I smiled and turned to leave. It seemed he hadn't managed to get into my head after all.

Armed with my two plates of nibbles, I headed towards a fire exit that was, perhaps unwisely, disguised in tinsel. Hopefully Dan had left it propped open and all I'd have to do was push it to gain access to the pool. I took a quick look around the hall – everyone was preoccupied – before shoving the door with my hip. To my delight, it opened and I was pummelled with the harsh scent of chlorine.

The majority of the lights were off in the swimming area, save for a few along the walkway and an eerie glow from the pool itself. I could just make out Dan, sitting on the edge, his trousers rolled up to his knees and his legs dangling into the water below. He saw me and waved. I began moving the plates away from my chest and back again while bobbing up and down – a sad, landlocked version of breaststroke – and Dan's laughter echoed around us. I shushed him, but it was too late. I heard the fire door opening behind me. I spun around, flinging cheese cubes in the process.

A foreboding silhouette greeted me. They were holding something that was reflecting the pool's light. We were well and truly busted.

'Forgetting something?' Michael asked.

I didn't know if I should have been relieved, but I was. I stepped forward. I was unsure if he'd noticed Dan and, if he hadn't, I was determined to keep it that way. We were both technically working that night, but only one of us had been employed (and could presumably be fired) by a member of the show committee.

'I know the food was your priority, but I thought you'd miss this,' Michael said, holding up my camera.

'Fuck,' I muttered to myself, helplessly looking at my still-full hands.

'Here,' he said, stepping towards me, before stretching the camera's strap out so he could place it over my head.

I sheepishly thanked him and ducked into the loop.

'Ladies and gentlemen,' his voice boomed around the pool as he placed the strap over my neck, 'presenting this year's Kiama Showgirl.'

'Ugh,' I groaned, doing little to hide my disdain. 'Just hang me with the sash instead.'

He smirked. 'I was wondering why you hadn't entered. I think I just got my answer.'

I realised what I'd said. 'Probably not the best thing to say to a psychiatrist, hey?'

'Not necessarily. You clearly feel strongly about it. Why is that, do you think?'

I wasn't falling for it that easily. 'Do you charge by the hour, doc?'

That smirk was back. 'Look, I know the showgirl competition can appear archaic to a person your age, perhaps even inherently misogynistic. But I'm quite surprised that an intelligent and driven young woman such as yourself doesn't see it for the opportunity it is.'

'Oh, please, save me that "betterment of the community through the betterment of our girls" drivel. I'm intelligent enough to know that being forced to shove my hand up a cow's arse before being lectured to about poise and etiquette is *hardly* an opportunity. I mean, maybe if you switched the makeup classes for self-defence ones? But that wouldn't go down so well with your sponsors and their lecherous meet and greets, now, would it?'

'You misunderstand me, Marlowe. I'm talking in purely pragmatic terms. The showgirl competition is just another bullet point on your CV. You may decry it, but there's no denying its heritage. It holds weight far beyond rural towns like Kiama. It could even be the difference between getting a job or it going to someone else.'

'Like Lily?' I asked, reading between the lines. She'd just been offered her cadetship and the wound was still fresh.

'Perhaps.'

'And here I thought the only thing holding me back was not having a rich daddy with media contacts . . .'

The smirk had graduated to a broad and bemused smile. Michael leaned in and placed his hand on my shoulder. I instinctively recoiled.

'Oh sorry,' he said, sensing my discomfort. 'Just trying to get that chip off your shoulder.'

I couldn't help but smile.

'Come on, Marlowe, you're better than that. And, although it may not seem like it, you do have at least one thing over Lily.'

I raised an intrigued eyebrow.

'*Tenacity*. You're a fighter. Lily's never had to be one. She's lucky, but luck runs out eventually – a fighting spirit never does.'

I didn't know what to say.

'Anyway,' he continued, 'I'll let you get back to your little poolside picnic. I've wasted enough of your time so I can avoid going back in there. Tell your friend I'll cover for him for the next hour or so, but we'll need help cleaning up.'

I thanked him and he headed back towards the fire exit. Just as I turned towards the pool, he called my name.

'Marlowe?'

'Yeah?'

'I'll suggest the self-defence classes.'

CHAPTER 12

Needless to say, once Dan and I had returned from our chlorinated cheese binge, there was little I could do when Lily's dad insisted I participate in the picture that now graced the photo lab's window. At the time, it had frustrated me. He was clearly throwing his weight around because he knew he could, but I was now thankful for the image. It was a reminder that, as much as I had envied her success, we'd actually made a pretty good duo once. I was going to miss that. I was going to miss her. I took one final look at the photo and continued on my way to the terrace houses, passing by the town's monolithic memorial arch and the surprisingly quaint masonic temple.

The crystal store was the very last shop on the so-called 'historical sandstone walk', and I had to navigate through clusters of immobile tourists on their Sunday strolls. The terrace houses were another oddly dissonant feature of the town, undeniably tied to its history but rarely utilised by locals. That had less to do with the stunning restoration of the nineteenth-century quarry cottages and more to do with the overpriced junk spruiked as 'souvenirs' by the inhabiting gift shops.

I finally made it to the end of the strip. The tourists' interest had waned with each store, meaning that the eastern end was almost a ghost town in comparison to the west. I stepped onto the crystal store's verandah before pushing through the beaded curtain that hung in the front door. The beads trickled over my body – mimicking the sound and sensation of rain. It was pleasant until I was overwhelmed by the cloying scent of incense.

There were two other customers in the store, a young couple. One was clearly into crystals, while the other was not. The latter looked at me pleadingly as I entered. He then attempted to use me as an excuse to leave but I told them I was only browsing and that there was no rush. If looks could kill, I would have been eviscerated on the spot. I glanced at the woman they were talking to, dwarfed by the crystal-covered counter. She was presumably the proprietor and looked exactly how you'd expect a crystal store owner to appear.

I walked to the back of the store, which contained a large bookshelf filled with alphabetically ordered titles. My eyes scanned the names. They ran the gamut from *1001 Uses for Crystals* to *Zodiac: A Beginner's Guide*. I wasn't entirely sure what I was supposed to be looking for. After all, it was all bunkum to me. I zeroed in on a book on symbology while the couple finished up their purchase. They'd spent a ridiculous amount of money on nothing more than rocks. Sure, they were pretty rocks, but rocks, nonetheless.

As the trickle of the beaded curtain signalled the couple's exit, I wrestled the large symbology book off the shelf. It was covered in a thin layer of dust, assaulting my already incense-aggravated sinuses and sending me into a sneezing fit.

'I was wondering when you'd come.'

I kept staring at the book jacket. Despite knowing that there was no one else in the store, I assumed the owner wasn't talking to me.

'The seeker of truth.'

Again, I ignored her, but I was feeling decidedly unnerved.

'Your pretty blonde friend looked at that book too.'

I spun around, perplexed. The crystal store owner was clearly pleased with herself, a wry smile gracing her features. I walked over to the counter. I looked into her eyes but I realised she wasn't looking at mine. Instead, her gaze was lower. She was looking at my chest, or – more specifically – my necklace. She recognised it and, therefore, recognised me.

'It's a beautiful piece,' I said, gesturing to the pendant. 'I was delighted to receive it.'

'I'm pleased to hear that. She agonised over it. She said it needed the perfect stones to help you with your task.'

'My task?'

'Solving the mystery.'

My eyebrows knitted in confusion. I felt like the beaded curtain was running over my body once more.

'What do you mean?' I asked.

She looked confused. 'She asked for a stone that would help someone solve a mystery – something that would allow them to see the truth beyond deception – while also protecting them. She said she had a friend who needed it. A writer who was going to expose a horrible secret.'

I felt like the store was closing in on me. 'She knew,' I mumbled. 'She fucking knew.'

The woman looked concerned. 'Are you all ri–'

'She died last night. She was killed.'

Her eyes widened. 'The body at the showground? I only heard about it on the radio.'

I nodded.

'Jesus. I – I didn't know, I swear.' She looked me up and down. 'Are you a cop?'

I shook my head and she looked relieved.

'Look,' she began, 'I don't live here. I'm just a shop owner. I don't believe in any of this stuff. I'm just trying to make a living off tourists and cashed-up new agers. I thought she was the latter. When she was talking about 'mysteries' and 'secrets' I just assumed she thought your boyfriend was cheating on you. I humoured her.'

I sighed. The book was about to slide out of my fingertips. I held it up to the owner. 'Why was she looking at this?'

'She was asking me questions about symbols. She had photos of them.'

I put the book down on the counter and pulled a piece of paper out of my pocket. I had attempted to draw the markings I'd photographed on Lily's body. They weren't a perfect match, but they were close enough.

'Did they look similar to this?' I asked, holding the drawing up.

She shook her head almost immediately. 'No, they were bigger than that and less letter-like. It was kind of like a bunch of circles that sort of looked like a flower. They were carved into something.'

My blood ran cold. 'Skin?'

She looked horrified. 'No! Wood, I think?'

I asked her to show me the symbols in the book, but she told me they weren't in there.

'There was one that was similar, in a different book about sacred geometry.'

'Can you show me?'

She shook her head. 'Your friend bought the only copy.'

'When was the last time you saw her?'

She took a moment to think. 'It's been a few weeks, give or take. Your necklace was the last thing she bought. So, before Christmas?'

I nodded. No new crystals had appeared on Lily's desk since then, so the shop owner was likely telling the truth.

'What was the significance of the stones she purchased for herself?'

The store owner's gaze dropped as if she could no longer bear to look me in the eye.

'They were all stones for safety and protection,' she admitted.

CHAPTER 13

I asked the store owner a few more questions, but she was clearly not the symbology expert I'd anticipated. She also didn't seem to know anything else particularly pertinent to Lily's death, or the reason why she had clearly feared for her life.

'I just thought she was being dramatic,' she said. 'I didn't know.'

Her words struck a chord with me and I'd been feeling similarly dumbfounded yet guilty since I'd exited the store. In hindsight, there had been signs that something was going on in Lily's life but I'd ignored them.

She knew she was going to die. Why didn't we?

Standing outside the crystal store, I looked at my phone. Dan had sent me multiple messages since the morning, and I'd ignored them all. The most recent one was asking me to call in to the bar where he worked because he wanted to see me. The Blue Diamond was just around the corner from the terrace houses, but I had no interest in braving its patrons and their gawking. Still, I needed someone to talk to and my childhood best friend sounded like a pretty good candidate. I texted him back: *Meet me at the bower in 5.*

The bower wasn't actually a bower, but a cluster of trees at the back of the Kiama Blue. The boutique hotel and reception centre were built on the site of my former infants school, and still contained the historic basalt buildings I'd spent my formative years in. It had been a tough adjustment. The Blue Diamond was the only decent bar in town, but it was difficult to kick back with a drink when my mind was telling me I needed to get to class. When Dan started working there, however, we realised his job came with a perk – we could now go to all the places we hadn't been allowed to as kids.

One of those places was the bower, an idyllic little cluster of trees located behind the administrative office, staffroom and principal's office. As kids, we'd been told the area was off-limits because a bowerbird had built its den there and we couldn't disturb it. The older students had said that was just an excuse so the teachers could have their privacy, but I was intrigued by the stories of the little bird decorating its den with stolen prizes – bottle caps, hair accessories and even craft supplies – all in the school's signature colours of blue and gold.

One day I saw my opportunity to finally get to the bottom of the mystery. Dan had been stung by a bee and we were in the school's makeshift sick bay waiting for his parents to pick him up. Someone in the office was supposed to be keeping an eye on us but when she left to go to the bathroom, I couldn't resist that opened back door. Dan watched on in horror as I disappeared towards the forbidden zone. I didn't look back.

Any nervousness I felt melted away the second I locked eyes on the intricately woven structure. It was just as they said it was, covered in blue and gold trinkets, and in the centre stood the most beautiful bird I'd ever seen. Royal blue highlights on inky feathers and piercing violet eyes. It seemed almost mythical.

I remember reaching into my hair and pulling out a small metal barrette that matched the bird's highlights perfectly. I was terrified of spooking it so I was careful to make my movements slow and non-threatening. The bird observed me intently but with curiosity more than fear. I gently bent down and put the hairclip on the footpath in front of me before slowly taking a step back. Almost immediately, the bird began hopping towards the clip. I held my breath. It picked it up and carried it back to its den, before putting it right in the centre. Pride of place.

When I returned to the sick bay, the office lady hadn't returned, so it was like it had never happened. I've never forgotten the feeling I had when I told Dan the story. His eyes grew wide and he completely forgot about his painful bee sting. I painted such a vivid picture that it was like he experienced it for himself. To my delight, the story became a thing of legend at my school, and one of my favourite pastimes was gathering a cluster of students and retelling my tale. Others tried, but ultimately failed, to see the bower for themselves. Its elusiveness just made my story all the more compelling.

Of course, by the time the Blue had taken over, the bowerbird's den had long since disappeared. But it was still my favourite part of the grounds, and Dan and I would regularly meet there on his breaks. He'd always been so jealous that he never saw the bowerbird for himself.

The first thing Dan did when he saw me was wrap his arms around me. I'd always favoured my personal space over his (typically adored) bear hugs, but that day I let go of my urge to fight my way out and submitted. There was comfort there, no matter how fleeting it felt.

'How are you?' he asked. It wasn't a standard greeting – he actually meant it.

'Okay. I think?'

'You should have come in. I was going to shout you a whisky.'

'I'm not really in the mood to deal with other people at the moment.'

He nodded understandingly before digging around in his pockets. 'I thought that might be the case, so here.' He passed me a minibar-sized bottle of Johnnie Walker. 'I mean, it's no Kilmagoon, but I'm kinda limited at this size.'

I smiled, taking the bottle and thanking him.

'You'd fit right in at the moment though. The whole hotel is filled with journos covering the story. I didn't expect it to blow up this quickly, but it's already national news. It's so weird seeing her face everywhere.'

I'd avoided any form of media up until that point but it was no surprise. She was sweet, pretty and had her whole life ahead of her. People ate that shit up.

'I don't know how well I'd fit in at the moment,' I said. 'Mark fired me.'

'What? When?'

'Last night, after I found her.'

'Why?'

'Because he's a fucking psychopath and probably killed her himself.'

'Seriously?' he asked, concerned.

'I dunno. He was drunk and upset. Called me a vulture for wanting to write about her before all these pricks,' I gestured in the direction of the bar, 'got wind of it and put their own spin on it.'

A grimace spread across Dan's face. 'Well . . .'

'What?'

'I mean, it *is* a little vulture-y.'

I rolled my eyes, cracked open the whisky and took a swig, hoping the burn would be enough to distract me from my overwhelming urge to punch Dan in his face.

'Look, I'm not saying you deserved to be fired, but I can kind of see where he was coming from.' He saw the look on my face and made a hasty retreat. 'Though he probably already regrets it and will be begging to have you back before you know it.'

I thought back to Mark's hulking form against mine – that warm, liquored breath. I wasn't so sure.

'Besides, not *all* the journos in the bar are pricks. The dude that helped you with your honours thesis is there – the Milat expert. What's his name, Jawline McGee?'

'Owen Archer?' I asked.

'Yeah. Seeing him in the flesh, I finally get the appeal. He looks like a living action figure.'

I laughed. It was an apt description. 'That's not why I asked for his help. He wrote the book on Milat, *literally*.'

Dan smirked, clearly not convinced. 'Maybe you should bump into him and say you're looking for a job.'

'I know there's an opening,' I said, grimly. 'He works for the same paper that Lily was going to do her cadetship at.'

Dan's grimace was back. 'Now *that* would be a vulture move.'

I agreed, and an awkward silence hung in the air. I took another sip of the whisky but immediately regretted it. It was too hot to be drinking it neat.

'Hey?' Dan asked. 'You wanna do something tonight – something to take your mind off things?'

I began shaking my head.

'We don't have to go out. I can come around to the cottage after work. Maybe we can get drunk and binge some Cordova films?'

'I'm not really in the mood for horror, Dan.'

'Shit.' He sighed. 'God, I'm so bad at this.'

'Yup.'

The awkward silence was back.

'Lo?' Dan suddenly asked.

'Yeah?'

'I'm really sorry about last night.'

'What do you mean?'

He looked at his feet. 'If I'd reminded you of the time like you'd asked me to, you wouldn't have had to go past the stables. You never would have found her.'

I thought of the implications of someone else finding the body – someone my dad couldn't control. The markings would have been public knowledge.

'No, it's okay,' I said. 'I kind of feel like it was meant to be, y'know?'

CHAPTER 14

After my conversation with Dan, I returned home. There was a cable news van parked outside and a reporter was being filmed in front of the station's picket fence. I politely stood to the side, waiting for her to finish, but when she swore loudly I realised it wasn't being recorded live and I walked through the shot. She glared at me, though it was difficult to see through her slowly melting makeup. It was moments like this which made me glad I'd opted to study print over broadcast journalism. I didn't want to be another bimbo with a mic, standing outside some shitty rural police station trying to look pretty in thirty-five degree heat.

According to Dan, the rest of the journos were all at the show-ground, crossing live every half-hour with pointless 'updates'. There had been no news since the original report, and there were only so many ways they could say that the body of the town's showgirl had been found in a stable. I'd expected the reporters to be filling the airtime with interviews from people with tenuous links to Lily, but it wasn't happening. Though not from lack of trying. Apparently, there had been some unspoken pact among the locals and they had closed ranks, refusing to speak to the media altogether. The town's typical 'us versus them' mentality was in full effect. I was surprised it was more potent than their thirst for relevancy.

I stepped into the doorway of the cottage and its coolness enveloped me. As much as I decried it, it often felt like an oasis away from the rest of the town. My eyes struggled to adjust to the drastic change in light, and I ran my hand along the hallway wall to orient myself. Everywhere I looked a bright golden orb obscured my vision. No matter how many times I blinked, it wouldn't go away.

The strange distortion made it all the more disconcerting when I finally noticed the frail figure sitting on the lounge in front of me.

'Mrs Williams?' I called out.

There was no response.

Eventually, my eyes grew used to the darkness and I could see her clearly. She was rigidly perched on our overstuffed lounge, staring into the distance – seemingly at nothing. She was wearing the same clothes I'd seen her in at the show the day before, but her hair was dishevelled and her makeup had been cried off. An overwhelming sense of pity crashed over me. I wanted to help her – to make her sorrow disappear any way I could, but I knew it was futile.

I called her name once more, but there was no response. I walked into her line of sight and tried again, but she looked through me as if I didn't exist. There was something eerily familiar in her gaze. She looked just like Lily had when I'd found her.

I squatted down next to her, my movements slow and purposeful so I wouldn't startle her. But no matter what I did, she remained unresponsive. I noticed a mug sitting on the coffee table in front of her and wrapped my fingers around it. It was cool to the touch and looked like it wasn't missing a single sip.

'Oh, this is no good,' I said, hoping to fill the awkwardly silent air. 'I'll get you a fresh one, okay?'

Unsurprisingly, she remained mute.

I was ashamed of how relieved I felt to be able to get away from Sharon. Despite losing an immediate family member at a young age, I was woefully unprepared to deal with other people's grief. Hell, I barely remembered how I dealt with my own. In the kitchen, I stared at the kettle, willing it not to whistle. If a watched pot never boiled, then I was determined not to take my eyes off it. Anything that got me out of having to return to that suffocatingly sad room and that broken woman.

I heard the front door open and breathed a sigh of relief. Two voices floated down the hallway. My dad's and Michael's. I retrieved an extra set of mugs from the cabinet and, the second I took my eyes off the kettle, it began to trill. It didn't matter any more though. I now had backup.

I carried a tray containing the teapot, mugs, milk and sugar, and set it down in front of Lily's mum and dad. Michael was also wearing the same clothes he'd worn the day before but looked less unkempt, even with the hint of stubble dusting his jawline. I smiled to myself as I noticed that he was tenderly holding his wife's hand. The smile dissolved when I realised he was actually checking her pulse.

'Is she okay?' I asked.

He looked up at me, as if only just noticing my presence, and gave a weary smile. 'I had to give her something pretty strong. She wasn't coping.'

I glanced at my dad, who was sitting in his easychair across from them. He nodded sympathetically.

'Did she say anything to you?' Michael asked me.

'Nothing. It was like she didn't even know I was here.'

'She's pretty out of it. But it's for the best. At least I can get her home now.'

I watched as he set about making a cup of tea – adding way too much milk – before dipping his knuckle into the liquid.

'Take this,' he said to Sharon. He manipulated her hands so that she was holding the mug. I was positive that the moment he removed his grasp she would drop it. However, it remained steady.

'Take a sip. Go on, it's not hot,' Michael gently commanded. Once again, she obliged, robotically bringing the mug to her lips and drinking from it.

Michael turned his attention to me, gently patting the vacant space next to him.

'Now, how are *you*, Marlowe?'

Defiantly, I pushed the tea tray over and sat on the coffee table. 'I'm the last person you should be worried about.'

He was giving me that look that I hated so much – the mind-reading one.

'You've been through something traumatic, Marlowe,' he said, leaning forward so that his knees brushed against mine. 'And that type of attitude isn't going to help you. People who witness or discover the aftermaths of violent crimes are the people most likely to be affected. And yet, support is seldom offered to them – no doubt further fuelled by their own belief that they are somehow less worthy of it than the family or friends of the victim . . .'

I squirmed uncomfortably and began shaking my head in protest, but he continued.

'But you fit in both categories, don't you? You knew her *and* you found her. You're doubly vulnerable. If anything, we should be worried about you more than anyone else. You need to know that it's okay to reach out. That there are people you can talk to.'

I finally met his gaze. 'I'm fine. Really, Doctor Williams. Growing up around here I've become desensitised to a lot of this stuff.' I winced. I'd just referred to his daughter's murder as 'stuff'.

If he was bothered, he didn't show it. 'We all know that you're tough, Marlowe. A fighter, right?'

My mind drifted back to our conversation at the show ball. What had he said about Lily and her luck running out?

'But even fighters need help sometimes. And there's no shame in asking for it.'

'I'll definitely ask if I think I need it but, at the moment, I feel like the best thing for me is to process it in my own way and in my own time.'

'Always so stubborn, aren't you?' he tutted, seemingly conceding defeat. 'But I respect your process. Everyone has different ways of coping. All that matters is that you know you have people who are here for you.'

'I do. And I really appreciate your concern. I still don't think it's deserved – given the circumstances – but I'm grateful for it.'

Without warning, he clasped my hand in his and, when I looked into his eyes, I realised that he seemed every bit as broken as Sharon.

'I'm not going to lose anyone else,' he whispered.

CHAPTER 15

Michael and my dad continued talking about the logistics of the case with a surprising amount of detachment. I was shocked to hear that the autopsy had already been performed and that Lily's body was almost ready to be released so her family could organise her funeral. While they talked, I watched Sharon. She seemed utterly unaware of the conversations happening around her. Occasionally her husband would pause to tell her to drink and she would always dutifully obey.

When they finally got up to leave, I followed them to the back door. More reporters had gathered out front and Michael and Sharon were cutting through our backyard so that they could be picked up from behind the station. My dad helped guide Lily's mum outside and Michael turned back towards me.

'Marlowe,' he began. Frustratingly, he often spoke in a soft voice that forced you to get closer to him. I leaned forward. 'Is there anything you can tell me about what you saw when you found her? Anything at all?'

Before I had a chance to answer my dad cut in. 'Jesus, Michael. She's a witness in an active investigation. You know you can't ask her stuff like that.' He sounded nervous and was looking at me pleadingly – he didn't trust me.

'No, it's okay,' I said, staring my father down before turning back to Lily's dad.

'Please, anything,' Michael implored. 'Anything that struck you as odd or suggested who did it?'

'Michael,' my dad interjected.

I was puzzled by his line of questioning. Was it merely the desperation of a mourning father, or was there something more to it? I thought back to my admission at the paper's office. Mark had cut me off before I'd fully spilt the beans about the markings, but had he spoken to Lily's dad since then and told him what I'd said?

It seemed unlikely. Sharon and Michael had spent the day being ferried between the Kiama and Warilla police stations, and Mark was no doubt nursing a significant hangover. No, it must have been my own paranoia. But still, I needed to be prepared in case Mark did eventually bring it up.

'The only thing that struck me as odd –' I began, sensing my dad's heart rate rise, 'was how beautiful she looked.'

I would remain steadfast in my story. Besides, Mark was so pissed he probably didn't even remember.

I heard my dad sigh a breath of relief, and Michael bowed his head and nodded. From somewhere behind him, there was a guttural moan. It was raw and animal-like and made the hair on my arms stand straight.

Lily's mum fell to her knees, sobbing violently. She began pounding at her head with her fists and screaming Lily's name. Her knuckles smashed into her skull, over and over again – like she was punishing herself for her daughter's death. Despite my father and Michael being twice her size, they struggled to subdue her. Each grabbed an arm and wrestled it away from her head, only for it to return. The free-for-all felt like it went on for minutes, but I think it was only seconds. She eventually tired herself out and went back to her catatonia, like nothing had ever happened.

'I'm so sorry,' I blurted out as they helped her to her feet. I'd been standing there – frozen – utterly unable to do anything to assist.

'Hey, it's okay,' Michael said, seeing how shaken I was. 'She's okay. It wasn't you, her medication's just wearing off.'

I felt myself nod but remained unconvinced.

I watched as the two men carefully guided her through the back gate to the waiting police car. Nathan was in the driver's seat and would be taking Michael and Sharon back to their home on Saddleback Mountain. It would be the first time they'd returned home since their daughter had died.

As they drove away, I noticed that I was shaking. My dad walked back towards me.

'Come on,' he said, opening the back door for me. 'We need to talk.'

I ducked under his arm and entered the cottage.

'What the hell was that?' he demanded, slamming the back door behind him.

'What?' I asked, bewildered by his tone.

'You didn't have to say anything to Michael. I covered for you.'

'Well, don't forget who's covering for you!'

His eyes snapped towards me. 'From now on, you keep your mouth shut. You've given your official statement. If anyone else asks, tell them it's none of their business.'

'Sure,' I said, feeling my temper flare. 'I'll tell Michael that his daughter's death is none of his business.'

'I already *said* I covered for you. You didn't need to lie to him.'

'A lie of omission is still a lie! He was obviously suspicious and you were making things a thousand times worse.'

'He wasn't suspicious. He just wants answers and justice for his daughter. Which – for the record – is all I want, too.' He sighed, rubbing both hands over his haggard face. 'I told you there were reasons why I did this. I'm sorry that you had to be involved, but your part in this is over. You don't have to lie because you don't have to answer. Forget about it, Lo. Just let me do my job.'

'But –'

'Look, I've got to get back to the station,' he said, turning to leave.

'No. You're going to stay here and you're going to tell me what the hell is going on.'

He turned back to face me. 'I can't, Lo. I'm sorry.'

'If you want me to keep my mouth shut you'd better give me a damn good reason why I should. I'm part of this whether you like it or not.'

He opened his mouth, seemingly to protest, but thought better of it.

'Okay,' he eventually said. 'I can't tell you everything, but I can tell you where we are with the case.'

It was a start, at least.

'I already knew about the markings on Lily's back,' my dad said after we'd both taken a seat at the kitchen table. 'They were reported to me a little while ago.'

'By who?' I asked.

'I can't go into specifics. I shouldn't even be telling you this much, but – at the very least – I have to keep names out of it.'

'Okay,' I said. I wasn't satisfied with his answer, but I knew not to push it – not yet, anyway.

'I thought I had a fairly good idea of who did the markings,' he continued. 'So obviously, when she turned up dead, we had a pretty clear-cut person of interest.'

'Who?' I paused, remembering I wasn't supposed to ask for names. 'I mean, can you at least tell me if I know them?'

He shook his head.

'No, you can't tell me? Or no, I don't know them?'

'Lo . . .'

'All right.' I sighed.

'Detective Leary got them into the Warilla station earlier today. Not for a casual chat like your interview. The two of us went at them – hard – trying to get answers.' He paused.

'And?'

'It looks like the person's got a pretty solid alibi for last night.'

'Oh.'

'Like, an airtight alibi. They were at a crowded place, multiple people saw them, there were photographs taken – the lot. That's actually why I need to get back to the station. The photos should have been sent through by now. And if the person is in them – which it sounds like they will be – we're kinda back to the drawing board.'

'So, what will happen if that's the case?'

He ran his hand through his hair. 'I haven't got the official figures for last night. But, typically, the show sees around ten thousand people through the gates. Every single one of them is a potential suspect.'

'But surely you have more to go on than that. I mean, it has to be connected to those marks on her back, right? Maybe someone else carved them? What if your person of interest was the wrong person?'

'Nah,' he said, shaking his head. 'They all but confessed to that. Still not enough to actually do something about it, mind you. But I'm confident we pointed the right finger.'

'So . . .' I paused to think. 'They had an accomplice then?'

'Maybe, but I'm beginning to wonder if it's unrelated to the markings.'

'Why?'

'The preliminary coroner's report hasn't been officially released yet, but I got the main gist when I was up at Warilla.'

I looked at him expectantly.

'She died of blunt force trauma to the head. It was pretty straightforward – a single blow did it. No sign of the murder weapon, but we've got a pretty good idea what it was. There were crystal fragments embedded in the wound.'

I thought of my dream – Lily jumping to her death onto crystal cliffs. I shivered.

'Crystals?'

'Yeah.' My dad nodded. 'She had a whole heap of them on her desk at the paper, didn't she? Mark mentioned it.'

'Yeah, bu–'

'We've seized them all, and the lab rats are testing to see if any match. Girls sometimes carry that shit round with them, right? Like a lucky charm or something?'

I thought of the crystal store owner's words. 'For protection,' I said.

My dad rolled his eyes.

'So, what about all that makes you think it has nothing to do with the markings?' I asked.

'Because it clearly wasn't premeditated. I'm not even sure if the person who did it intended to kill her.'

'In what way?'

'The evidence suggests that there was some sort of scuffle before the killing blow landed. Either the person started something and Lily fought back, or she instigated the action in the first place.'

Neither option seemed particularly likely to me. That just wasn't the type of person Lily was.

'Either way, she probably tried to use the crystal as a weapon and it backfired.'

'What makes you think Lily fought them?' I asked.

'There was blood on her dress. Only a drop, but it was somewhere that blood from her temple wound couldn't have reached. DNA profiling hasn't come back yet, but we know it doesn't match her blood type.'

'So, it belongs to her killer?'

'Almost definitely. And I'll bloody DNA test everyone in the town if I have to. But it would be a lot simpler if we could narrow things down. And that would be a hell of a lot easier if I wasn't fighting *you* every step of the way.'

'I'm sorry.'

'It's okay.' He sighed. 'It's a complicated situation. But we both want the same thing – for Lily's killer to be found. So please, Lo, just let me do my job.'

I nodded.

'All right,' he said, standing up to leave. 'I'm going to get back to it.'

CHAPTER 16

I remained at the table long after my father had left, trying to process all the information I'd just learned. The more I thought about it, the less the crystal story made sense. The stones on Lily's desk were relatively large – at least fist-sized. And while there was no denying a crystal that size could have caused her head wound, it didn't make sense that she'd be carrying one around the showground. She certainly hadn't been holding anything when she'd fled from the ghost train.

But, if that were the case, then my father's theory had to be wrong. The killer had to have brought the crystal with them, which only made sense if Lily's murder was premeditated. Plus, there were a million other things they could have used to hurt her – the crystal was clearly chosen to send a message. Lily's killer knew she was scared and knew she had been using the crystals to make herself feel safe. Did they also know that she intended for someone to investigate her death? Was *that* person who the message was truly for?

Was it all to scare me off?

When I finally mustered the energy to stand up, I went to retrieve my phone. I'd left it in the kitchen when I was getting tea for Sharon and I'd missed a few text messages since then. The first two were from Dan. One was a badly shot photo of Owen – the journalist staying at the Blue – that looked like it had been taken by a stalker, while the second, sent sometime later, contained a short yet emphatic statement.

omg owen drinks the same whisky as u!
u r soulmates!!!

I was already thinking of a sarcastic reply when I opened the next message. It was from a number I didn't recognise but that didn't really raise any red flags. Unfortunately, that indifference only served to make the content all the more shocking.

The words were all in caps and seemed to jump out at me from the screen. My mind translated them into a deafening shout that reverberated throughout my head. I struggled to come to terms with what I was reading.

SHE KNEW SHE WOULD DIE
SHE WANTED YOU TO HAVE THESE
MEET ME AT THE LIGHTHOUSE AT MIDNIGHT
COME ALONE
NO ONE IN KIAMA CAN BE TRUSTED

I frantically reread the message over and over again. When I finally processed what it was saying, my gut reaction was that it must have been some kind of cruel prank. Dan had told me that, while my name hadn't been mentioned in the press yet, every local knew that I was the one who had found Lily. I didn't think that I had any true enemies in the town, but I also wouldn't have put that kind of thing past people. Kiama could be a suffocatingly boring place – I knew that as well as anyone – and I knew how alluring the potential for drama or excitement could be. Anything to distract from that mind-numbing monotony.

Just when I was convinced the message was the product of some drama-starved troublemaker and nothing to worry about, I finally noticed that it was actually an MMS. I selected the attachment icon and watched the video download, hoping that a familiar face would pop up on the screen. A 'gotcha' moment that, while admittedly twisted, would have been far better than the alternative.

But when I saw the diaries – those leather-bound journals I'd given Lily as a Christmas gift less than a month earlier – I knew the message was real.

It was a short video but it still packed a punch. A gloved hand appeared from off-screen and picked up the top journal, before slowly flipping through its pages. Each contained writing or sketches, sometimes both, and I squinted at the screen trying to decipher the messages contained within.

I'd often had to transcribe Lily's notes at the paper so I knew the handwriting was hers. But the sketches were surprisingly foreign – frenzied, fluid and inky – almost comic book-like in appearance. I was puzzled. They were a far cry from the photo-realistic pencil illustrations Lily drew in art class. And yet, something tugged at my mind when I looked at them. Had I actually seen them before?

I needed to see the video in more detail so I retreated to my room and tethered my phone to my laptop. I shut my bedroom door. It was unlikely that my dad would return but I wasn't taking any chances. When I returned to the computer, the video was autoplaying and I maximised it before pausing on the page that had originally caught my attention. It was unmistakable in full screen – a flower-like symbol made up of interconnecting circles, surrounded by the exact same markings that had been carved into Lily's back.

I sighed, running my fingers through my hair and staring helplessly at the ceiling. I knew that the answers I wanted were inside the journals, but I was hesitant to seek them out – particularly by myself.

What if it was a trap?

I didn't doubt that Lily wanted me to have the journals. Her comments about having a better use for them and her conversations with the crystal store owner both suggested that she'd always intended for me to investigate her death. But who was to say whether the person who now held them was a friend or a foe?

What if it was her killer?

I googled the phone number that the message had been sent from but came up empty-handed. I decided to go through the video frame by frame, trying to decipher any clues as to the sender's identity. They'd gone out of their way to cover their tracks. The background was non-descript – a wooden table with no identifying features. Similarly, the gloved hand could have belonged to anyone. The black leather added both bulk and length to the person's fingers, meaning that I had no idea whether they were a man's or a woman's.

On my umpteenth view, I noticed something. The gloved hand paused on one page longer than the others and tapped twice on a particular bit of Lily's writing that had been underlined. I squinted at the screen, trying to make out what it said, but the quality wasn't good enough. I looked at the overall page. It seemed to be a list of some sort. I could just make out part of the title, scrawled in jagged, capital letters: MEMBERS?

I took the clearest screencap of the page I could before upping the contrast and printing it off. I hoped that the list would be easier to see like that and began searching through one of my drawers as the printer chattered away. When I finally felt my fingers brush against the cool metal of the Swiss Army knife – a gift from my father – I smiled to myself and pulled out its magnifying arm.

I pulled the page from the printer and was pleased that most of the writing was now much easier to see. It was a list of people from the town. Lily's mum and dad were there, as was Mark. The mayor and the local member of parliament were also featured. In fact, I noticed it seemed to contain almost every high-ranked member of the community.

Which was why I was surprised when I recognised my own name on the list. It was the one the gloved hand had tapped. However, while the nine letters that made up 'Robertson' were clear, the first name was harder to see. I had first mistaken it for an 'L' and an 'O', and had assumed it was referring to me, but when I used the magnifying glass the letters revealed their true identity: J – O – H – N.

John Robertson, aka my dad.

I stared at the list, an unsettling feeling bubbling somewhere deep within my mind. I wondered what the list signified and why the keeper of the journals had gone out of their way to show me my dad was included. I decided to go over the entire page with the magnifying glass to see if I could find anything else. That's when I first noticed it – four faint letters that preceded the word 'members' at the top of the page: C – U – L – T.

I immediately reached for my phone and replied to the text.

I'll be there.

CHAPTER 17

At 11.45 pm, I quietly snuck out the back door of the cottage, making a beeline for the side fence. I climbed it and dropped down into the post office's parking lot to avoid detection. I preferred the iconic building at night. Its hideous pink hue softened in the moonlight, and you couldn't tell that the clock's hands were always far behind schedule. Perplexingly, the tower's bell sounded at twenty-three minutes past the hour, a feature that the tourists found charming, but which infuriated the locals. Not me though. I didn't even hear it any more. My years spent living next door had made me immune to its jarring *bongs*, and they had become nothing more than white noise.

The time since I'd replied to the anonymous message had been a blur. I must have sat for hours staring at the list, willing my dad's name to fade away. But it was there, and it was unmistakable. Suddenly his actions made so much more sense. And yet, my mind was flatly refusing to genuinely think of the implications. Every time I tried I would lose time. It was like I couldn't even consider the possibility.

I needed more evidence.

I needed those journals.

Nathan had come around, sometime in the evening, with hot chips and potato scallops drowning in chicken salt. He was just dropping them off and letting me know that my dad was back up at Warilla and wouldn't be home until later that night. I thanked him before telling him that I'd be going to bed early. It had been a rough couple of days, y'know? He'd nodded understandingly, and I hoped he'd relay the message back to my dad.

After finishing my meal, I returned to my bedroom. I turned all the lights off and sat in complete darkness to give the illusion that I was asleep. Just after 10.30 pm, my dad returned and I dived under the covers. I heard him opening the front door, putting his keys down, walking to my door and pausing, just outside. I held my breath as the handle quietly turned, snapping my eyes shut as my door slowly opened. My heart was pounding and it felt like I could hear my blood rushing through my brain. He watched me for far longer than I thought he would. My skin crawled.

I refused to open my eyes, even when the door slowly shut. It wasn't until I heard the shower running that I finally dared to move. Something had changed. No, something was missing and I knew that I'd never get it back: trust.

I threw back the covers and pulled my knees to my chest, wrapping my arms around them as I strained to hear his movements. Eventually, he got out of the shower, cleaned his teeth and retreated to his room. Minutes later, I heard the familiar sounds of his snoring. Years of working nightshifts had left him with the ability to fall asleep almost instantly. It had always been an enviable trait to a night owl like me.

Now, crossing the road in front of the post office, I stuck my hand into my pocket and wrapped my fingers around the Swiss Army knife. I was still concerned that the meeting could potentially be dangerous and, while I had initially considered whether to tell my dad about it, obviously that was no longer an option. I wasn't stupid though, I had written out the details – the time, the location, the person's phone number, etc. – and closed the note inside my laptop. If something happened, I knew it would be one of the first places the cops would look.

I'd also considered checking in with Dan, telling him to raise the alarm if he didn't hear back from me after a certain time. But I knew there was no way of doing it without sounding suspicious, and I was worried that he'd go behind my back and tell someone out of fear for my safety. I also wasn't particularly comfortable involving him. Those powerful names on the list frightened me, and I didn't want to risk losing another friend.

I decided to bring the Swiss Army knife and promised myself that I'd use it if I needed to. It may have been tiny, but I knew it could be incapacitating if I was quick and caught the person by surprise. I left the blade sticking out, which was probably not the safest thing, but I couldn't risk accidentally pulling a nail file on someone. In reality though, the knife was nothing more than a totem for my safety – no more protective than the lapis lazuli stones hanging around my neck. I rubbed my thumb along the cool metal like it was a worry stone, but I kept worrying.

I approached the entrance to the harbour, ready to embark up the long, gradual slope to the lighthouse. I stopped and looked out over Storm Bay. It was a little-known secret that the cove happened to be positioned at the exact same angle as the ocean entrance to the town's infamous blowhole. Which meant that you could use it to predict the intensity of its spray.

Watching the waves violently crash over the rocks of the bay, I knew that the blowhole would be putting on a show tonight. I would have loved to pretend that, after twenty-two years of observing the spectacle, it no longer impressed me. But there was something about that column of water – shooting twenty-five metres up into the air, accompanied by a deafening roar – that brought out the kid in me.

The blowhole was an intrinsic part of the town, but unlike the twee historic buildings painted in photo-op ready hues and the hulking monuments to long-lost ghosts, its reverence was actually deserved. There was something primordial about it. It was formed aeons ago – when Saddleback Mountain was still a volcano. A lava flow that cooled as it touched the ocean and created the perfect structure to channel waves inside its cave and up through its spout. It had always been there, and it always would be. The same couldn't be said for the people of the town and their manmade structures.

The lighthouse rose ahead of me up the hill – a towering white monolith framed by rows of Norfolk pines. It was still a working lighthouse – a beacon to warn ships of the dangers of Blowhole Point – but it hadn't been manned since the early 1920s, meaning that, most nights, the area was deserted. There'd been storms earlier in the evening and the downpours and southerly winds had dissipated the day's warmth. I pulled my jacket around myself – though whether it was from the temperature or nerves, I couldn't tell.

At the top of the hill, I scanned for a figure, but there was no one around. Even the car parks overlooking the blowhole were empty. I pulled out my phone, leaning up against the lighthouse's hexagonal fence: 11.58 pm. My mystery person was nowhere in sight. The blowhole whooshed from behind the lighthouse, startling me. I tried to laugh off my skittishness, but it didn't do much to help.

When the clock struck midnight, my phone buzzed in my hand. A message appeared on the screen:

COME TO LOOKOUT

I continued past the lighthouse, walking up to the edge of the blowhole's top viewing platform. I placed my hand on the salt-slicked railing and heard the telltale gurgle of a wave entering the ocean cavern. Seconds later, I was pummelled by sea spray, which plastered my hair to my face. Scraping the strands away from my eyes, I peered out at the lookout.

Floodlights illuminated the general area until 1 am, but the lookout itself was shrouded in shadow. Still, I could tell no one was there, and the fact that there was only one path in and out made me uneasy. If I went down there first, the person I was waiting for could easily block my exit and trap me. The only other way out would be down – off the jagged cliffs into the surging water below. I tried not to think of my dream; of my decision to jump.

But then I saw it. A flash of light next to the lookout, up on the rock shelf. The area afforded a far better view, but it was treacherous, especially at night. Signs warned of its danger but that seldom stopped people. Two entire families had drowned there after being swept off the cliffs in the nineties, and countless rock fishermen had met their demises in the murky water below. After being on the body recovery teams, my dad had taught me to respect the area and recognise its danger and unpredictability. I would have normally rebelled against that kind of advice, but I'd come to fear the blowhole on an almost primal level.

I continued watching the light. It was slowly pulsing on and off, almost mimicking the pattern of the lighthouse. But it was obviously something small, like a handheld torch. Before I knew it, the light stopped and I frantically tried to search the darkness for any further sign of its source. Suddenly, my phone vibrated and I jumped so hard I almost dropped it over the railing into the gaping hole. I looked at the screen.

DON'T WORRY
I DON'T BITE

I wasn't so sure, but I knew if I wanted answers I'd have to go down there. I inhaled deeply, feeling the ocean air brine my lungs. I put my phone back into my pocket and wrapped my other hand around the knife. The salt on my fingertips made it tacky to the touch. I slowly began my descent down the blowhole's sweeping staircase, pausing at the end to let the next jet of water explode. It was spewing over the walkway's railing, drenching the entire path, and I'd have to be careful not to slip.

I was cautiously making my way along the footpath when a towering humanoid shape sprouted from the clifftop. I froze. The person was still only visible in silhouette – ageless, genderless – but they were tall, thin and imposing. The figure effortlessly slithered down the rocks onto the path. A long jacket. Hood up. My fingers tensed around the Swiss Army knife. My breath was ragged.

By the time I heard the gurgle, it was too late.

The water crashed over me. It dumped on top of my head, drenching every part of my body. I gasped at the pressure of the ice-cold ocean, coughing and spluttering, disoriented by the sheer magnitude of the wave that had engulfed me. Had I been sucked into the blowhole? Was I actually drowning?

But then I heard it. Shrill laughter pierced the night air. I was still on land. I inhaled deeply. Oxygen instead of water this time. I was out – it was over – but then the pain seared.

I pulled my bloody hand out of my pocket, splaying it open so that the Swiss Army knife fell to the ground. I couldn't tell how deep the wound was but it sure as hell hurt. The laughter stopped.

'Shit. Are you okay?'

The figure rushed towards me and I finally saw his face.

'*Jarrah*?' I asked, shocked.

CHAPTER 18

The last time I'd seen Jarrah Watson, he'd been sitting on my lounge, a distant and defeated look on his face. He was two years older than me – in year twelve when I was in year ten – and had been expelled from school for attacking a classmate. However, there was more to the story.

Jarrah was openly gay, and his peers had hurled homophobic slurs at him since kindergarten. It may seem preposterous to think of a six-year-old spouting hate speech but kids are impressionable creatures and Kiama was the kind of town that bred and nurtured prejudice. Any 'differences' were seen as traits to be stomped out. Even if you were born with them. The bullying was just the first step. The town would wear you down until you changed or left. There was no other alternative.

Despite all this, Jarrah was an exuberant and confident kid who always struck me as someone completely comfortable in his own skin. He was a larrikin who loved to make people laugh, but he also never shied away from a debate and was quick to become political. He would question his teachers, almost constantly, loathing their black and white approach to the world. But he adored the arts and his talents were nurtured by a select few members of staff who recognised his tremendous potential. Drama and visual arts were his domain, and he was often selected to represent the school at various camps, workshops and exhibitions.

However, his projects were not without controversy. For his year ten major visual arts work, he arrived at the school in the early hours of the morning to hang hundreds of blood-soaked tampons in the school's trees. As the sun rose over the main quad, the streaks of blood he had poured onto the concrete glistened. They spelled out the words 'Mother Nature'. He always claimed that the blood was real, sourced from a nearby abattoir, but the school's official statement was that it was fake. Seeing the way the flies flocked to it as it slowly congealed in the morning heat suggested otherwise.

Despite his flair for the dramatic, Jarrah had put up with a lot over the years: being tied to a basketball hoop and left for hours in the scorching sun; having his artwork destroyed and utensils stolen; and seeing his name scrawled next to homophobic graffiti all over the school. But he never fought back – at least, not until that day.

He'd been using the urinal when three of his year's most popular students had entered the bathroom. They were walking clichés – sporty, rich, dumb – and possessed the unflinching arrogance of true privilege. The ringleader of the group (who also happened to be the school captain) sidled up behind Jarrah, pressed his body against him and whispered in his ear: 'Does this make you hard, f*ggot?'

Jarrah remained silent as the captain's companions laughed and egged him on. The captain's hand snaked its way up Jarrah's back before grabbing a fistful of his hair. He pulled firmly, buckling his neck.

'I said,' he hissed into Jarrah's ear, 'does this make you hard, *f*ggot*?'

'Maybe you're not his type?' one of the other guys said, laughing.

The captain shot him a threatening look, before tugging harder on Jarrah's hair.

'Nah, he's too scared he's gonna jizz himself,' the second guy said, pretending to orgasm.

'Guess I'll have to check for myself then, won't I?' the captain asked, slamming Jarrah's head into the bathroom wall and reaching around to grab his crotch.

As soon as he made contact, Jarrah snapped his elbow back, knocking the captain to the floor. While the two offsiders looked on in shock, he quickly fastened his pants. The captain lunged for his legs but Jarrah sidestepped him, so he sprang to his feet and went in for a punch. It didn't land, and Jarrah grabbed him by the collar before pummelling him in the face. He felt the captain go limp and let go of him, watching as he slumped to the floor. Wordlessly, he stepped over the moaning body in front of him and walked out of the bathroom while the two grunts scrambled to help their friend.

Jarrah walked straight to the school's administrative office. He calmly strode up to the receptionist and asked for three things: an ambulance for the captain, an ice pack for his hand and to see the school principal. Even then, he knew that his time at the school had come to an end.

Of course, the official story never included the sexual assault. Instead, the captain and his goons claimed that they had been using the urinal when they had caught Jarrah perving on them. They'd confronted him, they said, and he'd just *snapped.* If their piss-poor attempt at corroboration wasn't enough to alert people to the lie then their outright bragging about the true story sure as hell did. The captain was untouchable – the son of the deputy mayor at the time, Peter Walsh – and he knew it. He freely admitted what he had done, but only after Jarrah had been expelled and his name had been dragged through the mud by the local paper.

My dad had tried to help him, but I don't think Jarrah ever saw it that way. Peter Walsh was champing at the bit to have him charged but my dad was able to talk him down. Both men knew who the real instigator in the fight had been. And my dad had calmly reminded Peter that if the three boys couldn't get their story straight during an informal interview then they'd never survive in court. But there was a catch – Peter would only agree to not press charges if Jarrah was expelled and forced to submit to a psychiatric assessment. My dad was the one who had to break the news.

That was the conversation I'd stumbled in on when I saw Jarrah sitting on my lounge all those years ago. His mother and father were there, looking just as defeated as their son.

'It's not fair,' Jarrah said to my dad. 'It was self-defence.'

'I know, mate.'

'Then why won't you let me fight it? If we go to court and win, they'll let me graduate. I only have six months left!'

'It's not worth it, son,' my dad continued. 'If you lose, you could go to jail. You're underage now, but I know for a fact they'll be pushing to try you as an adult.'

Jarrah looked at his parents pleadingly. Tears streamed down his mum's face, while his dad stared at him, helpless.

'Please,' he begged. 'Let me try.'

'I'm sorry, mate.' My dad sighed. 'But it's not your decision. You're only seventeen so it's your parents' call.'

'You can't say that I'll be tried as an adult in one breath and then tell me I'm not old enough to make the decision in another!'

'He'll take the expulsion,' a small voice croaked. I was shocked to see the source was Jarrah's mother.

'What the hell, Mum?' Jarrah asked, stunned.

'You won't win, sweetie. You'll never win. Not against him. And I'm not having my only son go to prison.'

'Dad?' Jarrah implored.

His father sighed. 'She's right, Jar. You won't beat him. I know you didn't do anything wrong, but they're not going to see it like that.'

'But that's not fair,' Jarrah repeated, shaking his head in disbelief. 'You're all cowards.'

There was no reply from anyone.

For the first time since I'd entered the cottage, Jarrah finally noticed my presence. We stared at each other in silence. I hadn't realised I was crying.

Jarrah left the town – for good – not long after that. As soon as he turned eighteen, he moved out of his parents' house and began couch-surfing his way around Sydney. He was determined not to let Kiama get the better of him. Eventually, he enrolled in a visual arts course at TAFE, which he then used as a stepping stone to secure a scholarship to the National Art School.

In contrast, Jarrah's abuser became the dux of the school that year and received a full-ride scholarship to complete his undergraduate degree at Sydney's top law school. Rumour had it that he was involved in some sort of hazing scandal and that his father – once again – had to tidy things up. While his son was up to his old tricks in Sydney, Peter Walsh was eventually granted the mayorship of Kiama.

Even after the truth came out, nothing was ever done about it and Jarrah was never vindicated. It didn't matter that the town knew he was innocent or that he was now successful. It was fit in or fuck off, and Jarrah had never even *attempted* to fit in. His very identity was seemingly perceived as an affront to the locals – small-town xenophobia at its finest.

But, instead of letting his experience in the town destroy him, Jarrah used it as ammunition to fuel his creativity and drive. He quickly became a force to be reckoned with in the Australian art scene.

In the profiles written about him in national newspapers and art journals, he often joked that he was a disappointment to his family. After all, they had done everything they could to keep him out of prison, only for him to end up studying at the National Art School whose campus happened to be the old Darlinghurst Gaol. 'Guess it was my destiny,' he'd deadpan.

In truth, it was his family who were the disappointments to him. He largely shunned them after they vetoed his decision to take the assault charge to court. Jarrah loathed them for being so weak – for refusing to fight – and promised himself that he would never be like them. The town had done that to them – he was sure. He'd gotten out early enough to retain his identity, though, and he assured the world that he would never give it up.

It may sound messed up, given what he went through, but I envied Jarrah more than anyone in the world. I remembered the first time I saw him again, smiling back at me amid a group of emerging artists in a national newspaper. His signature curly hair had been completely shaved off, replaced by a glistening dome that looked slick to the touch. He dressed like a male model for some sports-luxe fashion brand, clean and futuristic, yet made it look effortless and inherently his own. He was the physical embodiment of my definition of success – he'd escaped – and I hated him for it.

Still, I followed his career closely, and he became my poster child for getting out of Kiama. When he wasn't in the media for his projects, you'd almost always still spot him in the social pages. He was a regular fixture at all the hottest parties and events, and I often caught him rubbing shoulders with some unexpected characters. He seemed to know everyone who was someone.

I was also pleased to see that he still had his flair for the dramatic. He became somewhat of an enfant terrible in the art scene, stirring up controversy wherever he could. His most recent stunt, at the end of the previous year, could have potentially involved jail time, but he was able to twist the whole thing into a discussion about the true value of art in Australia. The crime itself was minor. He'd taken grant money he'd received from the government and – quite literally – turned it into art by painting thousands of banknotes and using them in a mosaic.

Technically, it was defacing legal tender, which carried a potential fine of five thousand dollars and up to two years in prison. But, once it had done the rounds on talkback radio, inspired countless opinion pieces, and prompted the minister for the arts to initiate a formal investigation into the accountability of grant recipients, Jarrah had turned up at the gallery with a laundry bucket, washboard and soap. He sat there for a week restoring each note to its former self. He pulled down the last note from the wall and scrubbed the last remnants of paint from it, then stood up and said two words: 'Money laundering'.

I remembered watching the livestream and being so utterly floored by the moment that I went straight to Mark and begged to do a profile on Jarrah for the paper.

I'll never forget the way my editor looked at me. The disbelief that graduated into that smarmy smirk.

'Nobody in this town gives a shit about that f*ggot,' Mark spat.

CHAPTER 19

'*Jarrah*?' I asked, shocked.

He came towards me, quickly bending down to pick up the Swiss Army knife, before gently grasping my uninjured hand and pulling me out of the blowhole's splash zone. He grabbed his torch and shone it on my palm. Fortunately, the wound wasn't deep.

'I don't think you'll need stitches,' he said, examining the cut.

I nodded. I was still in shock.

'Was this for me?' he asked, turning the Swiss Army knife over in his hand before carefully folding the blade away and holding it out to me. 'Jesus, Lo, didn't know you had it in you.'

'You told me not to trust anyone,' I managed to reply, taking it with my good hand.

He nodded. 'No, it's good, I suppose. Lily said you were tough; I should have believed her.'

'I didn't even know you two knew each other.'

'We didn't – not really – at least, not until recently. We both did a couple of art camps and workshops together back at school, but I tended to avoid her. She was such a fuckin' goody-two-shoes back then.'

A small smile washed over his features, but it was gone as quickly as it had come.

'She turned up at one of my exhibitions last year, completely out of the blue. She was the only person from Kiama who ever came to one. Not even my own family. But that was my call, obviously.'

I nodded, wrapping my arms around myself. I was so cold and wet it was becoming difficult to concentrate.

'We started hanging out more and more. She hated this place,' he said, gesturing all around him. 'So, she'd crash with me up in Sydney when she wasn't working.'

I tried to focus on what he was saying, but I couldn't. My teeth were chattering violently.

'I have some spare dry clothes in my bag if you want them,' he said, concerned.

My head was nodding before I'd even had a chance to think of my response.

Jarrah unzipped his backpack before handing me a sloppy joe and a pair of tracksuit pants. They both looked like they could have come from Lowes but the tags were designer. It was only then that I finally noticed what he was wearing – a long black hooded trench coat, skin-tight black jeans and platform boots with dolls' heads inside the heels. Columbine chic. At least the shoes explained his towering height.

I walked to the edge of the lookout and turned my back to him as I carefully peeled my sopping outfit off. My bra and undies were drenched, but they'd have to stay. Jarrah may have been gay, but that didn't mean I was comfortable enough to strip in front of him.

As it turned out, my paranoia was apparently founded. I carefully laid my singlet and jacket on the rock shelf and heard the torch click on behind me. He was pointing the beam straight at my back.

'What the fuck, dude?' I shouted, turning to face him while shielding my eyes from the light.

'Shit, sorry – couldn't resist. Thought I could be subtle.'

'I thought you were gay!'

That shrieking laughter was back. 'Don't flatter yourself, sweetheart. You're definitely not *my* type. I was just double-checking you didn't have the marks. Lily said you didn't, but let's not forget whose father was on that list.'

I defensively wrapped my arms around myself. I didn't know what to say.

'They brand their members,' he said. 'Lily had them. On the small of her back.'

'I know,' I replied, pulling the jumper over my head. 'I saw them.'

'What, how? When?'

I considered whether or not to tell him the truth. 'When I found her.'

'But –'

I interrupted him. If I was going to say what I was going to say I needed to do it quickly, like ripping off a bandaid.

'Her back was exposed when I found her,' I began. 'My dad covered it up before anyone else saw, and then made me promise not to tell anyone. But he doesn't know I took photos of them before I told him.'

'Oh.'

'Yeah.' I sighed. 'So, I'd really like to know what the fuck is going on here, and I figure you and those journals are my best bet.'

He nodded. 'I'll tell you everything I know.'

All of this had started over a drink or – at least – the ability to have one. Free booze was a fixture at the parties and events Jarrah attended and Lily had apparently become embarrassed about her teetotal status. When I asked Jarrah why I'd never spotted her in the social pages alongside him, he'd said that she'd always refused as she didn't want her parents to know she was there. It all seemed so out of character for Lily.

I'd never known or even questioned why Lily didn't drink. It kind of just fit with her personality. The town's golden child – sweet, innocent, chaste – was a good girl at heart and good girls didn't drink. It was the same reason why I'd never found it odd that she didn't date. Though, that may have also been because I knew there was no one in town good enough for her.

I was stunned to hear she was ashamed of those traits. But I was even more surprised when I found out the real reason why Lily didn't drink. Apparently, she'd been on high doses of antipsychotics for practically her entire life. And the older Lily became, the more she began to question why. Jarrah said that she'd often spoken of her father's controlling nature and the power he wielded over her and Sharon. So much so that, when Jarrah suggested that Michael may have been using the drugs as another way to assert his dominance, Lily had broken down and admitted it was something she'd always feared to be true.

I thought back to the heavily sedated Sharon I'd witnessed earlier that day. I remembered the way Michael was able to command her – like she'd been hypnotised by him. She was completely and utterly under his control. The thought made me uneasy.

Lily had apparently begged to come off the medication multiple times but her dad had always refused. She'd asked for a second and even third opinion from other psychiatrists. To his credit, Michael had happily obliged, but he was the head of psychiatry for the entire South Eastern Sydney and Illawarra Area Health Service, meaning that anyone she saw was technically his underling. They'd all told her horror stories of what would happen if she went off the medication – terrifying withdrawal symptoms far worse than the side effects of the drugs themselves – and they essentially frightened her into submission.

She admitted to Jarrah that she'd never been able to speak to anyone about it. I should have been there for her. We all should have. I began to wonder if I'd ever truly known the real Lily or just the smokescreen version of her cultivated by the cocktail of drugs that had been altering her brain's chemistry. What if she hadn't been the golden child – pleasant, placid, pliable – that the town knew and loved? What if that person never truly existed?

I felt myself getting frustrated, and my frozen skin, sopping hair and stinging palm weren't doing much to help. Sure, Michael's behaviour sounded reprehensible but being a controlling prick didn't automatically mean he was also a cult leader. Jarrah's flair for the dramatic was overcomplicating things. I needed to get him back on track.

'Stop burying the fucking lead,' I suddenly snapped. 'What does the cult have to do with all this?'

He visibly flinched at my words, before looking directly at me as though sizing me up. He smiled smugly. 'Well, if you'd let me *finish* . . .'

'I don't have all night. If you're supposed to be convincing me of something, then convince me.'

He rolled his eyes but continued. 'Long story short, she went off the drugs because I agreed to support her through it. I'd helped a few friends get clean over the years, and I spoke to a med student mate of mine.' He paused, looking suspicious. 'Okay, *technically* he wasn't a mate, he was my dealer, *but* –'

'Get. To. The. Point.'

'We slowly lowered her dosage so the withdrawal was negligible. She seemed to be responding really well, and I genuinely thought I was helping her, but . . .' He stopped mid-sentence, staring out over the ocean.

The roar of the blowhole masked my sigh.

'She started having these dreams,' he continued. 'Really bad ones. She was being chased through the rainforest up at Saddleback by these people in masks. They were dressed, like, weirdly formally. Red tail-coats with gold buttons. Long, black boots and gloves. They carried rifles . . .'

An image coalesced in my mind. I could picture the outfit so clearly. And the mask – black leather – with a sharp snout and pointy ears.

'Fox hunting attire,' I mumbled. 'With a black leather fox mask.'

Jarrah's eyes widened. 'How do yo–'

I shook my head back and forth. 'I – I don't know.'

'A memory?'

'*I don't know!*' I spat, frustrated at my mind more than him.

We stood in silence for an impossibly long time.

'Well, that's what hers were,' he finally continued. 'They got more vivid until she was finally out of the forest and in a clearing. There was a fire and so many people. They wore floral wreaths on their heads. The men's crowns had antlers from young stags, while the women's featured gazelle horns. Their masks were different now – a flower shape made up of layered circles.'

'The drawing from the diary?' I interrupted.

He nodded. 'The flower mask barely covered people's features and she began recognising them. Her dad, her mum. People from the town . . .'

'The people on the list?'

'Not all of them. She didn't have memories of everyone on that list participating in the rituals. But she thought at the very least they knew about what was happening and were potentially protecting the members.'

'Did she have memories of my dad there? I've seen his back; I know he doesn't have the markings.'

'Yes.'

My heart sank.

'But, for what it's worth,' he continued, 'she didn't think that he actively participated. She said he wasn't an *actual* member of the cult – he was just protecting them.'

'Is that supposed to make me feel better?'

He slowly shook his head, and I fought back tears.

'It's why she refused to involve the cops,' he said, after a while. 'She didn't know how far it went.'

I felt sick to my stomach. I didn't know what to say or do. It was crazy. The whole thing was crazy. But why did it seem so familiar to me? No. I was tired. I was in shock. It was just some weird form of déjà vu.

'They were just dreams,' I told Jarrah. 'I don't doubt that they were super vivid but withdrawal dreams often are, aren't they? It was all in her head.'

'She thought that at first, too. Until that dream in the clearing. She was kneeling before the fire – her father standing over her – when she suddenly felt this horrible pain in the middle of her back. She woke up and rubbed her hands over the spot. For the first time, she felt them – those jagged scars on her back. The markings were real. They weren't dreams; they were memories.'

'You can't really expect me to believe she never noticed that she had symbols carved into her back until that moment, right? That's absurd.'

'It's the truth though. She jumped out of bed, ran to the bathroom and looked in the mirror. There they were, plain as day. And at that moment, years' worth of horrors came flooding back to her. You can't deny it, Lo. You saw them yourself.'

He had me there.

CHAPTER 20

'Look,' Jarrah said, 'I know this is a lot to take in, and I kind of feel like I'm not really doing it justice. Just, *please*, read the diaries. It's all in there. As soon as she realised it was real, she started making detailed accounts of everything she remembered.'

He bent down and removed the journals from the bag before holding them out to me.

'She said she wanted you to have them if something happened to her. That you were the only person in town she trusted to get to the bottom of things.'

I looked at his hands. 'Why did you let her come back here if she thought she was going to be killed?'

He stared at me for a long time before slowly shaking his head. 'Fuck, Marlowe.'

'I'm sorry. But she knew she was going to die. I just feel like – I mean – maybe it could have been stopped?'

'I tried,' he said, his voice quavering. 'Believe me.'

I nodded, but I mustn't have been very convincing.

'Seriously, Lo. I did everything I could. I said she could stay with me for as long as she wanted. I said I'd protect her – that I'd get her out of the fucking country if I needed to – but she refused. She kept saying, "We just have to wait until after the show."'

He was choking up. Tears were pooling in his eyes and the dam was threatening to burst.

'She said she didn't want it to look suss – like she was fleeing. So, she was going to wait until she'd started her cadetship. Like, Jesus, she was supposed to move to Sydney next weekend. It was just one more week . . .'

I nodded, feeling horrible for questioning him.

'She was so proud of that cadetship,' he said, smiling to himself. 'She felt like it was the only thing in her life she'd ever truly earned by herself. Y'know, without her dad pulling strings or interfering? She was amazed that her parents had agreed to let her take it. She thought that if she could get out of town that maybe things would be okay. Kinda like how they were for me.'

'I'm really sorry, Jarrah.'

'No, it's okay. I know how it looks. And I don't think I'll ever live a day where I don't regret not standing up to her and convincing her to stay in Sydney.'

After we both stood in silence, staring off the cliff's edge, I finally took the journals from Jarrah and ran my fingers over the covers. The leather felt like it had aged decades since I'd given them to her. She'd clearly handled them often, the oil from her skin polishing the grain from rough to smooth. I hugged them tightly against my chest.

'To be totally honest,' Jarrah began, 'I thought sharing this with you was a bad idea. Like, seriously, she thought your dad was involved – why pick you? But she was adamant that you'd do whatever it took to find out the truth. She said you were tenacious.'

I smiled, before realising Michael had said almost the exact same thing.

'Lily's lucky, but luck runs out eventually . . .'

'She's right though,' I told Jarrah. 'I *am* tenacious.'

'Yeah, maybe. I mean, the knife was a good start. But if you're serious about protecting yourself, you'll need an upgrade. Do you want me to try to get you something? I might know a guy.'

'A knife guy?'

'More like a "miscellaneous illegal accoutrement" kind of guy.'

I laughed. 'Kiama's a hunting and angling town. You'd be surprised how easy it is to get knives here. Also, my dad has a stash of confiscated weapons in our back shed. I found a grenade in there once. He's adamant it's decommissioned, but . . .' I shrugged.

We both chuckled, but at almost the exact same time it petered out and became awkward. It didn't feel right to be joking about my dad, not after what I'd learned that night.

'Speaking of hunting,' Jarrah began. 'You're going to have to prepare yourself for what's in there.'

I looked down at the journals.

'It's really fucking bad, Lo. Like, PTSD-inducing, you-will-never-sleep-again, burn-the-world-to-the-ground bad. I mean, it sounds so innocuous when they refer to them as "fox hunts", but then you find out that they don't even hunt foxes, they hunt fucking –'

In the split second before he finished his sentence, an image popped into my head: a little girl in a forest, dressed in white, with a blood-red fox mask covering her face.

'Kids,' I blurted out, finishing his sentence but wishing that I hadn't.

How did I know that? How could I possibly have known that? It was enough to make me want to bend over the lookout's railing and vomit into the ocean below.

Jarrah was understandably suspicious, but I genuinely had no idea how I kept filling in the blanks. The details didn't even feel like memories. Instead, it was like a static image had been implanted in my mind – fully formed, devoid of any context. There was nothing connecting it to anything else. No web of memories for me to get tangled in. I tried to explain that to Jarrah, but it just made him even more convinced that I was involved.

'I'm not in a cult,' I protested, dumbfounded that I even needed to say the words out loud. 'I swear.'

He stared at me for an uncomfortably long time.

'Yeah, I think I believe you.' He sighed. 'But that doesn't mean you're not involved. Like, I don't think *you* believe you're part of all this. But, let's be real, Lily would have said the exact same thing a few months ago.'

'What are you trying to say?'

'Think about it, Lo. You're both the daughters of prominent members of the town, you're both the same age and you both have fragments of this horrifyingly specific scenario that was apparently just waiting to be unlocked inside your mind. What if you're part of it and you don't even know?'

'No,' I said. It was supposed to sound firm, but it came out as a whisper. 'I'm not on any medication, and while my dad may treat me like a child, he *isn't* controlling. Seriously, he doesn't give two shits what I'm up to. Oh, and I don't have fucking satanic symbols carved into my back!'

'What if not everyone's brandings are in the same place? What if they're somewhere else on your body?'

'And I've just never noticed them?'

'Lily didn't.'

'I'm not drugged up to my eyeballs on antipsychotics or whatever the hell she was on,' I protested. 'I know what my own bloody body looks like.'

'It wasn't only the drugs, just FYI. In the diaries, Lily talks about these weird therapy sessions she remembered having. They were kind of like a mixture of hypnotism and meditation, and she thinks her father was using them to make her forget things. She did some research into it, and it sounded like this super full-on mind control thing the CIA apparently used back in the day.'

'Oh, so now I've been brainwashed? Fucking fantastic!'

'Look, I'm just saying that it seems like there's a pretty definitive way to tell if people are a member or not. It would make things a lot easier if we knew for sure.'

'Stop beating around the bloody bush. What are you asking?'

'Y'know . . . Strip.'

'Piss off!'

He exhaled exasperatedly. 'So, you know I'm going to have to ask for my clothes back, anyway, right?'

'Oh, for fuck's sake!' I shouted, before peeling off the outfit.

'*Buh bah bah bah buh tss tss*,' he hummed, clapping his hands and mimicking the sounds of a slow strip show.

I dangled his clothes over the edge of the lookout before throwing them at his shocked face. He caught them and flipped on the torch, shining it over every inch of my body – just like my father had done to Lily. I was standing in only my bra and underpants. When I reached around to unclip my bra, he turned the torch off and covered his eyes with his hands.

'Ugh, no, that's enough,' he said, repulsed. 'I'm convinced, okay!'

'Are you sure this time?' I snapped.

'Yeah. There's no way they'd be able to brand those mosquito bites you call tits anyway.'

I gave him the finger and reached for my singlet. Somehow it seemed even more waterlogged than before.

'What are you doing, dumb arse?' he asked, before holding out the clothes I'd just removed. 'You can keep these. I was just trying to see if you had the marks.'

I snatched the clothes back from him. They were damp where my bra and undies had soaked through but were still infinitely warmer than my wet clothes.

'It's good news though, right?' he said. 'I mean, you're *probably* not in the cult?'

'Yay,' I flatly replied, pulling the sloppy joe over my head again.

'In all seriousness though, you're going to have to try to figure out how you know those things. Maybe reading through Lily's diaries will jog your memory?'

'Maybe.' I shrugged. Picturing that little girl in the fox mask, and the marks on Lily's back, I wasn't entirely sure if I wanted my memory to be jogged.

'Anyway, I'm going to need to head off if I want to make the last train out of this shithole.'

I nodded, secretly wishing I could join him.

'Oh, wait, Jarrah.'

'Mmm?'

'Her funeral is scheduled for Thursday. Are you coming?'

'Nah, I'm good. Lily wouldn't want to be remembered being stuck in this town for all eternity, anyway.'

I nodded. I knew the feeling.

CHAPTER 21

I managed to make it home in one piece, and I was doubtful anyone saw me or even noticed I had gone. The streets of the town had been well and truly empty – not that it was a surprise that early on a Monday. My dad was still sleeping when I crept past his door, and the booby traps I'd set up to alert me if anyone had entered my room remained undisturbed. The cottage's creaks and groans felt louder that night. To say I was on edge was an understatement.

I had a long shower and the warm water added colour and heat to my mottled skin. I could have stayed in there forever but as soon as I heard the hot water system begin to thump and shudder, I relinquished my sanctuary. I couldn't risk waking up my dad. I wiped the condensation off the basin mirror and examined my body from toe-to-tip. I knew Jarrah had already checked but there was still some part of me that was sure I would suddenly see Lily's marks carved into my own pale flesh.

To my relief, there was nothing. But that just raised more questions. How could I possibly have known the things I did if I wasn't involved in some capacity? It didn't make sense. There had to be some other explanation – one that didn't involve my father and half the town being part of a fucking cult. I tried to rekindle the spark that had set off those original images in my mind's eye, but I couldn't trigger them myself. Maybe they needed outside stimulation.

I was terrified to let Lily's journals out of my sight so I'd brought them into the bathroom with me. I stared at their bulk now; I knew

I wouldn't be getting any sleep that night. After bandaging my hand and putting on pyjamas, I retreated to my room and climbed under my covers.

I opened the first journal and flipped through until I found the start of an entry.

I could hear dogs barking, somewhere in the distance.

I opened my eyes, but my vision was blurry. I was groggy and disoriented. The air was hot and humid, but the ground I was sitting on felt damp and cool. I looked down at my bare feet and was surprised to find them covered in mud and leaves. Sighing, I stretched my face skywards, feeling my head gently thud against something hard. There was no sky, only the green canopy of the rainforest, seemingly stretching on forever.

Even with my hazy vision, I could tell I was sitting with my back against a towering fig tree. I was safely nestled between a pair of large buttress roots, like two arms wrapped around me. Pockets of sunlight filtered through the treetops, creating dappled spotlights among the bracken. The air was filled with birdsong, and I was bombarded by the scent of soil and decaying greenery.

A loud crack bellowed from somewhere behind me, silencing the forest's soundtrack. I thought I heard a scream. I replayed the sounds in my head, becoming more and more convinced that the crack had been a gunshot and the scream had come from a child. My heart was pounding. I didn't know if it was better to try to run or stay and hide.

'Over here!' a voice called out. It was impossible to tell which direction it had come from.

I dived onto my stomach so that the buttress roots hid me from all angles. A piercing horn reverberated throughout the forest, the sound ricocheting off trees and echoing all around me. The dogs' barking was getting louder and I could hear twigs snapping as footsteps powered forward. There were so many people in the forest, frantically searching for something or someone. It was easy to assume that they were looking for me.

After a few minutes, I heard the soft padding of footsteps on leaves immediately to my right. There was a louder sound as something thudded to the ground, making my heart leap. Then the sounds of someone weeping – snivelling gasps and mewling. I had to look.

A little girl was on her knees, looking towards me, a red fox mask bound to her face. Pale skin, with constellations of freckles and frizzy red hair. She was wearing a white pinafore dress that looked like it had been tie-dyed brown and green by the forest floor. Her hands were clasped behind her back which gave her a reverent air. She stared at me, her hypnotic green eyes filled with tears, before faceplanting into the dirt in front of me.

I gasped. It was only then that I realised her hands had actually been bound behind her, secured with clear cable ties. I also noticed something else – the plume of a bright pink tranquilliser dart hanging from her neck. I couldn't tell if she was dead or knocked out, and I struggled to consider which fate was worse. Just as I was contemplating running to her aid, I heard more footsteps. I ducked down. There was a hole in the root I could use to see the girl without exposing my hiding spot.

'Aikya! View-holloa!' a voice shouted. It sounded eerily familiar.

Two German shepherds burst through the tree line. They were bound together by harnesses, and both sported leather muzzles. They were attached to a long leash and, as they descended on the girl, their handler came into view. He was in full fox hunting attire, with a black version of the girl's fox mask covering his features. He reeled the dogs back towards him, patting and praising them for their find. They wagged their tails excitedly.

More fox hunters arrived, each in the same outfit. They were all different shapes and sizes, and the group contained both men and women. I could still hear others in the distance and it seemed like the group was just a small cluster of a much larger party. One of them blew a funnel-shaped horn, while another approached the girl – a gun aimed at her head. He pressed the rifle's muzzle against the back of her skull before turning to the other hunters.

'BANG!' he shouted, before descending into a fit of cruel laughter. A few of the other hunters joined in.

In my shock, I'd loudly gasped. I clasped both hands over my mouth. Only the hunter with the horn looked in my direction. I prayed it was just a coincidence. Thankfully, he turned back to the girl.

The hunter with the rifle used his foot to expose the girl's face. Her eyes were shut, a pained expression etched on her unconscious features. He kicked her in her stomach, but she didn't even flinch.

'She's out,' he announced to the group. I was horrified to recognise the voice. It was a man my parents knew. He edited the newspaper.

The hunter with the horn squatted down next to the girl, gently brushing her hair out of her face and tucking it behind her ear. He removed his glove and placed two fingers on her throat. With his other hand, he removed an ornate timepiece from his breast pocket. I realised he was checking her pulse. He removed the dart from her neck and placed it in his pocket. Without a word, he nodded to Mark, who bent down and grabbed a fistful of the girl's hair. He dragged her motionless body back the way they had come. The rest of the group followed.

'One more to go,' I heard someone excitedly utter.

To my horror, the hunter with the horn had stayed behind, his eyes scanning the roots of the fig tree.

'You coming?' someone called from the pack.

'Nature calls,' the horn-blower replied. 'I'll catch up.'

It was my father.

I was debating whether or not to run but I was still feeling so lethargic. Maybe he wouldn't see me? It was a stupid and naïve thought, but I didn't feel like myself in that moment.

After a few minutes of silence, it was becoming obvious that my father had no intention of relieving himself. Instead, he stood where the girl had fallen, staring towards me.

Finally, he broke his silence. 'I know you're there. It's okay, you can come out.'

I didn't move.

'Come on, Lily, sweetie. It's Daddy, you're okay. No one's going to hurt you.'

He unclipped the bottom section of his mask. He was smiling warmly, his arm outstretched – a hand waiting to be clasped. Without thinking, I rose from my hiding place and approached him before placing my tiny palm in his. It fit so perfectly. Like they were made for each other. A feeling of warmth and comfort spread throughout my body. I felt safe, even after everything I'd just witnessed.

In one sweeping motion, my father scooped me up into his arms. He gently cradled me before carefully sitting down on the root I'd been hiding behind. I was perched on his lap sideways, my legs dangling over his forearm. He gently picked the leaves off the soles of my feet, and I giggled at the ticklish sensation. He smiled. A tender, fatherly smile.

'I'm so sleepy, Daddy,' I said.

'I know, Vixen. You've had a big day, haven't you?'

I felt myself nod. 'It was so scary, Daddy. They hurt that other girl. I thought they were going to hurt me too.'

'Oh, Vixen,' he replied, sounding genuinely heartbroken.

'We'd never hurt you like that. You're special. More special than all the other little boys and girls.'

'I am?'

He nodded before reaching up to my face. He swept my curls away before carefully removing my mask. I hadn't even noticed I'd been wearing one.

'See?' he said, holding out the mask. 'You're a white fox. That means that you're special – pure – not like the others. They might still hunt you, but they'll never hurt you. You're too important.'

'But I don't want to be hunted.'

'I know, sweetie. Nobody does, but you should think yourself lucky that you have a pretty white mask and not a bad red one like the other little girl.'

I reached out and touched the top of his mask.

'You want a black mask, like mine?'

I nodded.

'Well,' he said, leaning close to my ear and whispering, 'I'll tell you a little secret. When you're a big girl, you'll get a black mask of your own. You'll get to dress up like Mummy and Daddy, I'll teach you how to use a gun and you'll get to hunt instead of being hunted.'

He squeezed me tight. 'How does that sound, Vixen?'

'But what if I don't want to hun–'

Before I had finished my question, my throat was already throbbing. I looked down and saw the pink plume at the end of the dart embedded in my neck. He'd stuck it in so quickly, I'd barely registered the movement of his arm. My father held me closer and began slowly rocking me backwards and forwards while shushing and tutting away my terrified protests. He began reciting scripture, like a soothing lullaby, and gently stroked my hair. I recognised it – the 'Song of Solomon'.

'Catch us the foxes, the little foxes, that spoil the vines: for our vines have tender grapes.'

CHAPTER 22

My eyelids sprang open and I gasped for air, feeling like I'd been holding my breath for an impossibly long time. I was in my bed, having just woken up from another strange dream. I lay there, recalling every moment. It had been a mishmash of all the horrifying details I'd read in Lily's journal, translated by some peculiar type of dream logic.

I rubbed my eyes much harder than I should have. I felt like I hadn't had even a second's worth of slumber, but that was clearly not the case. I never thought I would have been able to fall asleep after the things I'd read in the journals, but –

Wait, the journals.

Where were they?

I threw my covers back. They were nowhere in sight. I tried to remember if I'd fallen asleep with them in my arms but came up empty. I leaped out of bed and began searching the nooks and crannies of my bedroom. All my usual hiding places were empty. Panic gripped me. I'd been so out of it, what if my dad had come in and taken them? The thought made me nauseous. But then I noticed my pillow was missing its case.

A memory sparked in my mind. I had finished reading the journals and decided to hide them. I'd stuffed them into the pillowslip, and – ?

What, exactly?

I rubbed my temples, trying to will the memory to form. In a huff, I slammed down onto my bed. My mattress felt different. I hadn't heard the telltale sound of the bed boards creaking. Something had cushioned the blow. I jumped to my feet before lifting the corner of my mattress. I let out a huge breath of relief as I pulled the pillowcase towards me. Three black journals. Safe and sound.

I climbed back into bed and flipped through the journals. Lily's illustrations merged together like I was watching an animatic for the most horrifying children's cartoon. A picture book come to life.

I slowly turned the pages, reacquainting myself with the contents. I'd tried to be as pragmatic and objective as I could when I read the journals. I questioned everything and tried to ensure my emotions never clouded my judgement, but it seemed Lily had taken the same approach. Every single time I questioned the legitimacy of something, the next sentence would contain a rebuttal or an explanation.

She'd thought of everything, it seemed. I wondered if it was because she was looking for an out – something that proved her memories were false. I know I'd rather believe I was delusional than face the truth. But still, there was some part of me that refused to believe what I'd read. It was just too out there – too crazy.

According to the journals, the 'fox' hunts occurred on the eve of Beltane, a neo-pagan celebration that had Gaelic roots and typically revolved around fire-based protection and fertility rituals. In Australia, Beltane festivities commenced at midnight on the first of November and were usually conducted on former volcanic sites, making Saddleback the perfect location. But while most modern Beltane celebrations forwent any form of human sacrifice – only ever going so far as to simulate it – that wasn't the case for the Kiama rituals.

Historically, Beltane had a dairy-based origin so I was unsurprised to learn that both the Williams and Rose families had apparently been instrumental in introducing the rites to Kiama. They were also generous enough to share their hectares of land for conducting the hunts and ceremonies.

According to Lily, the rituals were as old as the town itself and had been shaping the lives of its inhabitants for just as long.

At the conclusion of each year's celebration, a branding was bestowed on the participants to render them complicit in the cult's practices. Although they 'hunted' children every year prior to the midnight ceremony, they didn't necessarily sacrifice them with the same frequency.

Instead, Lily's diary suggested that it was only when a member had completed their eighth hunt that they would sacrifice that year's red-masked child. By single-handedly killing the victim, they would signify their dedication and commitment to the cult, and they'd receive their eighth branding. It was larger than the rest – a circle that connected all the other symbols together. A sickening souvenir embedded in flesh.

The 'fox' hunting formed the pinnacle of the Kiama rituals and seemed to be the result of a somewhat peculiar interpretation of the 'Song of Solomon'. The scripture's meaning had been twisted and bastardised by the cult, seemingly to justify the monstrous child abuse Lily had described.

The words from the 'Song of Solomon' had undeniably held great power over Lily. I'd lost count of how many times she'd written the verses in her diaries, often filling up multiple pages with her frenzied repetitions. The pages were also covered in drawings of the branding – the flower-like symbol made up of interconnecting circles – that she had come to learn was called 'The Seed of Life'.

It was easy to assume that Lily was most traumatised by her time allegedly spent being hunted by those frighteningly familiar men and women in masks. Drugged, pursued and forced to watch unimaginable acts of violence against other children. But, according to her journals, Lily's real problems emerged shortly after her sixteenth birthday when her father's promise came true and the hunted became the hunter.

Reading the things she wrote, I began to wonder whether her father would have even needed his so-called CIA quackery to make Lily forget. Surely a mind as pure as hers would rather destroy itself than face up to those alleged memories? Maybe she weaponised her amnesia and used it as a tool to protect herself? Maybe the trauma itself *was* the mind control technique?

But – regardless of whether or not she remembered it – every year after her sixteenth birthday, Lily was certain she was forced to participate in the hunts. After all, every year, she would return from the rainforest bearing more scars – both emotional and physical.

I thought of my photographs of Lily's back. Seven symbols equalled seven years, seven hunts and seven ceremonies. If what Lily was saying was true, then she would have been due to sacrifice a child at the end of this year. I'd felt goosebumps when I had read the eerily prescient words Lily had written next to that revelation: *'I'd rather die than receive that mark.'*

No matter how much I was questioning her words, I had to acknowledge that her wish had come true.

CHAPTER 23

After placing the journals back under my mattress, I walked into the kitchen for a late breakfast. Once again, I had slept until the afternoon, and I thought I could counter my lack of energy with a large serving of extra sugary cereal. I poured way too much into a bowl before heading for the fridge. As I opened the door, I swore under my breath – no milk.

Out of sheer laziness, I considered eating the cereal dry but knew there'd be a fresh bottle of milk next door. Without bothering to change out of my pyjamas or put on shoes, I walked out my back door, cereal bowl in hand. I entered through the back of the police station and headed straight to the small break room.

Nathan was sitting at the tiny dining table, an opened newspaper and cup of coffee in front of him. When he saw me, he smiled, before spending way too long staring at my body. I crossed my arms over my chest, but he didn't seem to take the hint.

'Sleeping beauty's finally awake, eh?'

I ignored him, heading straight for the fridge.

'*Someone's* in a grumpy mood this morning,' he tutted.

I gave him the finger without bothering to turn around. I reached into the fridge, unscrewed the milk bottle's lid and poured a generous splash onto the cereal. It crackled like a freshly lit fire.

Nathan sighed loudly and I heard him lift up the paper, rustling its pages overdramatically. When I turned back around, I almost dropped my bowl. I was stunned to see Lily. She was on the front page, fleeing from the ghost train. Two bold words hung above her terrified face: 'KILLER CARNY?'

'That's my fucking photo!'

Nathan examined the front cover, perplexed. 'But this is national, not the local rag.'

I slammed my cereal down on the table before snatching the paper from Nathan's hands.

'Hey!' he shouted in protest.

I squinted at the byline. The article had been written by Owen, but the photo was credited to Mark. A sense of panic gripped my entire body. How the hell had he accessed my photos? But then I remembered I'd left the bloody memory card in one of the paper's computers that night. I'd been so scared by Mark's outburst that I hadn't even realised.

'What I wouldn't give for five minutes alone with that sick fuck,' Nathan growled.

I thought he was talking about Mark. But when he continued I realised what he meant.

'I knew it was gonna be an out-of-towner. Pricks think they can come in, assault our women and piss back off to whatever shit stain of a town they come from.'

I cringed at the possessive use of 'our'. Lily didn't belong to the town, and she certainly didn't belong to its men. Ignoring him, I slumped down into a dining chair as my eyes scanned the article. I couldn't believe what I was reading.

> ***KILLER CARNY?*** **by Owen Archer**
>
> 21 January 2008
>
> It was supposed to be one of the happiest days of her life. But when Kiama's reigning showgirl, Lily Williams, plunged into the dark depths of the show's ghost train on Saturday night, she could never have predicted that she'd come face to face with her potential killer.

Kiama police have named 26-year-old ghost train employee Steve Masters as a person of interest in Miss Williams' death after it was alleged he indecently assaulted her during her time on the ride.

Along with two other showgirl finalists, Miss Williams rode the ghost train as part of a photo opportunity for the local paper. But, once she entered the ride, things took a terrifying turn. Approximately halfway through the train's short journey, the entire attraction was plunged into darkness, which is believed to have been caused by an electrical fault.

It is alleged that Mr Masters, whose official role on the ride is to hide in its shadows and scare patrons, took advantage of the situation and proceeded to assault Miss Williams. The 22-year-old showgirl was heard screaming by those outside the train before she left the cart and ran to the exit. That horrifying moment was captured by an employee of the *Kiama Gazette*.

As the paper's editor, Mark Thompson, confirms: 'I was standing outside the ghost train with the operator, waiting for the showgirls to emerge. Suddenly, all the lights and sounds went out before a loud scream was heard. Shortly afterwards, Lily burst through the ride's doors, clearly terrified.'

That moment is believed to be the last time Miss Williams was seen alive by members of the public. Less than an hour later, her body was discovered inside one of the showground's historic stables by an unnamed Kiama resident.

'We tried to find her,' Mr Thompson recalled. 'I informed her parents about what had happened, and we all scoured the grounds. But, at that stage, we hadn't realised what had occurred on the train. We didn't know she'd been assaulted.'

That scenario was only suspected once police interviewed the two finalists who'd accompanied Miss Williams on the ride.

'In hindsight,' Mr Thompson admitted, 'I should have known something terrible had happened. She was obviously so frightened. I just wish we'd been able to find her before he did.'

Police have confirmed that Mr Masters did not have an alibi for the time between the incident on the ghost train and the discovery of Miss Williams' body. He was last seen heading alone towards his family's caravan, which was parked in close proximity to the stables where the murder took place.

It is alleged that the police sought a voluntary DNA sample from Mr Masters yesterday evening. However, it is believed that the suspect refused this request. Local police inspector, John Robertson, declined to confirm Mr Masters' refusal but did admit that DNA would play a significant role in the conviction of Miss Williams' killer.

'We can confirm that blood we believe to belong to the killer was found on Miss Williams' clothing, and that we typically seek volunteer samples from persons of interest to try to clear suspects' names as quickly as possible,' Inspector Robertson said. 'However, it's important to remember that refusing said sample is not an admission of guilt and should not be treated as such. If a suspect refuses a voluntary DNA test, the next step is to pursue a warrant.'

Time will tell if Mr Masters will be forced to submit to the test. However, the shocking crime and news of its potential perpetrator are rumoured to have made the closeknit community even more wary of outsiders. The small coastal municipality, approximately a 90-minute drive south of Sydney, typically boasts a population of just under 20,000. However, during the holiday seasons, that number triples due to the influx of tourists.

Mr Thompson, who had mentored Miss Williams at the local paper, expressed his shock at the violent crime and recalled the showgirl fondly.

'It's honestly unfathomable,' he said. 'She was the youngest journalist ever hired in the history of the *Gazette*. Lily had limitless potential. She was a tremendously talented writer and a genuinely kind and compassionate young woman. It feels like a piece of the town is missing. Like we woke up one morning and the blowhole was gone.'

Tributes continue to flow from around the country as the harrowing story of the young showgirl's senseless demise resonates in the hearts and minds of the entire nation.

Anyone with any information regarding Miss Williams' death is urged to contact Crime Stoppers on 1800 333 000.

CHAPTER 24

'Oi, I was still reading that!' Nathan yelled as I stormed out of the break room with the paper under my arm.

'Is Dad here?' I called back to him.

'Yeah, in the office. But he's on the phone.'

I ignored him and headed straight towards the inspector's office. Only minutes earlier, I would have gone out of my way to avoid seeing my father, but all of that was out the window now. I just wanted answers. Real answers, this time.

I pounded on his door, slightly surprised to see it shut. There was no response. I inhaled deeply and knocked one more time, before slowly turning the handle. The door clicked open and I carefully pushed it forwards.

'What?' my dad mimed from behind his desk before aggressively pointing at the phone.

I held up the paper and angrily prodded at the front page. 'What. The. Fuck?' I mouthed.

He shook his head, before waving me away with a dismissive flick of his hand.

I plonked myself down on the rickety chair positioned in front of his desk. I leaned back and crossed my legs defiantly, trying to make it clear that I wasn't going anywhere. He pinched the crease between his brows, before pointing to the phone and gesturing for me to wait. I nodded, satisfied.

As I watched him conduct the one-sided call – which seemed to have something to do with the DNA test warrant – I scanned his familiar features. The person I'd observed sitting on the bonnet of that police car – grey sideburns and lined jowls – looked positively youthful compared to the man before me. He'd aged a decade in just two short days. But guilt would do that to you, wouldn't it?

I softly sighed to myself, and he frowned at me. I was still struggling to associate the man who had raised me with the heinous acts described in Lily's journals. Jarrah had been right. Lily didn't think that my father belonged to the cult, but he definitely knew what they'd been up to. He'd been with them in that rainforest. He'd witnessed the ceremonies. He hadn't even *tried* to stop them. It didn't make any fucking sense.

I honestly couldn't decide what was worse. Being a member and participating in literal child sacrifice, or being a police officer who, while not *technically* participating, knew everything and still did nothing to stop it. I mean, logically, the obvious answer was the first. Still, there was something so unforgivable about being in a position to actually stop the cult and, instead, choosing to use that power to protect its members.

I wanted to leap across the desk and grab him by that blue collar. Tear off those three stars on each of his shoulders and ask him, 'Why?'

Why would he fucking do something like that?

And yet, there was still some part of me that refused to believe it. The part of me that was sitting there, wringing my hands, staring at that headline and begging some unseen force for it to be true. That Lily really *was* killed by a random out-of-towner, and that everything else was . . .

What, exactly? A misunderstanding?

I closed my eyes and saw those little red foxes fleeing through the forest. I still had no clue how I'd known the details of the hunts before Jarrah had told me everything. And yet, to my surprise, the journals hadn't triggered any further recollections – if that's even what they'd been in the first place. It still didn't make sense. None of it made sense.

I ran my hand through my hair, squeezing my skull to stop the throbbing that was resonating from somewhere deep within. My dad was finally wrapping up the call and I stared at the embroidered patch on his sleeve, the New South Wales Police crest. It featured an Australian wedge-tailed eagle carrying a blood-red sash in its talons. You couldn't tell on the patch, but the sash contained a single word: 'Nemesis'.

'Finally!' I exclaimed as he hung up the phone.

'Don't ever do that again,' he snapped. 'And for god's sake put some bloody clothes on if you're leaving the house.'

I looked down at my camisole and shorts and scoffed. I knew his demand had less to do with the clothes I was wearing and more to do with the body they barely concealed. It was the same absurd reasoning that saw a bikini ban at my school's swimming carnival while the boys were allowed to parade around in nothing but budgie smugglers. I mean, at least a bikini left *something* to the imagination.

'What the hell is all this about?' I said, tossing the newspaper onto his desk.

'What do you mean?'

'All this stuff about the ghost train scarer. You don't really believe that's who's responsible, right?'

'Well, we'll know for sure once we get this warrant. If the blood's a match, that's our man.'

'Where exactly was the blood on Lily's dress?'

He furrowed his brow. He seemed to be trying to figure out my angle and was clearly debating whether or not to tell me.

'Between her shoulder blades,' he finally admitted.

I allowed a small smile to grace my lips. 'Which would have been the exact place it landed when she threw her elbow back and hit him in the face.' I paused. 'Back on the ghost train, *before* it even blacked out.'

My father's mouth gaped.

'And wouldn't it have made more sense,' I continued, 'if the bloodstain came from a time when Lily's hair was pulled forward, exposing her back? Like when she was about to have her photo taken for the local paper, emerging from the ghost train? After her sleazy boss had spent way too much time fussing over her hair? Pulling it forward to show off the lengths while also framing her chest because, *god* forbid, she wasn't showing at least a *hint* of cleavage?'

'Who told you she hit Masters in the face?' he asked, coolly.

'The carny who operates the ghost train.'

'When?'

'After it happened, obviously. And before I found her.'

'That's funny,' my dad said, folding his arms across his chest and leaning over the desk towards me. 'You never mentioned it in your statement.'

A moment of panic struck me, but I was able to recover. I mimicked his posture and leaned towards him. 'I mean, it's not the only thing I didn't mention in my statement, is it?'

'When did this conversation take place, *exactly*, Marlowe? And why didn't you tell *me* about it all those times we were running through your story?'

'I didn't think it was pertinent to the case.'

'Bullshit. He only told you after the fact, didn't he? After we started sniffing around the carnies, right? Once they got their story straight.'

'No. It was on Saturday night, just before I found her. Dan was there. You can bloody ask him if you want. He'll tell you the exact same thing.'

He seemed utterly bewildered by my words. 'Jesus, Lo, why didn't you say this at the time? I don't care what you and Dan were up to, just tell the bloody truth.'

I didn't want to be a narc, but I didn't have much of a choice.

'Dan was looking after my bag while I was on the Hurricane. When I went to find him afterwards, the ride operator told me he was round the back.' I sighed. 'Look, Dan and the ghost train carny were sharing a joint. There was no deal or anything, just two dudes chilling, looking out over the ocean and apparently talking about Lily going nuts on the ghost train. When I got there, the carny repeated the story.'

My dad shook his head, but he didn't try to question whether I had also been smoking pot. He always preferred the 'don't ask, don't tell' school of parenting.

'The carny freaked out when he found out I was a cop's daughter and, after everything that had happened, I didn't want to get the poor guy in trouble. I mean, he'd had a pretty shitty night after Mark's stupid photo stunt broke his ride.'

'So, he knew you were a police officer's daughter, then?'

I nodded, frustrated. I had just said that.

'And, timewise, this was immediately before you found her?'

'Yeah, I got your text while we were talking and left straight afterwards.'

He laughed hollowly and shook his head. 'You got played like a bloody fiddle, Lo.'

'Wait, what?'

'The ghost train operator is Steve's father,' he began, condescendingly. 'And I imagine by then he already knew what his son had done. I still think the kid didn't know his own strength, but the dad knew that wouldn't mean much to us. And then you come along – the police inspector's daughter – the perfect person to sell his sob story to.'

I opened my mouth in protest.

'You really think Lily was the type of girl who'd fight back? Unless she *really* needed to?'

My words to the carny echoed in my mind: '*Lily's not like that.*'

'Tell me, Lo. Did the carny say anything when he saw you heading through the restricted section towards the stables?'

My face told him everything he needed to know.

'Tried to stop you, didn't he?'

'But, what about the positioning of the blood?' I asked, albeit meekly.

'It's an interesting theory. But if it really did happen on the ghost train,' he pulled open the drawer beside him, removed something from its depths and threw it on the desk in front of me, 'why didn't his mask have any blood on it?'

'*Fuck.*' I stared at the well-worn gorilla mask inside the evidence bag.

CHAPTER 25

I was headed towards the showground. My dad had explicitly told me to 'Stay the fuck out of police business and let me do my job' but I couldn't. My instincts were telling me that the ghost train operator had been telling the truth. Or maybe I was just too proud to admit that I'd been played. Either way, I was determined to find out.

The main gate to the showground was being guarded by police, and I assumed the same could be said for the other entrances. I didn't want any cops reporting my presence back to my dad, so I made a beeline towards the cheap motel that backed onto the fairground. There was a seldom-used thoroughfare there that granted access to Surf Beach, and with all the rides and trailers parked on the oval, I knew I could pass through undetected.

I ducked under a short wooden fence and stepped onto the fairground, marvelling at how different it looked with all the rides and attractions packed up. It was now basically just a convoy of large trucks. The hulking arms of rides like the Hurricane had been retracted and flattened for easy transportation. It was hard to believe they could be transformed so dramatically.

The majority of the carnies were there, helping ensure everything was secure and ready for the road. They were supposed to be heading south to an even smaller town for the next show the following weekend but the investigation was holding things up. The entire showground had been declared a crime scene and they'd been told they weren't allowed to leave until the investigation was complete.

I rounded a corner of trucks and was surprised to see that the ghost train was still fully intact, police tape lining the doors that I'd watched Lily both disappear into and emerge from. There didn't seem to be any cops around though. In fact, there didn't seem to be anyone around.

'You right, love?' an ocker voice called out from somewhere behind me.

I turned around to see a shirtless bear of a man with a long mullet and copious tattoos.

'Just trying to find someone,' I said, trying to sound more confident than I felt.

'Oh, yeah? Who?'

'Ghost train operator. Uh, didn't catch his first name, but his last name's Masters, I think?'

The carny strode towards me, sizing me up the whole way. He was covered in sweat, which made his tattoos glisten in the sunlight. Half of them were borderline pornographic: pinup-style damsels in distress bound in ropes, their breasts bulging in gravity-defying ways.

'You a journo?'

'Nope.' I resisted the urge to add, *Well, not any more.*

He took a step closer, invading my personal space. I wanted to step back, but I held my ground. Suddenly I felt a hand on the small of my back and let out an audible gasp.

'Leave her alone, ya lug. She's cool. She had a cheeky sesh with Baz on Satdy.'

It was the carny from the Hurricane who'd caught me when I'd almost fallen.

'Oh, shit. Sorry, love,' Mullet replied, immediately taking a step back. 'Don't like your chances at the moment though. More pig arseholes than a sausage factory, if ya catch me drift.'

'For what it's worth,' I began, 'I made sure no one saw me. Snuck in through the back of the motel.'

He crossed his arms in front of him and made an impressed grunt.

'I think something can be arranged,' the Hurricane carny whispered in my ear. 'Follow me, gorgeous.'

Mullet had watched the interaction closely, tracing his chapped lips with his tongue while his eyes greedily surveyed my body. He winked at me and I noticed that his breathing had grown ragged the closer his mate got to me. The bound women silently screamed from his sweat-slicked skin.

With his hand still on my back, the other carny guided me towards the ghost train. I fought the urge to throw my elbow back and run – just like Lily had. But I needed answers, and I was prepared to do whatever it took to get them.

When we passed by the ghost train, I started to get nervous. I was being corralled, away from the fairground and up to the restricted zone. We were basically following the same path I'd taken when I'd discovered Lily, but nobody was forcing me then. The carny was immediately behind me, so close that I could feel his breath on my neck. With every step forward, I regretted my harebrained reconnaissance mission more and more.

As we traipsed through the narrow corridors between trailers, I was so fixated on where he was taking me that I didn't notice the pile of power cords that were coiled on the ground like a neon snake. I tripped – badly. But, before I could even register what had happened, I was surprised to feel two large arms wrap around my waist and effortlessly lift me into the air. The carny carried me to the end of the passageway and carefully deposited me back on solid ground.

'You got two left feet or something, darl?' he teased.

'Nah, just unco.'

He laughed, and I tried to look around surreptitiously. I may not have wanted the cops to see me before, but now I would have been relieved to see a familiar face amid those eerily foreign trailers. The entire area was deserted. When I turned back around, the carny was staring at me, a puzzled look on his face. He had apparently sensed my discomfort.

'Don't tell me I'm going to have to give you a bloody piggyback.'

I didn't laugh. 'Uh, where are we going?'

'Back to mine for a quick root, yeah?'

My mouth gaped but, before I'd even considered telling him to fuck off, he'd doubled over in laughter.

'I'm just taking the piss. I'm sorry, I couldn't resist.'

I still wasn't laughing.

'Jesus Christ, love, you really do need that pot, don't you? So bloody uptight!'

I crossed my arms over my chest and stepped towards him. 'Can you fucking blame me after what happened here?'

His eyes darted in the direction of the stables, and then back to me. 'Shit, sorry,' he said, struggling to retain eye contact. 'D-did you know her?'

'Everyone did.'

'I'm just taking you to Barry's trailer,' he said, pointing into the distance. 'See the one with the Rabbitohs' flag?'

I looked at the red and green flag flapping in the sea breeze. It was on top of a large caravan parked close to the pavilion. I must have run straight past it just before I found her.

'Barry's missus will be there, too,' he said reassuringly. 'And their . . . uh . . .'

'Son?'

His eyes scanned my face. Then he nodded, glumly. 'Don't believe everything you see on the news, darl. He's a good kid. It's all just a bloody stitch-up.'

I nodded. 'If the locals didn't have an outsider to blame, I think they'd tear each other apart.'

'Probs best if you don't bring it up with Baz though, yeah?'

I didn't answer. Instead, I started walking towards the Masters' trailer. The carny sighed but dutifully followed. I felt terrible for what I knew was about to happen.

CHAPTER 26

'That better not be a bloody journo, Johnno!'

The voice belonged to a shrill woman in a Bintang singlet, who was sitting on a camping chair in front of the Masters' trailer. She glared at me as we approached.

'Nah, she's cool,' the carny replied. He mimicked smoking a joint. But it wasn't enough to stop the woman from scrutinising me.

'She's a fucking liar if she told you she wasn't,' a voice from somewhere inside the caravan growled. Johnno turned to face me, a look of betrayal plastered on his sunburned face. The flyscreen door flung open and Barry Masters locked eyes with me. His anger was palpable.

'Let me guess. She also didn't mention she was the inspector's daughter, did she?'

Johnno grabbed my arm and pulled me towards him. 'You sneaky little cun–'

'Hands off. *Now!*' Barry commanded, stepping down onto the ground.

Johnno relaxed his grip and dropped my arm but got into my face. 'I should have let you fall, you stupid little bitch.' He spat at my feet, before walking away. I tried to pretend I hadn't noticed it had hit my boot.

'Why are you even here?' the woman asked. 'Haven't you lot hurt my family enough?'

'I'm not here as a cop's daughter.'

'Well, if you think you're getting an interview you can piss right off,' Barry spat.

'I'm not here as a journalist, either. I wasn't lying – I was fired.'

'Oh, boo fuckin' hoo, darl,' the woman replied.

I exhaled slowly. 'I'm here as the person who found Lily's body. I'm also here as the person who was fired for asking too many questions about her death . . .' They were both rolling their eyes, but I continued. 'But, more than anything, I'm here as the only fucking person in this entire town who is even *prepared* to consider that your son may be innocent.'

Barry's eyes flicked to his wife. She glanced from him to me, before finally nodding.

'What do you want?' he asked.

'Answers.'

'You're gonna have to be a bit more specific than that, love.'

'Okay, why did Steve refuse the DNA test?'

For the second time, he turned to face his wife. She nodded once more.

'Because it's gonna match the blood on the girl's dress and they're gonna arrest him.'

'How *did* his blood get on her clothes?'

'You know the bloody answer to that! When she attacked him in the ghost train!'

'That's what you told me, yes. But there was plenty of time for you and your son to have come up with that story. And then I came along – the inspector's daughter – the perfect person for you to sell your sob story to.'

I hated myself for parroting my father's words.

'Are you thick or something, love?' he asked, frowning at me. 'I'd already told your mate what had happened, long before you ever showed up, and he's not a cop's son s'far as I know.'

'You could have been testing the waters? Laying the groundwork?'

He was growing frustrated. 'Look, I told your editor the exact same story *straight* after it happened. She'd only just run off then, and Steve was still standing behind me with bloody tissues stuffed up his nose. Your boss saw him.'

My heart rate rose. 'Mark knew that Lily attacked Steve?'

'Yeah, the prick wasn't gonna give me a cent for the ride's downtime, but when I mentioned getting the cops involved about the showgirl, out comes the wallet. Tried to say she had a panic attack or some shit. That it was an accident and not a police matter.'

'And you agreed?'

'I try and avoid the pigs as much as I can for, uh, *obvious* reasons. So, I took his cash.' He glanced at his wife and slowly shook his head. 'Biggest fuckin' mistake of my life.'

I stared up at the Norfolk pines above me and sighed. They were swaying in the breeze and raining their needles onto the showground below. The noise they made when they hit the caravans sounded like metal hail. It was pleasant – almost relaxing – until I heard her sobbing.

Barry squatted down next to his wife and wrapped his arms around her. She clung to him so desperately that I felt the need to turn away. The moment seemed far too intimate for an outsider to observe, and I wanted to remain respectful.

I kicked a bottle cap in the dirt while reflecting on what Barry had told me. My gut instinct – that he'd been telling the truth – had only grown stronger. He had absolutely no reason to lie about informing Mark about Lily's outburst. In contrast, Mark had countless reasons for never bringing it up.

Or maybe he did bring it up.

Maybe he told my dad and, just like with me seeing the markings, my father somehow convinced him to keep it to himself. He changed the narrative once more and, in doing so, condemned an entire family. Steve was the perfect patsy. An outsider for the whole town to rally against. And with the markings never made public knowledge, who would question it? After all, his blood was on her clothes.

I remembered I still had one more question for the Masters family and spun back around before clearing my throat.

'Steve wears a mask when he's in the ghost train, doesn't he?'

Barry let go of his wife and turned to face me. 'Yeah. So?'

'If Lily attacked Steve on the ghost train,' I began, 'and that's how his blood got on her dress, then why wasn't there any trace of blood on the mask?'

Barry opened his mouth to reply but froze, apparently dumbfounded. He turned to face his wife, who looked equally perplexed.

'Because I wasn't wearing it then,' a low voice announced from somewhere inside the caravan.

A tall, lanky guy emerged. He seemed uncomfortable in his own body, like a baby horse trying to make sense of its oversized limbs. He had a cut on the bridge of his nose and the hint of a black eye. Both seemed to have come from a single blow.

'That's their smoking gun, isn't it?' he asked me.

I knew I shouldn't have answered, but I nodded.

'Shit,' he said, more to himself than anyone else. 'I'm fucked.'

'Why weren't you wearing it, mate?' his dad asked.

'You know how bloody hot it gets in there. And you and that newspaper bloke spent so long fucking around that I took a break.'

'What happened in there, Steve?' I asked. 'Tell me everything.'

He turned to face me. 'I was sitting on the milk crate near the door and had the mask off because I was having a drink. But then I heard the cart start moving and had to run to my first hiding spot. By the time I was in place, I realised I'd left the mask back at the front.'

'And then what?'

'The show went on. Tapped all three girls on their shoulders at the designated times, they squealed and laughed. They seemed to be enjoying themselves.'

'So, what? Lily just attacked you, completely unprovoked?'

'I wouldn't say it was unprovoked,' he said, distractedly touching his bruised eye. 'The blonde definitely seemed the most skittish, so I targeted her. There's a part where the cart stops and I creep up behind it and whisper something to whoever seems the most spooked. I put both hands on her shoulders, said the line and then, *bam*, she throws her elbow back and knocks me on my arse.'

'And you only ever touched her on her shoulders?'

'One hundred per cent.'

'What did you say to her?'

'Same thing I say to everyone,' he replied, before lowering his voice to a chilling growl. '*You're mine now. You'll never escape.*'

'That's really fucking creepy!'

'It's a bloody ghost train, it's supposed to be creepy!'

His mother let out a small laugh, and we both turned to face her.

'He's been doing it since he was a kid. The second his balls dropped, and he got that deep voice, we stuck him in the train. S'pose it was less scary when he wasn't grown.'

'I'm honestly amazed Lily was the first to lash out,' I said.

'I've had a few near misses. But nothing like that. The way she trampled over those other girls to get out . . .' He stared at the ground, obviously recalling what had happened. He kept shaking his head. 'And then when the emergency lights came on and lit up her face . . .' He shuddered. 'I'd never seen anything like it. She was like a wild animal.'

I thought back to the moment Lily had burst through the ghost train doors. It felt like a lifetime ago, but I knew exactly what he meant.

'I've scared a lot of people over the years,' Steve began, 'but her . . . That wasn't me, that was something else. Something terrible must have happened to that girl, and I'm not talking about her death.'

I wanted to tell him, but I knew I couldn't.

'So, you never saw her after that?' I asked.

'Nope. Stuck around while me and Dad tried to fix the ride but, when she saw my face, Mum told me to go clean up and rest. I went back to the caravan. Obviously, if I'd known I was about to be framed for murder, I would have made sure someone else came with me.'

'And you didn't hear anything?' I asked, thinking about how close the caravan had been to the stables.

'Yeah,' Steve replied, frustrated. 'I heard the argument.'

'What argument?' I asked.

'The one I told the cops about.'

CHAPTER 27

Steve hadn't paid much attention to the argument. At least, not at the time. It had happened not long after he'd left the ghost train, and about half an hour before the fireworks had commenced. He was lying on the caravan's sofa bed – the lights off and a cold can of beer pressed against his slowly bruising eye – when he'd heard a woman yelling.

It hadn't struck him as being particularly remarkable. He was used to life among the carnies and tensions were often high on show nights. But when the sirens came and the rumours started spreading, he knew he'd heard Lily's final moments.

'What was she saying?' I asked.

'I didn't get the full back and forth. I had some music on, but every now and again certain words would float through the window. Mainly, she kept repeating two things: "I know" and "I remember".'

'Anything else? Anything at all?'

'I think she said something like: "It's too late, people have already seen it".'

'Seen what?' Barry interjected.

'I dunno. She sounded kinda sassy, I guess? Like she was trying to piss the other person off.'

'What about them?' I asked. 'What did they sound like?'

He sighed. 'At the time, I thought it was two women arguing.'

'You think a woman killed her?' I asked, shocked.

'Dunno,' he said, shaking his head. 'The more I think about it, the less sure I get. Maybe I only heard one side of the argument, y'know? Just her voice?'

I nodded.

'Like, there were obvious pauses, which could have been when the other person was talking. Maybe they were just talking much quieter than her? I definitely heard someone try and shush her, but that just made her louder.'

'How long did it last?'

'Not long. A few minutes, maybe?'

'Did she scream?' I asked.

He shook his head. 'One minute she was yelling and the next she just – wasn't.'

I closed my eyes and tried to focus on the metallic clangs of the pine needles hitting the caravans. It was the only thing keeping me from imagining the sound Lily's skull must have made when it caved in. I could feel my lips quivering.

'Why didn't you know about this?' Barry asked. It wasn't until I opened my eyes that I realised he was talking to me.

'What do you mean?'

'Surely your father would have told you?'

I shook my head.

'It's the same reason why the news isn't reporting it,' Steve said. 'It doesn't fit the whole "killer carny" angle. They've got their suspect, why bother looking for anyone else?'

I nodded. He was right.

'There's no way to prove what I heard.' Steve sighed. 'It's my word against theirs – and with that fucking blood . . .'

'But that's not fair,' Mrs Masters said, tears still spilling from her eyes.

Steve walked over to her and wrapped his long arms around her shoulders, just as his father had. She clung to him even more desperately and, once again, I felt the urge to turn away. But when I did, I was surprised by what I saw.

A gaggle of old ladies were standing at the back entrance of the pavilion, staring straight at me. They all looked vaguely familiar, but I couldn't place them. Kiama was a town that skewed on the older side and was filled with identical looking blue-rinsers. They tended to blend into the background, which – given their propensity for gossip – was a dangerous thing.

'Yoo-hoo, Marlowe, dear?' one of them called out.

I responded with an awkward wave.

'Come over here, pet,' another called, beckoning me closer with her wrinkled hand.

I held up my index finger and mouthed, 'Just a sec.'

I turned back to the Masters. 'Look, I'm really sorry, but I have to go.'

'You said you'd help.'

I thought twice about correcting Barry. 'I'm doing my best here.'

'You don't give two shits about us,' Steve's mother spat.

'Hey,' Steve interjected. 'She's the only person who's asked to hear my side of the story. Cut her some friggin' slack.'

'Yeah,' Barry growled. 'Probably so she can sell it to the highest bidder.'

'I'm not going to write about it. I promise.'

'Maybe you should write about it,' Steve replied, earnestly. 'No one else is going to get my side out there.'

'Marlowe?' one of the old ladies yelled again. Her saccharine voice echoed around the caravans. I needed to shut her up.

'I'm sorry, I've really gotta . . .' I pointed behind me.

Steve nodded, smiling understandingly.

I turned towards the pavilion. I wanted to help the Masters but if the old lady brigade didn't zip it I wouldn't be able to. I still didn't know where all the police were, and it wasn't like Marlowe was a common name. I couldn't risk any cops reporting back to my dad.

I walked towards the elderly women, racking my mind for a good excuse to explain why I had been talking to Lily's alleged killer. Something to do with the paper was the most logical, but I had no idea if news of my firing had made its way around town. My dad certainly hadn't mentioned anything to me but that didn't mean much. He'd rather pretend something hadn't happened than deal with the emotional aftermath.

'Sorry to disturb you, pet,' the leader of the group said as I stepped through the pavilion's arch, 'but we wanted to catch you before you left.'

'What's up?' I asked. I braced myself for the interrogation but, to my surprise, it didn't come.

'We've been trying to get a hold of your father all day, but we keep getting the runaround.'

'We understand how busy he is,' another interjected, 'with everything that's happened. But we really need to sort this out sooner rather than later.'

'There are cops on every gate,' I said, gesturing behind me. 'I'm sure if you ask one of them –'

'We have,' the leader snapped. 'They're useless.'

'Margaret!' one of the others chided.

'I'm sorry, dear,' she said to me. 'We're all just a bit on edge.'

'Yeah. I know what you mean.'

I could see the realisation dawn on her face.

'Oh – I mean – oh – of course,' she spluttered. 'This is *nothing* in comparison to what you've been through.'

The ageing clones all made the same sympathetic noises and nodded their heads.

'Hearing the news itself was bad enough,' Margaret continued. 'But to have been the one to find her. I can't even begin to imagine what you're going through, Marlowe.'

'And to already be back at work,' another chimed in, nodding in the direction of the Masters' trailer. 'And forced to interview the sicko who killed her!'

So, news of my dismissal hadn't made its way around town.

'You're certainly a bigger person than I am,' Margaret mused. 'I can't even bear to look at those monsters. I have no idea why he hasn't been arrested yet – he clearly did it.'

'I'm just trying to do everything I can to ensure the truth comes out and Lily's killer is brought to justice,' I said. I was somehow able to resist the urge to add, 'whoever they may be'.

'Now,' I continued, 'how can I help you?'

Without warning, she grabbed my wrist and began leading me towards the main hall of the pavilion. I followed, but it wasn't like I had a choice.

The main hall was dominated by everything from clusters of floral arrangements and oversized vegetables to tiered cakes and gaudy quilts. The longer I stood in the area, the more I became aware of the faint hint of decay scenting the air. Flies had descended on the perishing food items and the flowers were slowly starting to wilt.

The winners of each category were obvious, marked by smaller versions of the sash that had draped Lily's lifeless body. The same royal blue ribbon had also been slung over prize-winning cattle, swine and dogs. I recalled a photo I had taken of Lily and the winning beef heifer – their matching sashes on proud display. Mark had insisted I take it and, at the time, I'd found the irony absurd. But now it took on a different meaning: two animals judged and rewarded for their breeding and beauty but, ultimately, destined for slaughter.

'You see,' Margaret began, interrupting my thoughts, 'normally all the competitors would have picked up their entries yesterday and everything would be packed away by now.'

I nodded.

'But the police are refusing to let members of the public enter the gates so we're stuck with everything.'

'I mean,' I began, 'if the cops have said people can't come in, I'm not sure what you think I can do to change their mind.' I was frustrated that I'd been pulled away from the Masters for something so pointless.

'Oh no, pet,' Margaret said, shaking her head. 'We understand why the police can't let everyone in. It's just that we thought it would be nice to decorate the stables with the flowers as a type of memorial.'

'We don't think they'll last until the funeral and we didn't want them to go to waste,' another woman chimed in.

'Oh,' I replied, slightly ashamed of my frustration. 'What do you need me to do?'

'Well, we obviously don't want to disturb the crime scene,' Margaret said. 'But it seems like everyone's finished there and we'd just like confirmation.'

'We got a different answer from every policeman we spoke to, so we thought we'd better go straight to the top,' the same woman as before added.

I nodded, trying to think of a way to ask my dad without admitting where I'd been.

'I'll ask him.'

'Oh, thank you, pet,' Margaret said, clasping her papery hands over mine. 'I'll keep you in my prayers. I know you've had a lot of tragedy in your life but, if you keep following the Lord's light, I'm sure you'll find your way.'

'Thanks,' I replied, desperately trying not to roll my eyes.

I said my goodbyes and turned to the back of the pavilion. Then I froze. Something had caught my attention. Or, more accurately, the absence of something.

'I'm such a fucking idiot,' I muttered under my breath.

I stared at the wall of artwork I'd photographed the day before Lily's death, and finally realised why the inky sketches in her journals had seemed so familiar. I'd seen them before, hanging on the wall in front of me. It was also how I had known about the fox hunters' attire and the true identity of their prey. Jarrah had been right. The flashes had been memories, but they didn't belong to me.

She drew it – she fucking drew it – and hung it for the whole town to see.

And yet it wasn't the sight of Lily's drawing that had reminded me. Instead, I had noticed the blank spot it had occupied. It was the only entry that had been removed, making its absence all the more obvious.

'Um, excuse me?' I said, turning back to face the women.

'Yes, dear?' Margaret responded.

I pointed to the blank space. 'I thought you said no one could pick up their entries? What about that missing picture?'

'Oh, I hadn't even noticed,' Margaret said, surprised. Watching the way she struggled to squint at the vacant spot, I believed her.

'That one was gone before we got here,' one of the other women said.

'Yes,' another added. 'It drove me crazy, threw off the symmetry of the entire room. Shoddy planning to leave a gap like that.'

'It had nothing to do with the planning,' a stern voice called out from behind a row of oversized pumpkins. 'The entry was removed because it was deemed ineligible.'

I recognised the voice. It was the town's mayor, Peter Walsh. The father of the school captain who had assaulted Jarrah, and yet another name on Lily's list. I hadn't even noticed he'd been there, but his presence now felt as oppressive as the rotting scent that lingered in the hall.

'It's a shame,' I said, staring him straight in the eyes. 'It was a beautiful piece.'

A slight twitch in his eye and a stiffening of his posture told me everything I needed to know, but he tried to cover up his reaction by giving a nonchalant shrug.

'Why wasn't it eligible?' I asked.

He spoke exasperatedly, like every millisecond spent talking to me was a waste of his time. 'Because it was submitted anonymously.'

'Oh,' I replied. 'That's funny. I could have sworn it had a name on it when I saw it.'

'It didn't.'

'Hmm,' I murmured, replicating his smug shrug. 'Guess I'll have to double-check the photos I took.'

The twitch was back. He was clearly rattled. I needed to get back home and check the photos straight away, but his reaction had already given me my answer.

CHAPTER 28

I didn't bother sneaking out of the showground. My presence had clearly been noted by someone on Lily's list, so there didn't seem like much point. It also meant that I could exit via the main gate and not have to worry about dealing with the Masters. I felt guilty for bailing on them. But, at that stage, there was little I could do. My time was far better spent on other things – like finding the photos of Lily's illustration.

I'd taken the photos early on the first morning of the show, well before the gates had opened. I hadn't been back into the pavilion for the remainder of the event, so I was unsure when it was taken down. I thought back to Steve's recollections of the argument he'd heard. Was the picture what Lily had been talking about? The thing she'd allegedly antagonised her attacker with?

Maybe she didn't know it had been removed? Maybe it *hadn't* been by that stage? I kicked myself for not pinning anyone down. I was unlikely to get any concrete answers after so brazenly rubbing my suspicions in Peter's face. It had been stupid and sloppy.

As soon as I got home, I opened up my laptop and began scrolling through the photos. Lily's illustration was there, just as I had remembered it. Unsurprisingly, particularly given its subject matter, the picture was not a prize-winner. However, I could see that the small label beneath it clearly bore a name. Peter had lied – it was definitely not submitted anonymously. I zoomed in on the caption: 'Catch Us the Foxes' by Lily Williams.

The style was identical to the sketches in her journal, save for extra splashes of colour. It depicted a little girl in a white dress sitting on the ground, her bare legs awkwardly crumpled beneath her. A mass of curls protruded from behind the red fox mask that obscured her face. Behind her, a group of people in traditional fox hunting attire loomed ominously. All wore a larger version of her mask, its black hue a stark contrast against their bright red hunting coats. Some held rifles. Others had whips.

There were no identifying features but, based on the descriptions in the journals, I knew the one in the centre was supposed to be Michael. A golden hunting horn hung from his gloved fingers and protruding from his breast pocket was the telltale pink plume of a tranquilliser dart. I thought about the journal entry and reflexively rubbed the spot where Michael had plunged the dart into Lily's neck.

I felt horrible for even acknowledging it but I experienced an overwhelming sense of relief. The memories weren't mine. They were never mine. I wasn't a part of the horrors that took place in that rainforest.

No repression.

No brainwashing.

I wasn't one of the little foxes that spoiled the vines.

It was selfish, but I felt more comfortable around my father knowing I hadn't been part of the cult's hunts. It didn't excuse his alleged involvement, but it was a relief to know he'd protected me. I thought back to what he'd said when he'd asked me to lie about the markings – that keeping me out of things was all that mattered. I began to wonder if he still was.

When I returned to his office to ask about Margaret's memorial idea, I was prepared for a fight. I made it sound like I'd just randomly bumped into her on the street, but I knew he knew I'd been at the showground. He didn't say anything, though I wasn't sure whether that was due to his typical 'don't ask, don't tell' fathering style or because he didn't want to admit that he'd been keeping tabs on me.

Forensics had finished processing the scene, and he agreed that the idea was a nice gesture so he gave it his blessing. He radioed all the cops at the showground, telling them about the plan so they wouldn't give the women any trouble. When he finished, he shouted Nathan's name.

'What?' Nathan's muffled voice sounded from down the hall.

'C'mere!'

'I'm on the bog!'

I grimaced.

'Need a favour when you're done,' Dad bellowed.

There was no reply so the two of us sat in silence for an awkwardly long time. The newspaper was still lying on my dad's desk and I reached for it before smoothing my hands over its crumpled front page. Every time I saw the photo I'd taken, Lily somehow looked more scared. My dad may have kept me out of that forest, but he hadn't protected her. And he certainly hadn't protected all those other kids in their blood-red fox masks.

What had Lily's journals implied they were?

Impure.

'It would make a great photo,' my dad suddenly announced.

'What?' I asked, looking up from the paper.

'The flowers on the stables. We're not letting press through so you can snag the exclusive. I bet Mark would appreciate it.'

There was something in his tone that sounded forced. He knew Mark had fired me and was clearly trying to trap me.

'I –' I was interrupted by two wet hands slapping against my cheeks. 'What the *fuck*?'

Nathan cackled behind me. 'Just proving I washed my hands.'

'You're lucky he actually remembered this time.' My dad laughed. 'I've had to keep nagging him like I'm his bloody mum.'

'Don't fucking touch me!' I barked, wiping my cheeks. My dad and Nathan simultaneously held up their hands in surrender and then laughed at their dual reaction.

'Told you she was in a fuckin' mood today,' Nathan mocked.

I quickly got up from my seat and walked to the door.

'Wait, Lo,' my dad called out.

I paused in my tracks but refused to turn around.

'I'm sending Nath up to tell Margaret they can decorate the stables with the flowers and to give them a hand.'

'Piss off.' Nathan groaned. 'I'm not a bloody florist.'

'You should go with him, Lo. Then you can take your photos when you're done.'

'Are you fucking kidding me?' I spun around and saw the shock register on both their faces. They hadn't realised I'd been crying.

'Are you all –'

'How could you possibly think I'd ever want to step foot in those stables again?'

'I just –'

Before he had a chance to finish, I walked away. Neither man tried to stop me. The station's back door slammed behind me and I looked down at the paper in my hands. When my eyes scanned over the article's byline, I knew what my next step would be.

CHAPTER 29

'Phwoar!' Dan groaned. 'Why don't you ever dress up like that for me?'

'Because I don't need anything from you,' I replied sweetly, perching on a stool in front of the Blue Diamond's bar.

'Did you stuff your bra?' he asked, leaning in close.

'Push-up,' I whispered. 'Is it working?'

'Hasn't taken his eyes off you since you walked in. I s'pose if I were that handsome, I wouldn't feel the need to be subtle either.'

I laughed loudly.

'Ooh, do that again. He just gave me the filthiest look for making you laugh. Wouldn't have pegged him as the jealous type.'

I didn't tell Dan that I'd been counting on it.

'Anyway, the usual?'

I shook my head. 'Nah, need to keep my wits about me but don't want him knowing that. Can you make me a mocktail that looks like the real deal? Maybe something fruity? Feminine?'

Non-emasculating, I thought.

'Ah, one bimbo beverage coming right up!'

I picked up the bar's menu and began scanning the list of cocktails. They all had cheesy local names that the tourists no doubt found charming. The mirrored wall of the bar offered the perfect vantage point of my mark. Between a bottle of Chambord and Midori, I could just make him out in the reflection. He was sitting by a window overlooking the harbour, his laptop opened in front of him and a glass of whisky by his side.

Owen Archer was staring so intently at the back of my skull that I felt goosebumps ripple over my skin. For a second, I wondered if he had recognised me. But I knew it was impossible. During the research for my thesis, we'd only ever spoken via email and phone. I'd tried to arrange a face-to-face meeting multiple times but he'd always said he was too busy. Though, seeing the way he looked at me now, I was frustrated to realise that all it would have taken was a figure-hugging dress and a pair of heels.

I'd begrudgingly spent the evening preening myself, and I was pleased to see that my effort had not gone unnoticed. Owen had garnered a reputation for being somewhat of a playboy and, despite pushing forty, appeared to have a penchant for significantly younger women. It was a weakness that I'd hoped to exploit, and it seemed to be working.

I was thankful that Dan was helping me – tracking Owen's movements and reporting in. I'd been getting worried that he wouldn't show up at the bar that night but about forty-five minutes before closing time he'd sauntered in and ordered a nightcap. I'd practically sprinted the short distance from the cottage when I'd received Dan's text:

the chiselled eagle has landed

Dan was right, Owen was exceptionally handsome – even more so in real life – but he also knew it. His pride was palpable; an overinflated ego that I longed to puncture. He was the type of guy that I'd usually go out of my way to ignore, just for the fun of it. And, as I watched him watching me – casually leaning back while his index finger circled the top of his empty whisky glass – I relished the power I held over him.

It was going to be even easier than I thought.

My eyes flicked to Dan. He was showing off – effortlessly spinning and flipping the cocktail shaker around him, while 'seductively' dancing to the mellow jazz spilling from the bar's speakers. On any other night, I'd be rolling my eyes, throwing coasters and booing loudly but I giggled coquettishly, applauding the spectacle. In the bar's reflection, I caught a flash of anger illuminate Owen's face, and watched him physically puff up in some primal display of dominance. Dan quickly spun around.

'He's coming over.'

'Good job.'

Dan placed a large tulip-shaped glass in front of me and poured the peach-hued liquid in. A garish umbrella skewer, loaded with fruit, completed the illusion but I was dreading drinking the sickly sweet concoction.

'Sex on Bombo Beach,' Dan announced, winking. 'Just how you like it.'

Owen sidled up beside me and I took an exaggerated sip.

'Mmm, perfect,' I purred.

It wasn't perfect. It was orange juice and grenadine.

'Probably would have tasted better if Tom Cruise here hadn't manhandled it,' Owen chided. 'You don't *shake* a Sex on the Beach.'

Dan opened his mouth to reply, but I interrupted him.

'I asked for a show and Daniel was gracious enough to oblige.'

Owen scoffed and his jawline tensed. He had the type of 'effortless' permanent five o'clock shadow that only came from a fastidious grooming routine.

'And a *Cocktail* reference, really?' I teased. 'Bit before our time.'

I had hoped to deflate him, but that flash of pearly whites – potentially veneers – told me he was into it. He clearly enjoyed being the older man. I made a note of it.

'Dan? Can you please get the gentleman one of whatever he's drinking? My treat. But, god forbid, do it right or prepare to face a barrage of outdated insults.'

'I don't think even *I* could stuff up Kilmagoon on the rocks.'

'Wait,' Owen said, shocked. 'I was coming over to buy *you* a drink.'

'And maybe if you'd spent less time insulting the bar staff you would have beaten me to the punch.'

'You're seriously buying me a drink?' Owen asked. He looked genuinely puzzled – that same incredulous expression men get when a woman holds the door open for them.

'Yeah. I actually owe you one.'

There was a flash of panic in Owen's steely gaze as he desperately scanned every millimetre of my face trying to recall it.

'Don't worry, I'm not one of your one-night stands.' I leaned towards him and whispered, 'Well, not *yet*, anyway.'

I watched his Adam's apple bob up and down as his breathing became heavy.

I laughed loudly. 'I'm taking the piss, Owen. You helped me with my thesis last year. *Bylines from Belanglo*?'

'Oh shit,' he said, laughing. 'Yeah, Wollongong Uni, right? Don't tell me your name, I'll remember it.'

I knew he wouldn't, but I kept up the charade. The longer he struggled, the more indebted to me he'd feel.

'Uh, it was something weird.'

I laughed. He wasn't wrong.

'Fuck, what was it?'

He stared at my face like the answer would reveal itself. He looked at Dan pleadingly.

'Don't even think about it,' I threatened.

'Oh!' Owen suddenly exclaimed. 'Raymond Chandler! Uh . . . Uh, Philip . . .' He snapped his fingers and pointed at me. 'Marlowe!'

I smiled to myself, surprised that he'd actually remembered.

CHAPTER 30

We retreated to the corner where Owen had been drinking. His computer was resting on one of his competitor's newspapers, and Lily's serene smile peered out at me from the front page. I thought what an attractive couple she and Owen would have made. Classic, yet wholesome good looks – fit for the poster of a Hollywood rom-com.

He saw me looking and attempted to tidy up. But, before he closed his laptop, I spied a blank word document. It was reassuring to see that even the pros suffered from the occasional bout of writer's block.

We spoke about my thesis for a while, and I was surprised to discover he'd actually read the whole thing. I'd emailed it to him but, much to my disappointment, had never heard back. He swore he'd replied, but I could tell he was bullshitting me. Still, it was nice to hear him discuss obscure points I'd made, and my chest swelled when he praised my writing.

Sure, he obviously wanted to fuck me, but at least he'd actually read the bloody thing. The same couldn't be said for my dad, editor or friends. In fact, up until that point, the only person other than my supervisor who had bothered to read it had been Lily.

'How the hell did you get Milat to talk to you?' Owen asked. 'He fucking hates journos.'

'I know. I used it against him. Pretended I was on his side and was only interested in exposing the unfairness of his trial due to the media's involvement.'

'Shit.' Owen laughed, looking me up and down. 'You're ice cold, kiddo.'

'To be one hundred per cent honest, I only sent him the letter to impress my supervisor. I never thought he'd actually get back to me. And then, next thing I know, I'm pen pals with a bloody serial killer!'

'Let me guess, top of your class?' he asked, flashing that artificial smile.

I laughed dryly. 'Yeah, you'd think so, wouldn't you?'

He raised a surprised eyebrow.

'A *very* close second,' I replied, holding my glass up in a mock toast.

'Who was the prick who beat you? Want me to get him blacklisted?'

'*Her*,' I corrected. 'And I don't think –'

'Come on, screw the sisterhood.'

'No, it's not that.'

He crossed his arms and shook his head. 'And here I thought you actually had the balls to make it in this industry.'

I twirled the umbrella in my mocktail and sighed, wishing I'd ordered a real drink.

'Go on,' he goaded. 'Just give me a name, and it's done.'

I reached across the table, picked up his whisky and downed it in one gulp.

'Lily Williams,' I replied.

'God.' Owen sighed. 'I forgot how incestuous small towns are. Should have made the connection with your age though. You must've grown up together, right?'

I nodded.

'Were you two close?'

'She was my best friend,' I said. It wasn't technically a lie – we had been best friends before my mum died.

'Shit. Sorry.'

I shrugged and ran my finger along the rim of the whisky glass. Owen looked uncomfortable. It was the perfect time to pounce.

'I want to write about her. It feels like the only thing I can do, y'know?'

He broke my gaze. 'Have you chatted to the *Gazette* editor? He'd probably be your best bet, I imagine.'

'The one who fired me for even suggesting writing about her?'

'Wait, you're the one who took the photo? The one we used on the cover?'

'Yup, that was me. Thanks for the attribution, by the way.'

'Hey, I tried.' He held his hands up defensively. 'Believe me. Your editor said he'd had a falling out with the intern who took it, and that they were no longer employed by the paper. He refused to give me a name. I wanted to track you down but the deadline was looming and my boss ordered me to just run the thing under Mark's name.'

'And you dutifully obliged?' I mocked. 'S'pose it's been a few decades since you spent any time in an ethics class.'

That too-perfect smile. 'Let's just say your former boss led me to believe you weren't worth my journalistic integrity.'

'Let me guess. Said I was a vulture, right?'

'Among other things.'

'Do you still believe him?'

He rested his cheek on his fist and stared at me. Piercing slate-grey eyes.

'No. Men like Mark are part of the old guard, still intimidated by young women such as yourself: the go-getters, the ball-busters, the ones who refuse to take no for an answer.'

I rolled my eyes, trying not to let on that he'd hit the nail on the head.

'The way he spoke about Lily though. She sounded like your antithesis. Sweet. Compliant. Unquestioning. Got the job done without ruffling any feathers. By the sounds of it, he hired her because he wasn't threatened by her.'

'No one was.'

'It may have helped her get a job over you but it's also probably the same thing that got her killed.'

'Fuck, man. For someone who just critiqued "the old guard" that's a backwards-arse view that sounds a lot like victim blaming. Lily didn't "get" herself killed. She was murdered. Are you really trying to say that if she was a bit more of a bitch she wouldn't have been targeted?'

Owen was flustered. 'No, that's not what I meant. It's just – fuck. I wasn't victim blaming, okay? I know it wasn't her fault. Obviously.'

I saw my chance and took it. 'This, *this* is why I should be the person writing her story. You're a phenomenal journalist, Owen. I've admired your work since I was a kid. Fuck, I wanted to *be* you. But you didn't know her, and you don't know this town. The drivel that men like Mark are spouting isn't real. We're not all reduced to some shitty binary. Lily – the good girl; me – the bad. She was a *real* person. Help me show the world who she was.'

I was worried that I'd laid it on a bit thick but then I noticed his puffed up chest and boyish grin. He'd taken the bait.

'Look,' Owen sighed, 'you're a talented writer, Marlowe. Your thesis was exceptional, but the kind of piece you're suggesting just doesn't sell papers. Even if I put a good word in, I know Paul – my editor – would never go for it. People *want* that binary; they don't care that Lily was a multifaceted person.'

I opened my mouth to reply, but he continued.

'They want this,' he said, picking up the paper and pointing at Lily's smiling showgirl portrait. 'And this.' He opened the cover to reveal a grainy yet foreboding photo of Steve Masters. 'Good versus evil. As simple as that. They're *not* real people. Not any more. They belong to the masses.'

'That's bullshit.'

'I know. But it's true. And, if you want to make it in this industry, you're going to have to start viewing the world a little more black and white.'

'Good versus evil?' I scoffed.

He nodded. 'It's what all crime reporting boils down to.'

I flipped between Lily and Steve's photos and tried to hide my smile. 'And images that capture that dualism, they're important?'

'Hell yeah. It's a cliché, but as writers' copy shrinks in favour of ad-space, a picture really is worth a thousand words – sometimes more.'

'So, what would the holy grail be? Like, a picture of some poor dead girl with satanic symbols carved into her flawless flesh?'

'A little on the nose, but, yeah, that shit would sell.'

'Well,' I said, leaning back casually, 'I guess it's a good thing I took photos of the symbols on Lily's back when I found her.'

That chiselled jaw almost hit the floor.

CHAPTER 31

'Bullshit!' Owen spat.

'If you say so. I'm more than happy to go through your editor instead.'

'I've seen the coroner's report. There was nothing on her back.'

'What's the best way for me to get in contact with him?'

'Look, I don't know what the fuck you think you're playing at, but –'

I pulled my phone out of my bag and selected the photo of Lily I'd uploaded before I'd come to the bar. Even on the small screen, you could see the symbols – jagged and angry. I held the phone out to Owen.

'What the fuck?' he said, reaching for it.

I snatched it back. 'Eyes, not hands.'

He nodded, and I held the screen out to him once more.

'How the hell did you – wait. Goddamn it. Marlowe fucking *Robertson*, right?'

I pulled the phone back. 'Yeah, so what?'

He laughed dryly and shook his head. 'None of us could figure out why they were keeping the person who found her under wraps. The logical answer was that they were a suspect but when Masters' name started floating around we knew that wasn't the case.'

I frowned at him, puzzled.

'The other theory was that the cops were protecting someone. Either someone close to the Williams family or close to the investigation. Y'know, someone like an inspector's daughter.'

'Oh.'

'Shit,' Owen said, shaking his head. For the first time, he actually looked his age.

I took a sip of my mocktail, pondering what to do next. The bar was completely empty, save for Dan behind the counter. He tapped his watch and I nodded.

'Look, I'm not denying anything,' I said to Owen. 'But you know there's a third option, right?'

'Yeah? What's that?'

'Maybe it's less about the cops protecting a specific person, and more about them protecting themselves.'

'Fuck, Marlowe, what are you saying?'

'I'm not saying anything. At least, nothing on the record.'

Owen ran his fingers over his stubble. 'I know what my editor would pay for a photo like that. It would set you up for life. You could get out of here.'

I shook my head. He placed his hand on mine, and I fought the urge to recoil.

'We can protect you,' he said, squeezing my palm. 'Keep your name out of it?'

I finally pulled away. 'I'm the only person who could have taken that photo. If it's published, they'll know it was me.'

'Who're "they"?'

I stared him down, making it clear that I wasn't going to answer.

'It doesn't make sense,' Owen said. 'Where does Masters fit into all of this? Some travelling carny cult?'

I stared at him in disbelief. 'You know those marks weren't fresh. You can't seriously still think he actually killed her, right?'

'I mean, the cops certainly do.'

'He didn't do it. But he heard who did. The cops aren't mentioning that, are they?'

'His blood was on her dress, Marlowe.'

'She attacked him, on the ghost train – when I took your cover picture. He never saw her after that.'

'But why would she attack him?'

'Because she was scared. Scared of the people who did that to her.' I gestured at my phone. 'She knew she was going to die.'

'And how do *you* know that?'

'I have more proof,' I said, tracing the droplets of condensation on the table. 'Lily kept diaries, she named names.'

'Jesus,' Owen said. He was acting shocked, but there was something else there. A glimmer of excitement. He was no doubt thinking of his next Walkley award.

'I obviously want her killer to be punished, but I need to think of myself as well,' I began. 'If I blow this thing open, my life is over. I need assurances. I need a job. And I need to be the person telling this story.'

The faintest smile flickered along Owen's jawline. 'I'm guessing this ultimatum is what pissed Mark off so much?'

I shook my head. 'I hinted that I may have had access to further information but didn't go into specifics. No one knows about the photos. Or the diaries.'

'Why me, then?'

'I told you. I want to be you. I wasn't talking out of my arse. I want it all. The job, the Walkley awards, the book deals. Fuck the old guard.'

He laughed, his eyes sparkling, and stretched out his hand. 'Welcome to the vulture club, kiddo. You're a shoo-in.'

The Blue Diamond's lights began flickering on and off. Owen stared up at them, bewildered – like they were part of the conspiracy. I looked over at Dan, who stopped flicking the switches.

'Sorry, guys,' he shouted. 'Closing time.'

Owen looked at his watch. 'It's bloody ten o'clock!'

Dan shrugged. 'In Kiama-time that's, like, three am.'

'The council's really strict here,' I told Owen. 'The oldies in the houses across the road stay up just to report if there are still people in the bar after close. The hotel's received heaps of fines over the years. Don't take it out on Dan. It's not his fault.'

Dan had already walked over to our table and was clearing away our drinks. Owen looked like he was going to punch him. To my surprise, Dan was unintimidated.

'Seriously, Lo,' Dan said. 'You guys need to go *now*. I'm not getting in the shit for this.'

Owen locked eyes on me. '*You* still owe me a bloody drink.'

'Pfft! Good luck getting one now.'

'Oh my god, stop flirting and just *go*,' Dan demanded. 'Take her back to your friggin' suite, she'll shout you a drink from the minibar.'

He always had been a good wingman, even when I didn't want him to be. I raised my eyebrows at Owen.

'All right, deal,' he said. 'Come on.'

We exited onto the Blue Diamond's back terrace and Dan slammed the glass doors behind us. I stared up at the oak tree I'd spent countless recesses sitting under. Its leaves rustled in the clammy sea breeze.

'I'm surprised the bartender suggested you come back to my room.' Owen smirked. 'I thought he had the hots for you.'

I laughed. 'I'm not his type, trust me.'

'I don't believe that for a second,' he said, looking me up and down. 'I don't think there's a man alive who wouldn't consider you his type.'

I ignored the comment. He was trying way too hard.

'Dan and I grew up together. We're practically siblings.'

His smile was iridescent in the moonlight. 'I thought you small-town folk were into the whole incest thing.'

I laughed, genuinely shocked by the comment. 'Fuck you!'

'If you insist.'

I was about to reply when something hit the top of my head. I looked up and felt a second glob of sap land on the hollow of my throat.

'Goddamn it.' My chin was beginning to stick to my neck.

Owen licked his thumb, wrapped his fingers around my throat and carefully wiped the sap away. His hand lingered there for an uncomfortably long time, and I felt goosebumps radiate from his touch. He pulled me close and whispered in my ear.

'Guess you weren't joking about being my next one-night stand. Were you, kiddo?'

That fucking smile.

CHAPTER 32

I didn't want to sleep with Owen, but some part of me enjoyed the fact that he clearly wanted to sleep with me. It had been like that for as long as I could remember. I adored the chase – being wanted – and being wooed. It made me feel powerful. But the second they touched me everything changed. It became too real. That want – that need – was never reciprocated. There was simply nothing there.

It took me a long time to figure out that my feelings, or lack thereof, were not the same as others'. I thought I'd had crushes on people – powerful, talented men like Owen. But I soon figured out that, unlike everyone else, I didn't want to be *with* them, I wanted to *be* them.

At its most benign, it manifested in simple things like wanting to get to know them and to learn from them in the hopes of bettering myself. But there was also something deeper there. Something that scared me sometimes.

I wanted to consume them.

Everything they were, are and would ever be. To devour their very essence like a dominant twin absorbing its weaker sibling in the womb. I was the first to admit that it was unfathomably fucked up.

So, as I stood in Owen's hotel room, staring over his shoulder at the warning lights flashing on the harbour buoys, I allowed him to slip the straps of my dress down as he caressed my neck. His touch felt like insects burrowing beneath my skin.

'You're so fucking beautiful,' he growled in my ear, before running kisses from my jaw to my collarbone. I closed my eyes. Not out of enjoyment but to avoid looking into his – and seeing that hunger I could never return.

To my surprise, my phone began vibrating and I dropped my purse.

'Shit,' I mumbled, reaching for it.

'No, no, no, no, no,' Owen whispered, his lips pressed against my throat as he deftly kicked my bag away.

I sighed. I actually sighed. Like a petulant teen being lectured to. His kisses stopped and my eyes sprang open.

'You okay?' Owen asked.

No, I thought.

'Yeah.' I nodded. 'Sorry.'

He could see it. They always could. Some guys were into it but, to others, it was a deal-breaker. An insult. *She doesn't want me.* I had finally deflated that overblown ego, and I didn't even get to feel good about it.

I put my hand on his body, feeling its firmness, and began tracing shapes on his dress shirt. I was horrified when I realised that I was mimicking the symbols on Lily's back. He pulled me close to him, and I rested my head on his broad chest. He tenderly kissed the top of my head and I tried not to flinch. He slowly began rocking us backwards and forwards. I wanted to feel safe in his arms, but I didn't.

On the floor, I could hear my phone buzzing away.

'Hey, I was thinking,' he mumbled into my hair.

'Mmm?'

'How well do you know Michael Williams?'

What the fuck? I thought, pulling away.

'Why?' I asked.

'It's just, he'd probably be a good person to have onside. You know I'll try and help you as much as I can. But my editor and I have a somewhat contentious relationship. And we've been explicitly warned to tread lightly in our coverage of Lily's death. I just feel like having one of Paul's mates on board couldn't hurt.'

'What do you mean "one of his mates"?'

'Oh, sorry, I thought you knew that they were friends. It's how Lily got her cadetship. Nepotism at its finest.'

'I had no idea,' I replied, shaking my head.

I thought back to what Jarrah had said: *She was so proud of that cadetship. She felt like it was the only thing in her life she'd ever truly earned by herself.*

Lily hadn't known that her father was still controlling her.

'Yeah,' Owen replied. 'The two of them go *way* back. They're old hunting buddies. Paul comes down here every year and they go out into the rainforest together. He's a different man when he comes back. Best week of the job for the rest of us.'

I tried to hide my shock. Behind Owen, the warning lights on the harbour blinked on and off.

I didn't know what to say. I felt like I was being baited. Did Owen know about Michael's involvement? Was he warning me? Or worse, threatening me? Could he have been a part of the cult too? I thought back to Lily's list of names. Owen's definitely hadn't been on there, but neither had his editor's. Was the whole thing even more insidious than I had originally thought? Did it go far beyond Kiama and its inhabitants?

I needed to get out of that suite.

'Probably worth a try though, yeah?' Owen asked.

I nodded while my eyes scanned the moonlit room for my purse. It was behind Owen's feet, nestled next to the bed. The photo of Lily was in there, on my phone. I couldn't leave without it.

I was contemplating my next move – Owen's eyes still greedily surveying my body – when the sound of sirens filled the air. Two fire trucks sped past the window, and Owen turned to face them.

'Someone's burnt their toast.' Owen laughed. His smile fell when a police car and ambulance closely followed. 'Shit, you think something's up?'

I shrugged and he slid open the room's floor-to-ceiling glass doors before walking out onto the balcony. I took my chance, diving for my purse and pulling out my phone. I was alarmed to see several missed calls from my dad, along with a single text message:

Where are you? Get back to the cottage NOW. Stay away from the showground. It's not safe.

As I stared at the screen, puzzled, more sirens spilt into the room. I walked out onto the balcony and watched as more fire trucks, police cars and ambulances sped along Terralong Street.

'This isn't normal, right?' Owen asked.

I didn't answer. Instead, I leaned over the balcony railing and scanned the small car park across the road. There, sitting on the bonnet of his car, smoking a joint, was Dan. I knew his post-work routine too well. After all, I'd joined him for enough of them.

'I've got to go,' I said to Owen, already walking back into the room.

'Wait, why? What's going on, Marlowe?'

'I've gotta go,' I repeated.

'No,' he commanded, following me.

I laughed and threw open the door. 'Just try and fucking stop me.'

The door swung shut behind me but Owen grabbed it.

'Who was trying to call you, Marlowe? Your father? Something is happening, isn't it?'

I was already dialling Dan's number, but I turned to face him. 'Let's just say it's a good thing I stole your second drink. You're still under the limit so you can drive yourself there.'

'Drive *where*, Marlowe?'

Dan had answered, so I turned away.

'Hey Dan,' I said. 'I need a lift.'

'Oh god, don't tell me Jawline McGee's *that* quick in bed. Like, yeah, he's old, but at least have some common courtesy and buy Viagra. Isn't it cheap when you're on the aged pension?'

'Uh . . . you're on speakerphone,' I said, looking over at a clearly mortified Owen and pretending I wasn't secretly cheering inside.

'Fuck,' Dan swore. 'I'm never getting tipped again, am I?'

Owen stepped towards me and needlessly shouted into the phone. 'I'll give you the biggest tip of your life if you give me a lift too.'

'Sorry, dude,' Dan's mellow voice droned. 'Don't swing that way. But good for you, man.'

I burst into laughter. Owen was unimpressed.

'Not that kind of tip,' he growled.

Dan was giggling like when we were kids. I looked in the direction of the bower. Behind us, more sirens screamed.

'Oh, for fuck's sake,' I said, grabbing Owen's wrist and leading him towards the fire stairs. I didn't have time to fight with him. 'Come with me.'

'Where are we going?'

I held up my finger and spoke into the phone. 'We'll be there in a sec, Dan. Need to get to the showground ASAP. Something big's going down.'

CHAPTER 33

Dan looked sheepish as we approached his car.

'Sorry, dude,' he said to Owen. 'Just takin' the piss, y'know?'

'I'm thirty-eight,' Owen spat, defensively.

'And I'm sure you go like a fucking jackhammer,' I replied. 'Can we chill with the fragile masculinity for five seconds and get in the bloody car?'

Owen was sulking like a sullen teen. Slamming the door, crossing his arms in his lap and pouting. It was hard to believe that minutes earlier I'd been scared to be in a room alone with him. Apparently, all I'd needed to do was insult his virility. And yet, up until that point, he'd seemingly found all my jibes about his age endearing. I didn't get the double standard until I realised it had also come after my perceived 'rejection'. I sighed. I didn't have time for that bullshit.

'So,' Dan said as we pulled out of the car park and headed towards the showground. 'Gonna tell me what the hell is going on?'

'Pfft.' Owen seethed, kicking the back of my seat like a toddler. 'Good luck getting anything out of her.'

I rolled my eyes, pointed my fingers at my head and pretended to shoot myself. Dan giggled.

'Got a text from Dad,' I said to Dan. 'Telling me to stay away from the showground because it was dangerous.'

'God, he's an idiot. It's like he doesn't even know you.'

I laughed. It was true.

The emergency vehicles had seemingly stopped their onslaught and the streets of the town were deserted. We drove past the police station and I noted that the cottage's lights were out and that the driveway was empty. My dad was no doubt at the showground, dealing with whatever dangers lurked there.

Dan flicked his indicator on as we approached the roundabout next to the post office.

'Nah, straight ahead,' I said. 'Go in the back gate.'

'It'll be locked.'

'It won't. They need to get the emergency vehicles in.'

'If you say so.'

We drove past Storm Bay, and I noticed that the ocean was eerily calm. If I'd met Jarrah that night, I would have escaped my drenching. I couldn't believe that it had been less than twenty-four hours since I'd come to possess Lily's journals and even less time since I'd learned the true extent of the horrors they contained.

'You think it's another body?' Dan asked.

I shook my head, thinking of the procession of cop cars that had descended on the showground when I'd found her.

'Too many fire trucks and ambulances,' I replied.

The Norfolk pines grew denser and the town's pure-white Anglican Church peered through the tree line, appearing to glow in the moonlight. I'd once taken maths tutoring there and remembered watching the embers of the show's fireworks landing on the roof and praying that the whole thing would go up in flames. As we rounded the corner and the showground came into view, I immediately regretted that thought.

My dad was right, the danger was clear.

'Fucking hell,' Dan gasped.

I felt Owen's hand on my shoulder as he scrambled to see out the front window.

'The pavilion?' he asked.

I shook my head, staring at the smoke billowing from the other side of the showground.

'The carnies' caravans.'

We sped through the northern gate, heading towards the smoke. A large group of townspeople had gathered – something closer to a mob than a crowd. Staring at them, I could tell they weren't just looky-loos who were there after the fact. They were the instigators. The flashing lights of the emergency vehicles cast eerie shadows on their faces, making them appear even more animal-like. There was something wild about them. Something primal.

A makeshift barricade separated the mob from the firefighters attempting to extinguish the blaze. Police officers lined the divide – a human shield against the surging masses. My dad was front and centre. He was calling for calm but it didn't seem to be doing much.

Dan pulled to a stop behind the mob and I threw open the passenger door. The smell of burning metal and the chants of the townspeople filled the air.

'Murderer! Murderer! Murderer!'

For a moment, I thought they were referring to my dad. But when someone hurled a beer bottle over the barricade and screamed, '*Die, carny scum!*', I realised they were screaming about Steve.

Without warning, Owen jumped out of the car and attempted to enter the crowd. He used his height and strength to strong-arm his way in. Throwing an elbow here and there for good measure, seemingly pleased to be taking out his frustration with the town on its inhabitants. It wasn't a tactic that would work for me.

I turned to face Dan, still wisely tucked away in the safety of his car. He pointed towards the grandstand, and I nodded. I kicked off my heels, draped my bag over my shoulder and slammed the door shut behind me. Without bothering to check on Owen, I dived under the show ring railing and sprinted towards the grandstand. It was the reverse version of the shortcut I'd taken when I'd found Lily, and would lead me past the stables, straight towards the Masters' trailer. I hoped they'd managed to escape in time.

I ran towards the hollow passage, the ground turning from grass to mud under my bare feet. It was pitch-black beneath the grandstand and it was like entering an unknowable void. I ducked my head to avoid the rows of tiered seating above and continued forward. The mob's violent jeering grew fainter with each step.

I burst out the other side of the grandstand and the tops of the stables came into view. So much for never going there again. And yet, rather than taking the road my dad and I had driven down, I decided to slide down the small embankment and land behind them. It was a stupid decision. My dress was torn, my legs covered in streaks of mud and my hair was filled with pine needles. I looked like one of those feral forest children, raised by wild animals.

But then I heard a voice – a man's – coming from the other side of the stables.

'Fuck, man. What do we do?'

And then, another. 'Get the bloody cuffs off, *now*.'

I knew who it was before I rounded the corner. And yet, I could never have anticipated what would be lying at his feet.

CHAPTER 34

Steve Masters was slumped in front of Nathan, blood spilling from a wound on his head, eerily similar to Lily's. They were positioned in front of her stall, but the stables were barely recognisable since the last time I'd seen them. Each cage now bloomed with the pavilion's mismatched flowers. A patchwork of foliage reminiscent of the gaudy quilts entered in competition. It looked like a wild, overgrown garden. A twisted fairy tale of a memorial.

Steve's eyes were shut, but he looked less peaceful than Lily had. There was tension in his face. As if it were still responding to the pain he'd obviously felt. Why had I not gone back to him and his family earlier that day? I'd told myself my time was better spent doing other things.

Like what? Spending the evening flirting with a journalist and shamelessly using a dead girl as a bargaining chip? Mark was right, I was a vulture. And here I was once again circling a corpse.

Nathan's partner kneeled down and clumsily removed the handcuffs from behind Steve's back. His arms violently lolled forward, no longer controlled by their owner, and hit the concrete with a sickening *thwack*. In the moonlight, his blood shimmered like molten metal. I was going to vomit and I didn't even have the Hurricane as an excuse.

'Get someone!' Nathan shouted at his partner.

The other cop nodded and ran off towards the fire. Nathan stared down at Steve, kicked the ground beside him and swore under his breath.

'What did you do?' I growled, stepping out from the end of the stables.

'Who's there?' Nathan yelled, his hand reaching for his holster.

'What the *fuck* did you do?' I shouted, undeterred.

'Lo?' he asked, holding his hands up towards me. 'Look, it's not what –'

My body was no longer my own. I had lost all control. I felt my legs power forward, my bare feet slapping against the concrete, and my fists pummelling.

I heard my voice scream, 'What the fuck did you do?' over and over again.

He didn't fight back. Didn't even try. Instead, he took my beating. My arms thrashed against his shoulders, neck and head, the latter of which he meekly tried to protect. It was a cathartic yet wholly ineffective fit of rage.

'Lo, please,' he pleaded. 'It wasn't me; it was them.'

'You fucking piece of shit,' I screamed. 'I know. She knew. Everyone's going to fucking know!'

My throat was raw from the smoke and tears streamed from my eyes, but I continued my onslaught.

'What the hell are you doing, Marlowe?' a voice hissed somewhere behind me.

Two large arms wrapped themselves around my waist, dragging me off Nathan.

'Don't fucking touch me,' I screamed, kicking and squirming, trying to escape the person's grip.

'You're assaulting a police officer!' Owen yelled into my ear.

He carried me away from Nathan, back behind the stables. I was furious he'd followed me.

'He's not a cop,' I spat. 'He's a coward!'

'You're going to get arrested,' he said, wrestling me as I writhed in his arms. I hated the fact that he was so much stronger than me.

'I don't fucking care!'

He put his hand over my mouth, pressed his lips against my jaw and whispered, 'Calm down, right now. Do you actually want to expose these bastards?'

I wriggled and he squeezed me tighter.

'Answer me.'

I stopped fighting and nodded.

'Do you think that's something you'll be able to do from prison?'

He squeezed again and I shook my head.

'Then calm the fuck down, kiddo. And let's get these pricks.'

Owen eased me onto the ground and I slumped to my knees, coughing, spluttering and crying. I was shocked by what I had done. By what had come over me. But when I thought of Steve's body – lying so close to where hers had been and bearing the same injuries – my actions seemed completely reasonable.

'Are you okay, Lo?' a voice above me whispered. I was shocked to see it was Nathan.

'She's fine,' Owen answered.

'Lo? Do you know this guy?' Nathan asked, seemingly concerned.

I managed to nod my head as I got to my feet.

'Look, I know you're upset,' Nathan said. 'But your dad'll be here any second, and he'll bloody kill you if he sees you came. I saw him text you, I know he told you not to.'

'I think he's right, Marlowe,' Owen said. 'It's probably best if no one knows you were here. I assume you'll keep this incident to yourself, officer?'

The way he said it pissed me off.

'Yeah, mate.' Nathan nodded. 'Just a misunderstanding. No need to get anyone else involved.'

I laughed hollowly. 'No need to let anyone else know there was a witness to you murdering someone, you mean?'

Nathan crumpled like I'd punched him in his stomach. If I hadn't known better, I would have sworn I saw tears in his eyes. He beckoned me closer, placing a finger over his lips, and pointed past the side of the stables. Curiosity got the better of me and I crept up to the edge and peered around.

'He's not dead,' he whispered as I watched the paramedics transfer Steve's unconscious body onto a stretcher. 'And I wasn't the person who did that to him.'

He carefully pulled me back behind the stables before anyone noticed me.

'Bullshit,' I spat.

'It's true,' Owen said, behind me. 'People in the crowd were throwing things – bottles and rocks. One of them hit Steve as they were arresting him. I saw it.'

'Well that's fucking convenient, isn't it?'

'I don't get it, Lo,' Nathan said. 'He killed Lily. Why do you care?'

'Fuck. You.' I spat, feeling that other part of me begin to take over again. That loss of control.

'Marlowe . . .' Owen threatened.

'Look,' Nathan said, 'I've gotta get back. The ambulance will be coming this way any second. You guys have to go before someone sees you.'

Owen grabbed my wrist but I snatched it back. He sighed loudly.

'Marlowe, we *have* to go. The entire crowd saw Steve being struck. They know it wasn't Nathan. Your statement won't do anything other than incriminate you.'

I ran my fingers through my knotted hair, feeling tree sap, pine needles and god knows what else. I sighed – a deep, guttural exhale that seemed to expel all the energy from my body. I just wanted to sleep. To close my eyes and forget everything. To give up. My gaze leaped to the cliff face and I pictured the roaring ocean below. I thought of my dream. Of Lily jumping, and my decision to follow her – to end it.

I didn't want to die. I just wanted to disappear for a while.

CHAPTER 35

I left with Owen. Or tried to, at least. We retreated back under the grandstand, hoping to head back to Dan's car. But Owen suddenly stopped and I ran straight into his back. The spice of his aftershave intermingled with the damp smell of the earth beneath our feet. It was oddly comforting.

'Fuck,' he whispered.

'What?'

'Everyone's gone.'

I squatted down and peered out. He was right. The entire mob had disappeared, replaced by roving police officers cordoning off areas and directing the retreating fire engines. I couldn't see from where we were, but it appeared that the fire had been extinguished. None of it seemed like a problem until I realised Dan was also gone.

'Shit,' I muttered, pulling out my phone, and withdrawing back into the depths of the grandstand's underside. I had several missed calls and a message.

soz something happened & the crowd bolted
had 2 get out of there
im at the church if u can get here

We couldn't. Not with that many cops around. I couldn't risk them telling my father that I'd been there after he'd explicitly told me not to come. I didn't want to admit it, but regardless of the extent of his involvement in the cult, I was still scared of him. I wrote back to Dan and told him to go home.

'What the hell are you going to do?' Owen asked, watching the cops. 'Without the crowd, there's no way you can get out without someone seeing you.'

I didn't know. Didn't care. It all seemed so futile. So unwinnable. I was powerless, and it was killing me. I slumped down onto the ground. It wasn't like my dress could get any dirtier.

'Marlowe?' Owen whispered, spinning around.

'Just go,' I said. 'I'll stay here and wait them out.'

He eased himself onto the ground beside me. It was probably good that he couldn't see me roll my eyes. I stretched my head skyward and stared into the nothingness, imagining the canopy of the rainforest. I jumped at Owen's touch, his knee lightly brushing mine.

'You okay, kiddo?'

No.

'I just want to go to bed,' I replied.

'Here,' he said, elbowing me in the side and patting his shoulder. 'We'll be here for the long haul. You should rest.'

To my surprise, I surrendered. It helped that I couldn't see him and that he couldn't see me. We sat there like that, with my head rested on his shoulder – in complete silence – for the longest time. But just as I was on the precipice of sleep, I heard Owen sigh.

'You really think the carny is innocent, don't you?' he whispered.

'He *is* innocent,' I sleepily replied.

Owen gently rested his head on top of mine.

'Not going to lie, kiddo, didn't think you had it in you. But you're one scrappy li'l fighter, aren't you?'

I tried not to think of Michael's words.

'It was stupid,' I replied. 'But seeing him there, just like her . . .'

'I think that cop was quite disappointed when I pulled you off him. I mean, not retaliating in *any* way?' He elbowed me in the side again. 'Think he was enjoying himself a little too much. If you catch my drift.'

I pulled my head away from his.

'Let me guess? You're not his type – right? Like the bartender? He just sees you as a sister?' He scoffed to himself. 'You're kidding yourself, Marlowe. Bet half the bloody town's in love with you, and you can't even see it.'

'You don't know shit about me or this town.'

Even in the darkness, I could sense that counterfeit smile. 'Then tell me, kiddo. Let's start right here.'

'The showground?'

'No, *here*. Underneath the bleachers. Bet this place has seen a lot of action over the years.' Owen leaned in close. 'Pretty sweet hook-up spot.'

He was trying. He was still fucking trying.

Before I had a chance to reply, Owen was already kissing me. His mouth firmly pressed against mine, his tongue tentatively exploring the unwelcoming cavity.

There was only one thought in my mind: *Bite – hard.*

Thankfully, I quickly quashed it before any lasting damage was done.

I didn't pull away, but I wasn't exactly an active participant. Something was being done *to* me, rather than *with* me. I had hoped that the darkness would make it easier – that he wouldn't be able to see my lack of interest. Similarly, I'd hoped that, by not having to see the unrequited hunger behind his eyes, I wouldn't have to experience the suffocating feeling of the associated guilt.

And yet, there it was.

I knew he could sense it too. That *lack* of something. But, unlike the hotel room, he powered through. His mouth became more ravenous, and his hands began to softly trail over my body. My skin screamed.

'Come on,' he growled. 'I know you want me.'

I didn't know who he was trying to convince more.

'Owen,' I began.

'Shh, shh,' he hushed, moving his lips from my mouth to my ear.

'You'll never *be* me, kiddo,' he whispered, his hand snaking up my thigh. 'But this is the next best thing.'

I grabbed his hand, wrenching his fingers off my bare skin with an alarming amount of force.

'No. I can't.'

He snatched his hand away from mine and slammed back into the wall behind him. I could feel his pent-up aggression wheezing out of him like a deflated balloon.

'I'm sorry,' I muttered, frustrated with myself the second the words escaped my lips.

'What's the issue?' he asked exasperatedly. 'Are you gay?'

Ah, yes. The only conceivable reason a woman would ever turn down a man, especially one as used to getting his way as Owen.

'Nope,' I replied.

The truth was, the only thing I was less attracted to than men was women. But I knew that telling him was pointless. People just didn't get that type of thing. Hell, I barely got it.

'Then what?' he asked. His voice had faltered ever so slightly. He was genuinely hurt.

I found him so pathetic. How could someone so intelligent, so powerful, be brought to his knees by something so mundane? I could feel him staring at me through the darkness, desperately looking for an answer that would assuage his dented ego. I knew what I had to do.

'A person I spent almost every day of my life with was murdered here,' I began. 'Like, ten metres away. I found her mutilated corpse two nights ago. So, I'm *really* sorry if I'm not in the mood to fuck you right now.'

It wasn't the right answer, but it was probably a better one.

'Well, *fuck*, Marlowe,' Owen hissed, leaning in close. His breath was hot on my neck. 'Maybe you should think of that shit *before* you lead a bloke on.'

CHAPTER 36

I ran. Away from the grandstand. Away from the showground. And away from Owen fucking Archer.

Nobody stopped me or even tried to. It's possible they didn't notice me, or simply didn't care. The police had thinned out during my time under the grandstand, more interested in keeping the rapacious media at bay. And the ambulance containing Steve Masters' unconscious body had long gone. My dad definitely hadn't seen me though, and that was the most important thing. He wouldn't ask, and I wouldn't tell.

I made it home, somehow. As if I'd teleported there. But the sore soles of my feet suggested I'd run the entire distance. The house was empty – the lights still off.

I peeled off my dress and hopped into the shower, hoping to wash away the evidence of the evening. It wasn't so much the showground's dirt I was trying to get rid of but Owen's touch. The presumed possessiveness of it still lingered on my skin.

I was furious at him for blaming his desire on me. For suggesting that I had somehow been asking for it. And yet, deep down, some part of me recognised that he was right. I *had* wanted him to want me. But nothing more. It wasn't exactly fair to him, but that didn't mean he hadn't been a world-class prick.

I wanted to cry but couldn't muster it. It seemed to be too much effort for my overtired mind. And yet, I craved that release. Without it, I thought I might implode.

I spent the rest of the night curled up on the lounge watching the intermittent news coverage of the night's events. The mob, the fire and Steve's 'accident'. The reports corroborated what Owen and Nathan had alleged, but that didn't mean the situation wasn't suspicious as all hell.

The crowd had shown up earlier in the evening. A large group of local men who had taken it upon themselves to 'protect' the women of the community. If Steve wasn't going to be arrested, then they were going to ensure that he wouldn't have the opportunity to kill anyone else.

It had started off innocently enough – puffed chests, glaring eyes and whispered insults. But, when the carnies emerged from their trailers, the police had to step in to avoid an all-out brawl. There was posturing from both sides – hurled abuse, threats of violence, a bit of push and shove – but it wasn't until a Molotov cocktail landed on the top of the Masters' trailer that all hell broke loose.

Witnesses could describe the roaring fireball emitted from the caravan's gas system with an alarming amount of clarity. And yet, strangely, not a single witness could recall a specific person throwing anything. Yes, one person had said, the Molotov had definitely come from the mob, but there was no way to tell who had thrown it, and you couldn't possibly expect the police to arrest *all* of them, could you?

It was the same with the object that had allegedly struck Steve: the community banding together – us versus them. The sickening thud the rock had made as it hit Steve's skull was enough to spook the mob though. They'd fled before anyone had a chance to point fingers, and the police seemed wholly unmotivated to find the perpetrator. As far as anyone was concerned, justice had been served.

There was something biblical about it – an eye for an eye, a public stoning.

An innocent man silenced.

The pressure from the mob was rumoured to have fast-tracked Steve's arrest warrant. And my dad's name was thrown around as the person who'd made the call to take him into custody during the fire. Whether he had any say in Nathan's decision to perp-walk Steve past the crowd remained to be seen. Maybe if he hadn't been handcuffed, he would have been able to protect his head.

The news posited that the arrest had occurred because there was concern Steve would use the fire as a way to escape. One witness even went so far as to accuse the carnies of lighting it themselves as a distraction. It didn't matter that there was absolutely nothing to support the claim – the news channels still reported it.

The ambulance that picked Steve up only drove him the short distance to the harbour's helipad. The closest hospital – some twenty minutes away – didn't have the facilities to deal with his injuries, so the rescue helicopter transported him to Wollongong Hospital, where he was placed in intensive care.

I was sickened by the way the journalists crossing live from the front of the hospital reported Steve's prognosis. The glee in their eyes as they told the world that the monster who had murdered the beautiful showgirl was unlikely to ever wake up. And, perhaps more importantly, was unlikely to ever be able to defend himself against the allegations.

I thought of the last words Steve had said to me.

'Maybe you should write about it. No one else is going to get my side out there.'

CHAPTER 37

I awoke in my bed and the onslaught of images contained in my dreams blossomed in my mind. The hunger in Owen's eyes. The carnies' caravans burning. The jeers of the mob. And Steve's slowly swelling skull.

Only they weren't dreams – they'd actually happened. For the first time since Lily had died, I'd slept a dreamless sleep and was instead recalling the previous night's memories. It was as if the evening's events had overwhelmed my mind and it had shut down somewhere at the showground. I struggled to piece the rest together. Fragments – their sharp edges dulled by an overwhelming sense of apathy.

The cottage was creaking and groaning, the hot water system protesting my father's morning shower. It had obviously been what had woken me up, and I cursed him under my breath. I just wanted to sleep – a few more hours, a few more days – at least until the funeral. We'd had countless fights about the noise of his showers over the years. So many that he'd actually become pretty good at finishing up before the thudding started.

Today was the exception though. Maybe he needed more time to scrub away his guilt.

I suddenly remembered that we'd spoken the night before. Or, at least, that he had spoken to me. To my surprise, I'd woken up in his arms as he was gently carrying me to bed. He'd found me on the lounge and, after prying the remote out of my fingers and turning off the television, had taken me to my room. I'd squirmed and fought, but he'd hushed me and gently stroked my hair.

It had felt so familiar – so comforting. I tried to remember the last time he'd carried me like that. It had been in the rainforest. When he'd found me hiding among the buttress roots. Wait, no. That wasn't me. That was Lily. And it wasn't my father, it was Michael. Or was it? I couldn't remember. Everything had felt like a dream.

'Shh,' he whispered. 'It's okay. It's all over now.'

'Huh?' I groaned.

'We got him, Lo,' he said, pulling the covers over my shoulders. 'He can't hurt anyone else.'

'Michael?' I asked sleepily.

'No, Steve. Her killer,' he said, tucking my hair behind my ear. 'It's all over, Lo. You don't have to worry any more.'

'But . . .'

'Shhh,' he hushed again, patting my shoulder. 'Get some sleep. Everything's going to be okay now. You're safe.'

I'd tried to fight my fatigue, but it was impossible. I had fallen into a deep slumber, the remnants of which still clouded my mind. Curled up in my bed now, I considered returning to sleep but knew it was impossible. I wasn't like my father. I couldn't just fall asleep at the drop of a hat, no matter how exhausted I felt.

I rubbed my eyes a little too vigorously, the pressure simultaneously bringing both pain *and* relief. They still stung from the smoke at the showground the night before and were no doubt bloodshot. I began digging through my bedside drawers for eye drops but remembered they were in the bathroom cabinet. I sighed to myself. My father was finally out of the shower but I could hear him shaving at the basin. That telltale clink of the razor as he tapped it against the sink.

My phone was sitting on top of the drawers next to me. I tried to wake it but it was dead. My dad must have placed it there but clearly hadn't had the foresight to charge it. I plugged it in and reached for my laptop instead.

I squinted through my stinging eyes at the top news articles on my homepage. Steve was still in a coma. I knew his chances of waking would be nothing short of miraculous, but that wasn't what shocked me. I was surprised he was still alive.

But I suppose it didn't matter. Either way, he'd been silenced. Which meant, as horrifying as it may have seemed, that they'd managed to get away with it. The thought made me sick to my stomach. Why hadn't I gone back to talk to the Masters? Could I have done something to prevent it?

I clawed at my eyes, which were filling with tears. I scrubbed at them with my fingertips until the stinging became unbearable. I tried to tell myself it was just the smoke, but the sobs choking out of my throat suggested otherwise.

My father was still in that fucking bathroom.

I leaped out of bed and threw open my bedroom door, before stomping down the cottage's cramped hallway. I needed it to stop.

Tink, tink, tink.

My father's razor ricocheted off the cracked porcelain.

Bang, bang, bang!

My fist pounded on the peeling bathroom door.

'For fuck's sake,' I shouted. 'Hurry up!'

I was prepared for a fight. A screaming match. For him to swing that door open so violently that the entire house shook.

Instead, I heard him calmly stride to the door and I watched as the handle gently turned. I placed my hand on the knob to open it quicker but stopped when an unfamiliar pair of feet came into view. I stepped back as my eyes swept up the rest of the body and finally rested on his face.

Those fortune-teller eyes. All-seeing. All-knowing.

'Doctor Williams?' I asked, shocked.

Michael was standing in the small bathroom, wearing nothing but a towel slung around his hips. His hair was messy and damp, and remnants of shaving cream still clung to his face. But, even in his state of undress, there was something commanding about his presence.

I crossed my arms as if to hide my pyjama-clad body. I was wearing far more clothes than he was and yet still felt underdressed. The thought felt absurd when I remembered the things that I had read about him. The things his own daughter had accused him of doing in that rainforest. It took all my willpower not to slam the door in his face and bolt to safety. But nowhere in that town was safe. Not any more.

'My apologies, Miss Robertson. I didn't mean to impose.'

'No, I'm sorry,' I replied, caught off guard. 'I just assumed you were my dad.'

'He did warn me to keep the shower short,' he said, before leaning towards me. 'Or face your wrath.'

I felt my face flush and could sense that he'd noticed it too. The faintest smile flickered on his lips as he pulled away.

'I'm sorry if I woke you. With everything that happened last night, I didn't get the chance to go home. Your father suggested I freshen up before the final press conference.'

'The fin–' A large tear fell down my cheek, and I sniffed loudly. Michael reached for one of the towels on the rack next to him and handed it to me. I took it and dabbed at my still stinging eyes.

'Don't get too excited there, doc,' I said, looking at the concern on his face. 'I'm not actually crying – your services won't be necessary.'

'I may be a shrink, but I still have enough medical training to help treat smoke exposure.'

I tried to hide my stunned reaction before he noticed.

'Don't worry,' he said, smiling wryly. 'Your father doesn't know you were there.'

'But you do?'

He nodded. 'You and that himbo journalist, right? The pretty boy?'

I could still feel Owen's hands on my skin but didn't answer.

'Were *you* there?' I asked. Had he been the one who'd thrown the rock that had hit Steve? It would explain why the town had refused to give him up.

'No. I was at Warilla police station when it all happened. They called me in to tell me about the arrest warrant.'

'Then what makes you so confident *I* was there?'

'Come on, Marlowe,' he tutted. 'You know what this town is like. Eyes and ears everywhere. It wasn't the first time you paid those caravans a visit, was it?'

I thought back to the pavilion. To the mayor, Peter Walsh. There was no point in arguing.

'So what if I did?' I asked, surprised by my boldness.

He reached for another face towel and began wiping the shaving cream off his jawline. He seemed to be trying to cover up the sneer he'd been fighting ever since he'd opened the door. His arrogance was suffocating. But I suppose if *I* had just succeeded in framing someone for murder, I'd feel cocky too.

I turned to leave, pulling the door shut behind me, but then stopped.

'Oh, duh – I forgot,' I said, pushing it back open. 'Can you please pass me the eye drops in the cabinet behind you?'

Unsurprisingly, Michael remained frozen in place. He crossed his arms over his bare chest. The amused smirk slicing his lips suggested that he knew exactly what I was trying to do.

Or, more specifically, what I was trying to see.

CHAPTER 38

I was so sure they were going to be there.

The marks that had been carved into Lily's back. The same ones that she had claimed both her mother and father had. But, when Michael turned around, his back was bare. No matter how hard I stared, the markings would not manifest. There was simply nothing there.

I wanted to reach out. To run my fingers along his flesh. To make sure I wasn't missing anything. Instead, I remained frozen in place, feeling my heartbeat pulsing in my ears. I suddenly felt very cold and meekly rubbed at my arms. It did nothing. I felt numb. Betrayed.

She was wrong.

He was already back facing me. His eyebrow arched; his smile wry. He could sense my shock. My disappointment. He knew he'd won. Yet again.

He proffered the small white bottle like it was a lost treasure. 'The solution you seek,' he said, smiling knowingly.

I took the bottle from him, and he took the towel I'd been holding.

'One moment, Miss Robertson,' he said, walking to the basin and dousing the towel in cold water. He wrung it with a fluid twist of his wrists. The veins on his hands bulged with the pressure. I imagined those same powerful hands wrapped around my throat. My skin shuddered.

'Flush your eyes with the solution and then lie down for a few minutes with your eyes closed,' he said, handing the towel to me.

'Put this over your eyes and press, very lightly. It should stop the stinging and help with the redness.'

I draped the damp towel over my hand. It clung to my skin.

'Thanks,' I said, heading back out the door.

I did what he said. I flushed my eyes with the solution before lying down and draping the damp towel over my face. I gently pressed it against my eyes, fighting the urge to rub them. My entire body was covered with goosebumps, but I couldn't tell whether it was from the coolness of the towel or Michael's presence. Through my bedroom wall, I could still hear him pottering away in the bathroom.

Our encounter had been unsettling. But the most disturbing thing had been the absence of the markings. I began to question the reliability of my eyes. After all, they were damaged by the smoke. Swollen. Watery. Blurry. I'd only been able to look for a few seconds before Michael had turned around again. Had I somehow missed the marks?

I'd also made the mistake of expecting them to look like Lily's. But Lily had said that the brandings typically occurred between the ages of sixteen and twenty-three. Which meant Michael's scars would have been decades old.

With my face still covered, I ran my fingers along the waffle-shaped scars on my forearms. They'd faded considerably since I'd worked at the ice-creamery and were now a muted, silvery colour that blended into my pale skin. People had long stopped commenting on them. Was it because they could no longer see them?

Plus, Michael's skin was far more sun damaged than mine. The dairy farmer's son – a childhood spent in paddocks. Could his freckles and pigmentation have been enough to camouflage those incriminating marks? Or had he even gone so far as to have them removed? It sounded absurd, but I couldn't help but think it was a possibility. After all, why would he have risked exposing his back to me unless he was sure I wouldn't see them?

It was at that moment that I realised how peculiar the whole situation had been – how convenient it all was. Had I been set up? How long had he been in that bathroom, banging around until I woke up? He'd said that my father had warned him about facing my wrath. He knew I'd confront him if he made enough noise.

He knew Lily knew. He knew I did, too. And he knew I wouldn't be able to resist him standing in that towel – the answers to my questions within reach. Hell, he wouldn't have even had to remove the marks, he could have just covered them with makeup. He certainly made sure I only saw his back for a moment.

It was the perfect way to gaslight me into being sceptical of her claims. To plant those seeds of doubt deep within my mind. If the marks weren't there, then what else had she been wrong about?

An overwhelming sense of lethargy crashed over my body. I was so tired of fighting. I pressed the towel into my face. I just wanted to sleep.

That is, until I heard my door creak open.

At first, I thought I'd imagined it. My overtired mind playing tricks on me. But then I heard the footsteps heading towards me. Panic rippled through my body. I felt frozen in place.

'Doctor Williams?'

'Shh, shh, shh,' he hushed.

My eyes sprang open, but my sight was still obscured by the towel draped over my face. I went to raise my arm to remove it but discovered I couldn't. No matter how hard I tried, my limbs remained firmly locked in place. My entire body was paralysed.

I was suffocated by dread. My breath began to choke out of me in frenzied gasps. I could feel my torso rising and falling erratically. My heart was pounding against the wall of my chest so violently that I felt certain it would burst through.

Had this been how Lily had felt before she died?

'What the fuck did you do to me?' I managed to spit.

'There's no point in fighting it, Miss Robertson.'

I could hear he was closer to me now. Standing over my bed. I tried to lash out at him. I focused all my energy on propelling myself forward – thrashing my appendages towards him – but it was pointless. I had zero control over my body.

'The eye drops . . .'

He didn't answer me. Instead, I felt the mattress depress as he kneeled beside me. With one fluid motion, he swung his other leg over my hips. He was straddling me, pinning me in place.

'Get off!'

His body pressed against mine as he leaned his head down towards me. His breath sliced my throat. Tears streamed from my eyes.

'You're mine now,' he whispered into my ear. 'You'll never escape.'

'Please,' I begged. 'Please don't do this.'

'Come on,' he growled, 'I know you want me.'

I screamed. I screamed louder than I'd ever screamed before. I had no idea if my father was at the station – if anyone was – but I had to try. My voice was the only weapon I had.

He slammed his hands down over my face, pressing the towel into my mouth and nostrils. I had been mid-scream, and the air from my lungs was almost fully expelled. I stopped, but he didn't.

'Shh,' he whispered.

He pressed down – harder and harder. Even if I hadn't been paralysed, I would have struggled against his strength. He had rendered me completely and utterly powerless.

I was going to die. Just like her.

'Not much of a fighter now, are you?'

As the last remnants of air choked out of my lungs, and my consciousness slipped away, I could hear someone pounding on my bedroom door.

'Marlowe!' they screamed.

But they were too late.

CHAPTER 39

Just when I thought I'd exhaled my last breath, a surge of adrenaline took over my body. I inhaled deeply, feeling the towel suck into my mouth from the force of my lungs. I coughed and spluttered, and ripped it off my face, shocked that I'd somehow regained the use of my limbs.

Michael was gone.

'Marlowe! Marlowe, are you okay?' his panicked voice called from behind my bedroom door.

My body shuddered as I tried to control my breathing. Tears still streamed from my eyes. I watched as the doorknob frantically turned. It dawned on me that I'd locked it before I'd even lain down.

He'd never even stepped foot in the room.

I'd dreamed it.

I'd dreamed the whole fucking thing.

My mouth felt dry and coarse like it had been scrubbed by the towel. The pressure in my head was nauseating. I began coughing violently. My throat was red raw.

'Marlowe, please. Can you hear me? Are you okay?'

'I'm 'kay,' I managed to choke out.

'Are you up to opening the door? I just want to make sure you're okay.'

'I –' my coughing fit returned, 'am!'

'Please, Marlowe. You were screaming.'

Fucking great.

'Hang on,' I shouted, still trying to catch my breath.

I swung my legs over the side of the bed, my bare feet hitting the cool floorboards below. My breathing was still erratic and my head was spinning from the lack of oxygen. I noticed that my phone's screen was lit up. I unplugged it from the charger.

There was a message on the screen all in caps:

FOR FUCK'S SAKE
ANSWER YOUR BLOODY PHONE!!!

'Marlowe?' Michael called again.

'Fuck. Hang *on*!'

I put my phone down before walking to the door and unlocking it. As my fingers pulled at the latch, I noticed how much I was still trembling. I shook my hands, trying to stop them jittering, and slowly turned the doorknob.

'Marlowe . . .' Michael began, his face etched with concern.

'Look, I'm fine,' I interrupted. 'It's not what . . .' Seeing him after my dream made my skin crawl. 'I – I was . . .'

'Asleep. I know.'

My eyebrows knitted. I noticed that Michael had changed and was once again presenting as his dapper self. His hair was completely dry. I'd apparently slept longer than I'd realised.

'They've become worse, haven't they?' he asked.

'What?'

He shook his head, seemingly frustrated. 'He still hasn't told you, has he?'

'Stop talking in fucking riddles!' I barked, before descending into another coughing fit.

Michael reached his hands out but stopped short of touching me.

'Come on, sit down,' he said, corralling me to my bed.

I did what he said. But only because I was worried that I might pass out. I perched on the side of my bed and buried my head in my hands. I felt the mattress sink next to me as Michael sat down. My mind flashed back to my dream, and my breathing became ragged once more.

'Shhh,' Michael hushed, next to my ear. 'It's okay. Just breathe.'

His words and his proximity only made things worse.

'Come on, Marlowe. I need you to lift your head up and look at me. Can you do that for me?'

I sighed a jagged breath, before raising my head and looking into his eyes. They were as iridescent as moonstones. Hypnotising.

'That's it,' he continued. 'Now breathe. In-two-three, out-two-three.'

I tried to match his count, but my breaths choked out early. He kept repeating the mantra until my body slowly adapted to the rhythm. I could feel my chest loosening.

'I'd like to check your pulse. If you don't mind?'

I nodded and held out my hand. My entire arm was still shaking. I pumped my fingers in and out of a fist trying to stop the tremors.

'Your neck would be easier. With your permission, of course.'

I slowly nodded, and he reached towards me, carefully tucking my hair behind my ear. When his fingers made contact with my flesh, it was like a zap of static electricity. I clamped my eyes shut.

'That's it,' he whispered. 'In-two-three, out-two-three.'

I kept breathing in sequence as he monitored my heartbeat. Eventually, he removed his fingers from my neck. My eyes sprang open. The area he had grasped still bore the sensation of his touch. I reached my hand up and rubbed at it, trying to disrupt the strange feeling that lingered on my skin.

'Do you remember what you dreamed about?' he asked.

I locked eyes with his. Had I only screamed in my sleep, or had I called his name? His expression gave nothing away, so I averted my gaze and softly sighed.

'I don't know,' I lied. 'I never remember my dreams.'

'You've been having them ever since you found her,' he explained. 'You scream her name in your sleep, and his – her killer's. Your father has had to wake you up multiple times. He said he didn't think you remembered anything. From the sound of it, you've also been experiencing sleep paralysis.'

'Why am I hearing this from you and not him?' I asked accusingly.

'Come on, Marlowe. We both know your father lacks the emotional intelligence to deal with something like this. There's no denying he's somewhat –' he paused for a second, searching for the word, 'detached.'

I thought back to a conversation I'd had with my father when I was still in high school. I'd been debating whether to study journalism or psychology, and he'd 'helped' me by sharing an anecdote about his mental health assessment prior to enlisting in the police force. After a string of interviews, questionnaires and tests, the psychologist had diagnosed him as a psychopath. I'll never forget the pride in his voice as he gloated about his diagnosis: 'They said I'd be perfect for the job because I don't have a conscience.'

I could hardly talk though. The fact that my first thought was, *Goddamn it, that shit's hereditary*, probably summed up my own psychopathology.

'He's worried about you, Marlowe,' Michael continued, interrupting my thoughts. 'We all are.'

'For the last time, Doctor Williams. I'm fine.'

'But you're not *really*, are you? The night terrors are just the start of it. There's also the lethargy, the anxiety attacks, the paranoia and the fits of aggression.'

I opened my mouth to protest, but he continued.

'In my professional opinion, Miss Robertson, you appear to be experiencing symptoms of post-traumatic stress disorder.'

I could feel my rage bubbling under the surface. I wanted to yell – to scream – to tell him I knew exactly what he was trying to do. But I knew that was precisely what he wanted.

'Think about it, Marlowe. I mean, *really* think about it. Be honest with yourself. Be honest about what you've experienced these last few days. I know it's a difficult thing to hear for someone so used to being in control, but I think if you let go, you'll realise what I'm saying is true.'

Before I'd even had a chance to process his words, my phone began to ring.

'I'll leave you to get that,' Michael said, standing up. 'I've already intruded enough on your time. I also need to prepare for the press conference, but I do hope you'll consider what I've said. You need help, Marlowe – and you have a support network who are willing to provide it, if you let us.'

He left before I had the chance to tell him to go fuck himself.

CHAPTER 40

As soon as the door clicked shut, I reached for my phone. I hadn't had time to see who the text messages and phone calls were from, but the capitalisation suggested Jarrah. I scrolled through the myriad messages I'd missed while my phone was dead. My suspicions were correct.

He was furious about Steve's arrest and 'convenient' injury. We'd texted back and forth the previous day, after Owen's article was published, and Jarrah had shared my suspicions that Steve was being framed. Now that the carny had been silenced, Jarrah was baying for blood. He wanted proof of the cult, and he thought he could get it – with my help.

I walked to my door and pressed my ear against it. I couldn't tell whether or not Michael had left.

I walked back to my bed and slumped down on the mattress. I picked up my phone and dialled Jarrah's number. He answered on the first ring as if he'd been sitting there, waiting for my call.

'I thought you were *fucking* dead!' he shouted.

'Nope, just my phone,' I replied. I cupped my hand over my mouth and whispered as a precaution, but it was unlikely Michael could hear me even if he were still in the cottage.

'Why are you whispering?' Jarrah asked.

'Lily's dad was here. I'm not sure if he's left.'

'What? Why was he there?'

'To have a shower before the press conference,' I began. 'Oh, and to tell me that he thinks I have PTSD.'

'Shit,' Jarrah murmured. 'He's gaslighting you. Just like he did with her.'

'Yeah, I'm not fucking stupid.'

'Jesus, Lo. Please be careful. You've read the journals; we both know what he's capable of.'

'Yeah, I know.'

I thought back to my dream and felt my chest tighten once more. It was as if I could still feel the pressure of Michael's body pressed against mine.

'Anyway,' I continued, 'about this plan of yours, what do you need?'

'You,' he replied. 'You've been to her house, haven't you?'

'Yeah. I mean, it's been a while, but yeah.'

'Lily talked about the place they held the ceremonies – the ones they did after the hunt. She said it was on their property. A big clearing in the middle of the rainforest. I've looked on Google Maps. You can see it.'

'Uh, so?' I asked. 'According to her journals, the last hunt was in October. I hardly think there's still going to be evidence there.'

'But what if there is, Lo? It could corroborate the journals. You could go to the media with it all.'

I hadn't told him about my encounter with Owen, or of his editor's connection with Michael.

'I still don't understand what you need me for,' I admitted.

'I need backup, Lo! I'm not going into that fucking rainforest by myself after the things I've read. Plus, you've been on the property before.'

'I haven't been through their whole section of rainforest though. It's like hundreds of acres!'

'So? Weren't you ever a Brownie or a Girl Guide or whatever the fuck the female version of a Scout is?'

'Pfft, no!'

'Then why the hell do you have a Swiss Army knife?'

'My dad gave it to me. Until I sliced my hand open with you, I'd only ever used the bloody bottle-opener.'

'Well, shit.' He laughed.

I joined in.

'Come on, Lo,' he said after our laughter had died down. 'We've gotta do it. For her.'

I sighed. 'When?'

'Today? I can come down right now.'

'No. If we're doing this, we're doing it properly. We need more time to plan. I need to look at the maps and figure out the best way to get there without alerting Lily's parents to our presence. We'd need an early start, too. By the time you come down from Sydney, it'll be way too late today. I mean, I sure as hell wouldn't want to get stuck up there after dark.'

'Okay, sure,' Jarrah eagerly replied. He'd given in way too easily.

'Jarrah, I'm not saying I'll one hundred per cent do it. Okay? Just that I'll look into it. I mean, I wanted to see it for myself the second I read the journals, but Saddleback's rough, man. Like, *without* the whole death cult thing.'

'That's why I need you there, Lo. You were the only person Lily trusted, so you're the only person *I* can trust.'

'Yeah, I know. Turns out she's just as much of a pain in the arse to me dead as she was alive.'

I laughed, but he didn't. The silence was uncomfortable.

'She thought so highly of you, Lo,' Jarrah finally said. 'I dunno if she was the kind of person who'd ever say it to your face, but I hope you know it. I think she thought that if she were more like you none of this would have ever happened.'

'That's not true . . .'

'She was so scared, Lo,' Jarrah said, his voice small and brittle.

'I know.' I sighed, feeling tears bite at the corners of my eyes. 'Anyway, I've gotta go check if Michael's actually gone. Send me a photo of the clearing you were talking about. I'll call you later. After I've had a chance to figure stuff out.'

'Thank you, Lo. And please, be careful with Lily's dad.'

'Trust me, Jarrah. I can handle him.'

CHAPTER 41

The Williams family lived on a vast piece of land located on the western face of Saddleback Mountain. It was nestled underneath the Barren Grounds plateau but had sweeping, uninterrupted views of the South Coast. Everything felt limitless up there. The rainforest trickled into the fields, the fields into the beaches, the beaches into the ocean and the ocean into the sky. On clear days you could even see all the way to Ulladulla.

However, to say it was remote was an understatement. To get there from Kiama, you had to travel in a needlessly complicated U-shape. Driving down the Kiama bends, before heading past Gerringong, then back up the mountains via Foxground. It was easily a twenty to thirty minute trip, depending on how comfortable you were tackling steep, winding roads.

Looking at it on Google Maps didn't do the place justice. You couldn't get a feel for just how big it was – or how isolated. I stared at it on my computer screen and realised why Jarrah had been so flippant. He simply couldn't grasp what it was really like up there. How *wild* everything was.

Being on that land gave me the same feeling as being at the blowhole. There was something primordial about it. Something to be feared. Something that made me feel tiny and insignificant in the grand scheme of things. Like I was nothing more than a blip on a radar – come and gone in a millisecond.

And yet, Lily's house itself was a sanctuary. Perched on the edge of the rainforest. A modern, pavilion-style home fit for the front cover of an architecture magazine. A sprawling monolith designed to effortlessly blend into the landscape with an infinity pool that made it feel like you were floating on the edge of the world.

I suppose you actually were.

But therein lay the problem. It truly was like another world up there, and not one that could easily be ventured into. For starters, the property was on a private road, with an imposing security gate kilometres away from the house itself. If you didn't have a key or weren't admitted entrance via the intercom, the property was virtually impenetrable.

At any other time, I could have driven up to the gate, leaned out the window and pressed the buzzer, before waving at the security camera as I watched the gates spring open. I didn't have that luxury now. Jarrah and I would have to find another way in. Staring at the map, things weren't looking good.

That is, until I received Jarrah's text message.

GOOGLE HODDLES TRACK

After a cursory search, I discovered that Hoddles Track was located at the summit of Saddleback Mountain and stretched west before splitting in two directions. The top path would take you up into the escarpment, bordering the Barren Grounds, while the bottom would take you down into Foxground. Looking at the map before me, I realised that the latter portion actually joined onto the Williamses' private road. It was a potential entry point that I doubt many people knew about. I know I certainly hadn't.

It was perfect.

While the track had originally been used in the 1800s to transport produce from the Southern Highlands to Kiama, far better routes were established and the trail fell out of use. Its only purpose now was to pose a challenge to the more 'hard-core' tourists Kiama attracted. Adventure-seekers who turned their noses up at Saddleback's wheelchair-accessible lookouts because they weren't 'challenging' enough.

Apart from historical accounts regarding the trail's founding surveyor, Robert Hoddle, the track was only mentioned on bushwalking websites. Scrolling through the hiking forums, I grimaced. While the top track was undeniably the steeper one, the bottom would still be a long and arduous walk. It wasn't something I was particularly looking forward to.

But, as I clicked through the galleries of images proudly posted by hiking enthusiasts, I noticed something. There were tyre tracks on the ground in each shot. It didn't make any sense. The road simply didn't go up that far. You could drive to the summit of Saddleback, but not any further west. The road formed a loop around the phone towers perched on the mountain's peak, directing you back down the slope.

There was a fence at the western-most point.

No . . . A gate.

A strange sensation tugged at my mind. I got up from my computer, opened my door and walked into the hallway. Thankfully, Michael was long gone. I began rummaging through a chest of drawers in the lounge room. The top two had been officially designated the 'junk' drawers, but the remaining ones looked identical. There was no rhyme nor reason to their contents. Just a mishmash of household detritus, slowly gathering dust.

But then, under a pile of miscellaneous charger cables, I found it: a hulking metal loop filled with keys of all shapes and sizes. Thankfully, the key ring was better organised than the drawers. Each key was positioned next to a small plastic tag in a variety of colours. I flicked through each, squinting at my dad's messy handwriting, but quickly figured out the system.

I focused on the red tags – signifying fire trails – until I found the words I was searching for: 'Hoddles Track'.

CHAPTER 42

'Wait, you mean we can *drive* there?' Jarrah asked.

I'd called him straight after I'd found the keys.

'My dad has spare keys to all the fire trails around here,' I said. 'A lot of them are just old stock routes so I assumed Hoddles would be the same.'

'Isn't the path crazy steep though? How can you get a car up there?'

'The bottom track's better than the top but I assume we're taking my car, right?'

'Depends. What do you drive?'

'An ancient LandCruiser. She's not the prettiest thing, but she makes a fairly decent bush-basher.'

'I mean, anything that allows me to avoid physical activity is A-okay in my book,' he said, laughing. 'I wasn't looking forward to the hike.'

'You know we're not going to be able to drive the whole way, right? Once we get near their place, we'll have to go on foot.'

'Yeah, I figured as much. How are we going to get to the clearing from that angle though?'

'I honestly don't know. I mean –'

'Do you have the aerial shot in front of you?' he asked.

I looked at the map on my computer screen. 'Yeah, why?'

'Look at the back of their house. The rectangular bit at the southernmost point.'

'You mean the pool?' I asked, condescendingly, before remembering that Jarrah had never been there.

'Yeah. Go straight back from there. Look at the rainforest.'

I leaned closer to my laptop and squinted. 'What am I looking at, exactly?'

'Don't you think it looks like a trail?'

I zoomed in. I could kind of see what he meant, but it wasn't super clear.

'I guess,' I said. 'But a trail to where?'

'The clearings, Lo. It seems to go straight to the big one, and then that little one is off to the side.'

'Why would they need a track to the clear–' I cut myself off. I already knew the answer to the question.

The phone's crackling only emphasised our silence. It stretched on, punctuated by static.

'So, what would be the best way to do it, then?' Jarrah asked, seemingly talking through his ideas out loud. 'We enter via Hoddles Track on the eastern side of the property . . .' He paused. 'Then maybe hug the edge of the rainforest perimeter and walk down until we're lined up with the pool and hopefully find the track from there?'

'Mmm,' I murmured. I'd only been half-listening as I scrolled through pictures on the hiking forums. The rainforest was truly breathtaking. And yet, now knowing Lily's claims, utterly terrifying.

'Lo?' Jarrah asked.

'*Fuuuck.*' I groaned.

'What?'

I was looking at a photo posted by a disgruntled bushwalker. It was of a heavy-duty electric fence with a sign hanging on it. It read:

PRIVATE PROPERTY
TRESPASSERS WILL BE SHOT
SURVIVORS WILL BE SHOT AGAIN

I scrolled through the comments.

'Avoid the southern track like the plague. It's private property, and the owner's a bloody nutjob. There're ways to get over the electric fence, but it's not worth it. You don't want to come face-to-face with that prick and his gun.'

'Marlowe, what?' Jarrah snapped.

I didn't want him to chicken out. So, I lied. 'Nothing – sorry – my dad just sent me an annoying text.'

'Oh.'

I had no idea whether he believed me or not.

'Well, do you think that sounds like the best way?' he asked.

I thought over what he'd said. It seemed logical. 'Yeah, sure.'

'So, we're really doing it?'

I stared at the sign on my computer screen. 'Yeah.' I sighed. 'We're really doing it.'

'All righty then.'

There wasn't a hint of fear in his voice. I was worried that there should have been.

'If you're driving, I'll catch a train down first thing in the morning, so we can get up there nice and early. You cool to pick me up, Lo?'

'Yeah. But aren't you worried about someone seeing you?'

He went quiet for a second. 'Um, how about I get off early at Dunmore, and you pick me up there? That way we can head straight up Swamp Road and bypass Kiama altogether?'

It wasn't a bad idea. The station was only a ten-minute drive north of Kiama and almost directly across from one of the main access roads to Saddleback. But, most importantly, it would keep Jarrah away from the prying eyes of the town.

'Yeah, that's fine,' I replied. 'Just figure out which train you're coming in on and text what time I need to be there.'

'Sure, I'll let you know later on.'

'All right. I better head off. The final press conference is happening soon.'

'Shit. Already?'

'Yeah, I know.'

'Well, maybe by this time tomorrow there'll be more to report.'

My eyes flicked back to the computer screen.

SURVIVORS WILL BE SHOT AGAIN

'Yeah,' I replied. 'Maybe.'

I considered physically going to the press conference but I didn't think I could stomach it. Some police media advisor from Sydney had apparently had the tone-deaf idea to conduct it at the showground's stables. Something about the flowers on the stalls 'popping' against the baby-blue colouring of the police uniforms. All I could think was how the colour of Lily and Steve's blood had 'popped' against the stalls' pale concrete.

The whole thing seemed disrespectful.

I still watched it though, perched on the edge of my lounge. The New South Wales police commissioner had spoken, as had my dad. They'd reiterated that, based on DNA evidence, Steve Masters had been arrested for the murder of Lily Williams. There would be a formal investigation into Steve's injury, but Lily's case wouldn't be able to proceed until he was capable of being tried.

A neurologist from Wollongong Hospital had reminded everyone that Steve was unlikely to ever wake up. When asked whether his parents had been given the option to remove life support, the doctor had said that he couldn't divulge personal information. However, he did state that *if* that recommendation had been provided, it would be a decision the family members would have to live with. At that point, someone off-screen could be heard yelling, 'Kill the bastard'.

Michael had spoken next, playing the role of the grieving father to a T. It was an Oscar-worthy performance, and I felt enraged that, even through the television screen, he was able to invoke a deep feeling of sympathy from me. Sharon had stood by his side, her eyes even more glassy through the camera's lens. She'd said nothing and showed no connection to her husband or his words. No nodding in agreement, no supportive hand on his shoulder as his eyes filled with tears. She'd just stood there, staring into the camera. As if she were pleading at the faceless people sitting at home, trapped behind their television screens.

While everyone else had been quick to stick the knife in Steve and his family, Michael had taken a different approach. He'd condemned the attack on Steve, saying that it wasn't justice for Lily – it wasn't justice at all. At that point, Sharon had turned around and stared at the wall of flowers marking her daughter's place of death. She'd frowned and reached out her hand to tug on a frayed piece of rope attached to the stable's doors. When it wouldn't come loose, she'd abruptly walked out of shot. Michael had continued talking like he hadn't even noticed. But, when the cameras began panning away to follow Sharon as she ambled towards the cliff's edge, he'd hastily retrieved his wife before any further damage could be done.

The press conference had ended not long after that. But not before a final threat, masquerading as a plea, from the town's mayor. Peter said that the town needed a chance to grieve on its own. That the carnies would be moving on the next day, and that the press should too. He'd reminded people that Lily's funeral was only open to members of the town and that outsiders would not be admitted.

'This town has lost one of its own to an outsider,' he'd said. 'We need to be able to close ranks and heal as a community. Please respect this or face the consequences.'

I audibly laughed at the screen. Outsiders were the *least* of this town's problems. And, after tomorrow, everyone would know the truth.

CHAPTER 43

Dan texted me in the evening asking me to pop into the Blue Diamond to pick up the heels I'd left in his car. I didn't want to, but when I realised they were the ones I wanted to wear to the funeral, I texted him back.

I'll meet you at your car after work.
Not in the mood to see Owen TBH.

My dad was actually home that night so, as I headed out the door just before ten, I had to tell him where I was going. He was lying on the lounge reading a dog-eared paperback, a Raymond Chandler novel. In the background, the television blared poorly produced local commercials.

'Just popping down to the harbour for a sec,' I said. 'Have to get the heels I'm wearing to the funeral off Dan.'

'I didn't realise you two were the same shoe size.'

I realised he wasn't joking. 'No, they're my shoes,' I replied exasperatedly. 'I'm getting them back from him.'

'What did he need them for?'

'What?'

'Why'd he borrow your shoes?'

'He didn't! I left them in his bloody car.'

'Oh.'

My dad thought Dan was gay. Lots of people in the town did. Sometimes I felt like it was the only reason he was comfortable with us being so close. But it also often manifested in weirdly passive-aggressive bouts of homophobia, such as assuming Dan was a cross-dresser.

'You might have to get new ones,' he replied matter-of-factly. 'They're probably all stretched out now. Bet he couldn't resist trying them on.'

'Bye, Dad,' I said, turning my back to him and heading towards the front door.

'Wait, Lo.'

'What?' I sighed, turning back around.

'Did you speak to Michael?'

My dad had a nasty habit of asking questions that he already knew the answers to.

'Yep, sure did.'

'And?'

'And what?'

'Well . . .' He paused. 'Are you gonna, y'know, get fixed?'

'*Fixed*?'

'You know what I mean, Marlowe,' he said, far too aggressively. He often lashed out when he knew he was the one in the wrong.

'Have I really been screaming in my sleep?' I asked.

He nodded. 'It's real bad, Lo. Like how you were when your mum died.'

'What?' I asked, shocked.

He stared at me for a long time. 'You don't remember, do you?'

I shook my head. I truly didn't.

'You had nightmares – about the accident.'

My eyebrows furrowed.

'You'd scream your mother's name all night long.'

I had no recollection of what he was talking about.

He sighed. 'Michael fixed you then – he can fix you now, too.'

My mouth gaped. I tried to think back to the psychiatrist I'd been forced to see when my mother died. It hadn't been Michael. Had it?

I attempted to picture the person's face but drew a blank. But their voice. There was something about it. Something familiar.

'I've gotta go,' I said. I could feel tears forming in my eyes.

'Lo . . .' my dad began.

But I was already gone.

CHAPTER 44

Dan was sitting on the bonnet of his car, looking out over the harbour. It was still hot that night. No storm had come to cool everything off. A faint sea mist hung in the air. There was no wind, and the atmosphere felt oppressive.

As I approached his car, Dan picked up my heels and began to clap the soles together. He mimicked horses hoofbeats, speeding up the closer I got. I smiled.

'You're a fucking idiot,' I said, snatching them from him when I was within reach.

'And yet we're still friends. Who's the *real* idiot?'

I shook my head but smiled.

'How you holding up?' he asked.

'I'm getting pretty fuckin' sick of that question. I can tell you that.'

He held up his hands and mimed zipping his lips.

'A peace offering,' he said, opening up his backpack and revealing a small bag of pot and a couple of freshly rolled joints.

I went to reach in, but he snatched the backpack away. He looked at the hotel over his shoulder, before turning back to me and raising his eyebrows.

'How about a change of scenery?'

He slid off the bonnet and walked onto the harbour's flats, slinging the backpack over his shoulder. He beckoned me towards him. I followed, and he kept walking until he was standing on the footpath in front of Black Beach. When I caught up to him, he jumped onto the black sand below. The crushed basalt made a satisfying crunch as he landed.

Black Beach was an afterthought for the town. A tiny, uninviting shoreline on the harbour that could barely qualify as a beach. The jagged rock shelf below the waves made it an impractical choice for swimmers and surfers, and the rough, gravel-like sand was unpleasant to sunbathe on. Besides, with Kiama's numerous white sand beaches, there was always a better choice close by.

I always liked Black Beach though. It was yet another by-product of when Saddleback was a volcano and a reminder of the town's pre-historic origins. The fact that it was located directly across the road from the police station and cottage further fuelled my fascination. As a kid, I would spend hours sifting through the sand for treasure – namely, ocean-polished pieces of glass which I obsessively collected.

I sat down next to Dan, feeling my weight sink into the dark sand. I put my heels down next to me and dug my hands into the cool basalt shards; wiggling my fingertips deeper and deeper. Dan lit the joint and took a short drag before handing it to me. I pulled out my right hand – it was covered in tiny black specks that shone in the moonlight.

'So,' Dan began as I inhaled deeply, 'you wanna tell me what happened at the showground after I left?'

I held the smoke in my lungs, thinking about Steve's unconscious body slumped in front of Nathan. I finally exhaled – a long, slow sigh.

'Not really,' I answered, passing the joint back to him.

'Well, will you at least tell me what happened between you and Owen?'

I paused for a second – recalling the time under the grandstand – but quickly recovered.

'I don't know what you heard, man, but . . .' I shrugged.

Dan passed me the joint again. I noticed that he hadn't smoked it.

'Owen offered me fifty bucks to send that text message to you. Said he needed to see you again and asked me to lure you in. It was shady as fuck.'

'Nice to know the price you put on our friendship,' I spat, dragging on the joint once more.

'I didn't take his money. The second you replied saying you didn't want to see him I knew something was up.'

'*Wow*, how noble of you.'

'It's why we're here and not on my bonnet. I don't trust the bastard, Lo.'

Somewhere behind us, the basalt crunched.

'That's probably for the best,' a low voice growled.

Owen's presence startled me so much that I dropped the joint. By the time I retrieved it from the sand, it was coated in tiny black grains. I tried brushing them off but it was futile. I grabbed my shoe and snuffed out the end with my sole, before burying it in the sand.

While all that was happening, Dan had sprung to his feet. 'What the fuck are you doing here?' he asked Owen.

'I told you. I need to see Marlowe.'

'Yeah, well, she doesn't want to see *you*.'

'I think she can speak for herself, don't you?'

A memory blossomed in my mind. '*She* is the cat's mother,' I recited, before descending into a fit of giggles. I had no idea why I found the sentence so hilarious, nor where I'd heard it before.

'Seriously, mate,' Dan threatened in a surprisingly low voice. 'Fuck off.'

'Marlowe,' Owen exasperatedly droned. 'Can you please call your attack dog off?'

I was still staring out over the harbour. In the distance, a series of warning lights flashed on a rocky outcrop – the harbour's helipad. I thought of the look of pain branded on Steve Masters' face as he lay crumpled in front of the stables. I felt light-headed.

'Listen, pretty boy,' Dan said. 'You're a long way from home. So why don't you go back to your hotel room, pack your suitcase and get ready to check out with the rest of the vultures first thing tomorrow morning?'

I heard a single step crunch behind me as Owen moved towards Dan. 'I'm not going anywhere. Not now, and not tomorrow. I have a personal invitation from the Williams family to attend their daughter's funeral.'

Of course he does, I thought.

'And you really think calling me "pretty boy" is an insult? I think that says a lot more about you than it does me, *mate*.'

'The fuck's that supposed to mean?' There was an unsettling edge to Dan's voice.

'Let's just say this town talks. And tongues are certainly wagging when you're involved, aren't they?'

Another crunch as Dan edged closer.

'You got the balls to say what you actually mean, prick?'

'What's to say?' Owen asked. 'Personally, I find the whole country closet-case thing *so* passé. It's 2008, man. No one cares if you're gay.'

Even with my back turned, I knew the punch was coming long before it landed.

Owen was not a fighter. He'd never had to be one – certainly not like Dan had. He physically crumpled beneath Dan's fist, his knees buckling as he landed on the beach with a crunch. He let out a pained mewl so shrill it was pathetic. I felt an urge to kick him while he was down. Payback.

I slowly got to my feet and turned around. Owen was still kneeling on the sand; his hands pressed over the left side of his face. Dan had immediately backed off, genuinely shocked and disgusted by how quickly Owen had dropped. He looked at me, his hand still clenched in a fist, and sheepishly mouthed a single word: 'Sorry.'

I rolled my eyes and kneeled down in front of Owen.

'Let me see,' I said, reaching up to pull his hands away from his face. He physically recoiled under my touch, batting my hand away like a feral cat.

'Don't *fucking* touch her,' Dan shouted, and I watched with disgust as Owen flinched at the sound.

'Shut the fuck up, Daniel,' I spat. I reached into my pocket, pulled out my house keys and held them out to him. 'There are mixed veggies in the freezer. Get a bag and a tea towel to wrap them in, then come back.'

'I'm not leaving you with him.'

'Yeah, I think I'll take my chances with the guy who didn't just king-hit a bloke, okay?'

In the moonlight, I could see there was a hint of a smile on Dan's lips. He was clearly proud of himself.

'If you want to keep this bullshit bravado act up, at least do something useful and get the veggies.' I threw the keys at Dan, and he caught them. He slung his backpack over his shoulder.

'Are you sure you're okay with him?' he asked.

'Yes! Now, fuck off.'

Dan took one final look at Owen's cowering form, rolled his eyes and began jogging towards the cottage.

'Wait,' I shouted, picking up my heels. 'Take these, too.'

He spun back around, begrudgingly snatched the shoes from me and headed back off.

'My dad's home,' I called out to him. 'Don't bloody tell him what happened.'

He ignored me, but I knew he was likely to heed my advice.

'Now,' I said, turning my attention back to Owen. 'How you holding up, slugger?'

'He's a fucking psychopath!'

'Yeah.' I sighed. 'This town breeds 'em. Now, let me see how bad it is.'

'It's really bad,' he whimpered.

'I'll be the judge of that. C'mon, Owen, take your hands away. I need to see.'

He slowly removed his trembling hands.

My eyes widened at the sight.

CHAPTER 45

From all the fuss, I'd expected blood and broken bones. A crushed eye-socket, haemorrhaging nostrils and maybe even a cauliflower ear. Instead, there was some minor swelling and the beginnings of what was sure to be a pretty decent shiner.

Dan had obviously held back.

'Oh my god,' I said, raising my hand to my mouth.

'What?' Owen panicked.

'You're fucking hideous. He's ruined you.'

I saw realisation slowly dawn on Owen's face and began laughing. He raised his fingers to his eye and lightly dabbed at his skin before examining his fingertips. He'd clearly expected to see blood. A hint of embarrassment flushed over his cheeks.

'How many fingers am I holding up?' I asked, flipping him the bird.

'Just one,' he replied, giving me the finger back.

'Do you think you're concussed?'

He shook his head, wincing as he did.

'Name, location and current prime minister, please?'

He looked up at me and sighed. 'Owen Archer, literal hell and Kevin Rudd.'

'Yeah, you're *way* too sassy to have a concussion. I don't think we'll be needing an ambulance, do you?'

'It still bloody hurts,' he huffed, though there was a hint of shame in his voice.

'I'm happy to call a doctor if you want to get it checked out but I'm pretty sure they'll just say to ice it.'

I wasn't actually happy to call a doctor. I wasn't happy to call anyone. I didn't want people asking questions about Dan's involvement or encouraging Owen to report the assault. I needed to downplay things and using Owen's embarrassment against him seemed like a solid plan.

'Seriously,' I continued, 'it's really not that bad. I'm sure it hurts like hell, and you'll have a pretty nasty bruise for a few days, but it'll heal up fairly quickly as long as you get the ice on it nice and quick.'

'Yeah,' he said, gently prodding at the swelling with his fingertips. 'I guess you're right.'

We sat in silence for a while as he continued to absentmindedly touch his eye. I couldn't tell what he was thinking, but, as the minutes stretched on, I became worried that he was reconsidering his need for medical intervention. Behind us, the harbour's waves gently lapped at the blackened shoreline.

'I know this is the last thing you want to hear,' I began, 'but you're pretty lucky he went so easy on you. I've seen him do far more damage than that.'

He raised a bemused eyebrow then immediately regretted it. 'Is this the moment where you tell me what a pussy I am?'

I was shocked that he had managed to see straight through me but I was able to recover.

'God, no! I know how fragile a man's sense of masculinity can be. And – unlike *some* – I'm not stupid enough to question it.'

That gleaming smile was back. 'I clearly hit a nerve though. Didn't I?'

I gently reached out for Owen's jaw and tilted his slowly bruising eye towards me. 'Yeah, and Dan clearly hit more than that on you.'

He locked eyes with me, and I realised how close our faces were. I watched as his pupils darted down. His lips parted as he stared at mine. That longing, which I found so repulsive, was back.

I traced my fingertips up his face and could sense his breathing becoming shallow. I could feel his bone-structure underneath his taut flesh – those high cheekbones that formed the scaffolding for his good looks. There was a sense of architecture to his face. I could acknowledge the beauty of it, but nothing more.

He leaned closer to me, and the shifting of the sand beneath us sounded like rain. Strangely, I didn't feel that horrible sensation on my fingertips. Maybe because I was the one touching him. I was the one in control.

He tilted his head.

Opened his mouth.

And yelped, as I prodded the delicate flesh under his injured eye.

'What the fuck, Marlowe?' he spat, lurching backwards.

'I was trying to feel if the socket was still intact. I thought maybe that's why it hurt so much, but it feels fine.'

'To you, maybe!' he snapped, dabbing at his watering eyes.

'Sorry.' I shrugged.

He went to open his mouth but was interrupted by the sound of something substantial hitting the sand next to him. We both jumped a mile.

'Fore!' Dan shouted, up on the footpath.

I reached out and picked up the cold package, concerned that it had burst on the sharp sand. Thankfully, it was still intact.

I passed it to Owen, who held it against his eye before immediately hissing in pain.

'Fuck, it's cold!'

'That's kinda the point,' I said, smiling sympathetically.

'It's got bloody sand all over it, too!'

I sighed and pulled off my flanno, taking the package from Owen and wrapping the shirt around it. I passed it back to Owen and tugged awkwardly at my singlet. My arms and chest felt exposed.

'Thanks.'

'I always thought you must feel safe living at the cottage,' Dan called out as he jumped down onto the beach. 'I mean, it's next to the police station, and you have your own personal inspector guarding you.' He walked closer to us and I could see that he was sucking on a blue Zooper Dooper that he'd clearly stolen out of my freezer. 'But considering I just walked through your unlocked front door, raided your freezer and walked back out while your dad snored on your couch, it's a bit of a worry.'

'Did you at least bring enough for the class?' I asked, pointing at the ice-block.

'Nope, fuck y'all. This is *my* reward.'

'Your reward for what?' I snapped. 'Assaulting someone? You're lucky he's not fucking pressing charges, Daniel!'

'I didn't rule that out,' Owen said, peering out from behind the bag of vegetables. 'I only refused the ambulance. After all, there's a police station right across the street.'

I'd expected him to flash that smug smile, but he didn't. It seemed it wasn't a joke. I nervously looked at Dan.

'You said it yourself, Marlowe,' Owen began. 'He assaulted me. I have every right to report it.'

'But you won't, right?'

'I don't know, I guess that's up to you.'

There was something in his voice that put me on edge.

'What do you mean?'

'Well, I mean, your friend was certainly willing to do a lot to protect you. I guess I'm just curious what you'd be prepared to do to protect him?'

It felt like something was slithering underneath my skin. Something that would never go away, no matter how hard I scrubbed. My eyes darted between Owen and Dan. I didn't want to be there. I wanted to sink into the sand. To go back to when Saddleback was still a volcano.

To be alone.

Anywhere but with Owen.

CHAPTER 46

'You *fucking* creep,' Dan seethed at Owen.

'Marlowe,' Owen began, his smile saccharine, 'why don't you send your mongrel away, so we can talk?'

'I'm not going anywhere!' Dan spat.

I looked at Owen. He was staring at me with that nauseating smile. I could feel my heart pounding against my chest. I wanted to leave – both of them – to get up, walk away and not turn back. But Jarrah's story was too fresh in my mind, and I knew I could stop it this time.

'He doesn't have to go far, just out of earshot,' Owen continued. He turned around and surveyed the foreshore. 'There,' he said, pointing at the swing set past the footpath. 'Is that somewhere everyone feels comfortable with?'

I looked at Dan, and he shook his head.

'Go, Dan,' I said, trying to sound calmer than I felt. 'It's fine.'

'No!'

'Then how 'bout we all head over to the police station?' Owen asked. 'Though, it'd be a shame to have to wake up your father, right, Lo?'

'Dan. Go. *Now.*'

He started to open his mouth.

'Do it!'

He finally turned on his heels and slowly walked up the beach towards the playground.

'Good boy,' Owen said, his smile transformed into a cruel smirk.

I watched Dan's fist clench into a tight ball, but he didn't turn back around. For a split second, I wanted him to. The sounds of the sand crunching beneath his feet grew fainter with each step.

Owen carefully peeled my flannelette shirt off the frozen veggies and handed it back to me. It was already wet, and yet I still slipped it over my arms. Anything to put a barrier between my bare skin and his. He removed the tea towel and pressed the bag of vegetables directly against his eye. Streams of condensation dripped down his forearm. The bag had already begun defrosting in the warm night air.

He turned to face Dan and, when he saw him slump down onto the swing's seat, he gave a condescending wave before spinning back to me.

His entire demeanour had changed.

'Listen to me, Marlowe,' he said, his voice unsettlingly cool. 'You have to accept –'

'I'm not accepting anything. Not until I know exactly what it is you want.'

His eyebrows buckled and he winced in response. 'What?' he asked, seemingly puzzled.

'Cut the shit, Owen. What's it going to take for you not to report Dan?'

He burst into laughter, and I felt an overwhelming urge to claw at his swollen eye.

'Fuck, Lo,' he said, still chuckling. 'You know I don't give two shits about your mate, right? I was just trying to get him to piss off so we could talk.'

I stared at him. 'You're not going to report him?'

'Nah. You said it yourself, I was asking for it.'

'I didn't actually say that.'

'It was *heavily* implied.'

I looked over at Dan. Owen followed my gaze.

'The bloke needs serious help though. Anger management treatment at the very least.'

'You have no idea what it's like growing up here. It's fit in or fuck off. And if you can't . . .' I trailed off, thinking about Jarrah.

'So,' Owen broached. 'I take it you still want to get out of here?'

'More than anything.'

He removed the bag from his eye and gently dabbed the excess moisture away with his sleeve. The bruising had taken hold – a deep purple hue that only served to highlight the arresting colour of his eyes. His expression had grown serious once more.

'Then accept what Michael said, Lo, and drop all this Lily stuff. If you agree that you're unwell, he'll give you everything you want – far more than you'd ever get by selling her story. He got her the cadetship; he can get you one too. You'll finally be able to escape from here.'

Owen's words hit me like a strike to the head. I felt dizzy – like the whole world was spinning – but I was somehow able to get to my feet.

He knew.

Owen knew.

But had he known the whole time?

'Marlowe?' Owen asked, springing to his feet. 'What are you doing?'

I ignored him and began walking towards Dan.

'Marlowe, stop,' Owen said, stepping in front of me. 'We need to talk about this.'

'I just want to go home, please.'

'Lo, listen to me,' he said, placing both hands on my arms, effectively holding me in place. 'I'm trying to help you. You need to forget about the marks, forget about the journals, and do what he says. Please, you have to trust me.'

'I can't trust anyone.'

'Yes, you can. He'll take care of you. He'll give you everything you want. You just need to let all this go. It will all make sense, I promise.'

'Let me go, Owen. I need to go.'

He stared into my eyes pleadingly but finally relaxed his grip. I pushed past him and headed back towards the police station. I didn't turn back.

'What happened?' Dan asked as I stepped onto the pavement. He looked over my shoulder down onto the beach. It seemed like Owen hadn't followed me.

'Nothing. I just want to go home. Give me my keys.'

'Jesus, Lo. Tell me.'

I brushed past him and continued walking. He ran to my side.

'What the fuck did you agree to?' he asked, panic-stricken.

'Nothing,' I replied, honestly. 'He was just trying to scare you. He had no intention of reporting you.'

'Then why are you acting so fucking weird?'

'I'm not,' I replied, but immediately recognised how robotic it sounded. 'I'm just tired. I want to go home. Please give me my keys.'

He passed them to me but looked me up and down suspiciously. 'You're really freakin' me out, Lo.'

'I'm fine. Seriously, go home. And *don't* start shit with Owen on the way. He was willing to let it slide once, but I don't think it'll be a repeat offer.'

'I don't think that'll be a problem. He's already fucked off back to the hotel.'

I turned around to make sure he wasn't lying. To my surprise, there was no sign of Owen.

'Good,' I said, pausing at the bottom of the steps up to the main road. 'Now seriously, piss off.'

I began climbing the stairs and Dan sighed below. 'One of these days you're going to tell me what the fuck has been going on, Lo.'

I ignored him and darted across the street.

I walked up the steps to the cottage's verandah and opened the front door. Dan hadn't bothered to lock it. My dad was still fast asleep on the lounge, the television blaring in the background.

I turned off the television, but my dad didn't stir. I walked to my bedroom, peeled off my soggy flanno and flopped down onto my bed. I stared at my heels, which Dan had carefully placed on my bedroom dresser. I felt sticky from the sand and sea salt but was too exhausted to shower. I just wanted to sleep.

After all, in spite of Owen and Michael's threats, Jarrah and I still had an early morning the next day.

Nothing was going to stop me from exploring that rainforest.

CHAPTER 47

'You look like a fucking Irwin!' Jarrah said as he climbed into the Land-Cruiser at Dunmore Station the next morning.

I looked down at the khaki-hued hiking ensemble I'd chosen, and realised it was an embarrassingly apt statement.

'At least I don't look like a futuristic, Bowie-arse star child. What the fuck are *you* wearing?'

Jarrah was dressed in head-to-toe black save for an oil-slick sun visor that hung low over his eyes, and a matching pair of iridescent Doc Martens. His pants were skin-tight – shiny and ruched – and his long-sleeved top was made out of some strange fabric that mimicked the look of chain mail.

'Doc Martens, Sass and Bide, Alexander Wang and some obscure little shop in Tokyo that I can't remember the name of,' he said, pointing at each item.

'What part of "hiking appropriate" didn't you get?'

He looked at me, puzzled. 'But I followed your directions perfectly. Long pants, long sleeves, boots and a hat.'

'*Hiking* boots! And an *actual* hat that covers your bloody head!'

'Same diff.' He shrugged.

When he pulled on his seatbelt, I realised that his top was completely sheer with tiny holes in the fabric exposing his flesh.

'You're gonna get burnt to buggery in that,' I said, tugging at his sleeve.

'Not everyone has pasty skin like you, darling.'

He smiled sweetly. I rolled my eyes and couldn't help but laugh.

'You really have no idea what it's like up there, do you?' I asked, suddenly serious.

'I dunno. Like *FernGully*, right? Just with more child murder?'

I didn't laugh, and the weight of his words hung in the air. I turned the key in the ignition and pulled away from the station. In the distance, the escarpment loomed. I could feel a sense of regret creeping in but tried to ignore it.

We turned off the highway onto Swamp Road. It was a twisting goat track of a path that sliced through pastoral farmland and eventually led to the tiny town of Jamberoo. We'd turn off before then though, and slowly climb Saddleback's northern face. The mountain would gradually rise before us – the flat fields slowly transforming into dense and hilly rainforest.

'What is it you think we'll find up there?' I asked Jarrah after the silence had become unbearable.

He turned towards me, but I kept my eyes on the winding road.

'Proof.'

'But what?'

'I dunno. It's just this gut feeling that I have. After everything that's happened the past few days – framing the carny, silencing him, getting away with murder – I just feel like they're untouchable.'

'Then why the hell are we even bothering?'

'No,' he said. In my peripheral vision, I could see that he was shaking his head. 'That's not what I mean. I feel like if they *are* as untouchable as they seem, then maybe they get complacent about stuff – especially up there. I mean, there's no one around for miles. It's private property. No one's going to accidentally stumble onto those clearings.'

'I guess . . .'

Even I was shocked by how unconvinced I sounded.

'Like,' he continued, 'I don't think we're gonna suddenly stumble upon some mass grave of their victims or anything. I don't think anyone could be that complacent. But, based on what Lily told me and what was in the journals, I just feel like there'd have to be some sort of evidence of what goes on during those rituals.'

'Even all these months later?'

He nodded. 'There's tradition and meaning behind why they conduct the rituals – a sense of mythology to their beliefs, no matter how crazy: the "Song of Solomon", the volcano, the symbols. It's almost like a religion. The area is clearly significant to them in some way. Maybe there's stuff there year round? Stuff that marks what the area is used for?'

'Like what though?'

'Jesus, Marlowe,' he snapped. 'I don't fucking know. It's why we're bloody going – to see what's there!'

I thought of telling him about the post on the forum – about the electric fence, threatening signs and stories of the 'psychopathic owner with the gun' – but decided against it. He'd find out the first two once we reached the border of the property. I just had to hope that he wouldn't come face-to-face with the third.

'I'm sorry,' I replied, turning towards him. 'It's just – this whole thing, it's –'

'Utterly terrifying?'

Before I had a chance to reply, I slammed my foot on the brakes.

'For fuck's sake!' Jarrah spat, as I instinctively put my arm across his chest to stop him from propelling forward.

I hadn't been able to see what was ahead as we'd rounded the blind corner. Fortunately, we hadn't been travelling fast. Still, it caught us both by surprise.

The farmer in the middle of the road stared angrily at us, and I felt like it was warranted. After all, I'd seen the signs – the big yellow ones with pictures of cows – and still hadn't slowed down. I held my hand up in an apologetic wave, and he shook his head and muttered something before turning back to the cattle slowly meandering across the road.

'Ugh,' Jarrah groaned, looking at the snaking trail of cows in the field beside us. 'We're gonna be here all bloody day!'

'You were the one who said we should go this way,' I pointed out as I turned the engine off.

'Can we at least leave the friggin' air on?'

'You can wind your window down if you want. But it's gonna reek of cow shit.'

'Ugh,' he repeated. 'I hate this fucking hellhole *so* much.'

'Spare a thought for the suckers who are still stuck here. We can't all be modern-art wunderkinds.'

'Don't give me that shit – I paid my dues. I did the whole couch-surfing thing. Hell, I sucked dick for free accommodation.'

I visibly grimaced, and he laughed.

'Okay, maybe the accommodation was an added bonus, but the sentiment is there. You've gotta do what you gotta do. If you truly wanted out of this place, you'd have done it by now.'

'Fuck *you*,' I intoned, crossing my arms against my chest.

'*Speaking* of sucking dick. You still BFFs with that cutie? What's-his-name . . . uh, I wanna say, Dan?'

'Yep.'

A cow had stopped in the middle of the road and was staring right at me. Without warning, it lifted up its tail and took an almighty dump on the bitumen. The farmer was unbothered, lazily swatting flies around his head.

'He single?'

'I think so.'

'He come out yet?'

I turned to face Jarrah. 'Dan's not gay.'

He burst into laughter, and I felt frustrated on Dan's behalf.

'Seriously, he's not.'

He continued laughing. 'How the hell does his supposed best friend not know he's gay?'

'Because he's not.'

'Oh, okay,' Jarrah said, nodding overdramatically before miming zipping his lips. 'I getcha.'

I was getting sick of the rigmarole. 'He's not, Jarrah. Seriously.'

'Sure,' Jarrah continued, still nodding campily. 'Yeah, I'm sure that time we fucked back in the day was just a *big*, totally straight accident, right?'

I blinked in disbelief.

CHAPTER 48

'Wait,' Jarrah said, his eyes scanning my face as his brows furrowed in confusion. 'Shit, you genuinely didn't know?'

I shook my head.

'How could you not know?' Jarrah asked, bewildered. 'You're his best friend!'

The temperature in the car was slowly rising. Even with the windows closed the smell of manure lingered in the air. I wiped the sweat from the top of my lip and leaned my head against the window. Jarrah stared at me expectantly.

'He tells people he's straight,' I said, staring out at the cows. 'Everyone in town thinks he's gay, but he says he's not.'

Jarrah continued staring at me, seemingly puzzled.

'I dunno,' I said, lifting my head up and slowly shaking it. 'I guess I thought I was doing the right thing by being the only person who actually took him at his word.'

There was more to it than that, of course. Dan's so-called 'red flags' had made me feel better about myself growing up. While the rest of the town whispered about his lack of interest in girls, I'd assumed he was like me. Not straight, not gay – just *nothing*.

The fact that he was practically the only guy my age who hadn't ever tried to crack on to me had been the cherry on top of our friendship. I felt safe and comfortable around him. But, beyond that, being friends with him changed the way I thought about myself. I wasn't alone in my detachment. There was someone else in that tiny hole of a town who was just like me. Or so I had thought.

'I don't get it,' Jarrah said, shaking his head. 'He's a grown-arse adult now, why doesn't he just come out?'

'You've gotta be fucking kidding me, right?'

'What do you mean?'

'Think about it, Jarrah. Who the fuck would ever come out in this town after what happened to you?'

He didn't answer me, but I could tell my words had shaken him. There was something distant in his eyes, something closed-off. We both sat silently, staring at the cows as they moved like lemmings across the road. Their pace was glacial.

'This is getting fucking ridiculous!' Jarrah snapped. He pointed at the farmer, whose back was still turned to the LandCruiser. 'He can make them go faster than that, he's just being a prick and punishing us for driving too fast.'

'How exactly do you expect him to make the cows go faster?'

'I don't know. A whip? A cattle prod?'

I rolled my eyes again and yawned. How was I still so sleepy?

'I know what'll move 'em,' Jarrah said, propelling his hand towards the horn.

Thankfully, I was able to grab his fingers before he made contact.

'Don't even think about it,' I said, squeezing his hand harder than I should have. 'You'll spook them. And then they'll stop producing milk, and the farmer will put a bloody bullet between their eyes.'

'I don't give a flyin' fuck about Daisy,' he said, reaching towards the horn once more.

I bent his fingers back. 'I will break your fucking fingers if you try again.'

He snatched his hand back. 'Jesus Christ, Marlowe. It was a bloody joke!'

I raised my eyes back to the road and noticed that the farmer was staring at me. There was something about the look in his eyes that felt disconcerting. I wondered if he was a relative of the Williams family, and whether his name had been on Lily's list.

Did he know who I was?

Did he know what we were about to do?

A feeling of dread wrenched at my body and then the farmer broke into a twisted smile.

He knew. And soon they would all know, too. I was sure of it.

The last of the cows slowly trundled across the road, and we were finally able to continue our journey. When we passed the farmer, climbing back into his ute, he looked at me with that same manic smile and wiggled his fingertips in an odd sort of wave. There was a sense of finality to it that put me on edge. Though, much to my frustration, Jarrah hadn't seemed to notice.

After a few minutes of silence, he turned the radio on – without asking – and spent the remainder of the trip flipping through stations while bemoaning the quality of the local content. It was mainly vapid breakfast shows where the shrieky hosts shouted over each other, and local bogans called in to win movie tickets to the latest Hollywood drivel. The only music came in the form of jingles for used car dealerships and hardware stores. It was an aural nightmare.

There was fog on the mountain and the higher we drove, the more we encountered. I eased the LandCruiser into the white pockets slowly and was thankful that they were always short-lived. My dad had insisted on me learning to drive in all weather conditions and on all types of terrain, so I was quite used to navigating in poor visibility. Jarrah, on the other hand, seemed utterly bewildered by his surroundings and would mumble under his breath every time the car was engulfed.

'Fuck this spooky *Silent Hill* shit,' he muttered to himself, wrapping his arms around his body.

I chuckled. 'Pyramid Heads are the least of our concern,' I said, my eyes still firmly trained on the road. It was meant to be reassuring but, the second the words left my lips, I realised it wasn't.

'What the fuck are we supposed to do if we can't see our bloody hands in front of our faces?' he asked.

My eyes quickly jumped to the clock on the dash and then back to the road. 'It's still early. Worse comes to worst we'll just have to sit tight and wait until the sun burns the fog off.'

He shook his head and tried to change the radio station once more. The breakfast show hosts were being drowned in static the higher we climbed, and he flipped through as if the brash sounds of their conversations brought him some form of comfort. In contrast, I welcomed the serenity of the white noise.

CHAPTER 49

Even through the smattering of fog, I could tell that Saddleback's car park was deserted. There was likely no one around for miles. Still, we took a cautious loop around the phone towers at the top to make sure there was no one lurking in the mist.

'Is that it?' Jarrah asked, pointing through the fog towards the western gate.

'Yeah. Let's just pray the lock's the same or we're in for a bugger of a walk.'

I drove past and Jarrah looked at me, perplexed.

'Uh, Lo? Where we going?'

'I'll drop you off at the car park. You can keep a lookout while I try to get the gate open. Let me know if you see anyone, okay? We can't risk a ranger or someone else seeing what we're up to.'

'And how exactly am I supposed to let you know?'

'There's this great new device called a mobile phone. I really think they're gonna take off.'

'Fat lot of good a mobile is when there's no reception, eh?'

'We're *literally* next to the phone towers!'

'Don't take my word for it.' He shrugged, before passing me my phone from the tray in the dash.

I slowed the LandCruiser to a stop and peered at the screen. Sure enough, I had no bars.

'That doesn't even make sense!'

'This thing got a CB radio or something?' Jarrah asked, squinting at the dials on the LandCruiser's dashboard.

'Jesus Christ, I'm not *that* bloody country!'

'So that means . . .' Jarrah trailed off.

'We have no way of contacting anyone while we're up here. Fuck.'

Jarrah leaned his head against the headrest and let out a long sigh.

'Having second thoughts?' I asked. I sure as hell was.

'The fog – now this. It's less than optimal, to say the least.'

'Yeah.'

He ran his hand over his shaved head before turning to me. 'Why don't we at least try the key? Then decide from there?'

'So, what? If it doesn't work, it's a sign?'

'Yeah. Something like that. These things do tend to come in threes.'

I reversed the car back up to the gate, pointed the LandCruiser's nose towards the opening and turned the engine off. The fog moved quickly up there on the peak. One second you'd be shrouded; the next it was gone.

'Here,' Jarrah said. As if sensing my reluctance, he held his hand out. 'Gimme the key. I'll try the gate.'

'Thanks,' I replied, before digging it out of my pocket and passing it to him.

He took a deep breath and opened the door, before stepping down onto the ground and slamming it shut. Even in the short time the door was open, I could tell how cool it was outside. The air that entered the car smelled fresh and wet and seemed to slide down my throat like a menthol cough drop. I wound my window down. Somewhere in the fog, a lone bird called – a peculiar creaking noise that sounded like someone winding a spring.

My eyes flicked back to Jarrah. He walked in front of the Land-Cruiser and completely disappeared from sight. It was like he had been engulfed by a cloud.

A single thought entered my mind: *Drive off without him.*

I felt my fingers tense against the car keys, still in the ignition, as Jarrah reappeared and kneeled down in front of the gate. Before I knew it, the gate was swinging open and a wide and inviting path seemed to part the fog.

There was a strange feeling somewhere in my chest. It took me a while to recognise it as disappointment. I'd been secretly hoping the key wouldn't work.

Jarrah stood up and gave an animated shrug as if to say, 'So much for that excuse'. He began walking back towards the car, and I tried to think of a way to convince him to leave. Another pocket of fog engulfed him. It was as if he'd been wiped off the face of the earth.

When he finally reappeared, it was like I was looking at an entirely different person.

Jarrah stood frozen in the centre of the road, his face mask-like. He was staring off into the distance, somewhere behind the LandCruiser. I watched as he slowly raised the palm of his hand – signalling me to stay put – before lifting his index finger to his lips.

Just as a look of concern washed over his face, the LandCruiser was engulfed in fog. I couldn't see anything but whiteness outside the windows. The only sound I could hear was my pulse in my ears. When the fog finally cleared, Jarrah was gone.

'Go, now,' a voice hissed beside my window, causing me to clasp my hands over my mouth.

'Get out of sight,' Jarrah continued. 'I'll catch up.'

Before I'd had a chance to even process what he'd said, he'd run off into the fog, back towards the car park. I turned the engine on, grimacing at the sound, and looked at the open gate before me. The only way forward was through the gate and into the rainforest.

As if sensing my hesitation, the fog cleared in front of me, revealing the path. And yet, all I could see in the rearview mirror was white. Jarrah was nowhere in sight. I eased the LandCruiser up onto the fire trail and drove through the gate.

The fire trail was muddier than I'd expected, and I began to worry about getting bogged. I'd driven on similar terrain in the past, but only ever with my dad and the assurance that he could help push it out if needed. No offence to Jarrah, but I doubted I could say the same for him.

Even if that were an exaggeration on my father's part, at least with him I knew that a four-wheel drive full of cops could be radioed in and be there within minutes. Not only did Jarrah and I have no way of contacting anyone, but we also couldn't risk doing it in the first place. It was essential no one knew what we were doing up there.

I carefully drove over the muddy tracks and pulled the Land-Cruiser to the side when the path curved. I turned around to ensure it was protected by the tree line, though I don't know why I bothered. It certainly wasn't like anyone there would have been able to see me through the fog anyway.

I turned the engine off, but almost immediately regretted it. I didn't want the sound to draw attention, but I also wanted to be able to get out of there as quickly as possible if I needed to. Behind me, the fog still swirled.

How long would I have to wait for Jarrah?

What if he never came back?

I tried to push the thoughts out of my mind, feeling my chest tighten with anxiety. What had he heard out there? A car? A person?

I decided to roll my window down to see if I could hear anything. That icy mountain air caressed my face and goosebumps crept down my spine. I could hear the rainforest – bird calls, rustling leaves, the wind – but nothing else.

Then there was a loud scraping sound somewhere behind the LandCruiser.

The gate.

Someone was closing the gate.

And I no longer had the key.

CHAPTER 50

I was trapped. Panic gripped my body as my mind struggled to think of a solution. Should I reverse back up there? Shout out that someone was still on the trail and needed to be able to get back out? Or drive – drive as fast as I could away from the person who was trying to trap me?

What if it was the farmer? Had he followed us up there in his ute, obscured by the fog? Or had he called someone from Lily's list? Michael, Mark, my dad?

I could run. Away from the LandCruiser and into the rainforest. I had supplies. I could hide or even loop back around to one of the lookouts. But I might get lost or trip and break my leg in the fog. No, it was best to stay with the car. At least Jarrah could find me then.

I cursed myself for not bringing a weapon and quickly scanned the LandCruiser's interior for something. There was nothing except Jarrah's visor and my backpack full of useless non-lethal objects.

I wondered if Jarrah's bag had something before realising that it was gone. But why would he have taken it with him if he was only opening the gate? I felt my stomach drop and choked back a gasp from my quivering lips.

It was him. He hadn't heard anything. He'd just wanted to lock me in. To trap me here.

But why? Why would he do that?

And then, it hit me. My initial instinct had been correct. The first anonymous message about the journals *had* been a trap. Just one with a slightly slower payoff. He'd built up my trust. Spun his lies. And lured me to that fucking rainforest.

For them. He was one of them.

It all made sense. Why he'd come back after all these years. Why he had Lily's journals. Why he'd been so insistent that we go into the rainforest. And his success – the profiles in the papers and photos in the social pages – the involvement of Owen's editor was proof the cult had ties to the media.

So *that's* what it took to escape this town – you had to sell your soul.

I felt like I was going to vomit. My hands were shaking, and tears were streaming down my cheeks. I was on the brink of hyperventilating. How could I have been so blind?

I fought to get my breathing under control and the LandCruiser was once again swallowed by the fog. And then, I heard them – footsteps approaching the car. I turned to face the passenger door and lunged towards the lock.

But it was too late. Someone was already opening the door.

I immediately unclipped my seatbelt and scrambled out the driver-side door as the fog cleared around me.

'What the hell are you doing?' Jarrah asked, peering around the front of the car. He was looking at me like I was crazy.

'I know you locked the gate.'

'Uh, yeah? I didn't want anyone to see it was unlocked and then come up here and find the car while we were out searching.'

'Then why'd you take your bag with you?' I hissed, fighting back tears.

'What? My bag's behind my seat. I haven't touched it since I put it there at the station.'

I peered through the window to where he was pointing. Sure enough, his satchel was wedged underneath the back of his seat. I had no idea how I'd missed it.

'Are you okay, Lo?' He was talking to me like I was a wild animal he was trying not to spook. I was getting sick of people treating me like that.

'Why'd you tell me to drive up here, then?'

'Because I heard something?' It was as if he was unsure why he was answering the question. 'Seriously, Lo, what the fuck is going on? You're acting super sketchy.'

'*I'm* acting sketchy?'

'Uh, yes! *Super* sketchy!'

'What did you hear?' I snapped.

His face contorted in confusion once more. 'A car, and then a dog barking. Did you seriously not hear it?'

The hunting hounds, my mind whispered, and I fought back the urge to vomit.

'Are you crying?' Jarrah asked, walking around the front of the car to get closer to me.

'Stay back!' I barked, and he stopped dead in his tracks.

'Lo . . .'

'What kind of dogs?' I shouted.

'Dog – singular. And I dunno the breed. Little yappy thing, ankle-biter, y'know?' He bent down and hovered his hand a short distance from the ground.

The air was too thin. Too cold. I couldn't get enough of it into my lungs. I felt like I was going to pass out.

'It was there with its owners – an elderly couple,' Jarrah continued. 'They parked in the car park and then walked it up to the northern lookout. When I saw them go down the path, I ran back to lock the gate before anyone saw it open.'

I stared at Jarrah's face. I believed he was telling the truth. He was too confused. Too scared. And everything he said was entirely logical.

I rested my head on the LandCruiser's door. I'd been using it as a type of shield, as well as a way to prop myself up. My legs felt like jelly.

I didn't have the strength to pull myself back into the car so I slumped to the ground.

Jarrah ran towards me. The grass felt damp against my pants, but I didn't care. I tried to suck that crisp mountain air into my hyperventilating lungs while Michael's words echoed in my mind: *The night terrors are just the start of it. There's also the lethargy, the anxiety attacks, the paranoia and the fits of aggression.*

Was he right? Was all of this just the symptoms of PTSD?

CHAPTER 51

'Are you sure you still want to do this?' Jarrah asked. 'Why don't you stay in the car and I'll take your camera into the ritual area and take pictures of what I find there?'

We were both sitting in the LandCruiser in a small clearing just before the fork in Hoddles Track. It was the point of no return where we'd have to ditch the car and take the lower path down onto the Williamses' property by foot. In the rainforest, somewhere below us, the electric fence and warning signs loomed.

'I said I'm *fine*. We're doing this. Both of us.'

After my legs had buckled, Jarrah had rushed around the front of the LandCruiser. He'd grabbed my backpack from the car and fished out my canteen. He'd then gingerly held the bottle up to my lips and I'd snatched it away. I was furious that he had seen me like that. So weak. So vulnerable.

In the end though, my rage and embarrassment were a help more than a hindrance. It was the only thing that got my breathing back under control and provided me with the strength to get back into the driver's seat. I pretended like nothing had happened and, for the most part, Jarrah did too.

But there was something about the way he looked at me that infuriated me. Like I was broken. Like he was questioning my capabilities, or worse, my sanity. He had lost faith after seeing me like that, and I tried to fight back the thought that maybe it was justified.

Had *I* lost faith in myself? The thought terrified me.

We'd driven along the fire trail almost in silence, and watched as the fog grew sparser and sparser the further we drove. It could have been chalked up to the passage of time, and the warming of the sun, but it was just as likely due to our gradual descent down the western face of the mountain. Either way, it felt like a sign – no excuses now.

'Well, as long as you're sure,' Jarrah said, shrugging.

But I wasn't sure. I wasn't sure at all.

'See, we're here,' Jarrah said, pointing at a map he'd printed off. 'Hoddles Track splits here, which is just up there.' He pointed at the fork on the map and then gestured through the tree line in front of the LandCruiser.

'And that's where the Williamses' property starts?'

'Nah, a bit further down. Should be a fence around here.' He tapped at the map once more.

I stared at it for a while, trying to get my bearings. 'Coming in from this angle puts us close to the house and its surrounds.'

'Yeah, but it will be much easier to find the track down to the clearings if we can use the house as a guide.'

'Sound travels differently up here. I think it's because of the echo off the plateau, but I can remember being all the way down at the waterhole and hearing Lily's parents talking on the back deck, clear as day.'

'Shit, seriously?' Jarrah asked, his eyes trailing the distance from the house to the waterhole on the map.

'Yeah. We're gonna have to be super quiet. I think we can get away with footsteps and twigs breaking and stuff – just because of how much wildlife is up here – but I don't think we can risk talking at all. At least, not until we get to the clearings. They should be far enough away from the house.'

'Aw, but what about our witty repartee?'

'I'm serious, Jarrah.'

'Ugh. Fiiiiine, I'll shut up, but *you're* the one missing out.'

I ignored him, but a smile tugged at the corners of my lips. It was hard to believe that only moments earlier I'd thought he was trying to kill me.

He still could be, my mind whispered.

I immediately quashed the thought, physically shaking my head as if to dislodge it from my mind. The past few days had taught me what it was like to not be able to trust anyone, but the thought of not being able to trust my own mind was an entirely new concept. Had this been what Lily had felt while the town gaslighted her into submission?

No. I couldn't think like that.

'So, we're good to go?' Jarrah asked. He was once again looking at me like he thought I might be insane.

'Yeah, I . . .' I began. 'No, actually, wait. Can you please pass me the little bottle of salt from the glove box?'

His face contorted in confusion, but he opened the compartment.

'Why do you have salt?' he asked, reaching in and taking out the bottle.

'Because my dad always says the fish and chip shops don't put enough on.'

'And, what exactly does that have to do with us now?'

I grabbed the bottle from his hands, checked that the lid was properly closed and placed it in my backpack. I took a deep breath before staring Jarrah straight in the eye.

'Because,' I began, my voice tinged with embarrassment, 'I'm going to use it to cast a protection spell.'

His eyes widened.

'If I sprinkle it behind us as we walk, and say an incantation, then no one who means us harm will be able to follow us.'

'Really?' he asked breathlessly.

'No, you fucking idiot. It's for the bloody leeches. There's no way they're gonna get through your skin-tight pants, but the little suckers love attaching themselves to my ankles. There's something about my blood that they apparently find irresistible.'

He snorted with laughter. 'See?' he said, pointing back and forth between us. 'How could you *possibly* want to silence this?'

I could think of one reason – Michael's gun.

'Let's go,' I replied, secretly wishing that protection spells were real.

CHAPTER 52

We broke the tree line and went down Hoddle's bottom track, where we were almost immediately engulfed by the rainforest. Its canopy was so dense that you couldn't see the sky, and yet the sun still managed to filter through the leaves in discordant patches. The spattering of pale light cast eerie shadows on the leaf litter covering the ground. The soundscape was mesmerising – like the backing track of a meditation tape – and I was lulled by it.

I didn't have much faith that Jarrah would be able to keep quiet for long, which was why I was so surprised when we finally stumbled upon the border of the Williamses' property. The clearly marked electric fence appeared exactly how it had in the photo on the hiking forum, but there was a new addition to the sign threatening trespassers – a well-placed bullet hole.

It was impossible to hide my shock.

In contrast, Jarrah casually strode over to the sign and stuck his pinkie finger through the hole before turning to face me and raising his eyebrows. I pointed at the small yellow sign warning of the electrical current, and he nodded before lifting his index finger – seemingly signalling me to wait. It was at that moment that I realised I had no idea how we could navigate the fence. The hiker on the forum had said that there were ways around it but had never actually elaborated.

I gritted my teeth, furious that even with all my planning I hadn't considered that we'd need a solution to getting over the fence. How could

I have been so stupid? Or did it just prove that, deep down, I never actually thought I'd be standing there?

While I was busy berating myself, Jarrah had kneeled down in a plant thicket that resembled a cross between palm fronds and tall grass. He plucked one of the long green tendrils and walked back towards the fence, before squatting in front of it. Before I had a chance to protest, he carefully looped the greenery around the fence's wire and gently held each end in his fingertips.

I walked towards him as he delicately pulled the loop so that the plant came into contact with the wire. I held my breath, but he remained completely still. After a few seconds, he turned to face me and smiled.

'What the fuck?' I mouthed, crouching down beside him.

'It's not on,' he mouthed back.

I stared at the fence then turned back to face him. 'Are you sure?'

He nodded and gestured for me to touch the plant. I shook my head, and he shrugged before dropping it onto the ground.

'Watch this,' he whispered, and I stared in horror as he gently placed the back of his hand on the wire.

It was too late to stop him – his entire body had already gone rigid.

I clasped my hands to my mouth, trying to stifle the gasp that had escaped my lungs. Jarrah's eyes had rolled into the back of his head, and his entire body was shuddering. I went to touch him but immediately stopped myself. I stared helplessly at his twitching face as his mouth contorted into . . .

A smile?

He winked at me, that shit-eating grin spreading further over his face, and I slapped the back of his head – hard.

'You fucking prick,' I hissed, my heart still pounding.

He raised his index finger to his lips while trying to stifle his own laughter. I punched him firmly on his arm, and he fell into the fence.

There was nothing funny about his actions. What if I'd screamed? The entire mountainside would have heard me.

Part of me wished we would come face-to-face with Michael and his gun – just so I could take it off him and put a bullet between Jarrah's eyes. What was all of this to him? Fun? A fucking adventure? How could he claim to care about Lily, and bringing her killer to justice, while pulling stunts like that?

I left him on the ground, still trying to control his laughter, and carefully climbed over the fence. Tears were beginning to pool in my eyes, and I felt my breath growing ragged. I was on the brink of another anxiety attack – I could feel it – but one that was also fuelled by rage. I was genuinely scared of what I was capable of.

When we reached the perimeter of the homestead's cleared land, I was surprised that Jarrah didn't even pause to look at the property. Instead, he turned ninety degrees and began heading south, just inside the tree line. I suppose there was no need for nostalgia if you'd never been there before.

In contrast, I noted that if we continued along the track, we'd eventually end up on the Williamses' driveway. Right outside their front door – like we were just popping in for tea. As I scanned the familiar landscape, I felt an overwhelming urge to do exactly that.

Let's go and see Lily, my brain seemed to think. *Just like old times.*

It felt like a cruel trick, and I tried to push the thought away, but it all came flooding back. Lily and I had been so close as kids. I'd spent so many hours on this property. When did that stop? Why did it stop? When did she go from being my best friend in the world to being someone I deigned to tolerate?

I'd loved it here. I'd loved her family and I'd loved her.

What the hell had happened?

We continued down the edge of the rainforest in silence, while Jarrah munched on a muesli bar. We were hidden by the tree line but always kept the homestead in sight. Jarrah marched on, never pausing or slowing his speed. I assumed that he could hear my footsteps because he never turned around to check if I were still there. Maybe he didn't care.

When he finished his muesli bar, he dropped the wrapper on the ground. I picked it up and shoved it into my pocket. It wasn't just litter – it was evidence, and I found myself once again growing frustrated by Jarrah's flippancy. This wasn't real to him – not like it was real to me – it was just random scribblings and doodles in a diary. He hadn't had to come face-to-face with the perpetrators. He hadn't feared for his life.

He was a tourist here. Like all the others who descended on the town for brief holidays before returning to their normal lives. At the end of the day, he would get on that train, go back to Sydney, and everything would go back to normal. He didn't have to live with a person whose name was on that list. Or come home and find a gaggle of them gathered in his lounge room. And he certainly hadn't had to find her body – to see what they had done to her – those angry marks carved into that flawless flesh.

He didn't have to lie to them. He didn't have to be threatened by them. He didn't have to wonder if he was next.

What a luxury that must be.

As the forest began to curve, the waterhole and the back of the house came into view. There didn't appear to be anyone in the pool or on the back deck, but there was no telling if Michael or Sharon were behind those sprawling windows. I'd brought a small pair of binoculars but there was no point in looking. After all, the tinted glaze kept both the sun *and* prying eyes at bay.

Once again, Jarrah barely glanced at the house. Instead, he kept his eyes trained in front of him as he navigated the uneven terrain. His gait and pace were still languid – like he had all the time in the world. His head never turned when a branch snapped somewhere in the distance, or a bird let out a particularly piercing cry. He seemed utterly at home in that rainforest. I tried not to think of the implications.

But, as I watched the back of the pool slowly align with our position, he finally reduced his pace. He turned to face me.

'Told you,' he smugly mouthed, before pointing at the thin, snaking path to our right.

We followed it for a short while, but neither of us could have anticipated what we'd find at the end.

'Fuck,' Jarrah mumbled.

He had entered the ritual area first. There wasn't enough room on the makeshift path for us to stand side by side, so I had to crane my neck to see what he'd spotted. I hadn't noticed that he'd stopped dead, so I walked straight into his back. It pushed him further into the clearing. He stepped out of my way, and I could finally see what he meant.

'No . . .' I said. My voice sounded small and brittle.

'Fuck,' he repeated – louder this time.

We should have been well out of earshot of anyone on the Williamses' homestead but I still winced at the sound.

'What did you even think would be here?' I asked, staring at the clearing.

It was precisely that, nothing more than an empty void in the rainforest. There was absolutely nothing of note or significance. The area seemed entirely untouched by human hands.

'*Fuck!*' Jarrah shouted, running his hands over his head.

There was a log, not far from where we were standing – an old tree that had fallen at some point in the past. I walked over to it and sat down. I removed my canteen from my backpack and took a long drink. Jarrah remained frozen in place, his eyes frantically scanning the clearing as if some nefarious clue would present itself.

'But why would there be a path from the house to here?' he asked.

'I dunno, man.' I unbuttoned my shirt, frowning at the sweat-soaked singlet underneath.

He walked over to me and dropped his satchel onto the ground but didn't sit down. He kept scanning the clearing, growing more frustrated by the second.

'I really thought . . .'

'What?' I snapped. 'That there was going to be some satanic temple here? Goat heads impaled on spears? A bloody portal to hell in an old volcanic vent?'

'This doesn't mean that nothing happened here, Lo!'

'But it might as fucking well have. We needed this, Jarrah – *she* needed this. Without corroborating evidence, this is her word against theirs. The journals mean nothing if there isn't anything to back them up.'

'You can't really believe that, can you? For fuck's sake, Marlowe, you had memories of what was done here!'

'Well, I hope you weren't hanging on me being your star witness. Because the only thing I had memories of was a picture she entered in the show. It was just another bloody drawing like the ones in the journals. It's not *proof*, Jarrah.'

He opened his mouth to say something, but I continued.

'Look, I'm not saying I don't believe her – I do, wholeheartedly. But you have no idea what we're up against. This goes far beyond the names on that list. These people have friends in very high places. We only have one chance at this. And they'll tear us to shreds if we go in half-cocked.'

'How do you know all this?'

'I just do,' I replied. I didn't want to explain about Owen's editor – not yet, anyway. 'Okay?'

He stared at me in disbelief but eventually nodded.

'Fuck,' he sighed once again. 'I really thought there'd be something here.'

'I know. I did too.'

We sat in the clearing together for some time, sipping on our water bottles and nibbling on the food we'd brought in complete silence. Neither one of us seemed game enough to ask when we'd be returning to the LandCruiser. It would be admitting defeat, and we were both too stubborn to do that.

'I've gotta take a leak,' Jarrah announced, climbing to his feet.

'You're more game than I thought. I'd rather my bladder burst than risk pissing out here.'

'Why?'

I outstretched my right leg and pulled the bottom of my pants up to my shins. I tugged my socks down and examined my ankle. Jarrah looked at me like I was losing my mind, but I held up my index finger and repeated the process on my left leg. Sure enough, a leech was attached to the side of my ankle – already engorged on my blood.

Jarrah groaned, genuinely disgusted. 'How the hell did you not feel that?'

'They're like little ninjas,' I said, staring at the black blob. 'You don't feel a thing.'

A look of realisation washed over Jarrah's face. Immediately, he yanked his pants up. Fortunately, his ankles were bare, and he breathed a sigh of relief.

'I think it's almost full,' I said, gently prodding the creature attached to me. 'It'll fall off once it's finished.'

'No, you weirdo! Use the bloody salt and get it off you.'

'But he's my friend.' I pouted. 'I'm going to keep him as a pet.'

He rolled his eyes, but I could see that he was fighting back a smile.

'In all seriousness,' I began, 'removing them while they're still sucking can make them regurgitate everything back into your bloodstream, and you can get an infection. I might as well just let him finish.'

'All right. But he'll need a name if he's part of the team.'

I stared down at the slimy parasitic creature so desperately clinging to my flesh.

'Owen.'

'All right, Owen,' he said, addressing the bloodsucker. 'You take care of Lo while I take a piss. And tell your friends to stay away from *my* big leech.'

'Ugh, seriously?'

He laughed before heading towards the tree line.

I stared at the writhing leech's ever-increasing mass. I knew that, in the grand scheme of things, it was only taking a tiny amount of my blood, but there was still something predatory about it. A part of me was being harvested and would remain in that rainforest long after I'd left.

A blood sacrifice.

Lily was terrified of leeches.

The thought had popped into my mind out of nowhere. There was a memory attached to it – Lily's feet covered in the slithering inkblots as her cries and screams echoed through the rainforest. My feet had been covered with them too, but I'd been fascinated. I'd clasped my hand over Lily's mouth worried that she was scaring them. We were young – very young – but the memory felt fresh.

I recalled that, when we had returned to the Williamses' home, my dad had immediately busted out the salt. But Michael had insisted on us waiting them out. Lily had cried the entire time, but I had squealed with delight as they expanded before my eyes. I could remember Michael looking at me with those all-seeing eyes, a hint of something like pride lurking somewhere behind them. It horrified me to realise that I wanted him to look at me like that again.

As if appalled by the thoughts floating through my mind, the leech detached itself from my flesh and fell to the ground. A Y-shaped puncture wound was all that was left. I squinted at the bite mark, but looked up when I heard footsteps. Jarrah was sprinting towards me.

'There's something you need to see,' he breathlessly announced.

'What is it?'

'It's proof, Lo. It's the proof we need.'

CHAPTER 53

'You did this,' I said, staring in shock at the tree Jarrah had guided me towards.

'With what, exactly? My fucking dick? My bag was with you the whole time.'

I ran my fingers over the carvings in the tree – seven layered circles forming a flower-like pattern, encased in a larger circle. The same symbol that Lily had drawn in her journal – over and over again – and the same symbol that she had shown the crystal store owner. What had the woman said? That the symbol in the photo had looked like it was carved into wood?

Had this been what Lily had photographed?

'You really think *I* did this?' Jarrah hissed in my ear, making me jump. 'Look around.'

My eyes scanned the trees around me, and my heart began to race. Every single trunk bore the same symbol, eight perfect circles expertly arranged and carved deep into the bark.

We were surrounded. Each circle was like a piercing eye watching our every move. I could feel my breath getting caught in my throat.

'That's not all,' Jarrah said, gently pulling me through the trees.

Normally, I would have fought back, but I was so shocked by the prevalence of those symbols that I allowed myself to be led by him. Not that it mattered much. We certainly didn't have far to travel.

When we entered the second clearing, my mouth gaped. In my

earlier shock and disappointment, I'd completely forgotten it had existed. I imagined it from the only angle I'd ever seen it from, above – the view from Google Maps. It was much smaller, attached to the side of the main clearing like a misshapen tumour, and broken up by a cluster of dense trees that mimicked the rest of the rainforest. If you didn't know what you were looking for, you'd never find it.

It was utterly perfect.

'Look,' Jarrah said, pointing to the ground at the centre of the clearing.

I raised my hand to my mouth. Though whether it was out of shock or simply a precaution against the feeling of nausea churning my stomach remained to be seen. It wasn't a satanic temple, it wasn't a bunch of goat heads on spears, and it certainly wasn't a portal to hell. But it was proof – tangible proof of Lily's claims.

Jarrah was right – they *had* been complacent. And, as I stared at the eight giant circles worn deep into the ritual ground, I finally felt a sense of power surge through my body. This was it. This was exactly what we needed.

'And there,' Jarrah said, interrupting my thoughts and pointing to the southern end of the clearing.

I looked at the cluster of large stones and immediately recognised them from the doodles in Lily's journal. She had expertly recreated the peculiar natural formation that served as the ritual altar, and I pictured the tools she had drawn lying on top of the flattened stone. A chalice, a crescent-shaped boline knife and the circular branding iron used to inflict the eighth and final mark.

'Jesus,' I muttered as Jarrah pulled me towards the centre of the clearing.

It was difficult to tell from the ground, but the large circles formed the same flower-shaped pattern as all the other symbols. However, the imprints in the ground seemed to be the catalyst for those marks – what all the other instances were signifying. After all, in the centre lay the remnants of a large fire pit. Knowing what it was used for made my stomach churn.

'Fuck,' I said, choking back bile. 'That's where they . . .'

I couldn't finish my sentence and felt my body involuntarily double over as I began to dry heave. I wanted to vomit, but nothing would come out. Tears stung the corners of my eyes, and I spat onto the ground.

I'd always believed Lily's claims but, up until that point, that's all they'd ever been. They were stories. Horrifying stories, but stories nonetheless. It was like history books retelling holocausts, survivors of freak natural disasters talking about the aftermath, or the disembodied conversations between victims and emergency service dispatchers during terrorist attacks. They had undeniably happened, but it never quite seemed real to those who hadn't experienced it firsthand.

The gravity of what had happened in that clearing hit me and I crumpled to the ground. It felt like every ounce of my energy had been sapped from my body. I just wanted the earth to open up and swallow me whole – to obliterate everything I was and would ever be. I needed it to be over. I couldn't go on. Not when I knew what had happened here.

But then, I saw it – a glint of green shimmering in the sun's light. It looked like some kind of crystal, but I couldn't be sure. It was sitting at the edge of the fire pit and something about it called to me. 'This is important,' it seemed to say. I unsteadily climbed to my feet, but I could feel my energy returning. I had remembered why I was there. Not just for Lily, but for all the little boys and girls in those fox masks – the ones who had been hunted in that rainforest for decades.

They would be my strength. I would do this for them.

I walked over to the fire pit – trying to purge my mind of what was contained within the ashes – and bent down towards the illuminated green crystal. But it wasn't a crystal. It was glass. The broken shard of a wine bottle, not unlike the ones I had helped Michael clean up at the show ball.

'What is it?' Jarrah asked. I gasped before spinning around to face him. In my anguish, I'd completely forgotten that I wasn't alone. I was glad that wasn't the case.

'More proof,' I said, turning the shard over and laying it on the palm of my hand. 'Proof of what they do here.'

Jarrah walked over to examine it. Part of the wine bottle's label was still intact on the shard, and it bore an unsettling logo. The words 'The Foxes' could be seen underneath a familiar-looking crest. In the centre, there was an illustration of a person in fox-hunting attire, similar to the ones Lily had drawn, but not in her style. The top of the person's head had been broken off but, if I were to hazard a guess, I'd say that they had been drawn wearing a black fox mask.

'What the fuck?' Jarrah said, leaning in close and squinting at the shard.

'You know Lily's mum is a winemaker, right?'

'Yeah.'

I pointed at the crest. 'Rose Valley Wines – her winery – uses this crest on all their bottles.'

He nodded.

'But I've never seen this particular design before,' I continued. 'And I know their vintages pretty well. I think it might be the family's private label.'

'The ceremonial wine Lily spoke about in her journals? The one imbued with . . . ?'

'Exactly.'

'Fuck,' Jarrah said, physically recoiling from the shard in my hand. He stared down at the fire pit, as if only just registering its significance. 'Wait, Lo. Look.'

He kneeled down and pointed at the ash.

'What?' I asked.

He leaned his face towards the ash and gently blew.

'What the *fuck*,' I snapped, jumping away from the sooty plume.

'Look!' he repeated.

As the cloud of ash subsided, I finally saw what he was talking about. 'Fuck,' I gasped. 'Are they –'

'Bone shards,' Jarrah replied, confirming my fears. 'We've gotta get back to the car and call the cops. This is all evidence.'

I stared down at the white pieces, my pulse rattling in my head. 'But it'll go through my dad. As soon as he hears the location, he'll know. He'll cover it up – just like he covered up Lily's markings.'

'Then what, Lo? We can't just leave this here. You said we needed corroborating evidence – well, here it is!'

I could feel my chest growing tight and helplessly ran my fingers through my hair. My eyes darted from the fire pit to Jarrah's fraught face. He was right – this was everything we needed. But what good was that when my dad could make it all go away?

'Photos,' I announced. 'We photograph everything, and then we get out of here before anyone sees us. If we can't trust the cops, we've gotta go over their heads. We'll leak everything to the press – Lily's journals, the pictures of the marks on her back, and the pictures from here.'

Jarrah's face buckled. He seemed unsure of the plan.

To be completely honest, I was too. I didn't know how far the cult's reach truly was. Sure, they had connections to Owen's paper, but that didn't necessarily mean the entire Australian media was in their pocket. Surely if we were able to get the evidence to a broad range of national newsrooms, then someone would bite. And once they did, the police would have to act. It would make them accountable.

It wasn't a perfect plan, but it was the best one I had.

'I'll do it tonight,' I continued. 'The journals are still under my mattress, but I can photocopy the pages and compile the photos. Send it all by post so they can't trace it. Stick it all in the parcel boxes overnight so no one sees my face. Though, it's not like they won't know who sent it. I'm the only person who could have taken the photos of the marks on her back.'

'Then don't include them. Seriously, Lo. The pictures we take here and copies of the journals will be more than enough. No one knows we saw her journals, and no one will know we were here – you don't need to implicate yourself.'

I didn't have the heart to tell him that I already had – that Owen had likely already told them everything.

'No,' I replied. 'People need to see the marks – they need to see that my dad covered them up. It proves that the cops are involved in all this. They tie everything together.'

'I dunno, Lo . . .'

'Look, it's not going to come back on you, okay? It's my decision and I'll face the repercussions.'

'That's not what I –'

'I don't care,' I barked. 'Now, let's get these photos so we can get the fuck out of here before someone finds us.'

He opened his mouth to say something but seemed to think better of it.

I was glad he did.

CHAPTER 54

We spent the rest of our time in the clearing and its surrounds, painstakingly photographing everything we could. I used my camera, while Jarrah used his phone. We both carefully scrutinised the altar stones, but there was nothing that suggested anything untoward. It had been months since the last ritual and – even if it *had* fallen on a cult member's eighth hunt and featured an actual sacrifice – the blood would have long been washed away in the summer storms.

Speaking of storms, while we were hard at work, the sky turned from a pristine blue to a murky grey. It made things appear all the more ominous. The air felt charged. I just wanted to get out of there.

'What about the bone shards?' Jarrah asked.

'What about them?'

'What if they get rid of them before anyone has a chance to investigate?'

'I mean, the fact that they haven't done it before now shows that they probably won't. And tomorrow's the funeral. They're going to be distracted by that.'

'Maybe we should still take some? Just in case?'

I stared at the bone shards in the ash. The last thing in the world I wanted to do was touch them, but he was right.

'Have you got anything to put them in?' I asked.

He kneeled on the ground and began digging through his bag. I did the same.

'Nothing.' He sighed.

My hand brushed against the salt container, and I pulled it out. 'This might work.'

He stared grimly at me before nodding towards the pit. Apparently, I was the one who would have to do the deed. My stomach lurched.

I unscrewed the lid and poured the salt onto the ground, before grabbing a pinch and throwing it over my left shoulder. Jarrah seemed bemused.

'Hey, I'm doing everything I can. I can't risk any more bad luck at the moment.'

He nodded understandingly, and I kneeled in front of the fire pit before carefully scooping a small pile of ash into the bottle. Parts of it stuck to my fingers, and I once again fought back the urge to dry retch. I gently shook the bottle, making sure I'd caught a few pieces of bone – they looked even more horrifying close-up. I screwed the lid back on and noticed that my hands were shaking. I slapped them against my pants, trying to get rid of the excess ash.

'You should probably take a photo of the bottle next to the pit,' Jarrah said. 'Just so you can prove it came from there.'

It was a good idea, so I did what he said. But just as I pressed my finger down on the shutter, a harrowing scream pierced the rainforest.

It sounded like it had come from a child.

I lowered my camera and saw that Jarrah was staring at me with a horrified expression. I had secretly hoped that the sound had come from deep within my own mind, but that didn't appear to be the case. The echo of the scream still resonated around the clearing, and my pulse whooshed in my head.

'What the fuck was that?' Jarrah whispered.

'I dunno,' I said. But I certainly had a pretty good idea.

'Don't you think it sounded like a kid? Like a kid screaming?'

Before I had a chance to answer another scream rang out – it seemed closer this time – and was undeniably child-like.

Jarrah sprang to his feet, staring in the direction the scream seemed to have come from. I unzipped my bag to put my camera and the salt bottle back in, and Jarrah spun around as if startled by the sound. I held up my hands apologetically.

'Shhh!' he scolded.

I slowly got to my feet and pulled my backpack on, trying not to make a sound. Jarrah's eyes nervously scanned the tree line as he placed his satchel over his shoulder. I could see that his breathing had grown ragged, and I knew what he was about to do.

A third scream rang out.

'Jarrah, wait!'

But it was too late, he was already sprinting towards the tree line.

I followed Jarrah – I had to – but I didn't want to. It seemed like a stupid and dangerous idea. That part of the rainforest was dense and steep, and it would have been easy for us to lose our way. As we sprinted over fallen logs and past towering fig trees, I did my best to remember the transient landmarks. But everything looked the same.

And how did we know we weren't running straight into a trap?

The scream sounded again – as if it were right in front of us – and Jarrah jolted to a stop, slipping on the sodden leaf litter and falling to the ground. I was able to catch up to him and held out my hand. He sheepishly took it, and I pulled him to his feet.

We stood in silence. Waiting and listening. Trying to muffle the sounds of our heaving breaths. We seemed to be heading in the right direction, but I was glad we were taking a moment to get our bearings. I strained to hear something, but the pulsing of my blood sounded like flowing water.

Wait – no – it *was* flowing water.

I pushed past Jarrah and carefully stepped over the hulking buttress roots of a fig tree. The further I walked around the vast trunk, the louder the water sounded. I placed my hand on the cool bark and peered around it.

Behind the fig tree, a middling waterfall flowed down a series of moss-covered boulders before gathering in a pool at the base. It was beautiful, but I couldn't shake the feeling that I'd been there before. It was possible, of course. We were still on the Williamses' property, and the rainforest had been my and Lily's playground all those years before. Still, knowing how close it was to the ritual area made me uneasy.

The scream rang out once again, so close that I felt like it was a direct response to my presence. But, when I looked over to where I thought it had come from, there was simply no one there. It didn't make any sense.

A strange feeling swept over me as my eyes scanned the landscape. There was nobody there – I was sure of it. Then what was making that horrible noise? I tried to tell myself that it was just an echo bouncing off the plateau. That someone – somewhere – was screaming in the rainforest, just not where we thought they were.

It is *an echo*, my mind seemed to answer. *An echo from the past.*

I was hearing the disembodied voice of one of the hunts' victims. A ghostly impression that had been absorbed into the rainforest like the late morning heat. Those children were trapped there, forever – their screams ringing out for all eternity – and we were bearing witness.

I felt someone place their hand on my shoulder and jumped out of my skin.

'Look,' Jarrah said, leaning in close to my ear.

His hand stretched around my body, and my eyes followed to where his finger was pointing.

'No,' I said, shaking my head in disbelief. 'No way.'

CHAPTER 55

'A fucking *bird*?' I whispered, staring at the unassuming brown creature perched on one of the waterfall's boulders.

'Watch its beak,' Jarrah whispered.

Sure enough, at the exact moment another scream rang out, the bird had opened its beak. My eyebrows knitted in confusion as I stared at its fern-like tail feathers which had plumed before me like a peacock's. It seemed unfathomable that a sound like that could be produced by anything other than a human.

'Why the fuck does it sound exactly like a kid screaming?'

Jarrah leaned in close and I fought the urge to distance myself.

'Look at the tail feathers. It's a lyrebird.'

'So?' I snapped before the realisation hit me. 'Oh, fuck.'

The bird sounded exactly like a child screaming because it was mimicking one. That's what lyrebirds do. They copy sounds that they've been exposed to – collecting them like trophies to impress their potential mates – the more aurally distinct or striking, the better. I felt my hackles rise as the realisation dawned.

I truly *was* hearing an echo of the past – a ghostly impression that lived on via the rainforest.

'We should film it,' Jarrah said, before quietly removing his phone from his satchel. 'I'll do it.'

I nodded as Jarrah carefully stepped over the buttress roots, slowly inching closer and closer to the bird. Oddly, it didn't seem to notice his presence and instead stared at the rainforest's canopy as if it could hear something in the trees. The closer Jarrah got to the waterfall, the more slippery the boulders became, and I could tell he was struggling to retain his balance. I wanted to call out to him to avoid the moss but didn't want to startle the bird.

To my surprise, he was able to deftly traverse the area surrounding the pool of water and was in the perfect position to record the haunting scream. But just as he raised his phone in the bird's direction, an ear-splitting boom ricocheted through the air. I watched in horror as Jarrah's feet slipped out from underneath him – his back and head crashing down onto the rocks below.

The lyrebird let out a final piercing scream and leaped into the canopy.

'Are you okay?' I called out to Jarrah. The question echoed around the rainforest, startling me.

'Yeah,' he groaned, still lying on his back. 'Fucking thunder scared the shit out of me though.'

It had scared me too, but only because I'd initially thought it was a gunshot and had been expecting to see Michael emerge from the trees.

'Did you hit your head?'

'Nah. Satchel took the brunt of it.'

Jarrah started to sit up, and I began climbing over the buttress roots to get to him.

'Don't bother, Lo. I'm fine, and I don't want you slipping and breaking your neck.'

I appreciated the sentiment – I was definitely not known for my coordination – and Jarrah was able to carefully get back on his feet. I watched as he uneasily clambered back towards me, wincing every time he appeared to lose his footing. I noticed he was still clutching his phone.

'Amazed that didn't end up in the water or smashed against the rocks,' I said, pointing at it.

'Yeah. Still pissed I didn't manage to hit record though.'

'I'm not trying to make you feel bad,' I began. 'But you know no one's going to believe us about the bird, right?'

His brow furrowed.

'I mean, I saw it firsthand and I barely fucking believe it. I know they're good mimics, but that was – just – I dunno, man. It seemed so real, y'know?'

'It *was* real. That exact scream happened somewhere in this rainforest, at some point in time. The lyrebird essentially took a recording of it.'

He was right, but I knew that I'd never be able to truly capture just how convincing the lyrebird's shriek had been. I opened my mouth to say something, but another huge crack reverberated around us. It was like the sky was being torn in two.

'Fuck,' Jarrah spat. 'I felt like that one rattled my brain.'

'I just hope the rain holds off,' I said, staring up at the canopy.

'Uh, I hate to burst your bubble, but you do realise it's already raining, right?'

For once, I was the one who got to stare at him like he was insane. I held my hand out – unsurprisingly it remained dry. I raised a sarcastic eyebrow at Jarrah.

'Seriously, listen,' he replied.

I rolled my eyes but did what he said. To my surprise, it did sound like it was raining, though I'd just assumed the noise had been coming from the waterfall.

'The canopy's too thick to let it through here. It's probably pissing it down in the clearings.'

'Shit. We've gotta get back to the LandCruiser – *now*. The track was already super muddy. If we get bogged up there, we're screwed.'

'Fuck,' Jarrah replied, his eyes wide. He began scanning the area. 'I think if we head diagonally from here, we'll end up back near the fence where we came in.'

'No way in hell. We can't risk getting lost. We'll head back to the clearings and go back up the path.'

'All right. But it'll take heaps longer.'

'Then you better get your fucking skates on, hadn't you?'

Before Jarrah had a chance to reply, I began bolting back towards the clearing.

CHAPTER 56

We managed to make it back to the LandCruiser unscathed, albeit soaked to the bone. It had been easier than I'd thought to find the clearings again and running along the ritual path quickly put us back behind the Williamses' homestead where we were able to trace the tree line to our starting point. Though, having to climb back over the electric fence while sopping wet had been a worrying prospect. Thankfully, the electricity was still off.

Once we reached the LandCruiser, we were relieved to find that it wasn't bogged and were able to drive back along the fire trail to the gate. The fog had fully cleared by then, and the rain had driven away any tourists, so we were able to get out undetected. We'd left a pretty damning set of tyre tracks, but even if someone saw them I doubted that they'd be given a second thought.

Jarrah and I were surprisingly untalkative as we drove back down Saddleback's peak and headed towards Swamp Road. It was like the second we shut the gate behind us, the gravity of what we'd seen hit us. I was struck by a strange feeling of guilt for having wanted to see the things we saw. Like it made me culpable for what had happened there.

I imagined Jarrah was thinking the exact same thing as he silently stared out the window at the rolling fields of Jamberoo's outskirts. In the paddocks, the cows clustered in the rain. We'd both wanted it to be true. We'd both wanted that proof. Sure, it was to vindicate Lily, but what the fuck did that say about us?

'There's one thing I don't get,' I said, finally breaking the silence.

'Only one?' Jarrah asked, turning to face me.

'Well, the main one, I guess.'

'What?'

'This has been happening for decades, right?'

'Yeah. Lily said that families like the Williamses and the Roses brought the rites over when they migrated here. It's been happening since the town was formed.'

'And she said they sacrifice a child once each cult member has completed eight hunts?'

In my peripheral vision, I could see that Jarrah was nodding.

'So,' I began, 'that's potentially one child murdered for every person on Lily's list. Every single one is of age, they should have received their eighth marking by now.'

'I mean, excluding people like your dad, remember?'

'Yeah.' I nodded. 'But even excluding, say, a third of them – which from what Lily described seems pretty generous – you still have to count all the ones who came before them. Parents and grandparents who have long since passed away, y'know? Former family lines that died out and stuff? That list isn't conclusive.'

'I don't get what you're trying to say.'

'I mean, that's a *lot* of murdered children over the years, but the numbers just don't add up.'

'In what way?'

'When you were in the police station back in the day,' I began, 'in that little waiting room where they keep people?'

'Yeah?'

'Do you remember the missing person posters on the walls?'

'Uh, no. I mean, I was kind of distracted by the systemic forms of oppression being perpetrated against me by an inherently xenophobic police force.'

'Fuck, Jarrah,' I said, looking at him sombrely. 'I think about that day a lot. I should have said something, tried to back you up or –'

'Ugh. Can you please not do this? I should be able to say what I want to say without you making it about yourself.'

I opened my mouth to say something, but he continued.

'Look, the police force is fucked, this town is fucked and your father is fucked – albeit far more than I originally thought. But none of that is your fault, okay? I don't want or need your sympathy, and I shouldn't have to be the one who makes *you* feel better about yourself.'

'I'm really sor–'

'Just drop it, Lo,' he said, shaking his head. 'Anyway, what were you saying? Missing person posters?'

'Yeah,' I said, trying to recollect my thoughts. 'The station's covered in them. Which seems odd, y'know, because Kiama's so tiny? But that's the thing, they're not just for Kiama. And not even just the Illawarra. They're from the *whole* of New South Wales – and even a few from around the country. And, out of all those posters, kids make up the tiniest percentage.'

I could see Jarrah nodding to himself.

'Kids do go missing,' I continued. 'Even local kids. But they're pretty much always found in a couple of days. Alive. They've either run away from home or been taken by a family member during a custody battle. I guess what I'm trying to say is, I just don't understand how *that* many kids could have been taken and killed without anyone noticing.'

'I thought Lily had a pretty good theory about where they sourced the victims, didn't you?'

'What theory?'

'Oh shit, did she not put that in the journals?'

I shook my head. I had no idea what he was talking about.

'You know Lily thought Michael and Sharon weren't her real parents, right?' Jarrah asked.

I wrinkled my brow, still keeping my eyes on the slippery road. 'I know everyone in town thought she was adopted because Sharon couldn't have kids. But I never heard Lily mention it herself.'

'Yeah, well, growing up I don't think she ever believed it – or at least, never said that she did. I think maybe she was suspicious of it to some degree – like a niggling feeling at the back of her mind. But, when she went off the meds, she gained a lot of clarity about stuff. And that ended up being one of the first things that she questioned.'

'I mean, sure, she looks nothing like her parents, but that doesn't mean a whole lot. I sure as hell don't look like anything my dad.' I paused. 'Thank god.'

'Yeah, but do you look like your mum?'

'What? Like a charred corpse?'

'Jesus Christ, Lo. That's fucked up, even for you.'

'So sensitive! She's *my* dead mum, I'm allowed to make corpse jokes – it's literally all I have of her.'

'Well, in that case, I've been meaning to ask you some stuff about her but didn't want to bring it up because I assumed it was a touchy subject. What was her name again?'

'Tabitha.'

'Oh, yeah.' He nodded. 'And she died when you were – what – in infants school?'

'Mmm-hmm. Admittedly, I don't remember a whole heap from around that time though.'

'Do you think it could have had something to do with all this?'

'With what?'

'Y'know . . . *this*. If she was murdered because of her involv–'

'Jesus, are you asking me if my mum was in the cult?'

'I mean, it would explain why you had memories of –'

'Jarrah, I explained that,' I snapped. 'They weren't fucking memories, okay? Lily submitted a drawing of the cult to the show's art competition, and I saw it the day before she died. It was the only reason I knew what you were talking about.'

'Yeah, b–'

'And besides, my mum died in a bloody car accident. There wasn't anything nefarious about it. She was burned alive when she crashed on the Kiama Bends. She wasn't the first, and she wasn't the last.'

'Oh, shit. Yeah, I'd forgotten,' he sheepishly admitted. 'The black spot, right? Heaps of people have died there over the years. You'd think they'd bloody do something about it.'

'I mean, it hasn't formally been deemed a black spot yet,' I corrected. 'Apparently even more people need to be killed there before the council is granted government funding to even try and fix it.'

'Now *that's* fucked up.'

'Yup.'

An awkward silence hung in the air.

'But, um, did you look like her before then?' Jarrah asked. 'Before the accident, I mean?'

'I dunno.' I sighed. 'People who knew her say that I do. But, when I look at photos and stuff, I don't see it. She was, like, *really* beautiful.'

'Oh yeah? No way you look like her, then. Maybe you're adopted too?'

I gave him the finger without taking my eyes off the road. He laughed loudly.

'I mean, I *wish* I'd been adopted,' I admitted. 'Especially after learning all this. Maybe that's why Lily wanted to believe she was adopted too.'

'Nah, she had memories of really suss stuff. She didn't even think she was formally adopted. She thought she was stolen from her birth mother.'

'Like, kidnapped? I've seen photos of us together as babies, so I really don't think that's the case.'

'She thought she was taken from the hospital just after she was born. She said that's how they sourced the children in the hunts.'

'But surely the public would have heard about that, right? Even if the cops were somehow covering it up, how could they shut that many mothers up?'

'Think about it, Lo. There are potential scenarios where a woman wouldn't speak up.'

I still wasn't getting it. 'Like what?'

'Well, for starters, what if the mother was already giving the child away – either by choice or force or coercion? Like, what if she was deemed unfit to keep the child? Maybe by a certain psychiatrist we both know?'

'Shit. Is that what Lily thought was happening?'

'Among other things. Michael is associated with heaps of foster homes and orphanages. Those kids are basically ghosts, Lo. They get shuffled around so often that no one would ever question a sudden absence.'

I felt my stomach churn. 'You know who else has pretty close ties to those places? My dad.'

I'd heard countless stories from my father about having to take children away from their families and put them in places like that. He'd always maintained that they were better off, and I'd heard some sickening stories but did 'better off' mean dead?

'I guessed as much,' Jarrah said, nodding. 'That's why all this stuff needs to get out there. You *have* to do it tonight, Lo. We can't risk leaving it any longer.'

He was right, of course. It had to be tonight. And I'd have to be the one to do it.

CHAPTER 57

We finally turned off Swamp Road and approached Dunmore station. The realisation that Jarrah would be leaving me to do all the dirty work finally hit me. He truly was a tourist here. He would go back home, and no one would ever know of his involvement. He'd be completely safe, and he knew it. It was likely the only reason he came back here in the first place.

'You sure you don't want to come to the funeral?' I asked.

'Fuck, Lo. Don't lay the guilt trip on me. I know for a fact Lily wouldn't give two shits whether or not I was there.'

'I'm not trying to guilt trip you,' I said as I pulled up to the station's drop-off area. 'But did you ever think that I wasn't asking for Lily?'

'Then who the hell are you asking for? She's the only person in that entire shithole of a town I ever gave a fuck about.'

'Me, Jarrah. Did you ever stop to think that maybe *I* need backup, just like you did in that forest? Especially after what I have to do tonight.'

'I don't know what to say, Lo. You know I'm not welcome in town.'

I scoffed to myself, but it was largely to distract from the pain his words had dealt. I was shocked by his lack of support. Jarrah was only the delivery boy, and that job was done. He never had any intention of seeing the rest through. Lily had chosen me to expose the cult, and me alone.

'Look,' he began, staring at the train timetable on his phone. 'This'll make me sound like a prick, but the next train will be here any minute and it's a direct line with limited stops. I'd *really* like to be able to get on it.'

'You do that, then. Run on back to Sydney and forget all of this. Don't worry, I won't mention your name. They won't come after you – so you can continue doing your little art projects. Maybe you can make a piece in my honour when they kill me, huh? Bet it'll fetch a pretty penny at auction one day.'

'Lo . . .'

'Seriously, Jarrah, fuck off.'

'Don't be like this.'

'Like what? Honest? Scared for my life?'

'They're not gonna kill you, Lo.'

'That's pretty fucking easy for you to say, isn't it?'

'No, just – ugh.' He ran his hands over his head like he was the one who was frustrated.

'Maybe you're right,' I said. 'Maybe they'll just put me in a coma like Steve.'

'Stop being so fucking dramatic. They won't touch you, not with your father's protection. That's not a luxury all of us have, Lo.'

'I don't know why I wasted all those years feeling guilty about what happened to you in that station. Turns out you're just as much of a coward as your parents.'

His head snapped towards me. There was genuine rage behind his eyes. For a moment, I thought he was going to punch me. Still, I didn't back down.

'What is it you say in those whiny little interviews that those pretentious arts journalists lap up?' I hissed. 'That the town *made* your parents cowards. Though, not you, of course – you got out early enough, right?'

A frightening grimace was transforming Jarrah's pleasant features from soft to hard. The muscles in his neck were bulging, and his hands were balled into tight fists. I could tell that he was trying to control his breathing.

I went for the jugular. 'What a fucking hypocrite you are. At least you don't have to worry about being adopted though, hey? You're clearly your parents' son – just as piss-weak as they are.'

With a series of swift movements, he unbuckled his seatbelt, threw open the passenger side door, grabbed his satchel and stepped out of the car. I flinched at the flurry of activity, convinced that one of the actions would result in his fist connecting with my face. To my surprise, he didn't lash out and he remained silent the entire time.

He paused as he turned around to shut the LandCruiser's door, considering whether or not he should say something. I was ready for a fight.

'Marlowe?' he quietly said.

'Yeah, what?' I snapped. 'Finally grew some balls, did ya?'

'There's mud all over the bottom of the car. You should go to a car wash or something before you go home. Just so your dad doesn't ask questions.'

Before I had the chance to reply, he slammed the door shut and ran off to catch his train.

When I put my hands back on the steering wheel, they were shaking.

CHAPTER 58

As loath as I was to admit it, when I pulled into the police station's driveway, I was thankful that I had cleaned the car. Michael's four-wheel drive – a sleek black BMW that somehow still looked spotless in the rain – was parked in one of the vacant spots reserved for police cars. I'd hoped that it meant he was in the station, but from the second I entered the cottage I knew that wasn't the case.

Michael and my father were sitting in my lounge room, along with the town's mayor, Peter Walsh, and were having a heated discussion about Lily's funeral. Neither my father nor Peter noticed my presence, but Michael did. A small smile graced his lips as he wiggled his fingertips in the same odd wave as the farmer on Swamp Road.

He knew. He knew exactly where I'd been.

'Where the hell have you been?' my dad snapped, startling Peter. 'And why are you soaking wet, did you jump in the bloody harbour?'

'I was down at the Boneyard,' I lied, talking about the secluded beach. 'The rain came out of nowhere, and I knew that by the time I made it back to the car I'd be drenched, so I just stayed down there hoping it would pass.'

'What the hell were you doing down there? You know there's no reception. I was trying to call you.'

'I –'

'Oh, come on, John,' Michael interrupted. 'Cut her some slack for god's sake.' He turned to face me. 'It's good that you were taking some time for yourself, getting out of the house – clearing your head. Though you never really struck me as a "beachy" type of person.'

I struggled to meet his gaze. I was terrified that he was about to call me out on my lie. That he knew exactly where I'd been and the horrors I'd seen there. Instead, he smiled back at me like a proud parent. It didn't make sense. He genuinely seemed to believe my lie. I turned to face my father, who was still scowling at me.

'Well, can you take care of yourself in places that have bloody phone reception? I was worried, Lo.'

His response surprised me.

'Sorry, Dad. What did you want me for, anyway?'

His eyes flicked to Michael.

'I'm afraid that's my fault,' Michael said. 'I just wanted to ask you something, Marlowe. I was happy to wait, but your father insisted on calling. I didn't mean to cause such a fuss.'

Peter loudly cleared his throat before unsubtly looking at his watch.

'You can ask her when we're done here, Michael,' my dad said. 'She's not going anywhere.'

My father locked eyes with me, and I stubbornly crossed my arms over my chest.

'Can you leave us, Lo,' he said. It was a command rather than a question. 'We have a lot of things to sort out before tomorrow.'

'I need to take a shower anyway.'

I moved away. Michael caught my eye and mouthed 'Sorry'.

As soon as I was out of sight, Peter's voice boomed around the house. 'I don't care where you get the fuckin' money from, John,' I heard him spit. 'I want more cops at that cemetery. You really think the press is gonna play nice? This whole fuckin' thing has been a bloody circus. You know they're going to turn on us, and you need to get control of the situation before they do.'

'Or what, Peter?' my dad's voice snapped.

I paused in the hallway, straining to hear Peter's response, but the only sound came from the thudding of my heart.

I took a long shower, scanned my body for leeches and tried my hardest not to think about what I'd seen in the clearing. And yet, every time I closed my eyes, the fire pit was all I could see. I felt like the ash still clung to my body and wouldn't come off, no matter how hard I scrubbed.

I'd brought a change of clothes with me to the bathroom lest I come face-to-face with Peter or Michael roaming the cottage's halls. It was a good thing I had because, when I walked into my room, I discovered Michael casually perched on the end of my bed. The sheer audacity of his presence infuriated me.

'I'd tell you to make yourself comfortable,' I said, stepping into the room, 'but it looks like you already have.'

'Forgive my intrusion. I had to get away from those two, and there aren't many options in a place this small.'

'What are they arguing about?'

'The funeral. My family has a single plot left in the old portion of Bombo cemetery. It was always supposed to be mine, but . . .'

He paused for a while, absentmindedly running his hand along my bedspread.

'Anyway,' he continued. 'Because it's in the old section, that means that the funeral has to be held at the front, right next to the highway. They're worried about the media and looky-loos lining either side of the road – even rubberneckers driving past and causing accidents. The police can keep people off the cemetery grounds themselves, but everywhere else appears to be fair game. We'll all be completely exposed tomorrow.'

The faintest hint of a smile graced my lips. He had no idea how prescient his statement would prove to be.

'Oh, excuse my manners,' he said, gesturing at the bed before beginning to stand up. 'Do you want to . . . ?'

'No, it's fine.' I walked over to my dresser and gently perched on the edge.

He sank back down on the bed. It groaned under his weight, catching him by surprise. My eyes quickly flicked to my backpack. I'd repositioned myself so I could check on it – my camera was in there, full of the incriminating pictures from the clearing, not to mention the bone shards. Thankfully, it was still sitting slumped by the side of my bed – seemingly untouched. I breathed a short sigh of relief.

'So, what did you need to ask me, Doctor Williams?'

His brow furrowed as if he'd only just remembered that was the purpose of his visit. 'I just wanted to know if you'd like to say something tomorrow, at the funeral?'

'Say something?'

'About Lily. There's absolutely no pressure and, if you're not comfortable, I completely understand. But I just thought that it might be good for you – a way to properly say goodbye.'

'I –'

'It's just,' he interrupted, 'Sharon is in no condition to speak, and the only other people who have agreed are Peter and Mark.'

'The *mayor* is going to say a eulogy for Lily? And her boss? That's it?'

'Your father also offered. If need be. And I'll obviously be saying something, but – as you can no doubt tell – your voice and perspective would be very much welcomed.'

'I just –'

'You don't even need to come up with something yourself if you're not comfortable with that. Perhaps there's something you can read? A passage that you feel is appropriate? Something that you know was significant to Lily?'

'I –'

I had been about to turn him down but, at the last second, something popped into my mind.

'I think I have the perfect thing.'

Michael left shortly after that, joining my father and Peter who continued to argue all the way out the front door. I was glad to hear them go. I needed the house to myself to begin preparing the packages I would have to send that evening. Sure, I'd do the majority of it while my dad was asleep, but I still needed to source the addresses and get everything uploaded so I could print it all off.

And yet, I remained perched on my dresser, unable – or at least unmotivated – to move. My eyes kept being drawn to my movie posters. The ones that had adorned my walls during my formative years and had become so unassuming that I felt like I was looking at them for the first time in my life.

Would that be what Lily's death would become when the truth came out? Just another story, no more real than the latest horror flick? What had Owen said? That Lily wasn't real any more? That she belonged to the masses?

No, she wasn't just a story. She was a catalyst. A harbinger of doom, at least for the cult. She was the beginning of their end.

I'd make sure of it.

I finally mustered the energy to get down from the dresser and closed and locked my door. I grabbed my laptop and backpack and climbed onto my bed. It creaked and groaned – even more than it had with Michael – seemingly protesting my weight.

I'd missed the familiar noise while the journals had been under there, cushioning the blow. There'd been something comforting about –

Wait.

I sprang to my feet, ran around to the edge of my bed and lifted the mattress – right where Michael had been sitting. The pillowcase was there, but it was empty. The journals were gone.

Panic gripped my chest like a vice.

How could he possibly have known they were there? How could he have known what I intended to do with them, that very evening? Had he been there? In the rainforest? Watching? Waiting? Hearing our plans as we stupidly discussed them in the clearing? We thought we'd been out of earshot of the house, but we hadn't considered that someone could have already been out in the rainforest. Or worse, that someone had followed us.

My stops at the train station and then the car wash would have given Michael more than enough time to make it back to the cottage. I could feel my breath growing ragged. But at least I knew one thing I was sure Michael didn't – I'd already scanned every single page of Lily's journals and saved multiple backups. If this was his attempt to silence me, it would only make me louder.

CHAPTER 59

It was done. I'd compiled and posted the packages under the cover of darkness. Once again sneaking out of my house while my father slept, blissfully unaware. It was fortunate that the post office next door had two full-size mailboxes, and I'd filled them both to the brim. I'd been able to easily go back and forth between the cottage and the post office, carefully depositing the parcels in small batches. The packages would bypass the post office and be taken straight to the nearby distribution centre first thing.

I hadn't bothered climbing the back fence; I didn't really care whether I was caught in the act. That being said, the streets had been deserted and I hadn't seen a single person or car as I dutifully carried out my mission.

It was like it had never happened.

But it had. And I'd signed my name to it. Everyone would know what I'd done. But – more importantly – they'd know what *they* had done. There was no point in remaining anonymous. The cult would know it was me, regardless, and I could use my name as an insurance policy.

Sure, it might not be enough to save me from them. But, at the very least, it would mean that my death would not be in vain. If something happened to me, it would only solidify their guilt. People would *have* to ask questions.

I had no dreams that night or, at least, none that I could remember. To say that I was exhausted from the day's events, both physically and mentally, was an understatement. The second my head hit that pillow, I was out, and I seemingly hadn't moved a muscle until my alarm jolted me awake.

I tried to relish those few seconds between sleeping and waking. That twilight zone of preconsciousness where I was nothing more than a blank slate. But, soon enough, the memories crept back in and the realisation dawned.

Today was the day that everything would change. And it would be my doing. There was no turning back.

I got ready for the funeral on autopilot – showering, eating breakfast, cleaning my teeth and slapping on makeup. I only returned to the real world when I stood in front of my closet, trying to figure out what to wear. For most people, it was a straightforward decision. But, staring at the rows of all-black ensembles, I was spoiled for choice. The majority of my wardrobe was funeral appropriate. What the hell did that say about me?

I wondered what Lily had been dressed in before she was placed in her coffin. Probably something pure and white. If I dressed like I was constantly in mourning, then Lily dressed like she was heaven-sent. The town's guardian angel. Always looking out for everyone but herself.

I reached for a little black dress and a tear spilled down my cheek. It caught me off guard and I frustratedly wiped it away. There would be no waterworks at the funeral. At least, that's what I told myself. Of course, it would be easier said than done.

I found myself wondering what Lily's reaction would be if she knew I was crying over her. If it were me, I'd be royally taking the piss – especially after years of having to put up with my 'tough guy' act – but she'd probably cry on my behalf and apologise. She'd wrap her arms around me and I'd squirm and protest. Which would only make her cry and apologise more.

How could a person like that have come from a family like hers? How could something so good and pure be forged from evil? How had she survived as long as she had?

I think that was the thing about her death that I was struggling with the most. The sheer inevitability of it. The same scenario could have played out a million different times, in a million different ways, but the outcome would always be the same. She was destined to die. *She* couldn't live with *their* crimes.

I walked over to my mirror and took one final look at my ensemble. Something was missing. I carefully retrieved Lily's necklace from my dresser and fastened it behind my neck. Its weight was oddly comforting – like her arms were wrapped around my shoulders.

CHAPTER 60

Terralong Street was deserted.

Every single storefront was closed and the cafes' outdoor dining areas were eerily empty. Lily's funeral had – quite literally – shut down the entire place. Kiama was finally the ghost town it had been destined to become.

A lone figure stood on the corner of Terralong and Shoalhaven streets, standing guard over a pedestrian crossing that was unlikely to see foot traffic anytime soon. I stared at Daisy the cow, marvelling at her new coat of paint. 'RIP Lily Williams' was emblazoned along her side, while poorly painted calla lilies blossomed over her body. A flower crown of lilies rested on top of her horns – its ribbons gently blowing in the breeze.

I slowly drove over Terralong Street's seemingly unending speed bumps and was quietly unnerved by just how isolated the area was. It was truly uncanny – like the aftermath of an apocalypse and I was the only person left on Earth.

I relished the sensation.

I stared down at the clock on the LandCruiser's dashboard and finally realised why the streets were so empty. I was running late. The funeral was due to start any minute.

I put my foot down on the accelerator and swore under my breath. I was amazed that my dad hadn't called me, demanding to know where I was. But, when I remembered I'd already turned my phone off in preparation for the funeral, I realised that he probably had.

I couldn't believe that I'd fucked up so badly. I obviously didn't give a damn about what my father or the Williams family thought, but it seemed disrespectful to Lily. That is, until I remembered Jarrah's words: 'Lily wouldn't want to be remembered being stuck in this town for all eternity.'

I almost contemplated turning back. Doing a Jarrah and not bothering to show up. But when I thought of those men – Michael, Peter, Mark and my dad, John – delivering her eulogies, I knew I couldn't abandon her.

She deserved so much better than that – than them.

I sped down Bombo's southern headland and I could see the cemetery on the flats below – straight across from the beach and Bombo's tiny train station. Even from the hill, I could tell that there were rows of news vans in the station's small car park – their satellite towers ominously reaching towards the heavens. Peter had been right. The media hadn't heeded his warning and they weren't playing nice.

I turned onto the highway, past the iconic dry-stone wall inscribed with the town's name. Rows of people had gathered on the opposite side of the road. They were standing on the bridge over Spring Creek and had a perfect vantage of the south-east corner of the cemetery where the burial plots for the Williams family lay. To my horror, I noticed that the majority were holding either cameras or microphones.

They really were vultures, flocking around her corpse.

The traffic slowed while drivers gawped at the cemetery and I noticed that a cluster of police cars were parked in the driveway to the farmstead at the back of the grounds. The long passageway was right next to where the funeral was being held, and they'd attempted to park the cars so that they blocked the view from the media standing on the bridge.

The entrance to the car park was on the opposite side of the cemetery and parking there would only make me even later. Fortunately, I spotted Nathan standing guard at the farmstead's driveway.

He ran over to my window when I pulled in. When the LandCruiser slowed to a stop, he yanked my door open.

'Where the *fuck* have you been?' he spat.

'I –'

'Get out, you can leave it here. The car park's full. You're lucky your dad didn't send a bloody squad car to drag your arse down here.'

'But –'

'Go. *Now.* They're waiting for you. Your seat's next to your dad – he's not happy.'

I could see the cemetery lawn over the top of the police cars. It seemed like the entire graveyard was filled with members of the town, all in their sad mourning attire. Everyone was standing, besides Michael, Sharon, Mark, Peter and my father. Sure enough, there was a single spot left in the small row of seating – directly between my dad and Michael.

As I walked towards the crowd, my father glared at me but Michael gave a small, knowing smile.

It was almost like he knew exactly what I planned to do.

'Everything okay?' Michael whispered in my ear as I sat down. I could feel the eyes of the entire town boring into the back of my head.

'Yeah, sorry. I lost track of the time.'

My father crossed his arms over his chest and huffed loudly, shaking his head.

'Are you still comfortable with saying something?' Michael asked. 'It's okay if not.'

'No, I'm good – I want to.'

'Thank you, Marlowe,' he said, before gesturing to his wife. 'It means a lot to the both of us.'

Sharon was staring at Lily's coffin in an almost catatonic state. I doubted that my presence meant much to her, let alone my words. It was like she wasn't even there.

Michael stood up and walked over to the funeral director, who was standing in front of the coffin bookended by two large photos of Lily.

One was a striking portrait that I'd taken for the paper on the day that she'd died, while the other was the picture from the photo lab's window of the two of us at the show ball.

'Just had to make it about you, didn't you?' my father hissed in my ear. His breath was hot on my neck. 'Late to her *fucking* funeral. You should be ashamed of yourself.'

I opened my mouth to reply, but the funeral director's commanding voice boomed over the graveyard. The volume shocked me until I noticed the small speaker at his feet. But even with the microphone, it was unlikely that the whole crowd would be able to hear him. There were simply too many people on the cemetery grounds. Still, the droning hum of the town's chatter faded and Michael returned to his seat.

The sun blazed above and a refreshing sea breeze blew in from Bombo Beach. The sky was clear and blue, an endless ocean above our heads. The weather seemed inappropriate for a funeral, and yet, I suppose it was a fitting tribute to Lily.

A day as perfect as her.

I recalled that it had rained on the day of my mother's funeral and that someone had told me it was because the sky was crying. Who had it been? Surely not my father. I tried to catch the edges of the memory, but the funeral director started his spiel and everything else faded into the background.

Lily's funeral was non-denominational. A celebration of her life rather than an attestation of her continued existence in some made-up realm. If heaven were real, there was no doubt in my mind that Lily would have earned a VIP pass – but it wasn't. She was gone. Gone forever. The only remnants of her were lying inside that gaudy wooden box and, eventually, they would be gone too.

I'd never been particularly heartbroken about the fact there was no hereafter. But as I sat there, staring at her coffin – wedged between the men who had participated in both her death and its cover-up – I found myself mourning the afterlife. I didn't give a fuck about heaven – about the pearly gates, fluffy clouds or angel wings. I just wanted hell to be real.

And I wanted each member of the cult to rot there for all eternity.

CHAPTER 61

Once again, Michael played the role of the grieving father with aplomb. I cried – even though I'd promised myself I wouldn't – as he gave his rousing eulogy. Michael cried too; loud guttural sobs that wrung at his body. I couldn't believe how real his emotions seemed as he struggled to get through the crumpled page of handwritten notes clutched in his shaking hands. It was the perfect tribute to Lily – a beautiful, heartfelt speech. Until you remembered that she wouldn't have been lying in that box without him.

I couldn't fathom how he could do it. Standing up there, in front of the whole town, pretending to grieve. But, as my eyes slowly scanned the row of men next to me, I began to consider that maybe he wasn't pretending.

None of them were crying. Not my dad, Mark, or Peter. Instead, they sat there, stony-faced, their eyes trained on anywhere *but* Michael or Lily's coffin. They didn't care. Not like he did. Even Sharon showed zero emotion – her eyes fixed on her palms as if she were reading her own fortune – but, in all fairness, that could have just been the drugs.

It was only then that I realised I didn't know who had physically killed Lily. Obviously, it was someone from the cult, but that didn't mean that it had been Michael. What if he *was* truly grieving his daughter? His only child? What if he hadn't wanted her to die?

For a brief moment I felt a wave of pity crash over me. But, almost instantly, it turned to revulsion. I was furious that he was making me feel that way. Furious that I was falling for the act. Because, even if he genuinely *did* grieve her, even if he *hadn't* been the one who'd killed her – he was still protecting the people who had. If anything, that made it even worse.

Monsters can grieve, but that doesn't make them any less monstrous.

A spattering of light applause broke out at the end of Michael's eulogy. Which seemed weird and added to the strange, performative feeling of the whole thing.

It wasn't a funeral; it was a bloody stage production.

Michael returned to his seat and the funeral director introduced the next speaker. Mark rose to his feet and embraced Michael. It was a typical blokey hug, with rough back-patting and minimal bodily contact, but I was still surprised to see it. Once again, it didn't feel real. The whole thing was an act, but it was like I was the only one who could see through it.

That would all change though. As soon as my parcels were delivered, the illusion would finally be shattered. Everyone would see these men for what they were.

Mark sauntered over to Lily's coffin and put his palm on top of the polished wood. Michael took his seat and reached his hand out to his wife's – physically picking it up and placing it in his. I watched Mark mouth a silent prayer to the coffin before retrieving his own notes from his pocket. I was horrified to feel the back of Michael's hand brush against mine. He hooked his pinkie finger around my own and pulled my palm into his.

I wanted to yank my hand away, but when I turned and stared into his tear-filled eyes, I knew that I couldn't. Not with everyone watching. He gently squeezed my fingers, and I turned back to watch Mark. Out of the corner of my eye, I could see my father staring at my hand interlocked with Michael's. He was frowning.

Michael was undoubtedly a tough act to follow, but that wasn't the reason why Mark's eulogy was so paltry in comparison. It was just . . . bad.

The things he said were basically a rehash of the quotes Owen had published in the paper. The same meaningless drivel about Lily having had limitless potential and being the youngest journalist ever hired in the history of the *Gazette*.

He also repeated the same odd comparison he'd used in the interview with Owen. The one where he compared Lily's death to the town waking up and discovering that the blowhole had disappeared. I was amazed that nobody had called him out on the quote before then. He clearly thought it was gold but, if I'd still been working at the paper, I would have made sure he knew how dehumanising it was.

It didn't help that he appeared to be drunk. I'd caught a whiff of that familiar rummed breath when he'd hugged Michael directly in front of me, but it wasn't until he started talking that I realised how far gone he was. He was slurring and swaying. Not to mention sweating profusely. It gave him an unhinged air that everyone seemed to notice. Every time he tripped over his words or forgot his place, I could feel Michael's hand slightly tense against mine. Even my dad seemed disgusted by his actions, awkwardly shifting in his seat and sighing loudly.

Their precious performance was falling apart, and I hadn't even taken to the stage.

Halfway through some half-cocked spiel about Lily's inherent 'goodness', Mark froze. He was staring at the crowd behind our seats, his face pale and mask-like. It looked as if Lily herself had appeared to tell him how badly he was fucking her funeral up. Of course, the real Lily would never have done that type of thing.

Michael let go of my hand and turned to face the direction Mark was staring. I did the same, but the crowd was blocking my view. I turned back to face Mark, shocked that he was still frozen in place, although his face had contorted into an eerie expression of rage. Whatever he was looking at, he was absolutely furious about its presence at the funeral.

A gentle murmur began rippling through the crowd. My father and Michael exchanged a concerned glance, and Peter Walsh awkwardly cleared his throat. Thankfully, Sharon was still staring at her hands, blissfully unaware that her daughter's funeral was completely falling apart.

The funeral director, who up until that point had been standing next to Lily's coffin with his head respectfully bowed, walked towards Mark and gently placed his hand on his arm. Mark jumped at his touch and his expression transformed from rage to confusion.

He didn't finish his eulogy. Instead, the funeral director gently removed the microphone from his hand and carefully led him away from Lily's coffin and back to his seat. His gait was unsteady, his brow drenched in sweat. What the hell had he seen in that crowd?

Peter pompously got to his feet and fiddled with his suit buttons while Mark slumped down in the chair next to my father. The funeral director looked at my dad pleadingly but was cut off by the low growl from Mark's mouth.

'What the *fuck* is that f*ggot doing here?'

It didn't take a genius to figure out who he was talking about.

CHAPTER 62

Sure enough, when Peter had finished his eulogy-cum-tourism campaign, and the funeral director had introduced 'Lily Williams' best friend, Marlowe Robertson', I was able to confirm my suspicions. When I faced the crowd, I was immediately drawn to his presence. After all, he had no intention of hiding that day.

Jarrah was standing at the edge of the crowd, casually leaning against a small fence that surrounded an old burial plot. While the rest of the town had shied away from the area, either from respect or squeamishness, Jarrah seemed entirely unbothered. As always, he was dressed in head-to-toe black, in a perfectly tailored suit that only accentuated his slimness and height. It gave him a foreign, insect-like quality. The handle of a gothic parasol was balanced against his shoulder, the black lace umbrella shielding his bald head from the sun's harsh rays. In similar over-the-top fashion, a pair of impossibly large sunglasses hid half of his face.

It was a fucking ridiculous – albeit technically funeral-appropriate – outfit that simultaneously served to obscure its wearer while also drawing the most amount of attention to them as humanly possible.

And yet, I can't tell you how comforting I found his presence. He'd shown up. Not for the town – not for Lily – but for me. I wasn't alone in my horrible ordeal. Someone had my back after all.

I unfurled the page of notes I'd brought with me and was suddenly struck by the proximity of the coffin. It was as if, for the first time, I had truly grasped that Lily was lying inside of it. The Lily I knew.

The Lily I loved. The Lily I'd found. Everything she was and would ever be was locked away inside that box. All her potential. All her fears. All her dreams. All her secrets.

Well, not all *her secrets,* I thought as I stared down at the notes in my hand. I was shaking again.

'I am the rose of Sharon, and the lily of the valleys.'

As my voice resonated throughout the graveyard, I could feel my heart pounding against my chest. It was like someone was trapped inside my body, desperate to get out.

'As the lily among thorns, so is my love among the daughters.'

I was staring Michael Williams straight in his fucking creepy eyes.

Proud. Defiant. Tenacious. Everything Lily could never be. Not any more.

'As the apple tree among the trees of the wood, so is my beloved among the sons. I sat down under his shadow with great delight, and his fruit was sweet to my taste.'

Michael stared back at me – every bit as defiant – but there was something else behind those eyes. Bewilderment? Rage? *Pride?*

'He brought me to the banqueting house, and his banner over me was love. Sustain me with cakes of raisins, refresh me with apples: for I am sick with love.'

To my horror, I finally realised what it was – a deep, profound *sadness*. Michael was crying. And so was I.

'His left hand is under my head, and his right hand does embrace me.'

How could he keep doing this to me? How were his emotions so real? Why did I suddenly feel so guilty?

'I charge you, O you daughters of Jerusalem, by the gazelles or by the hinds of the field, that you stir not up, nor awake love, till it pleases.'

I had to tear my eyes away. I couldn't bear looking at that broken man for a second more. Somewhere in the crowd, a camera flashed. Owen *fucking* Archer was taking my photo.

'The voice of my beloved! Behold, he comes leaping upon the mountains, skipping upon the hills.'

I had no idea how I'd missed him there – standing directly behind Peter. Watching. Waiting. Documenting.

'My beloved is like a gazelle or a young stag: behold, he stands behind our wall, he looks forth through the windows, showing himself through the lattice.'

Owen removed the camera from his eye. He had a fully fledged shiner – the type that engorges half your face like some purple *Phantom of the Opera*-style mask. I inadvertently winced.

'My beloved spoke, and said unto me, Rise up, my love, my fair one, and come away.'

My eyes scanned the crowd before finally landing on Dan. He was standing with our small group of friends – Rachael and the rest of the gang I had been hanging out with on the night of the show.

The night that I'd found her. The night that I first saw those markings. The night when this had all begun.

'For, lo, the winter is past, the rain is over and gone.'

I noticed how bored my friends all looked. Of course, none of them had been particularly close to Lily. I was the only conduit between them. Maybe I should have tried harder to connect them?

I thought about how isolated Lily must have been. How sad it was that the only person she felt she could turn to hadn't even lived in the town. I should have been there for her. But I wasn't.

'The flowers appear on the earth; the time of singing has come, and the voice of the turtledove is heard in our land.'

My eyes traced back to Jarrah. His entire demeanour had changed. He was no longer lolling against the grave fence. Instead, he was standing completely straight, staring at me in shock. He let go of the umbrella's handle and raised both his hands like he was asking me what the fuck I was doing.

He had no idea I'd already signed my name to the dossier I'd sent to the media. Or that Michael had already stolen Lily's journals from my room. The eulogy was just theatrics – an extra way to stick the knife into the cult before the truth came out.

'The fig tree puts forth its green figs, and the vines with the tender grapes give a good smell.'

My eyes fell back on that row of powerful men. The ones on Lily's list. The ones my message was for.

'Arise, my love, my fair one, and come away.'

But, to my surprise, they didn't look angered by my words. Instead, they also appeared deeply saddened. Even my father – so quick to scowl, scoff or roll his eyes at my every action – looked utterly broken by my words. There were tears in his eyes.

What the fuck was happening?

'O my dove, in the clefts of the rock, in the secret places of the cliff, let me see your face, let me hear your voice; for sweet is your voice, and your countenance is lovely.'

But then I saw it. The rage I'd yearned for, the sheer hatred I'd expected was plastered on the face of one of the cult members.

'Catch us the foxes, the little foxes, that spoil the vines: for our vines have tender grapes.'

Just not the one I'd expected.

CHAPTER 63

Sharon Williams seemed completely lucid. Like her rage had sloughed off the fog surrounding her mind. Her eyes were no longer glassy – they were clear and piercing and trained firmly on mine. She was furious at me. Furious at the words I had spoken. She knew their true meaning, and she knew why I had chosen to repeat them in front of the whole town.

I thought I'd felt true fear in those previous days. Discovering Lily's body, reading her journals and seeing the remnants of the horrors that had occurred in that rainforest. But all that paled in comparison to the fear that gripped my body at that moment. My potential death never seemed more real.

If one of the men from the cult killed me, I found myself thinking, *it would be in cold blood.* A necessary evil – like cleaning up a spill. It would be pragmatic and detached, and I could almost imagine them whispering, 'No hard feelings,' as my last breath choked away. Maybe they'd show me mercy and make it extra quick.

Not Sharon though. Not with the way she was looking at me. My death at her hands would be fiery and passionate. A true revenge killing designed to be as painful and long-lasting as my pitiful body could bear. She would endlessly torture me until I begged her to finish.

Hell hath no fury like a grieving mother.

I felt a hand on my arm and jumped a mile. I was surprised to see the funeral director standing by my side, his face placid and his smile warm. He was attempting to wrangle the microphone off me, just as he had with Mark. And, as I stared out at the sea of concerned faces, I realised that I, too, appeared every bit as lost as my former editor. But hopefully not as drunk.

Instead of being led back to my seat by the funeral director, I left of my own accord. Walking past the men in the front row, I was once again struck by how genuinely saddened they appeared. My words had certainly not had the impact I'd expected.

But, perhaps more perplexing, was that Sharon had returned to her catatonia. She didn't even glance in my direction as I returned to my seat. Instead, her glassy eyes remained trained on her hands, still gently resting on her lap. She looked like she hadn't moved a muscle, and I wondered if I'd imagined the whole thing.

No. That rage had been real. Just as real as the fear that I had felt. I was sure of it.

When I sat down, the funeral director began his concluding remarks and Michael's knee knocked against mine. It had been a purposeful movement and, realising he was trying to get my attention, I looked up at him. There were still tears in his eyes.

'That was beautiful, Marlowe,' he whispered into my ear. 'But I wish you'd told me what you planned to read.'

'You said to choose something significant to Lily,' I whispered in reply. 'I know that passage was important to her.'

His brow furrowed slightly.

'After all,' I said, 'she'd written it enough times in her journals, hadn't she?'

I don't know who was more shocked – Michael or me. Michael seemed shocked at my mention of the journals, while I was shocked by *his* shock. Once again, I was at a loss as to what he was playing at. Why was he pretending that he didn't know?

That he didn't know that *I* knew?

He'd made it clear that he'd been the one who had taken the journals – sitting on my bed, right on top of where they'd been hidden, and stroking my mattress. Why the fuck was he playing coy now? Was this just another one of his mind games? To confuse me until I was under his control? Was this what he had done to Lily?

He started to say something but was interrupted before he had the chance. The funeral director had invited both Michael and Sharon to place the first flowers on Lily's coffin before it was lowered into the ground. Michael rose to his feet. His eyes were still fixed on my face, seemingly full of concern.

He broke his gaze and turned around to his wife. He held his hand out, but she ignored it, so he gently grasped her wrist.

'Come on, Sharon,' I heard him say. 'It's time to say goodbye to Lily.'

There was something about the innocuousness of the statement that enraged me. And yet, it seemed to be enough to coax Sharon to her feet. She dutifully stood before her husband and allowed herself to be led to her daughter's casket. I struggled to believe that the pure rage I had seen behind her eyes could have been produced by someone so frail.

How had I ever feared that husk of a woman? Was *I* losing my mind?

I felt something grab at my hand and was shocked to see my father's fingers interlaced with mine. I instinctively tried to pull away, but his grip remained firm. Puzzled, I stared into his eyes. I was horrified to see he was looking at me in the exact same way Michael had looked at Sharon.

'It's our turn, Lo,' he said, nodding towards the casket. 'Come on.'

I allowed myself to be pulled to my feet, and we walked hand-in-hand to Lily's coffin. A flash of a memory. My father and I doing the exact same thing at my mother's funeral. I looked up at the sky as if expecting rain.

I let go of my dad's hand and took the single white calla lily the funeral director was holding out to me. He gave a small, respectful nod before stepping to the side. I walked straight to the coffin and stood there for a few moments. In the distance – over the top of the police cars – I could see all the media's cameras pointed in my direction. I fought the urge to flip them the bird.

I stared down at the lily in my hand, saddened to see that there was a small tear in its pure white petal. I wanted to turn around and ask for a different one but realised it was an absurd request. Besides, what did it matter? The whole funeral was pointless. A ritual as meaningless and archaic as the ones held in that rainforest.

I gently placed the lily on top of the casket, turned my back and walked away.

Jarrah was wrong. Lily wasn't trapped in the town for all eternity. She was nowhere.

Lily Williams didn't exist. Not any more.

CHAPTER 64

The family had declined to host a wake, and – for some reason – the funeral party were required to dutifully stand to the side of the coffin while members of the town paid their respects one by one. The funeral director carried chairs over for Sharon and Michael, but the rest of us had to stand behind them while each well-wisher nodded sympathetically and apologised for their loss.

I didn't want to be there. Didn't want to be a part of their farce. Things hadn't gone how I had planned, and I couldn't figure out why.

And yet, I had the distinct impression that each of the men wanted to confront me over my choice of reading. But still, as the minutes ticked by, nobody made a move. I supposed they couldn't. Not with the eyes of the town, and the media, on them. Instead, they all stood in that line – their heads bowed, their hands reverently clasped: the perfect mourners.

Unsurprisingly, Mark was the first to break.

'The fucking nerve,' I heard him growl.

'Mark,' my father warned, his head still bowed.

'Don't you fucking "Mark" me. How the fuck did your men let that piece of shit in here?'

I raised my head. Sure enough, Jarrah was standing in the long line of people waiting to pay their respects. He was staring right at us – defiant – perhaps even goadingly so. My friends were immediately behind him, and Dan's eyes were scanning back and forth between

Jarrah and the funeral party. It was almost like he could predict what was about to happen.

'Mr Watson is a member of the town,' my dad began. 'He has as much of a right to be here as anyone else.'

'You can't seriously believe that, John,' Peter interjected. 'Not after what he did to her.'

'Need I remind the both of you that he had an alibi.'

'Just because he didn't do the deed doesn't mean he's not fucking responsible,' Mark seethed. 'You know she never would have lashed out on that ghost train if it wasn't for him.'

I could feel my face contort in bewilderment. What the hell were they talking about?

'He's right, John,' Peter said. 'He's every bit as responsible as the carny, and you know it. This is a bad look for you, mate.'

My dad finally raised his head. 'What the bloody hell do you expect me to do? Cuff him? Drag him out kicking and screaming? In front of the whole town? In front of the *media*? The fucker's got clout now. He's made a name for himself. He's not some scared little kid any more. You can't bloody bully him into submission this time.'

My eyes flicked to Michael and Sharon, who were still busy with the well-wishers. If the Williamses could hear the conversation behind them, they were pretending otherwise. One of the oldies from the show committee awkwardly wrapped her arms around Sharon. It looked like she was hugging a mannequin.

My dad appeared to have silenced Peter, but Mark was still going for the jugular.

'What if this was your daughter's funeral, huh? What if he had done it to her? Would *you* want that piece of shit here? Think about what this is doing to Michael and Sharon. Worst day of their fuckin' lives and you're making it even harder because you're scared of some p*ofter.'

My dad went to open his mouth, but Mark continued.

'You know what? Fuck you, John. If you haven't got the balls to do something, then *I* will. I don't give a shit if that fucker pulls the q*eer card. I'll publish what he did. I'm not scared of him. It's about time the artsy-fartsy cunts that support his work know what he's really like. This pathetic little vendetta he has against this town ends today. I'll make sure of it.'

Before my dad had a chance to reply, Mark was already walking towards Jarrah.

'Oi, f*ggot!' he shouted, spooking the long line of mourners.

'Oh, for fuck's sake,' my father muttered under his breath.

'Just remember, John,' Peter smugly interjected. 'You could have prevented this.'

There was a yelling match, but Mark was the one doing all the yelling. He was in Jarrah's face almost immediately and, from my view next to the coffin, I could see his spittle shining in the sunlight as it sprayed from his mouth. It was like when he'd confronted me at the paper the night Lily had died. Just after I had mentioned the markings. That pure rage.

Jarrah seemed entirely unfazed.

My dad, on the other hand, was furious. He was still standing next to Peter and me, but I could tell that he was itching to go over and grab Mark by the scruff. His jawline was clenched – the veins in his neck bulging – and his hand was balled into a tight fist. I was surprised at how much restraint he was showing.

That all changed when Mark grabbed Jarrah by the suit collar. To the media's cameras it would have looked entirely unprovoked, but everyone close by was able to see that Jarrah had whispered something. Something that had sent Mark into a blind rage.

My father ran towards them and I followed. I'd heard how they'd all spoken about Jarrah. I wanted to make sure that there was a witness close by. Especially after what had happened to Steve.

'Get your hands off him, *now*,' my father commanded.

Mark's eyes swept from Jarrah to my dad. I could see that Jarrah was smiling smugly. Mark's fingers tensed around the fabric of his jacket.

'Mark,' my father scolded.

Mark let go of Jarrah with a dramatic flick of his hands and let out a frustrated growl.

'Huh,' Jarrah said, addressing my dad while straightening his suit. 'That's funny. I didn't hear anyone call "Sooey".'

'You really gonna let him talk to you like that, John?' Mark snapped.

'Need I remind the *both* of you that this is a private funeral and that you will conduct yourself in a respectful manner or face expulsion.'

'I was just trying to pay my respects, officer,' Jarrah said with faux sweetness, 'when this Neanderthal *brute* came over and started hurling slurs at me.'

'I'll show you fucking slurs, you piece of shit,' Mark said, raising his fist towards Jarrah.

'Hey!' I said, stepping between the two of them. My voice had come out louder than I'd intended, but it seemed to do the trick. All three men stared at me, shocked. Like they hadn't realised I'd been standing there the whole time.

'Stop it,' I continued. 'All of you.'

'He's the one who bloody started it, Lo!' Jarrah protested.

'I know. But I'm going to be the one to finish it.' I turned to face Mark. 'I don't know what the fuck your problem with Jarrah is. But if the issue is him being here, then take it up with me. *I* was the one who invited him. He was friends with Lily. A better friend than I ever was.'

'I fucking knew it,' Mark said, shaking his head in disbelief.

My dad looked dumbfounded.

'A fucking friend,' Mark scoffed, before pointing at Jarrah. 'Are you going to tell her, or am I?'

Every bit of smugness melted away from Jarrah's face. He looked – scared.

'Tell me what?' I asked Jarrah.

He shook his head. He couldn't look me in the eye.

'Tell me *what*, Jarrah?' I repeated.

CHAPTER 65

'Mark,' my father warned.

But Mark ignored him. 'Last chance, Jarrah.'

Jarrah remained silent, staring at the ground.

Mark took a step towards me and leaned in, his breath caressing my skin. 'Who the fuck do you think carved those markings in Lily's back that you're so *goddamn* obsessed with?'

The shock was like a blow to my head. Immediately, I spun around to face Jarrah but he still couldn't bring himself to look at me. I turned to my dad.

'He was the person you questioned?' I asked. The day that Jarrah had given me the journals. The day that he'd sent me the text messages. He was already down here – in a fucking interview room at Warilla police station. 'He was the one with the alibi for her time of death?'

My father stared into my eyes for a long time before finally nodding.

'He might not have killed Lily himself,' Mark seethed. 'But he may as well have.'

'That's not true,' Jarrah protested. His voice was small, shaky.

'You *mutilated* her,' Mark spat.

'No. I – it wasn't like that. I *told* him,' he said, looking at my dad. 'It wasn't like that and you fucking know it!'

'But you did it?' I asked. 'The carvings on her back. The ones that I saw the night she was killed. The ones that started all this? It was *you*?'

'It doesn't change anything that I've told you. I swear, Marlowe.'

His eyes were filling with tears. I felt like I was back on the Hurricane. Disoriented. Nauseous. Confused. I remembered how hard he'd pushed for me to not include the pictures of Lily's back in my packages. The pictures of *his* carvings. I thought he'd been trying to protect me, but he was just protecting himself.

'Everything I've told you is real; everything in the journals is real,' he continued. 'The cult – it's them, Lo. It's all of them. This town. It – it's fucked.'

'Poisoning someone else with your lies, are you, Mr Watson?'

All three of us spun around at the sound of Michael's voice. I had no idea how long he and Peter had been standing there.

'Michael, hey,' my dad said, stepping towards him. 'This isn't for you to sort out – not today. Go back to Sharon. She needs you, mate.'

'From the sounds of it, your daughter needs me more,' he said, locking eyes with me.

My eyes darted between each of the men. I felt like I was drowning on dry land. Another wave of panic crashed over me.

'What the fuck is going on?' I pleaded.

'I'm so sorry, Marlowe,' Michael said, shaking his head. 'We shouldn't have kept things from you. We were trying to protect you, but I had no idea you'd been in contact with him.'

'I just thought it was because she'd seen the markings,' my dad said. 'I – I didn't realise.'

'We all should have realised,' Mark added. 'All the signs were there – the paranoia, the distrust. She was acting just like Lily.'

'No,' Michael said, sternly. 'Marlowe is stronger than that. Lily was sick. She was vulnerable. And *he* took advantage of that.'

'What the *fuck* is going on?' I repeated.

'This prick told you about the "cult", right?' Mark sneered, pointing at Jarrah. 'About us hunting children in the rainforest? The fucking ritual sacrifice? It's bullshit, Marlowe.'

'But, Lily's journals,' I sputtered. 'There's evidence.'

'Lily was sick, Marlowe,' Michael began. 'Very sick. She battled with mental illness her whole life and developed schizoaffective disorder as a teenager. It made her believe things that weren't true. Horrible things. They felt real to her though.'

'What?' I asked, shaking my head in disbelief. 'No.'

'It's true, Lo,' my dad added. 'We've all known for a very long time and have done what we could to keep her out of harm's way.'

'No,' I said, my voice breaking. 'She would have told me.'

'You know that's not true,' Mark said. 'You saw the way she looked up to you.'

'Bullshit.'

'She didn't want anyone to know.' Michael sighed. 'She didn't want anyone thinking she was broken.'

'But she wasn't,' I said, shaking my head. 'She seemed completely fine, up until the last couple of months.'

'She *was* fine,' Michael replied. 'When she took her medication. But the second that stopped her symptoms returned – the delusions, the hallucinations, the paranoia.'

I turned to face Jarrah. 'You were the one who made her go off her meds. So she could *drink* with you at your fucking parties . . .'

'No,' Jarrah said, stepping towards me.

I took a step back.

'She didn't need them, there was *nothing* wrong with her. It was just another way for these sadistic fucks to control her. She wasn't delusional, Lo. Everything she said is real. Don't let them gaslight you too.'

'As real as those marks you carved into her body?' Mark spat.

'Those were for her *protection*,' Jarrah hissed. 'She asked me to do it.'

'Just like she *asked* you to submit that inflammatory drawing into the show's art competition?' Peter Walsh asked, before turning to me. 'That's why it was removed, Miss Robertson. Because *he* sent it in under her name – without her permission.'

'She *did* ask me to.'

'But that doesn't make sense, Jarrah,' I said, shaking my head. 'You said yourself that Lily just needed to get through this weekend. That she'd be free after that and could move to Sydney. Why would she deliberately antagonise them if she was that scared of what they'd do to her?'

'Because she had bigger balls than *any* of you give her credit for. She wasn't some delicate flower. She was a fucking warrior, and she's going to bring you all down – even in death. Just you wait.'

'Wait for what?' Michael asked. 'The reveal of your little art project? That's what all this has been about, hasn't it? That and your vendetta against this town. Tell me, Mr Watson. Did her death ruin things for you? Or did it just make the final piece all the more powerful?'

Jarrah opened his mouth to say something, but Michael continued.

'I suppose at the very least you won't have to worry about crediting her for your ideas. For turning her nightmares into reality. I must say, I've followed your work for many years, and I think the things you did in that clearing are among your best.'

I gasped – I audibly gasped.

'So, Mr Watson,' Michael continued. 'When's the big reveal?'

CHAPTER 66

The packages.

The packages were the big reveal. I was a fucking pawn for some pathetic art project.

Jarrah had used me. Just like he'd used Lily. And it might have resulted in her death.

It was like a filter had been lifted from my eyes. I could see the world again. The real world. It all made sense. More sense than fucking child sacrifice and evil adults in fox masks. How had I allowed myself to be so blinded?

It was the markings. The markings that *he* had done. If I'd never seen them, I never would have believed the rest.

Of course Jarrah was the one who had defiled the clearing on the Williamses' property – just as he had defiled the flesh on her back. It had all the hallmarks of one of his artworks. Large scale, gaudy and fucking on the nose. It was why he had been so insistent on us going there. Why he knew to take Hoddles Track and had miraculously spotted the path from the back of the Williamses' homestead to the clearings.

It was because he had been there before. God knows how many times. Carving those fucking symbols into the trees and wearing the rings into the ground.

It was how he knew that there was no phone reception and that the electric fence was off. How he confidently strode through the rainforest like he fucking owned the place. And how he knew to take a piss right in the spot that led to the second clearing. He was leading me there. So I could document his lies. So I could make them seem more real.

It was also why he wasn't scared. He knew there was no threat because he'd made it all up. It was how he could laugh and joke in that rainforest. How he was able to look at those ashes without dry retching. Because none of it was real.

But what was the point of it all?

I stood there – staring at the men surrounding me – and the penny finally dropped.

It was revenge. Revenge for what had happened to Jarrah in the town all those years ago. Peter had been the father of his attacker and had insisted on him being expelled. My father had been the one who had ensured Jarrah's punishment happened, while also letting his attacker walk free. Mark had published a series of articles at the time that were essentially a smear campaign against Jarrah. And, if I were to hazard a guess, Michael had probably been the one who had conducted Jarrah's psychiatric assessment.

And me. I'd been there that day. I'd stood there in silence. I could have stuck up for him. But I never did. I was every bit as guilty in Jarrah's eyes.

But what about Lily? What could she possibly have done to warrant Jarrah's wrath?

Maybe she had nothing to do with his revenge. Maybe she was his muse. Maybe he fed and cultivated her delusions like a wild garden. Ensuring she'd point fingers in all the right directions. It was cruel. Sick. Almost as bad as the horrors Lily was convinced to believe.

Maybe her death *was* a blessing in disguise. A way to sever Jarrah's hold over her. A way to stop the horrible things that she believed to be true.

The things that never actually existed.

My thoughts stopped swirling and I could feel the sun on my skin and smell the salt from the sea spray in the air. Jarrah was still arguing with the men. Protesting. Denying. I hadn't listened to a word of it. I didn't really care. Not any more.

But then, there was a cacophony of gasps and screams from behind Lily's coffin.

The squealing of brakes and the honking of horns.

A vehicle smashing into something.

Then something else.

'Where's Sharon?' Michael asked, his voice tinged with panic.

I turned to face the chair she had been sitting in. It was empty. Michael was already running towards the road and the rest of the men followed.

'Wait, Lo,' Jarrah said, grabbing me by my wrist.

'You take your fucking hands off me,' I spat, before wrenching myself away.

He held up his hands defensively. 'Please, Lo. You have to trust me.'

'No, Jarrah, you were right. I shouldn't have trusted anyone.'

Before he could say anything else, I was already running towards the road.

CHAPTER 67

I didn't see the accident firsthand. But that didn't matter. I would see it over and over again in the coming days. Running on a loop on every news channel – stills splashed on the covers of every newspaper. Breaking news conveniently unfolding in front of rows of journalists, television cameras and true-crime paparazzi.

For a handful of lucky newsrooms, it was even broadcast live. The loud smash interrupting the monotonous drivel spouting from bored presenters struggling to fill airtime. It couldn't have gone better if it were planned. Peter had been right, the rubberneckers had been a liability.

Sharon was lying by the side of the road. Her body was crumpled – her right foot bare. A single black pump lay in the centre of the left-hand lane.

She appeared completely unscathed, albeit in shock.

Michael dived onto the ground next to his wife as a dazed Nathan slowly climbed to his feet.

'What the hell happened?' my dad asked.

Nathan stared at him like he wasn't really there. His entire body was trembling. His lips were moving, but no words were coming out.

My father gently placed his hand on Nathan's shoulder, and the contact seemed to bring him back to his senses. He looked out at the road and then stared down at Sharon. She was softly sobbing into her husband's chest.

'Is she okay?' Nathan asked Michael.

Michael nodded, his arms still wrapped around Sharon's trembling form.

'What about everyone else?' Nathan asked, his eyes scanning the cars involved in the crash.

'Mate, forget about that,' my dad said. 'I need you to tell me what happened.'

'Sh-she just walked out onto the road.'

My dad's expression buckled, and he turned to face Michael. Something important was exchanged in the glance between them.

'What do you mean, Nath?' my dad asked.

'I was watchin' her,' he said, shaking his head. 'She just started walkin' straight towards the road. I called out to her, but it was like she couldn't hear me. I thought maybe she was pissed off at the press. That she was gonna shout at them from this side of the road. But then I realised . . .'

Nathan's eyes flicked back to Sharon.

'Realised what?' my dad asked when he didn't continue.

'That she wasn't gonna stop.'

My dad and Nathan both looked at Sharon. Her face was still buried under Michael's chin. Her pained mewling sounded like a wounded animal.

'You saved her?' Michael asked.

'I mean, I just –'

'No, you *saved* her,' Michael repeated. It was a statement, not a question. 'Thank you.'

Nathan smiled sheepishly and allowed himself a small nod.

'I got to her the second she stepped onto the road. I grabbed her by the waist before the car even swerved and I just fell backwards with her on top of me. Are you sure she's okay?' he asked. 'We hit the ground pretty bloody hard.'

'Are *you* okay?' my dad asked.

'Yeah. Just . . . yeah.'

My dad slapped Nathan on the back. 'Good job, mate.'

Peter stepped out from next to me and shook Nathan's hand, his body positioned so that the press got the perfect shot. My gaze fell back on Sharon. She had turned her head and was staring straight at me. Her cold eyes fixed on mine as her husband slowly stroked her hair.

Her rage was back, and this time I understood why.

I had done this. I had made her try to kill herself. And Michael and my father both knew it. It was why they'd looked at each other the way they had. They knew I was to blame.

The eulogy. The fucking eulogy. She *had* been furious at me, just not for the reasons I'd originally thought.

If the rantings in Lily's journal had been a potent combination of schizophrenic delusions and Jarrah's influence, then me reading from them was a kick in the teeth to everyone who had loved her. Everyone who had been trying to protect her.

It was heinously cruel. Sick. Twisted. Detestable. I had shattered an already broken woman with my words. If it weren't for Nathan, Sharon's blood would have been on my hands. I was a monster.

And things were only going to get worse once my packages reached those newsrooms.

I ran to the LandCruiser. I had to get to the parcel distribution centre. I had to stop those packages from being sent. I would not be responsible for spreading Jarrah's lies any further. For his fucking revenge plan. Not after seeing how much damage it had already done.

With one final look at Lily's coffin, I sped away from that cemetery and from all the people that I'd hurt.

It didn't matter that it wasn't intentional. The damage was already done.

CHAPTER 68

'You right, love?' a gruff voice called out from somewhere behind me.

I was standing with my hand on the door handle of the distribution centre's office. I'd pressed down, but it hadn't budged. It was locked. I turned around to face the voice. It belonged to a middle-aged man in an orange high-vis vest. He was standing in front of a large roller door and smoking a cigarette.

'Our girl's still at the funeral,' he said, nodding towards the office. 'Dunno what she's bloody doin'. She was supposed to be back ages ago – the phones are ringin' off the hook.'

'There was a car accident,' I said, approaching him. 'Out the front of the cemetery. It's held everyone up. I only got out because my car wasn't in the main car park and I knew a back route.'

'S'that right?' he asked. 'Everyone okay?'

I nodded, but I knew it wasn't true – Sharon was far from okay.

'Good. The last thing this town needs is more bloody drama.'

I nodded again. He took a long drag on his cigarette and his eyes locked with mine. I looked away.

'You work here, right?' I tried to casually ask. 'Is there any chance you could give me a hand with something?'

He looked at me like I'd just asked him to prostrate himself before me.

'I'm on smoko,' he said, holding up the cigarette. 'Besides, I just sort packages. You'll have to wait for the girl if you want something. Not really in my job description, y'know?'

'It's about packages though,' I said, smiling warmly. 'Sounds like you'd be the perfect guy to ask.'

He laughed. 'Nice try, sweetheart, but I don't get paid enough to have to deal with people. Just wait for the bloody girl, okay? She can't be too far off.'

He dropped his cigarette and ground it onto the concrete with the heel of his boot.

'I'm on the clock, love. I gotta go.'

'Wait, please. I posted a bunch of parcels last night and I need to get them back. I know that they're here. Please help me. They can't be sent.'

He stared at me for a long time.

'Please,' I repeated.

'You're the copper's daughter, right?' he finally asked.

I nodded, slightly confused, and he appeared to think something over. I pounced while I still had the chance.

'There was a bunch of them. About this big,' I said, indicating the size with my hands. 'All the same, and all addressed to different newsrooms. I posted them in the parcel boxes outside the post office last night, and I know they come here.'

He squinted his eyes, though whether it was due to the sun or what I was saying, I couldn't tell.

'I mean,' I began, gesturing at the roller door behind him, 'they're probably still in there right now.'

He had absentmindedly retrieved another cigarette from his pocket and seemed shocked when it touched his lips. He removed it, frowning, before tucking it behind his ear. He gave a long exhale.

'Look, love –'

'*Please*. Please, just look for me. I've fucked up so badly. You have no idea what I've done. I *have* to stop them from getting out.'

'It's not that.' He shook his head. 'I'd love to help ya. But it . . . it's just . . .'

'What?' I asked. Tears were pooling in the corners of my eyes.

He gently placed his hand on my shoulder. I didn't have the energy to recoil from his touch.

'They're gone, darl. They're already gone.'

'No,' I muttered, shaking my head in disbelief. 'No, there has to be something you can do.'

'If there was, I would. I promise ya. But once they're on those trucks, there's no turnin' back. They went first thing. I've been here since four am.'

'No,' I whimpered, feeling my chest seize up and my breaths grow ragged.

'Come on, love,' he said, squeezing my shoulder. 'It can't be that bad.'

But it was.

I had to get away. I turned my back and walked towards the LandCruiser. The parcel sorter was calling out to me, but his words were white noise. All I could think about was the look on Sharon's face. That anger. That hatred. And how she had turned it on herself.

I climbed into the LandCruiser and pulled away from the distribution centre. I was heading back into town on autopilot, but I had nowhere to go. Not any more.

CHAPTER 69

I was back at the showground. Back where it all began.

And yet, I had zero recollection of how I'd made it there. I'd left the distribution centre and then – what? Driven to the showground, clearly. But why had I done that?

The carnies were long gone, and the entire area felt like a different place. It was so . . . normal. So nondescript. An empty oval – a car park – and a pavilion with all its doors locked. And, of course, those stables. The place where I'd first spotted those gold gladiator sandals.

One of my favourite things about the show had always been the way it transformed the area. It was almost like the atmosphere itself changed when the carnies rolled in. You could feel it there, among the rides, showbag trailers and food vans. It was something different – something electric – something so un-Kiama-like.

But Lily's death had transformed it again. The area would never be the same. The atmosphere was now one of deep grief and sadness. Heavy. Suffocating. When people went there, the only thing they'd be able to think about was her. Her death. Her body. And now, those fucking marks.

They'd haunt the nation just as they'd haunted me. Like a curse I'd unwillingly unleashed. They'd be forever tied to her like some grim legacy, and forever tied to the town.

Who would the public believe? I wondered. *Jarrah or the supposed cult members?* I knew better than anyone just how alluring a conspiracy theory could be. How easy it was to allow yourself to be blinded and consumed by it.

But, in the end, it didn't really matter who or what the public believed. The damage was well and truly done. There would be a permanent question mark over the town and the people on Lily's list. The people I'd unknowingly condemned. The people who were innocent.

No wonder my dad had tried to cover the markings up. He knew the damage that they would do. After all, he'd seen what Jarrah's lies had done to Lily.

He really had been trying to protect me.

I got out of the LandCruiser and walked towards the stables. The flowers adorning the stalls were all dying, and half of them had blown out of the caged doors. They formed a macabre red carpet, leading straight towards the cliff's edge.

I realised what I was doing there.

I'd come to the showground to kill myself.

The thought had popped into my mind like I was recalling an errand I had forgotten to do. There was something so mundane about it. Something so inevitable. I would die here – where she had – just like in my dream.

People say that suicide is a coward's way to die, but the decision was never mine. It was like a parasitic entity had reached its tendrils into my mind and affixed itself to my brain stem. I controlled it no more than I controlled the weather. No amount of wishing that the sun would come out could dissipate the storm clouds that were gathering in my mind.

Besides, I *wanted* it to rain – with calm and collected assuredness.

Nothing in my life ever felt easier. It made sense. I could understand what had caused Sharon to step out onto that highway. But this was different. Sharon had wanted to die because of someone else's mistake. *My* mistake. She didn't deserve to be punished.

But I did.

A gust of wind was channelled between the rows of stables, sending flowers and pine needles hurtling towards the cliff. Something else caught my eye – a glimmer on the old rope tied to Lily's stable reflecting the sun's light. Puzzled, I walked towards it and frowned. I remembered Sharon moving towards it during the press conference.

I reached out my fingers and touched it, surprised by the crispy yet sticky texture. My fingertips glistened in the sun. They were covered in tiny crystal-like fragments. I ran my other hand along the door of the stable. It was slightly tacky, but it didn't make my fingers shine. The substance on the rope wasn't sea spray but it was definitely salt.

My father was wrong. Lily hadn't been killed by one of her crystals. She was killed by a fucking salt lick, a rock solid chunk of salt that had been attached to the stable door. Which meant his original theory was correct. Her death wasn't premeditated. And the murder weapon wasn't a secret coded message to me. Once again, I'd been blinded by a ridiculous conspiracy fuelled by Jarrah's markings – a conspiracy I'd unleashed on the world.

I walked up to the cliff's edge, kicked my heels off and felt the spiky patches of grass prickle the soles of my feet. The sun was warm on my face and the cool ocean breeze was inviting. It drew me closer to the edge and the jagged rocks below.

I decided to leave my shoes and the small handbag I'd taken to the funeral by the cliff's edge so everyone would know where I'd gone in. It was likely that people would check the showground once I was reported missing. But, if for some reason my death went unnoticed, my body would probably eventually pop up on one of the town's many beaches. It would depend on the current but – based on the number of corpses my father had retrieved from there – I knew that Bombo was the most likely candidate.

For some strange reason, I found comfort in that. I'd always liked Bombo. Plus, that's where she was now.

I sat down on the edge of the cliff, my bare feet dangling over the rock shelf below, and I began drafting my suicide note in my mind. It would be my way of explaining things – of apologising to everyone I'd hurt – and I hoped that it'd be enough to mitigate the damage of my parcels.

What was more powerful? I thought. *A conspiracy theory or another dead girl?*

I pulled my phone out of my purse and turned it back on for the first time since the funeral. I'd decided to type my suicide note on it and email it to myself. I knew they'd check both my phone and computer. So, even if some lowlife decided to nick my phone, the cops would eventually see it.

Almost immediately, my phone began chirping away with missed calls and messages from people who had witnessed my hasty exit from the cemetery. I scrolled through them, barely taking in what they said. It was strange reading the last words these people would ever say to me. And yet, I still felt completely numb.

Until I saw the MMS.

The one containing a photo of the stolen journals and a short message:

meet me @ the bower
we need 2 talk

It was Dan. He must have taken the journals when he'd come into the cottage to get the frozen vegetables for Owen's face. After all, he'd returned my shoes at the same time. When I got home, they'd been in my room – on my dresser. He'd been in there. The evening *before* Michael had been sitting on my bed. He had to have taken them then.

How could I not have noticed? And, more importantly, how the *fuck* did he know that they were there, tucked under my mattress in a pillowcase?

I stared down at the rock shelf below, suddenly nauseated by the sight of the sheer drop below my feet. I was overcome by rage.

Jarrah. Fucking *Jarrah*.

He was the one who deserved to die. Not me, and certainly not Sharon. *He* had done this. And I was going to make sure the whole fucking world knew it.

CHAPTER 70

'You fucking piece of shit,' I seethed as I rounded the corner to the bower.

From the second I'd learned that Dan had stolen the journals, I knew Jarrah would be there. And, sure enough, the two of them were both casually leaning against the school building waiting for me. They were still in their funeral suits and made a striking pair. From just one glance, I could tell that they were completely comfortable in each other's presence. I felt a pang of envy. That was *my* best friend, and yet – as Jarrah had so gleefully pointed out – there were so many things that I didn't know about him.

It was Lily all over again.

'Whoa, Lo,' Dan said, his hands held up. 'You've gotta calm down, okay? I know you're angry b–'

'You have no *fucking* idea!'

'Lo!'

'How can you stand by him?' I said, shaking my head in disbelief. 'After everything he's done? After all the lies he's told and people he's hur–'

'I'm not *fucking* lying,' Jarrah interrupted.

'Did you, or did you not carve those markings in Lily's back?' I snapped.

His eyes flicked to the ground. 'Look, I . . . it's not that simple.'

'Did you do it? Yes or no?'

He shook his head in frustration and muttered something under his breath.

'What?'

'Yes, okay? But it's like I told your dad – she *asked* me to do it. *After* she got rid of the actual brand that they gave her. Y'know the circle thing that looks like a flower? The Seed of Life? The cult's symbol?'

I rolled my eyes. 'The symbol from the clearing, you mean? The symbol *you* carved into the trees? Your new art project?'

'No. Lily's dad is full of shit. I didn't do any of that. It was all them, Lo.'

'So, what? It was just a bloody big coincidence that you needed to take a piss in the exact spot where the markings were carved into the trees? I'm not fucking stupid, Jarrah. You led me to that second clearing. You knew about Hoddles Track, you knew about the trail from the farmstead to the clearings, and you knew the electric fence was off. You'd *obviously* been there before.'

He let out an exasperated sigh.

'You can't expect her to believe you if you're not honest about everything, Jarrah,' Dan interjected. 'You lied about the markings, you lied about being questioned by the cops, you lied about submitting Lily's picture and you lied about being in that rainforest.'

'I didn't lie. She just never bothered to ask. S'not my fault she's a shitty journo. Though, with role models like Mark and Owen, who can blame her?'

I opened my mouth to give him a piece of my mind, but Dan did it for me. 'Jesus, Jarrah. Don't be such a fuckwit. You're the one in the wrong here. You lied.'

'Oh, please. You don't get to play the BFF card now. If I've lied, then so has Marlowe. We *both* know that.'

'When the fuck have I lied to you?' I snapped.

'What about your little rendezvous with the hunky journo, huh? His hotel room, Black Beach, the showground? You two have become nice and cosy over these past few days, haven't you?'

My eyes flicked to Dan. He was staring at the ground. His betrayal had a perplexing physicality to it – like it was squeezing my chest.

'What the hell does any of that have to do with you?' I asked.

'I'm not stupid either, Marlowe. I know you'd do anything to get out of this place. I know you've been trying to sell her story and –'

'*Your* story, you mean.'

'No, Marlowe. *Her* story. The one she entrusted the two of us with. She chose us for a reason, and you're jus–'

'No, Jarrah. *You* chose us. Me and the men from this town. The ones who you feel have wronged you. The people on that list all deserve punishment for what happened to you but not like this. Lily was innocent. She was sick, and you took advantage of her. You poisoned her mind when she was at her most vulnerable. You made her believe the most horrifying things about her loved ones – the very people who were trying to protect her. For what? Some fucking vendetta?'

'Jesus Christ, Lo,' he said, his eyes wide. 'You really think I still give a shit about all that – about *them*? It was the best bloody thing that ever happened to me. It got me out of this hellhole. I should be fuckin' thanking them.'

'And yet, here you are.'

'For Lily, Lo. And for *you*. On the train trip back, I realised how fucked it was to expect you to face this on your own. I came here to support you. You said you wanted me at the funeral.'

I scoffed.

'It's true, Lo. And everything else is too. Do you genuinely think I'd do something like that to her for *revenge*?'

I stared at the man before me. He seemed like an entirely different person to the one who had been goading me and excusing his lies only minutes before. He was hurt. And shocked – shocked that I would even contemplate the things I had accused him of.

'Then why *did* you do it?' I asked. 'If it wasn't revenge? Giving me the journals, taking me to the clearings, convincing me to post the packages?'

'Because I believe Lily.'

A startling realisation dawned on me. It was a feeling deep within my gut that I just couldn't shake. Every time I attempted to quash the words in my mind, they would bubble back up to the surface – loud and assured.

Jarrah Watson was telling the truth.

I didn't understand it. I *couldn't* understand it. And yet, in my heart of hearts, I believed Jarrah. But still, none of it made any fucking sense. I slumped down under the shade of the bower's trees and gave Jarrah one final chance to explain things – to help me finally understand.

To his credit, he did.

Jarrah *had* been to the clearings before, but he swore that he wasn't the one who had carved the symbols into the trees or created the markings on the ground. He just needed to see the area for himself. When Lily had gone off the medication, and the memories had started flooding her mind, he'd been sceptical of her claims and had decided to take things into his own hands.

He went into that rainforest – without Lily's knowledge – having gleaned enough information from her to navigate the area. When he saw the clearings with his own eyes, he was appalled with himself for not believing her and for instead assuming she was losing her mind. He decided to do anything he could to protect her.

In theory, it made sense. But I still didn't know if I could trust him. I'd been fucked over far too many times. So, despite what my gut was telling me, I remained sceptical.

He also admitted to carving the marks in Lily's back. The ones I had seen and photographed. But he was adamant that Lily had asked him to do it, just like she'd asked him to submit her artwork to the show. The markings were protection runes, and he only carved them when Lily had threatened that she would do them herself if he didn't.

He took the threat seriously. After all, it wasn't the first time Lily had hurt herself.

The patch of missing flesh finally made sense.

CHAPTER 71

'She turned up on my doorstep the day she had the dream about the ritual in the clearing – the one I told you about,' Jarrah said. 'The same day that she first noticed the brandings.'

'Wait,' I replied. 'I thought *you* did them.'

'No, I did the rune carvings. The ones you saw. The cult's marks were different – like a cattle brand. It was the flower symbol in the clearings. The Seed of Life. You never saw it on her back, but I'm guessing you saw the remnants of it?'

I nodded, remembering the wound on the small of her back.

'She had seven circles,' Jarrah continued. 'One brand for every hunt she was forced to participate in. Just like she said in her diaries.'

'And what? She just randomly decided she wanted seven more and asked you to do it?'

'They were protection symbols, Lo.'

'Fat lot of good that did.'

'Not for her. For the children from the seven hunts she participated in. She knew they'd die eventually. After all, she knew she was supposed to kill her first victim this year – when she received her eighth branding.'

I remembered the words Lily had written in the journals: 'I'd rather die than receive that mark.'

Was that why she had made Jarrah submit her drawing? Because she knew the cult would kill her for exposing the truth? Was her death actually a suicide?

'I think she saw the protection runes as some form of atonement,' Jarrah went on, interrupting my thoughts. 'Carved into her flesh – just like the cult's brandings had been. It was stupid, but after what she did to her back, I wasn't gonna leave her to her own devices again.'

I looked over at Dan, and he nodded solemnly.

'When I opened my front door that day, she practically collapsed in my arms,' Jarrah continued. 'Which was when I noticed that her back was covered in blood. She'd tried to bandage it, but there was just too much – it had soaked through everything, even her clothes.'

'Jesus,' I said. 'Why didn't she go to the bloody hospital?'

'She was terrified, Lo. She didn't know who she could trust.'

'Please tell me you at least took her there?'

'I tried, believe me. But she wouldn't go. The closest hospital to me was still part of her father's network. Besides, she didn't want anything on her records.'

'So what? You just patched her up yourself?'

'No, my med student friend came over and helped her out.' I noticed he'd nervously looked at Dan. 'Y'know,' he continued. 'Cleaned it up, bandaged it properly, got her on some antibiotics.'

'Your drug dealer, you mean?'

He sighed and nodded.

'And I'm guessing he's not the kind of guy who'd feel particularly comfortable talking to the police or being an expert witness in a criminal case, right?'

Jarrah nodded again.

How convenient, I thought.

'At the very least please tell me you took photos,' I pleaded.

'Yeah, of course I did.'

'Then why the fuck didn't you give them to me to include in the packages? It's better proof than all of the other stuff combined!'

'Yeah, right. The only thing it's proof of is that I have photos of a dead girl's freshly mutilated back. So excuse me for not sharing.

It doesn't matter that she did it herself. Your fuckhead of a father and the rest of the pigs were already trying to pin her murder on me based on the runes.'

I opened my mouth, but he continued.

'You do realise that if I hadn't been photographed at that party on Saturday night I'd probably be lying in an intensive care unit now, right? And that everyone would have thought I was her killer?'

I didn't know what to think any more.

'Sure,' Jarrah continued, 'that poor carny would still be up and around. But if it's him versus me, I know which one of us I'd prefer to be a bloody vegetable.'

'I'm not talking about the photos of her back after she removed the cult's brandings,' I said. 'I'm talking about the photos *of* the brandings.'

'What photos of the brandings? There aren't any.'

'What do you mean?' I asked. A strange sensation crept along my skin. 'You didn't take photos of the brandings when you saw them?'

'No, that's the thing – I never saw the brandings themselves. Just the pulpy mess where they'd been. She started hacking away at her back the second she saw them in the bathroom mirror – after her dream. She told me she grabbed one of her dad's razor blades and just went to fucking town on it.'

I felt like the ground had fallen out from under me. I locked eyes with an equally bewildered Dan and realised that he was thinking the exact same thing. It made sense. It all finally made fucking sense. Jarrah hadn't poisoned Lily with his lies. It was the other way around.

'You never saw the cult's brandings?' The question felt like it was caught in my throat.

'No. I never bloody said I did.'

'Fuck,' Dan mumbled under his breath.

'What?' Jarrah asked, turning to face him.

'I thought you said you'd seen them. I mean, how else did you know about them?'

'Uh, because Lily told me? What the fuck's the issue?'

I could already feel tears forming in my eyes. My breathing had once again grown ragged. I needed to stop the panic attack, but it was already taking over.

I hadn't realised it, but I'd wanted to believe Jarrah more than anything in the world. Simply because it was the only thing that could possibly excuse what I had done to Sharon. The appalling words I had spoken that had driven her to attempt to take her own life.

And yet, in a cruel twist of fate, Jarrah's words *had* been true. But so had the things the men at the funeral had said. The men that Jarrah had condemned. They were *both* telling the truth, but neither realised it. Instead, they assumed the other was at best a liar and at worst a monster.

But there was a common denominator – the *real* monster.

Lily.

It was her. All of this was her. Or, at least, her mental illness.

'Will someone tell me what the fuck is going on?' Jarrah snapped.

I looked up at him through tear-filled eyes. 'They were telling the truth, Jarrah. Lily *was* sick.'

'No. No, she wasn't!'

'I mean . . .' Dan began.

'She *wasn't*!'

'The back incident happened after she went off her medication, right?' I asked.

'Yeah, obviously. But that doesn't m–'

'Doesn't mean what? That she suffered a psychotic break when she went off her meds and started self-harming?'

'Self-harm's slitting your bloody wrists and cutting your thighs or some shit. It's not fucking mutilating a huge patch of skin on your lower back for no apparent reason.'

'Her father said her illness made her believe things that weren't true.'

'But it *was* true!'

'The story about her not noticing the markings never made sense, Jarrah. I said as much when you told me. But I believed you because I thought I'd seen them for myself.'

'That's why I didn't bloody correct you! Because I knew you'd never believe me and I needed to get you into that clearing so you could see the *actual* proof.'

'Is it proof though?'

'Of course it's bloody proof!'

'I dunno, Jarrah. That part never really made sense either. Why would they mark the place like that – leave all that evidence lying around? If anyone stumbled across it, they'd be bound to ask questions.'

'Because it's the fuckin' middle of nowhere and they think they're fuckin' bulletproof!'

'Maybe. But there's still something off about those carvings in the trees. Why would there be so many of them? What purpose could they possibly serve?'

'I dunno. Maybe it represents every kid they've fucking sacrificed?'

'That symbol's all throughout Lily's journals – scribbled over and over again – just like the "Song of Solomon" verses.'

'So, what are you trying to say? That Lily did them?'

'I'm just pointing out that she was clearly displaying obsessive and compulsive tendencies. It could just be another symptom of her going off her meds.'

'No. She wouldn't do that. She wouldn't lie to me about it.'

'I'm not saying she lied, Jarrah. Her father said she was delusional. She might not have even known she was the person who had carved them.'

'Michael is the one who's fucking delusional! He's a monster, and I know how to prove it. He has the brandings, Lo. Lily was sure of it. I'll fucking kidnap the piece of shit and show it to the world.'

'I've seen Michael's back, Jarrah. There's nothing there – no brands, no symbols – *nothing*. Just like there wasn't anything on Lily's back. It was all in her fucking mind.'

My words rippled around the bower and silenced the two men. They stood, staring at me – a mixture of shock and confusion etched on their faces. They shared a brief glance before turning back to face me.

'Bullshit,' Jarrah seethed, the slight quiver in his voice betraying his conviction.

'It's true.'

'No, you're full of sh–'

'When did you last see Michael's back?' Dan asked.

'The day before yesterday.'

'Uh,' Dan began awkwardly. 'Do I wanna know how? Or should I just –'

'He showered in the bloody cottage before he got changed for the press conference,' I snapped. 'I needed to use the bathroom, so I pounded on the door assuming it was my dad. When he opened it, he was only wearing a towel.'

'Oh.'

'I got a good look at his back – there was *nothing* there. I'm sure of it.'

'You're a fucking liar,' Jarrah growled.

'Why the fuck would I lie?'

'I dunno, Marlowe. Maybe because you're one of them?'

'Oh, for fuck's –'

'Think about it, Dan,' Jarrah interrupted, turning to face him.

'Jarrah,' Dan warned.

'No, seriously. I mean, it all adds up.'

'No, it doesn't,' Dan replied. 'None of it does. You've gotta let this shit go. You're getting paranoid. Lily was obviously sick. And I know you thought you were helping her but – I mean – fuck, man . . .'

A flash of rage illuminated Jarrah's face, and he opened his mouth to say something.

'What?' Dan barked. 'You gonna accuse me of being a cult member too?'

He shook his head. 'You know what she's like,' he said, almost pleadingly.

'Yeah.' Dan sighed. 'I do. It's how I know she's not in a fucking cult.'

The dam finally burst as the realisation of what I'd done to Sharon hit me once more. Sobs were choking out of my mouth, and my arms were tightly wrapped around my knees. I couldn't even bear to look at Jarrah any more. I could see how delusional he seemed and was kicking myself for not recognising it before. I'd been so caught up by his story – by Lily's story. I had fallen for its allure, just like him. And it had almost killed me.

Jarrah took a step towards me and crouched down. He pointed a threatening finger right in my face. I refused to meet his eyes.

'Cut the fucking crocodile tears. I know what you're doing. I'm not fucking stupid, Marlowe. What did they offer you? What could possibly be worth the blood that's on your hands?'

He grabbed my wrists, and I tried to yank them away. He held both of my hands up to my face. Dan moved towards us.

'You see it, Marlowe?' Jarrah hissed. 'You see the blood?'

Dan grabbed him by the shoulders and pulled him back. I was finally able to wrestle my hands away, and I held them against my pounding heart. My breaths choked in and out. Tears streamed down my face.

'I'm going to show the world what's on your hands, Marlowe,' Jarrah threatened as Dan dragged him away from me. 'They're going to know exactly who you are and exactly what you did.'

'Shut the fuck up, Jarrah,' Dan shouted. 'Get the fuck off this property or I'll call the bloody cops. Get the first train back to Sydney and get some fucking help. You're losing it, man.'

Dan dragged Jarrah away from the bower and I could still hear him pleading his case. He was screaming about the lyrebird. If he'd still been there, I would have told him the mimicked screams were likely

Lily's – maybe even from the day we were accosted by leeches as kids. I stared down at the palms of my hands – just as Sharon had – they were shaking. Somewhere behind me, the sounds of footsteps echoed.

I spun around and was shocked to see the figure emerging around the corner.

CHAPTER 72

'You okay, kiddo?' Owen asked, his face contorted in concern.

'What do you want, Owen? Besides fucking eavesdropping.'

'I saw you come back here and wanted to talk to you,' he said, walking towards me. 'But when I saw who you were meeting, I thought I'd better stick around. Y'know, just in case.'

'Well thanks for stepping in, mate. You were a huge help.'

'I didn't think you'd want me to interfere,' he said, absentmindedly touching the bruise on his eye. 'Not after last time. Besides, your attack mutt seemed to have things under control.'

I rolled my eyes.

'Must be nice to know he chose you over his boyfriend.'

'Don't fucking start.'

He held up his hands and eased himself down onto the ground next to me. The scent of his aftershave made me feel sick. He knocked his knee against mine, and I pulled it away.

'I saw what happened at the funeral,' he said. 'So, they finally told you everything, huh?'

'Apparently so.'

'I tried to warn you, Lo. The day before yesterday. I said it'd all make sense.'

'What part of this makes sense?'

'Yeah,' he nodded. 'Fair call.'

'I just don't understand why they kept it all a secret,' I said. 'I mean, was it Michael? Was he scared it was going to affect his professional reputation if people found out his own daughter was a nutjob?'

'From everything I've heard it sounds like it came from your father – and that the rest of the police force backed him up.'

'But why?'

'Because they knew what would have happened if those marks got out there – no matter where they came from. The madness it would have caused. And when Jarrah was cleared, and the cause of death came in, they realised her murder was likely unrelated. They didn't want it distracting from finding her actual killer. They knew stuff would likely come out during the trial but, until then, they didn't want the media anywhere near it.'

'Then how the fuck do you know so much?'

'Because of you.'

'What do you mean?'

'The night of the attack on the carnies, I went back to my hotel and called my editor. I told him everything you'd told me.'

I frowned at him.

'Don't worry. I didn't tell him who my source was.'

I nodded – not that it mattered any more.

'Of course, at the time, I didn't realise you suspected Michael and the rest of those men. But Paul knew all about Lily's problems and accusations and knew what I was talking about. In fact, it turns out it was how she got the internship. Her father was convinced that if she got away from the town and had something to focus on she'd go back on her meds and everything would go back to normal.'

'What about Michael and Paul's hunts in the rainforest?' I asked.

'Yeah, in hindsight that was a really fuckin' unfortunate thing for me to bring up, hey?'

'No shit.'

'I mean, I've seen photos.' He shrugged. 'Whole bloody office is forced to sit through them when he gets back. It's mainly deer and roo, but I've seen a few rabbits and foxes – real ones. Y'know, bushy tails, pointy ears, whiskers? Cute little buggers. Frankly, I feel sorry for them.'

I let out a long sigh and stretched my legs out in front of me. The two of us sat there in silence. Both lost in our own thoughts. I closed my eyes and fought the urge to roll up into a little ball and sleep under the shade of the bower's trees.

'Do you still think the carny's innocent?' Owen asked. 'After everything you now know?'

My eyes sprang open. I didn't know the answer any more. Everything told me that Steve had been telling the truth – but I'd been wrong about so many things. About so many people. What I thought didn't matter. Not any more.

'I honestly don't know,' I said, after a while.

Owen began to nod but was interrupted by someone emerging from behind the school building. Dan.

Owen leaned in close. 'I think that's my cue to leave,' he whispered, before pointing at his eye. 'Not keen for another one of these.'

I nodded, and he quickly got to his feet before retreating in the opposite direction.

'Jarrah's gone,' Dan said, addressing me. 'Hopefully for good, but I'll walk you back to the cottage or your car just in case.'

I nodded, and his eyes fell on Owen's back.

'Oi, pretty boy. Wait up.'

Owen spun around, and I braced myself for what was to come.

'Sorry about your face, mate,' Dan said. 'Absolute dog act on my part.'

Owen nodded, slightly perplexed. 'Yeah, well I'm sorry for . . . I'm just sorry too.'

'Well, at the very least you now know that you'll never have to pay for another Kilmagoon at the Blue Diamond.'

That artificial smile was finally back. 'Is that so?'

'Yeah, just ask for a purple punch.'

Owen laughed. 'Just might have to take you up on that.'

He gave a final wave to the two of us and walked away. Dan sat down next to me. He wrapped his arms around me, but I didn't fight back. I didn't have the energy to.

'I'm so fuckin' sorry, Lo.'

When he finally pulled away, I could see he'd been crying. He went out of his way to pretend otherwise.

'Remember the bowerbird?' he asked, way too cheerfully. 'I was always so jealous that you saw it.'

I wiped my own tears away and took a deep breath.

'I never saw it, Dan.'

His brow furrowed. 'What do you mean?'

'It wasn't real. I made it up.'

'Bullshit.'

'There was nothing out here, Dan. No woven nest, no collection of blue and gold trinkets, and definitely no beautiful ink-hued bird.'

'But that doesn't make sense. Why did the teachers never call you out on it?'

'Because doing so would have exposed their lie.'

'Shit.'

'Yeah.'

He ran his hands through his hair and stared around the bower in disbelief. It was like the entire area had transformed before his eyes. As if it had lost its magic. He let out a small laugh and shook his head.

'Why'd you do it?' he asked. 'What was the point of lying about it?'

'I dunno, man. I guess because it was a better story than the truth?'

He looked like he'd just found out the tooth fairy wasn't real.

'I mean, I remember being so disappointed when I saw there was nothing there,' I continued. 'Like, I felt so betrayed that we'd all been lied to. And when I came back in, you were sitting on that sickbed nursing your bee sting and looking at me so expectantly. I didn't want to let you down – to make you feel the way that I had felt. The real story fuckin' sucked, so I just – I dunno – made up a better one?'

'Fuck, Lo.'

It was almost as if my childhood lie had been the most shocking reveal of the day.

We talked for a long time after that. About Jarrah – about Lily – about Owen, and about the ways we'd all been played. Dan said he hadn't seen Jarrah for years before he randomly showed up at the Blue Diamond the night after Lily's death – the same day Jarrah had been questioned at Warilla police station, and the same day he'd given me the journals.

They'd hooked up that night and, in the ensuing days, had spent a lot of time talking on the phone. Dan admitted that he'd been smitten by Jarrah's attention – it was just like old times. But he grew suspicious when Jarrah became increasingly fixated on me. He was clearly using Dan to gain more information. Combined with my own caginess and odd encounters with Owen, Dan realised that something was up. He was determined to get to the bottom of it.

He'd stolen the journals. Not for Jarrah, but for himself. Jarrah had already confessed that he'd given them to me but refused to divulge their contents. So, when the opportunity presented itself, Dan took it. He took *them*. Needless to say, he regretted it. And he had no idea what to do with the information he'd discovered.

Ultimately, he decided to wait until after Lily was buried – out of respect for her. But, when he witnessed the argument at the funeral, he finally had the courage to confront Jarrah and find out what the hell had been going on. While I'd so desperately tried to retrieve the packages, Jarrah had told him everything. And – for the most part – Dan had believed him.

It had been his idea to text me to allow Jarrah to plead his side of the story. But Dan *hadn't* told him what he had used to lure me there.

He assured me that the journals were still safely tucked away at his house. He also promised that he'd give them back to me straight away. But I no longer cared.

I mean, why would I? They were just the rantings of a madwoman.

After apologising for the billionth time, Dan finally walked me back to my car. Thankfully, there was no sign of Jarrah. He offered to escort me to the cottage, but I assured him that I'd be fine. I drove off, struck by the realisation that our friendship would never be the same.

I was too exhausted to cry.

CHAPTER 73

When I returned home, I was shocked to discover my father sitting on the lounge room floor. My packages were strewn around him. One of them was open and he was flipping through the scans of the photos and journal pages. He looked up at me – his face grave – and shook his head.

'Jesus Christ, Lo.'

'I'm so sorry. I, I thought –'

'You thought what? That this was real? That we were killing *kids*? My fucking name is in here.'

'I'm sorry,' I repeated, tears streaming from my eyes. 'I fucked up so bad.'

'How could you think this? I'm your *father* – I fucking raised you.'

'I didn't think you killed them. Lily thought you were just helping them to cover it up.'

'That doesn't make it any fucking better! You still *believed* that?'

'I *saw* you cover up her marks. You made me lie about them. What was I supposed to think?'

'That I was doing my fucking job?'

I broke down in tears as I slumped onto the floor in front of him. The sight of the packages made me physically ill. I wanted to vomit but, as my weeping racked my body, I could only manage to dry retch. I felt like I wasn't getting enough air and clawed at my throat.

'Breathe, Marlowe,' my father commanded.

I tried to nod, but my whole body shuddered with each sob.

'Oh, for fuck's sake,' my dad muttered, before climbing to his feet.

The pictures of Lily's mutilated back fell from his lap. They only made me hyperventilate more.

'I – I'm so sorry,' I wailed, as he kneeled beside me.

He placed his hand on my shoulder and I winced at his touch.

'Come on, Lo. Breathe.'

I tried to inhale deeply, but the air got stuck in my throat and I choked it out in pathetic sobs. I felt like I was about to black out. I was horrified to realise that I wanted to.

'This is getting fucking ridiculous. Calm. Down.'

I tried to respond to him, but the words wouldn't form. The corners of my vision began to fade. It was as if a lace curtain was slowly descending over my eyes. I couldn't even tell if I was *trying* to breathe any more. The world was slowly disappearing.

With one swift movement, my father slapped his hand against my back – hard. I slumped forward from the force, but the shock was enough to kick-start my breathing. I lay there, my face pressed against the carpet while the oxygen slowly returned to my brain.

My dad grabbed the back of my dress and tugged me upright.

'There you go,' he said, rubbing my back far too roughly. 'That's it. In and out. Nice and slow. You're okay.'

Nothing about this was okay.

I wrenched myself away from him and gulped down more air. The fog clouding my mind was slowly dissipating. My eyes scanned the parcels covering the floor.

'That's not all of them,' I managed to choke out. 'I sent more than that.'

'I know. I couldn't get them all. The bloke you spoke to at the delivery centre called me the second you left and handed over the ones that were still there.'

'But what about the rest?'

'It's too late. Some of the local ones have already been delivered.'

'Does the Williams family know?'

'No. But they will soon.'

'I have to warn them. I have to try to apologise.'

'No, Marlowe. You've done more than enough to that family. You're not going anywhere.'

He grabbed my purse from the floor and took out my phone and car keys.

'What the hell are you doing?'

'You can't be trusted,' he said, placing them both in his pocket.

'But I know what really happened at the showground that night. She wasn't killed by one of her crystals, she was killed by –'

'A salt lick. Yeah, we know.'

As I opened my mouth to protest, we both heard the back door open.

'Just me,' Nathan called out.

My dad got to his feet as Nathan walked into the lounge room. He noticed the parcels straight away and when he saw the picture of Lily's back, he looked at me.

'What do you want?' my father snapped.

'Oh – uh, you're needed at Warilla. Sounds pretty urgent.'

'I bloody bet it is,' my dad said, locking eyes with me. He turned back to face Nathan. 'Have you finished your incident report about the accident at the funeral?'

Nathan nodded.

'All right. I'm gonna need you to stay here.'

'The station? I wasn't planning on go–'

'No. The cottage. I need you to keep an eye on Marlowe.'

'Dad . . .'

'She's not to leave here. Understood?'

Nathan nodded, but he looked unsure.

'Right. I'm off.' My father sighed, before turning to face me. 'No doubt to clean up your mess.'

'I'm sor–'

'Yeah. You should be.'

He stormed out the door.

I stared at the packages. I had to do something. I had to warn the Williamses before it was too late.

'What the bloody hell was all that about?' Nathan asked me as the front door slammed shut.

'Where's Sharon?'

'I dunno, back at her house, I guess?'

'Why isn't she in the fucking hospital?'

'Uh, because *I* took the brunt of the fall? There wasn't a bloody scratch on her.'

'Shouldn't she be on suicide watch?'

'Wait, what?'

'She tried to kill herself in front of thousands of people!'

'What the hell makes you think that?'

'What do you fucking mean? She tried to walk out onto a six-lane highway!'

'Not on purpose. She was off her bloody tits. Poor thing didn't know which way was up.'

'No. She did it on purpose.'

'Why the fuck would she?'

'Because of me,' I said, tears brimming in my eyes once more. 'Because of what I said at the funeral.'

He shook his head. 'Can someone bloody explain what the hell has been going on?'

'I'll tell you everything if you take me to the Williamses' home. My dad took the keys to the LandCruiser, but I need to get there – *now*.'

'Fuck, no. He'll bloody kill me!'

I knew I had to appeal to his ego. 'You saved her once. Now's your chance to do it again. Local media have already received these parcels – when they begin reporting on them, it's going to push her over the edge.'

His eyes scanned the parcels.

'They're filled with Jarrah's lies,' I continued. 'The lies that drove Lily to self-harm and the lies that likely led to her death. The piece I read at the funeral came from them. I think it's what made Sharon try to kill herself.'

He stared at me for a long time, his eyes probing my features.

'There's no one next door,' he finally said. 'But I can get one of the other constables from Warilla to go up there and do a mental health check.'

'It'll take too long for them to get there – it might be too late. We're way closer.'

'Well, I'll bloody call them, then.'

'No. It *has* to come from me. I have to do it face to face.'

'Why?'

I looked down at the packages, then stared Nathan straight in the eyes.

'Because I was the one who sent them. And I'm the only person who can explain why.'

CHAPTER 74

Nathan and I jumped into his police car and sped through the streets of Kiama with the sirens blaring and lights flashing. I'd never travelled those familiar roads that fast before and, as we entered the Kiama Bends, I felt the telltale signs of a panic attack grip my chest. I clamped my eyes shut and tried to focus on my breathing, but that only amplified my motion sickness.

As we raced past the spot where my mother – and so many others – had died, a collision erupted in my mind. It felt so real that I physically flinched and, as if bracing for the impact, lifted my hands in front of my face.

To both of our surprise, I didn't vomit heading up the mountain to the Williamses' farmstead, though it was definitely touch and go for a while. When the road transformed from bitumen to gravel, Nathan reduced his speed, and we soon pulled up to the property's imposing gates. Nathan wound down his window and the fresh mountain air was like a salve for my nauseous body. He leaned over and pressed the intercom's buzzer. We both looked at the camera mounted above the gates. They lurched to life and sprang open before us – splitting the wrought-iron number nine in half.

We continued up the driveway until we finally broke the tree line. In contrast to the previous day's fog, everything was bright, crisp and clear. They really did live on the top of the world. And yet, I was drawn back towards those trees. Back to the clearings, and what Lily had done there. It had felt so real. I suppose because it was – at least to her.

We pulled into the farmstead's entrance and parked out the front of the self-contained guesthouse. The front door to the main house opened. To my surprise, Michael, Mark and Peter all emerged. But there was no sign of Sharon.

I noticed the confusion etched on their faces as we approached them. They looked back and forth between each other, their eyebrows cocked, waiting for someone to say something. Finally, Michael stepped forward.

'What are you doing here, Marlowe?'

'I need to talk to you. I need to tell you something. It's about Sharon.'

'Where's your father?' Mark interrupted.

The front door opened, and a solemn-looking man I'd never seen before emerged. He wasn't wearing black, so he clearly hadn't been at the funeral. There was something about him that I couldn't quite put my finger on.

'Are we ready?' He stopped when he saw me. 'What's happening?'

'Did John send you, Nathan?' Michael asked.

'Nah. I had to bring Lo up. She needs to talk to you.'

'It's really important,' I repeated. 'It's about Sharon.'

'Where is Sharon?' Michael asked the stranger.

'In her room.'

'And she's . . .' Michael trailed off. 'Everything's . . . ?'

The stranger nodded.

Michael nodded to himself and looked at his watch.

'Doctor Williams, please. I really need to talk to you. It's important.'

He looked at me as if he had only just remembered my presence.

'Marlowe, I need you to go inside for a moment, okay? Grab yourself a drink and make yourself comfortable in the living room.'

'No, I need to –'

'Please, Marlowe. I need to speak to Nathan for a moment. I promise I'll listen to whatever you need to say when I'm finished.'

'Well, can I at least stay?'

'For fuck's sake,' Mark spat. 'Just bloody go inside, Lo.'

Michael glared at Mark before turning back to face me. He placed his hand on my shoulder. There was something in his eyes – something that made me want to give in.

'Please, Marlowe.'

'Okay.'

'Thank you,' he said. I could tell that he meant it. There was a hint of relief in his voice. And yet, it still felt like it was something I was going to regret.

Peter opened the door and I begrudgingly walked underneath his arm. After it had slowly shut behind me, I turned and could see all of the men looking at me through the panes of glass. They were waiting for me to leave before they started talking. I sighed and walked away.

CHAPTER 75

It had been years since I'd been in that house, and yet it instantly felt familiar. I'd spent so much time there as a kid, it had clearly made its mark on my mind. The open-plan kitchen was immediately to the right of the short entranceway, so I walked to the cluster of cabinets lining the wall and pulled out a glass tumbler. I walked over to the large island separating the kitchen and the dining room and filled the glass with tap water from the sink. It was filtered and fizzed like champagne.

I carried my tumbler over to the sprawling glass doors and marvelled at the view. Below the tree line and rolling farmland, Seven Mile Beach looked like it stretched on forever. In front of me, the infinity pool glistened welcomingly in the sun. On any other day, I would have killed for a dip.

I walked over to the oversized leather lounge in front of the fireplace. I placed my glass down on a coaster and admired the strange statuette sitting on the coffee table. It was a bronze hare that was coquettishly looking over its shoulder. I picked it up – surprised to find that it was lighter than I anticipated. I juggled it between my hands wishing that the men would hurry up. I sat the hare back down and paused. Something had caught my eye.

I tentatively approached the mantel, as if mistrusting what I had seen. But the closer I got to the wine bottle, the surer I became. There was no doubt that it was the same type as the broken one I'd found in the clearing – the one with the person in hunting attire on the label.

My prediction had been correct – they were wearing a fox mask. A black leather one. Identical to what Lily had described and drawn in her journals. Exactly the same as the ones that she claimed the cult members had worn. I peered at the writing on the label. Having seen the bottom half in the clearing, I had a pretty good idea of what it said. Sure enough, those four familiar words were there: 'Catch Us the Foxes'.

'It's what started all of this,' a small voice said behind me.

I was so shocked that I jumped and swore out loud. Regaining my composure, I turned around. Sharon was standing next to the lounge wearing a flowing silk dressing-gown. Her feet were bare, which may have explained why I hadn't heard her approach.

'Mrs Williams.'

'You're welcome to pick it up,' she said, walking towards me and gesturing towards the wine bottle.

There was something strange about her movement. It was slow and languid, and matched the slight slur to her speech. Nathan had been right; she was clearly off her face.

And yet, as she walked towards me – seemingly floating across the polished concrete floor – I noticed how serene she looked. There wasn't a hint of the anger she had shown towards me at the funeral, nor the hysterical confusion she'd displayed as she sobbed in Michael's arms at the side of the highway. It was perplexing and utterly haunting.

'Go on,' she said, as she stopped beside me. 'It's my finest work. A private vintage grown on this very mountainside. The volcanic soil is particularly pure up here, and it gives the wine a delightful acidity. It lends it an almost savoury palate. It truly is one of a kind.'

I carefully picked up the wine bottle – cradling it as if it were a newborn child. Sharon seemed to appreciate the reverence with which I regarded it and stared at it like a proud parent. But then her expression soured.

'She must have seen that damn thing every day of her life. Before her broken mind twisted it into that horrifying tale.'

I looked into her eyes. Tears were brimming.

'How could she turn something so beautiful into something so heinous?' she asked. 'Where would such a thing even come from?'

She stared at me, expectantly. I realised that they weren't rhetorical questions.

'I – uh . . .'

She frowned at me, seemingly disappointed, and held out her hands. I looked at them, puzzled, before realising that she wanted the wine. I carefully passed her the bottle, and she ran her thumb over the label – encircling the person in the fox mask.

'When did you realise?' she asked.

For a second, I wasn't sure whether she was talking to the bottle or me. 'Realise what?'

'Who really killed my daughter?'

My face crinkled in confusion, but she was too fixated on the bottle to notice.

'It's why you read that poem at the funeral, wasn't it?'

'What? I –'

'You spoke to that poor young man, didn't you?' she asked, her eyes still trained on the bottle. 'He told you about the argument. Their caravan was so close to the stables, he had to have heard it.'

'Yeah, b–'

'You have to know I had no idea they'd retaliate like that. I mean, I didn't even know about the blood on her dress until it was too late.'

Once again, I opened my mouth to say something, but she continued.

'They wouldn't tell me anything. They deliberately withheld information because they thought they were protecting me.' She shook her head. 'If only they knew.'

She began to scratch at the label. As she dug her manicured thumbnail in, the head with the fox mask was severed. There was the most awful feeling in the pit of my stomach.

'If I'd known they were closing in on someone I would have said something,' she said. 'I just – I just needed more time – I thought I had more time.' She peeled the rest of the label away. 'And then that poor young man from the ghost train. I never meant for it to happen. I never meant for *either* of them to happen.'

She locked eyes with me. I knew what was coming.

'Please know that it was an accident, Marlowe,' she pleaded, tears streaming from her eyes. 'When I found her in that stable, she was like a feral animal. The things she was accusing me of – they were unspeakable!'

My mouth sprang open as my jaw quivered.

'She attacked me when I denied it,' Sharon continued. 'So, I pushed her – all I did was push her to stop her from hurting me – but she slipped. She slipped and fell on the pine needles and hit her head on –'

'A salt lick,' I said, surprised to hear my own voice.

She looked at me, wide-eyed, and nodded.

'What happened to it?' I asked. 'It wasn't there when I found her.'

'It broke in half when she hit it, and I panicked. I – I touched it. It was covered in her blood. I took the pieces and threw them off the cliff.'

I clamped my eyes shut and tried to control my breathing.

'I – I never meant to hurt her. I swear. Or that poor boy in the coma. If I'd said something sooner . . .'

I opened my eyes when she didn't continue. She wanted something from me. Forgiveness? Understanding? Atonement?

'I saw the police car pull up,' she said. 'I know they're here for me.'

Before I could say or do anything, she'd already smashed the bottle against the mantel. Wine and glass shards sprayed everywhere, and I instinctively raised my hands over my face. I could feel fragments embedding themselves into my forearms.

Then I heard the scream.

I pulled my hands away from my face and let out my own shriek. Sharon had plunged the top half of the shattered wine bottle into her neck. I watched on in horror as she ripped it from her flesh and collapsed onto the ground.

The blood.

The fucking blood.

I'd never seen anything like it before. It was far worse than anything dreamed up in a horror film. I stood there, dumbfounded, for far too long. It was like my body had forgotten how to move, and time had stopped. But, finally, I dived to the floor and crawled towards Sharon. Her eyes were staring at something unseen – just like Lily's had. I reached out to try and stop the blood gushing from her neck. Just as my hands touched the wound, I was shocked to feel a pair of arms wrap around my body and pull me back.

Nathan crouched down and wrapped his large hands around Sharon's neck. But it was too late – she was still staring at nothing. I allowed myself to be pulled into Michael's arms as he cradled me against his chest, just as he had his wife on the side of that road. I was screaming at the top of my lungs – over and over again – but I couldn't hear the sound.

I looked down at my hands. They were covered in blood. Just like Jarrah had said.

EPILOGUE

The Sydney Opera House's concert hall was completely silent. Every eye in the venue was fixed on Marlowe Robertson as she stared at the palms of her hands. Those in the front row could see that she was shaking.

A hand reached out from the seat next to her and grasped her palm. She looked up – shocked – as if she'd forgotten Michael Williams had been sitting next to her for the entire interview. The faintest smile graced her lips, and she turned to face the audience.

'I – I'm sorry,' she mumbled, her microphone only exacerbating the crack in her voice.

'We love you, Lo!' another audience member yelled, prompting further shouts of encouragement from the crowd.

She pulled her hand away from Michael and made a heart sign with her fingertips – holding it up to the audience. She could see on the monitor that one of the cameras had zoomed in on the gesture. On the live feed, the online chat began spamming '<3'.

'Are you okay to go on?' the presenter asked, no doubt wary of the time. 'I can't imagine how difficult this must be for you, even seven years later.'

Marlowe looked at the woman and nodded.

'That's actually why it's so important for me to be sharing this story,' she said, before turning to address the crowd. 'It's why I wrote my book. Because this type of thing *needs* to be talked about – even when it's difficult to do so.'

Marlowe gestured at the screen behind her, which still contained the front cover of *The Showgirl's Secret*. She knew that her publicist would be pleased to see her getting in an extra plug for her book. Michael caught her eye, and she nodded slightly.

'It's also why Michael and I started The Lily Foundation,' she announced, hoping that the techs had changed the graphic to display the charity's website and social media handles. 'It's all about destigmatising mental illness and educating people on how to support their loved ones when they're facing this battle.'

'Because ultimately,' the presenter interjected, 'it is a battle that can be lost, isn't it?'

'Yes.' Marlowe nodded, recognising that the woman was trying to get her back on track. 'Unfortunately, both Lily *and* Sharon lost that battle.'

'And what were you thinking at that moment? When you were cradled in Michael's arms, staring down at Sharon's blood on your hands?'

'Honestly? I thought I was being punished.'

'But I thought you said you didn't believe in a higher power?'

'No, not by God. I thought I was being punished by Sharon.'

'But why?' the presenter asked.

'Because, at the time, I thought that I was the only person she had confessed to. So, by her killing herself, I thought that she was leaving me with that burden. That she knew that no one would believe me after all my other claims proved to be false. All I'd wanted was the truth, and she'd given it to me – but there was nothing I could do about it.'

The presenter nodded solemnly.

'Or so I thought. When my father turned up with the rest of the police, moments after she died, I was so confused. I couldn't figure out how they'd made it there so quickly.'

Marlowe turned to face Michael. He was wiping tears from his eyes.

'But they were there to arrest her, weren't they?' the presenter asked.

'Yeah.' Marlowe nodded. 'She'd confessed before Nathan and I had arrived. It was why my father had been called away. She had a session with her psychiatrist – the man I hadn't recognised – after the funeral. And she had admitted everything.'

'And what had prompted that confession? All those days after Lily's death?'

Marlowe noticed the glint in the presenter's eyes. She swallowed the bile that was gathering in her throat. On the screen, the seconds to the interview's end ticked away.

Marlowe fought back tears. 'It was me. The reading I'd done at the funeral. She thought I knew – it's why she tried to kill herself then.'

Tears streamed down Marlowe's face as the presenter rose to her feet and walked to the edge of the stage. The cameras followed her. It looked natural, but it was all pre-planned.

'And if it weren't for the investigative skills of Miss Robertson, coupled with the valiant actions of Leading Senior Constable Nathan Campbell, the identity of Lily Williams' killer would have died with her mother. It was only through Marlowe's tenacity, and this young officer's bravery, that Steve Masters' name was cleared.'

Marlowe's eyes flicked to the monitor as she watched the cameras pan to the front row. They zoomed in on the man sitting towards the end of the aisle, bookended by Barry Masters and his wife. Nathan looked surprisingly dapper in his formal police uniform and visibly puffed up as the camera focused on the bravery medal attached to his chest. Both of the Masters proudly placed an arm around him, and his face slowly turned red. The three had become close in the years since Steve's accident – the family that Nathan never had – and the Masters truly believed that by saving Sharon and allowing her to confess, Nathan had also saved their son.

The camera panned to Steve Masters. Alive, but not well. His traumatic brain injury necessitated the use of a wheelchair, and he was propped at the end of the row like an afterthought. When the camera zoomed in on his vacant stare, Marlowe found herself unable to look at the monitor. The presenter was spewing more drivel, but Marlowe had tuned it out. She was sick of seeing Steve used as a prop.

The entire crowd was cheering for him, but he had no idea.

After the presenter had milked Nathan and the Masters for all they were worth, she returned to her seat. Marlowe picked up the mug on the table in front of her and sipped the water inside. She took a deep breath. She knew what was coming.

'Now,' the presenter began, her brow narrowing, 'I think it's time for the tough questions, don't you?'

'Wait, those were the *easy* ones?' Marlowe asked, prompting laughter from the crowd.

'I'm curious what you would say to your detractors? The conspiracy theorists who seem convinced that you are now part of the cult that Lily detailed in her journals.'

Marlowe took a protracted sip of water. She knew how to milk things too.

'After all, it's difficult to deny the fact that your life has drastically changed in the wake of Lily and Sharon's deaths. I think most would argue for the better.'

'Would they?' Marlowe asked before placing her mug on the table. She looked out into the massive crowd and smiled. 'Well, ultimately, I empathise with the conspiracy theorists. Because I once *was* one of them. I know more than anyone how beguiling a good conspiracy can be, and that's why I included the bowerbird story in my book and continue to bring it up in talks like this. It serves to remind people that sometimes the truth simply isn't the best or most interesting story. Sometimes bone shards come from cows, not humans; sometimes disembodied screams come from birds, not ghosts; and sometimes the most horrible things in the world come not from reality, but from the psyche.'

The presenter nodded sagely.

'The harsh reality is that mental illness remains one of this nation's most insidious and prolific killers. The fact that we prefer to imagine that Lily and her mother were the victims of some sort of satanic, child-killing death cult, rather than two women struggling with mental illness, speaks volumes about society's perceptions of these issues.'

A murmur made its way around the audience, and a spattering of applause broke out.

'The things we should fear don't lurk in rainforests,' Marlowe continued. 'They lurk in our minds, and in the minds of our loved ones. I mean, you only have to look at me. I had the most textbook, cut and dried symptoms of PTSD after finding Lily. Yet, for some fucked-up reason, I thought that the only person who was truly trying to help me was actually trying to kill me.'

She turned and faced Michael.

'No, I was also trying to kill you,' he said.

'Oh my god, don't!' Marlowe chided, playfully slapping him on the wrist. 'They don't need any more bloody ammunition for their conspiracy theories!'

The audience erupted in laughter, and Michael sheepishly shrugged at the camera that was trained on him. Marlowe turned back to the presenter. She was stony-faced, but that may have just been the Botox.

'Through your work with The Lily Foundation, you've spoken in-depth about your own mental health issues and treatment, haven't you?' the presenter asked.

'Yes. When Michael and I started the foundation, we knew that transparency would be tremendously important. Over the years, I've shared both the ups and the downs. But, the fact of the matter remains, I wouldn't be sitting here today if I hadn't gone into treatment after witnessing Sharon's death. It's something that I have to deal with every single day – even all these years later – and I think it's important to be honest about that. It truly is a lifelong journey.'

As if on cue, the entire audience broke into applause.

'The Lily Foundation and – of course – you and Michael have done so much for mental health awareness in this country, particularly for those in rural areas. And I really do encourage everyone watching this – both here and at home – to go out and support the charity in any way you can. They really are changing people's lives, folks, and could always do with more donations and volunteers.'

'Oh, thank you,' Marlowe said, smiling warmly at the presenter. She glanced at the clock on the stage – the numbers had turned red – there wasn't long to go. She resisted the urge to scan the crowd.

'No, thank *you*, Marlowe and Michael, for your time on what I'm sure is a very difficult day. It's quite incredible that with Lily Day you've managed to transform such a tragic anniversary into a force of good.'

'I honestly think it's what Lily would have wanted,' Marlowe replied.

'Bullshit!' a voice yelled from the crowd.

Even without seeing him, Marlowe knew who it was.

'Lily and Sharon's blood is on your hands!' Jarrah Watson shouted.

More people joined in. It was only a small fraction of the crowd, but it was enough. Their voices reverberated around the concert hall as they repeated the words over and over again. Marlowe's eyes flicked to Michael. He was watching a group of security guards exit the wings. He looked calm on the surface, but Marlowe knew that didn't mean much.

'P-please,' the presenter began, her harried voice joining the din. 'Please, may I ask you to stop? This is *quite* inappropriate.'

A few counter-hecklers had tried to start their own chant, but the lack of organisation meant they petered out before long. Still, there were boos and jeers attempting to drown out the sounds of the protesters. In the distance, Marlowe could see that a few had brought crudely drawn banners. She looked at the monitor on the floor – one of the cameras had zoomed in on Jarrah. He was halfway up the stalls, right on the edge of the row. The security guards were descending on him, but he stood strong and continued the chant.

The view on the monitor changed, and Marlowe noticed a camera was pointing at her. She could see someone approaching on her left-hand side and turned to face them. It was a young Asian woman with a choppy bob – the skittish stagehand, seemingly there to escort her back to safety. She wouldn't go though. She refused to be intimidated by Jarrah.

Then she noticed what the stagehand was holding.

Before she had a chance to react, the stagehand threw the contents of the bucket onto Marlowe. She held her hands up in front of her as she leaped to her feet, but it did little to stop the substance from hitting her square in the chest. A few audience members screamed, and it was enough to disrupt the chant – if only for a few seconds.

Marlowe stood there, mouth agape, dripping in blood, which she prayed was fake. Michael grabbed her by the wrist to pull her to safety, but she wrenched her arm away. She wasn't going anywhere. On the monitor, all the shots were of her. Standing on that stage – covered in blood – while the protesters' chants rang out.

A small smile graced her lips.

'I want that fucker *fried*,' Michael shouted into his mobile.

He was standing alongside Marlowe as they rode the private elevator to the Park Hyatt's penthouse suites. He'd finally managed to drag her off the stage, and – after being locked down in a dressing room together while security cleared the protesters – they'd eventually been escorted through the bowels of the Opera House to a waiting limousine. Its cream leather seats were now dyed red.

'I don't give a damn that it wasn't real blood,' he snapped. 'It's still assault. And I don't care that he wasn't the one who did it – the stagehand was obviously working under his order. The fucking protest was just a distraction.'

He begrudgingly listened to the person on the phone, examining his three-piece suit in the elevator's mirror. It had received its own fair share of fake blood, but nowhere near as much as Marlowe's clothes.

'We've been putting up with this prick for years. These stupid fucking stunts every time he has a new art show. He lost the libel case against Marlowe's book. I want an AVO this time. No excuses.'

Before the person on the other end had a chance to reply, Michael hung up. He sighed and looked down at his watch. There was a large streak of blood on its face.

The elevator doors opened, and Michael gestured for Marlowe to go before him. She'd removed her leather jacket not long after she'd left the stage and it was slung over her forearm. He noticed that her long hair was still slick with the fake blood and that her black singlet was clinging to her flesh.

She spun around to face him as he stepped into the private lobby. '*I* could have told you that it wasn't real blood. Some got in my mouth.'

'I'm not sure if you heard, but they don't know if they got all the protesters,' Michael replied. 'The cops are worried some may have slipped out in the confusion. But Jarrah and the stagehand, as well as the majority of the ones with the banners, have all been brought in for questioning.'

'You know he's not going to stop doing this shit, right?'

Michael's smile was wry. 'Not everyone's as tenacious as you, Miss Robertson.'

'I dunno. These stunts are getting more and more outlandish.'

'More and more *desperate*, don't you mean? Have you seen the kinds of gallery shows he's been landing lately? Let's be real here, he doesn't give a fuck about Lily – he never did. This is all about him. It always was.'

Marlowe glanced around the space before lowering her voice. 'I'm just saying maybe don't underestimate him, okay? The dude's a total wildcard. You just never know what he's capable of.'

Michael leaned in close. 'Hmm, who does that sound like?'

Marlowe rolled her eyes and stepped away from him.

'Are you still okay to go to Government House tonight?' Michael asked. 'I mean, they will have seen what happened. It's already all over the news. So, if you were looking for an excuse to get out of it, you definitely have one.'

'Nah, I'm looking forward to it. And I'm sure as hell not going to let Jarrah get in the way of things.'

'Well, in that case, we better get cleaned up.' Michael reached into his pocket and pulled out the key to his suite.

'Oh,' Marlowe said, seemingly taken aback, 'I was thinking I could just show up like this. It suits me, don't you –'

'We're going to be late, Marlowe.'

She locked eyes with him but eventually fished her key card out of the jacket still slung over her arm. The two of them walked to their respective suites. As Marlowe heard Michael's door snap shut, she pushed hers open.

The Sydney Suite's loungeroom overlooked the iconic building that she and Michael had just left, and the floor-to-ceiling windows provided the perfect vantage point. Ferries languidly bobbed along the water, while seagulls hovered in the air, and tourists cluttered the footpaths of Circular Quay.

She headed towards the master bathroom and was once again floored by the view – this time, of the Sydney Harbour Bridge. Tiny people in jumpsuits were slowly climbing the arch. They looked like they were all tethered together – completely at the whim of the people they were bound to.

At the centre of the room was a free-standing bathtub that could comfortably fit at least four people. Marlowe was surprised to see that the round vessel had been partially filled with water. A bottle of Kilmagoon and a crystal glass rested on the side of the tub.

She approached the bath and dipped her arm into the water. It was lukewarm, so she turned the tap, and hot water began pouring out of the spout. She began peeling away her clothes, quietly amazed by just how much of the fake blood had managed to permeate them. She was frustrated that she'd been forced to wear her signature all-black. Her impromptu *Carrie* moment would have looked so much more impressive in white.

Carefully stepping into the vessel, Marlowe watched as the water was slowly dyed red. The bloody plumes that spiralled off her legs were perfectly contrasted against the pure white of the tub. As she caught her reflection in the bathroom mirror, she was shocked that her hair had caused a large amount of the red substance to drip down the small of her back. She felt goosebumps ripple across her flesh when she realised how similar it looked to the wound on Lily's back.

She tried to push the thought away, but it was replaced by something even worse. An image of the man in the suite next to her – washing away Jarrah's fake blood from his own silvery wounds. The very wounds she'd been lying about for years.

She thought about the first time she'd seen the eight circular brandings on Michael's lower back. It was in the cottage. When he'd answered the bathroom door in nothing more than a towel. She could never forget the shock she had felt when she finally saw them. All her fears confirmed in an instant – her life forever changed.

She knew before then, of course. Her memories of her time in that rainforest had come flooding back the moment Jarrah had first spoken about the hunts. She wanted to believe that it wasn't real, but when she noticed that Lily had replaced the linings of her journals, Marlowe knew that there'd be something hidden within – something for her eyes only. After all, only the person who had given Lily the journals would know that they'd been altered.

And yet, when she peeled back the false lining and saw the polaroid picture of the four of them – Lily, Marlowe, Michael and Tabitha – she still didn't want to believe it. But what could possibly explain why the two children were dressed in white pinafore dresses while Michael and

Marlowe's mother were dressed in full fox-hunting attire? And those fox masks – white and black, respectively – the bottom halves unclipped so that their faces were exposed. What could possibly explain them?

Still in a state of disbelief, Marlowe had wanted to gather as much evidence as possible before she made a decision, but she'd never anticipated just how far the cult's reach was. If she'd never told Owen about Lily's journals, then Michael may have never seen fit to be in that bathroom the following morning – brazenly flaunting his brandings like they were a badge of honour. And those words – the ones that he had said to her – forever etched in her brain.

'Well, Miss Robertson. You finally got your answer. Now, what are you going to do about it?'

Like she ever had a choice.

Marlowe turned the tap off and eased herself into the bath. She began washing the blood off her lower back, exposing her own marks. They were so much rawer than Michael's – a swatch of angry pinks that seemed to radiate heat. She didn't have as many as him – only seven – the same number Lily had before she'd hacked them away and turned up on Jarrah's doorstep.

She traced over the brands with her fingertips – thinking of the nights she'd received them. Seven circles for every hunt she'd participated in since Lily and Sharon's deaths. The eighth branding – and everything it signified – was less than a year away. The mere notion made her sick to her stomach.

Marlowe thought about Lily and Sharon. About all the stories that she and the other cult members had spun about them over the years. The stories that so many people seemed to believe. The stories that had earned Marlowe fame, fortune and a plethora of awards.

Sharon Williams hadn't killed Lily. That was just another self-serving story fabricated by the cult. As real as the bowerbird and its nest.

Marlowe held her breath and disappeared under the water. She thought about the time that she and Michael had spent together while they'd been locked in the dressing room. How she'd inadvertently flinched when he'd kissed the top of her head.

'Your mother would be so proud of you, Vixen,' he'd whispered to her.

'Yeah,' she'd replied. 'Wish I could say the same about the living parent.'

'You can't expect John to ever understand this. He was never one of us; he just loved Tabitha. We should never have let you go when she died – it was your birthright, and it was taken from you.'

'I think he would have handled the whole thing a lot better if he knew Mark was actually going to be punished for Lily's death.'

'Marlowe.' Michael had sighed. 'How many times have we spoken about this?'

'He killed your fucking daughter!'

A hint of emotion had rippled across his features. 'She wasn't my daughter. You know that.'

'But you raised her.'

'And in doing so, I put everyone at risk. She could have destroyed it all. She wasn't cut out for it. Not like you – not like me – it wasn't in her blood.'

'So you think Mark did the right thing?'

'I don't know,' Michael had said, shaking his head. 'I mean, it brought *you* back to us.'

Rising from the water, Marlowe noticed that the bridge walkers were now descending the giant metal structure – still seemingly at the whim of their counterparts. A feeling of dread crept along her skin. She closed her eyes and willed one of them to jump.

ACKNOWLEDGEMENTS/APOLOGIES

One of the first things the team at Simon & Schuster asked me when I met with them was what I was looking for in a publisher. The question threw me for a loop because I thought the whole point of the meeting was for me to sell myself to them, not the other way around. 'Ideally,' I eventually answered, 'I'm looking for someone who I feel inherently "gets" the book.'

I regretted the words from the second they left my mouth. They felt too demanding – too *expectant* for an unsigned debut author. But, in the end, that's exactly what I received. Nobody gets *Catch Us the Foxes* like the S&S ANZ team do. Hell, sometimes I think they get it more than me. And I can't express how grateful I am to all of them for that fact.

To my powerhouse publisher, Fiona Henderson, thank you for your unwavering passion, dedication and enthusiasm, and for every second that you have invested into me and this book. You have been an absolute joy to work with, and I can't wait to get up to even more trouble with you in the future!

Thanks to Angus Dalton and Anna O'Grady for all their hard work behind the scenes to generate buzz for *Foxes* and get it into as many people's hands as possible. To the phenomenally talented Sandy Cull, thank you so much for your jaw-dropping work on the *Foxes* cover and your openness in sharing your creative process. Thanks to copy-editor extraordinaire Deonie Fiford for her eagle-eyed edit, as well as to Anthea Bariamis for nailing all things audio. To S&S's fearless leader, Dan Ruffino, thank you for your faith – it means the world to me.

And to everyone else on the S&S team, thank you for being you and everything you do!

To my agent, Tara Wynne, and the team at Curtis Brown, thank you for taking a chance on my weird little murder book and for believing in it enough to sign an unpublished writer with no discernible author platform. I am particularly appreciative of Tara for all her hard work and guidance in helping me find the perfect home for *Foxes*. It was neck and neck for a while there, but it really couldn't be a better fit.

To the lovely Patti Miller, I know this isn't the book you thought I'd be publishing, but I hope that you still count me as one of your success stories because I never would have had the confidence to start *Foxes* if it weren't for your mentorship. I promise I'll finish the memoir one day – made-up murder is just *so* much more fun than writing about sad real-life stuff! Thank you as well to my Faber Academy peers, Antoinette, Bev, Sabina, Shelley, Sue, Tegan, Tricia and Virginia. You were all so supportive and encouraging and helped me see that I could find success writing about what I loved instead of what I thought might sell (aka my sob story).

I'd like to thank Express Media and the Copyright Agency for giving me the opportunity to participate in the 2018 Toolkits: Fiction program. Through the program and my mentorship with the amazing Jennifer Down, I was able to complete the first draft of *Foxes*. If you would like to support the wonderful work that Express Media does for young Australian writers, please consider subscribing to their literary journal, *Voiceworks*.

I am similarly indebted to the Australian Society of Authors and the Copyright Agency after winning a place on the ASA's 2019 Award Mentorship Program. If you are an aspiring author, I cannot recommend the ASA's services highly enough and encourage anyone working on a manuscript to apply for an Award Mentorship. It could – quite literally – change your life.

Speaking of life-changing, my sincerest thanks to my ASA mentor, Monica McInerney. Simply put, this book would not have received representation or a publisher without Monica championing it every step of the way. In my brief time in the publishing industry, I have heard countless stories of her tireless dedication to and support of her writing peers. She truly is the patron saint of authors, and I feel so privileged to have had the opportunity to be mentored by her. You're a gem, Monica.

To Romy, thank you for being such a fantastic friend and my biggest cheerleader over the years (even when I drop off the face of the planet for months on end). To this day, I don't know if I would have survived a small town without a fellow weirdo like you. I also wholeheartedly apologise for leaving you with the longest cliffhanger in the world – at least you finally know who killed the showgirl!

To Dad, you've put up with a lot of eye-rolling over the years, but – in the end – I'm thankful for those hours and hours and *hours* of policing stories. This book wouldn't have existed without them, and I consider myself so lucky that I can pick your brain any time I have a weird question about the job. Not sure how thankful my editors are for me inheriting your long-windedness, though! But seriously, thank you for everything – your support has helped me achieve things I never thought were possible.

Similarly, I really did mean it when I said my mum is the best in the world and that she's always had my back. In fact, I could spend the entire length of this novel gushing about all the incredible things that she has done for me over the years and the sacrifices she has made. I wouldn't be here without her – in more ways than one – and I hope she knows how much I love and appreciate her. That being said, she's actually disappointed that I dedicated this book to her because, and I quote, 'I wanted you to name a dead body after me instead'.

You can all now see why I'm like this, right?

And finally, I'd just like to offer my sincerest apologies to the town of Kiama and its residents (past, present and future). Obviously, this novel is a work of fiction. And, while it's partly inspired by the local myths and folklore that I grew up hearing about the town and its surrounding rainforest, all signs point to them being precisely that – just rumours and urban legends. That doesn't mean that they didn't provide fertile ground for a twisty psychological thriller, though! What can I say? Kiama really is the perfect little murder town – my very own *Twin Peaks*.

I'd particularly like to apologise to the Kiama Show Society and make it clear that I hold no ill will towards the show or the showgirl competition. In fact – as a kid – the Kiama Show weekend was my favourite time of the year, and some of my fondest childhood memories took place at that showground. Unfortunately, the show was cancelled due to the bushfires in 2020 (for the first time since World War II) and postponed again in 2021 due to Covid-19. I genuinely hope that it's able to go ahead soon because I know how much it means to the community.

This is going to come off as a bit rich, given the terrible things that you've just read about Kiama in this book, but – in a twisted way – *Catch Us the Foxes* is actually a love letter to the town. I know, I know . . . Pretty messed up, right? But I'm hardly a romantic, and to quote iconic David Lynch villain, Frank Booth: 'You receive a love letter from me, you're fucked forever!'

No, but seriously, I grew up in Kiama, and it undeniably left its mark on me. I used to feel the identical way Marlowe felt – trapped and desperate to escape – and that feeling was the main catalyst for this book. But with a bit of time and distance, I've come to view that town in a way that I never thought was possible. It's not just the 'perfect little murder town' that inspired this book and allowed me to achieve my dreams – it's the place that made me who I am, and I'll always be grateful for that.

If you're *not* a local and have read this book, please consider visiting Kiama. It truly is one of the most beautiful places in the world, and the locals are actually lovely (but that doesn't make for a very good crime novel, does it?). If you do visit, please say hi to Daisy the cow for me, and be sure to treat yourself to some of the town's 'world-famous' ice cream. I personally recommend the 'Stairway to Heaven' from The Ice Creamery. Be sure to take a photo and tag me on social media @nicolawestbooks if you do.

Just don't stay too long – you may never leave!

ABOUT THE AUTHOR

Nicola West is the daughter of a third-generation police officer and grew up in a bucolic coastal town in New South Wales. After moving to Sydney to pursue a career in journalism, she vowed to be as far removed from both her hometown and her father's profession as possible – that is until she found herself writing a novel about both topics. In addition to being one of eight young writers chosen to take part in Express Media's 2018 Toolkits: Fiction program, Nicola was also selected for the Australian Society of Authors' 2019 Award Mentorship Program. She was a mentee of bestselling author Monica McInerney. *Catch Us the Foxes* is her first novel. She lives in Sydney and can be found on Twitter and Instagram @nicolawestbooks or via www.nicolawestbooks.com.